the
living
canvas

NEW YORK TIMES BESTSELLING AUTHOR

PEPPER WINTERS

The
LIVING
Canvas

by

New York Times Bestseller
Pepper Winters

The Living Canvas
Copyright © 2019 Pepper Winters
Published by Pepper Winters

Published: Pepper Winters 2019:
pepperwinters@gmail.com
Cover Design: Ari @ Cover it! Designs
Editing by: Editing 4 Indies (Jenny Sims)

Prologue

Olin

WHEN DID KINDNESS become weakness?

When did compassion become blindness?

I believed strength, *true* strength, came from seeing past someone's actions and trusting the goodness inside them. I believed words were just words and lies were just lies and they didn't really matter, because, in the end, the truth always came out.

A person was a product of their upbringing and society's doctrine, and so, I chose to see past that creation and see the real soul hurting underneath.

I chose weakness to be kind.

I became blind to show compassion.

It made a total fool out of me…

Chapter One

Gil

-The Past-

TALLUP DISAPPEARED.

Seven months, three weeks, and eight days after that God-awful night in Motel Gardenia, Tallup vanished from school. She'd ensured my life had remained an utter misery. Her attention constantly on me. Her threats chasing me, her rules hunting me.

She'd steadily let herself go—no longer wearing tight, prim skirt-suits but hiding her small frame in loose-fitting dresses. Her face fattened, along with her waistline, and fellow teachers joked that she'd reached middle-age spread.

I didn't care she no longer looked like a soul-sucking succubus. I was glad she resembled the rotting grossness inside.

Thanks to her, I could no longer look at Olin with Justin.

I could no longer pretend life was okay.

Distance hadn't healed my heart. Love hadn't triumphed over evil.

I found it excruciatingly difficult to keep my distance, all the while far too disgusted with myself to ever talk to Olin.

Every day, it grew harder and harder to stay in town.

I only had a few months until graduation. I honestly didn't know what kept me from leaving. I knew what I wanted to be now: I was an artist. It was the cure to my insanity. And artists didn't need degrees or university accolades. Artists were talented, or not—born with the gift or refused such a skill.

I had everything I needed to succeed.

And I needed to run. Run. *Run.*

Run far away and never look back.

But Olin…

I'd lost her but at least I could still protect her. We walked the same streets. Attended the same school. Lived in the same town. That tiny piece of togetherness sustained me and imprisoned me whenever I thought of leaving.

But then…Tallup vanished.

A new teacher replaced her. Education continued on as if nothing odd had occurred. And the principal made a half-hearted attempt at explaining the switch. Tallup got a job teaching English in Japan. She'd accepted. She'd be missed. Yada yada.

For a week, I didn't trust it.

Every day, I expected Tallup to be at the front of class, ready to stare me into submission, her smirk hidden at breaking Olin and me apart.

But Monday, Tuesday, Wednesday, Thursday, Friday…she didn't return.

The next week, hope did its best to make me drunk. Instead of listening to lessons, I plotted ways to talk to Olin. To explain. To *fix* us.

But each time I tried to catch Olin's gaze, Justin was there. Making her smile through her sadness, his touch soothing her sorrows away.

By the third week of Tallup missing, I grew braver.

She'd crippled me—taken my virginity, my goodness, my strength and left me lacking in every way. But…with her gone, I was free.

Free to chase Olin and claim her back.

But…I'm not free.

Because why would Olin ever forgive me? Why would she ever love me?

She'd given her heart to someone else, and as much as that crucified me—worse than any forced sex or drunken beating—I had to honour her choice.

I left school knowing I'd lost any right to her.

I went to bed so fucking sick of being weak.

I made a pact to talk to her on Monday.

To lay the truth at her feet.

To let her judge me, hurt me, hate me.

And then…I'd kiss her.

I'd kiss her.

Beg her.

Do anything to make her mine.

And if she forgave me, I would never, *ever* let go.

* * * * *

Sunday night.

Fate decided it hadn't finished toying with me, delivering its final blow on my tragic mess of a life.

I had a script planned. Every word and apology ready for Monday morning and making Olin mine.

But then, a visitor arrived.

Not a man looking for a whore, or a drug dealer looking for his cut.

Just a petite woman with the soul of the devil.

My teacher.

Who'd been missing.

Who'd come to finish me.

I'd answered the knock thanks to my father being drunk in his bed and his current whores having fifteen minutes rest before new clients arrived.

The house was quiet, for once, and I had homework to do before I left for an evening of graffiti.

But as I wrenched open the door, my fist curled around the handle and my heart stopped beating. Tallup stood on my dirty stoop, her hair dull and eyes angry. Her cheeks pinched with age and sleeplessness.

The fury inside me exploded outward. "What the *fuck* are you doing here!?"

We weren't on school property.

No one could hear us.

I refused to be polite to this bitch.

She hoisted something higher in her arms. A bundle of fleece and blankets. "I came to find you."

"Why?" My knuckles whitened around the handle, holding tight. If I didn't, I'd hit her, strangle her, *kill* her. "Leave. I have nothing to say—"

"Here." Her arms snapped forward, shoving her swaddled package into my chest. Instinct made me take it, clutching it tight as she ripped her touch away. It fell a little before I had full control.

The bundle was warm and heavier than I expected.

And it moved.

Fuck.

My eyes shot to hers. "What is this?"

She wiped her forehead with weariness, but her gaze was just as evil, just as cruel. "It's yours."

A small mewl sounded, ripping my eyes down and shooting me with dread.

No…

With sick urgency, I brushed aside the peach fleece and stared at the downy head of a newborn. I almost dropped it in my rush to give it back. "Take it."

Tallup shook her head. "I don't want it. I *never* wanted it." She laughed, a little crazed. "I was on the pill. This wasn't supposed to happen."

"You're saying it's *mine*?"

"That's what I said, didn't I?"

I gulped for air. "But that was months—"

"Nine months this week. It was premature. Eight days early. Guess it knew it wasn't wanted."

I turned stone cold. "How do I know it's mine?"

"Because I say it is." Her voice darkened. "It's yours."

"I don't want a kid."

"Neither do I."

"What do you expect me to do with a baby?" I narrowed my eyes at the blackened street. No neighbours spied. No one heard our dark conversation.

"I don't care." She shrugged. "I honestly don't care if you kill it."

"If you care so little for its life, why didn't you end it when—"

Her eyes snapped to mine. "I tried, believe me. I went to the clinic. I filled in the forms. I waited for a doctor to suck that nuisance straight out of me."

I couldn't hate her more than I did. A cold, oozing, insidious hate.

Her voice turned brittle. "I almost went through with it. but…I was raised better. We're Christian. Abortion is a sin."

I laughed out loud. I couldn't contain it. "And raping a student isn't?"

She stiffened. "I vividly remember you enjoying having your cock inside me."

"I vomited after each assault. Did that not hint that I couldn't stand you?"

Her face etched with fire. "You came." Her lips twisted into a nasty smile. "If you didn't, that thing wouldn't exist."

"That wasn't pleasure, you bitch. I came because you force-fed me Viagra—"

"I don't have time for childish nonsense." She looked at the starless sky, then back at the peach blanket forced upon me. "Just because I couldn't kill it doesn't mean I want it. I hate children. And the past week has proven just how much I loathe everything about them."

Instinctual protectiveness made my arm latch tight as if her words were spears. "Adopt it out then."

She rolled her eyes. "That would lead to questions about who the father is." Chilly calculation filled her face. "Do you want people to know it's yours, Gilbert? Do you want me to tell them you forced yourself on me and this is the result?"

I shook with rage. "*You* forced yourself on *me*."

"Yes, but who would they believe? Have you grown up so much you're willing to put your life on the line to prove…what? That this baby isn't yours? Because I promise you, a paternity test will undeniably show that it is."

My mouth went dry as the baby squirmed and cooed. It didn't know its very existence was being argued against. It didn't know it wasn't wanted.

Sadness filled me. Sadness for the life born from hate. A life that should never have been created.

"If you don't take it, I'll drop it off at the shelter. It can disappear into foster care. Maybe end up in a situation like yours—"

My blood ran cold. "You'd never do such a thing."

How could she? She was a teacher, for Christ's sake.

I clutched the blankets closer. "You teach kids for a living. Why can't you love your own?"

She smiled tightly. "It's *because* I teach that I don't want my own. I only teach because my mother was a teacher, and that was what was expected. I don't do it because I enjoy it. I've hated it since the moment I started."

I forced my anger to subside, doing my best…for our kid's sake. "This is yours as much as mine. Stop being such a cold-hearted witch. I know you could love—"

"Shut up, Gilbert. I'm not keeping her."

"Her?"

My insides bottomed out.

My world changed.

My priorities shifted.

Her.

A girl.

I have a daughter.

I grew up in an instant.

I was no longer a boy, but a man.

A *father.*

A father who would never be like his own. Never be a parent who didn't put their life on the line to protect his child.

I cuddled her close. So damn close.

Already in love with her and I hadn't even seen her face.

How was it possible to fall so fast? How could my heart abandon Olin and replace it with a newborn so quickly?

I didn't know how, only that it'd happened, and there was no going back.

Tallup didn't notice the change that'd happened in me. She nodded stiffly, glowering at my daughter. "It's a girl. A useless, loud, horrible little—"

"A perfect, *brilliant* little girl and you're throwing her away." I shook my head in disgust. I thought I hated this woman for what she'd done to me. I'd had daydreams of murdering her with my bare hands. I'd envisioned going to the police and having them on my side. Of explaining to O. Of winning her back and making my life right again.

But that hate was nothing, *nothing,* compared to my level of contempt now. I couldn't look at her without wanting to strike her. I couldn't stand her face, her smell, her soul. My voice vibrated with arctic snow as I looked down at the woman who didn't deserve to live. "Who the fuck are you?"

She sniffed and braced her shoulders. "I just want my life back."

I laughed darkly. "So do I."

"Oh, come on. You're still sore over losing Olin? She's a nobody."

"Don't call her that."

"I can call her whatever I want. I've accepted a job in Japan teaching English, now that this little…inconvenience is out of the way." She grinned. "My life will be my own again. But I'll still know if you've been naughty. You better not have been talking to her while I've been gone, Gilbert. Otherwise—"

"Stop."

This.

All of this.

It was stupid, pointless, *juvenile.*

Who cared about power trips and forced assaults and teenage hearts that were broken?

Who cared about right and wrong and justice?

The world didn't care.

Justice didn't care.

And I didn't care.

Not anymore.

The only thing I cared about was ensuring my daughter never had to suffer such things. She might've been born to a ruthless mother and a gullible father, but she wouldn't pay for my sins.

She deserved an empire.

She deserved stability and family.

Family.

O was once my family.

She always would be.

I would always love and care for her.

But I had someone else who needed me more.

And if her mother refused to give her the world; if her mother would rather throw her to the hounds of hell, then I would do it.

I would be there for her over my own messes.

I would fight her battles at the cost of my own.

I would *never* stop putting her first.

Above everyone.

"I'm done." I sighed, bored and no longer afraid of this sad, bitter woman. "Go away." Tucking my tiny daughter into my chest, I rocked her.

This was my legacy.

She was my reason for existing.

Tallup swallowed, watching me closely with a tilt of her head. "So…you'll keep her?"

I nodded with a stern stare.

"Will you tell anyone where she came from?" Her eyes might stay narrowed and full of threats, but her lips worried with consequence. She was afraid I'd tell everyone our story. That I'd drag my daughter through court cases, prison sentences, and foster care.

No way.

No *fucking* way.

I dropped my head and inhaled the sweet hair of my child. "I'm leaving. Tonight."

She froze. "Leaving? Where?"

"Don't know. Don't care." I looked away from her, brushing back the fleece to stare at my daughter's tiny, adorable face. She slept in my arms. Trusting me to hold her and not drop her. Believing she'd wake to warm food and unconditional love. Knowing I'd be there to keep her safe, just as I'd tried to keep Olin safe.

And I would.

Nothing would stop me from loving her.

She had me for eternity.

I'd failed O, but she had Justin now.

I wouldn't fail this new love of my life.

Tallup pointed a finger in my face. "If you say anything—"

"Enough." I just smiled. Totally unaffected and free from her wrath. "You'll never see me or my daughter again." Stepping back into the house I'd shared with drunkards and whores, I grabbed the door. "Goodbye, Jane Tallup."

I slammed the old wood in her face.

The rattle woke up my daughter.

Her eyes blinked with fuzzy sleep, her mouth opened like a tiny bird's, and her frustrated grumble made overwhelming affection and debilitating fear crest over me.

What did I know about raising a child?

What did I know about finding a place to live, a job that paid, childcare to source, food, diapers, medicine, kindergarten, and all the other things that came with a lifetime commitment to another?

I didn't have a clue.

I can't do this.

But then my daughter opened her eyes again, blinking and bold and huge.

And I knew that I could.

One day at a time.

For her.

Marching through the house, I grabbed a bag, stuffed some clothes, my art supplies, and the wad of cash my father kept from his johns into the depths.

It was the first time I'd ever stolen from him.

He'd promised to kill me if I ever did.

After tonight, he'd never find me.

Slinging the bag over my shoulder, I looked down at my daughter again, my heart fisting at her sigh of contentment.

Her big eyes were closed in slumber, quiet and safe.

She looked like a baby owl.

A big-eyed, intelligent baby owl.

Like the nickname I'd used for Olin.

Fuck, O.

My chest imploded as my heart stopped beating.

In a few short hours, I would've gotten on my knees before her and asked for a second chance. We might've found our way back to each other. We might've been happy.

But now...I'd never see her again.

I'd never be able to kiss her or beg for her forgiveness.

She would always think I'd abandoned her, turning her deeper into Justin's arms, sealing a marriage between them.

That was my only regret.

I'd leave this town, and O would never know where I'd gone.

She'd never know why I shut her out.

Never guess why I removed my love.

Never understand that the girl I held in my arms was the cause of all of it.

I'm sorry.

So fucking sorry.

With my meagre possessions and brand new baby, I slipped from the whore house, stole through the streets, and bought a train ticket to London.

I never looked back.

Chapter Two

Olin

-The Present-

"GIL...DON'T."

He gritted his teeth, wrapping the rope tighter around my wrists.

"Stop it." I wriggled and squirmed, trying to be free of him.

"Don't make this any harder than it is," he breathed, tying a knot and jerking me forward.

I fought against him, bracing against his pull.

His hand slipped on the rope, giving me a fraction of a second.

I spun and bolted.

I managed a few terrified strides before his boots thudded behind me.

He caught me so easily.

He spun me around, picked me up, and carried me to the podium. Big fat tears rolled down my cheeks, unable to believe what he'd done. In all the times he'd ever touched me, he'd restrained the power and violence he wielded so effortlessly now. He had a strength that controlled me with barely any effort whatsoever.

That alone sent my heart galloping uselessly in my chest. My back prickled with nervous sweat. My chest fluttered with anxious breath. And I moaned in disbelief as he plopped me onto the stage and kicked out my legs, forcing me to sit on the edge.

I sat with a jar, my teeth clacking together as I dared look up at the kidnapper I should've been afraid of but never suspected.

"Why do you get to decide what my life is worth?" My voice teased with a whisper but throbbed with condemnation.

He bit his bottom lip, his eyes narrowed and afflicted. "I don't."

"Yet you're playing God."

He reached for more rope. "I'm doing what's necessary."

"No, you're doing what he wants you to do." A fresh swell of tears tried to make me weak. "Don't do his dirty work, Gil. Don't—"

"I made a promise." His head hung, his hands feathering over my ankles as he wrapped the rope around them and tied an intricate knot. "I promised my daughter that I would always protect her. No matter the cost." His voice caught. "No matter the pain."

"What about *my* pain?"

His head dropped lower, his messy, tangled hair dancing with his eyelashes. "I've always caused you pain...this is no different."

"This is you taking my life, Gil. This isn't a breakup. This isn't some misunderstanding. You're tying me up to *kill* me." I tried to capture his gaze. "Listen to me. *Look* at me. Are you really prepared to kill someone who loves you? Someone you love?"

"I'm prepared to do whatever it takes to keep her safe."

Every muscle shut down. I swayed as his words fisted around my heart and squeezed its last beat.

His admission was the correct answer for a father in love with his daughter.

But his loyalties cost me so much trust. It siphoned out of me, slipped through the ropes, and puddled at my feet.

My trust in him, in *us*...was broken.

He'd just lost me.

Lost me worse than he ever did when he walked away without a goodbye.

You've lost me forever.

My heart restarted, drowning in horror.

Piece by piece.

Beat by beat.

I grew cold and empty.

Silence wrapped around us, stealing our voices, suffocating our thoughts. Quietness was easier to bear than his soul-shattering confessions, and I allowed it to hug me, trying to find comfort where there was none.

"I know you'll never forgive me," he murmured. "I know the

only place I can go is hell. And I know I've destroyed any hope of a future where we could all be alive and happy. This is entirely my fault. I'm the reason Olive was taken, and I'm the reason those girls had to die. I'm the one who should forfeit his life…and who knows? Maybe that will be his next request, but while Olive is alive…I have no choice." He stood on cracking knees, towering over me. "As long as she is alive…I have to try." His misery left me stamped and branded as he turned and walked through his office to the apartment beyond.

The second he was out of viewing distance, I scrambled to undo myself. I bucked and writhed on the podium, twisting and turning, desperate to escape.

But each imprisonment stayed steadfast, and the only thing I succeeded in doing was burning through valuable energy. Energy I couldn't afford to lose.

Whatever Gil was about to do to me, I had to be smart. Had to be brave. I wouldn't give up.

I would've fought every dragon and beast by his side. I would've given him everything to keep his daughter safe…if only he'd asked. If only he hadn't taken what wasn't his to take.

A single tear rolled down my cheek, icy and alone.

I wouldn't cry again.

He wasn't worth my tears.

He isn't worth my heart.

When he came back, his eyebrows tugged low, noticing my attempt at freedom. In his hands rested a plate of peanut butter and jelly sandwiches with a tall glass of water. The only two pieces of crockery he owned that weren't chipped or plastic.

A heavy thread of strawberry followed him as he lowered to his haunches before me.

Such a simple, innocent scent.

A berry reserved for hot summers and delightful picnics. It had no place in this chilly warehouse with ropes binding me to a terrible fate.

"Open," he murmured, holding the sandwich to my lips.

I shook my head, earning peanut butter crumbs on my chin. "What are you doing?" I kept my face turned away. "Stop it."

"You're hungry. It's my turn to feed you."

My eyes widened. I resisted the urge to morbidly laugh. "You're about to kill me, but you want to feed me first?"

His entire face blanched. He wobbled on his haunches and swallowed hard as if struggling to keep his own stomach contents down. "Don't. Please don't."

"Don't what? Make you face what you're about to do to me?" I swung my knees to nudge against his, my chin high and voice sharp. "You've tied me up against my will. You're going to gift me to him. You'll allow him to do whatever he wants. The least you can do is accept the gruesome details." My anger plaited with fragility, wavering a little. "Will he kill me or you? How will it happen? Slit my wrists and bleed me out like the last girl? Paint me and leave me to die like the ones before her?"

He groaned as if I'd butchered him. With his jaw locked, he shoved the sandwich into my mouth, forcing me to chew or choke. "Just eat, O. I need you to eat."

I fought to grab air not tainted with food, but he followed my head, keeping the awful sandwich pressed tight against my mouth.

We duelled for a while. I shifted my head left and right, up and down. He employed patience and followed. Crumbs and strawberry jam smeared my face. Embarrassingly, my stomach snarled to stop fighting.

To devour the offered energy because there must be a reason he wanted me to eat. Maybe he wouldn't be the one to kill me. Maybe he wanted me to have energy to fight.

I stilled. My body relaxed. I opened my mouth politely and took a dainty bite.

Gil tensed, his eyes never unlocking from mine as I ate every inch. I swallowed it down, then waited for him to wipe my cheeks and chin free from the mess.

He did with a shaky hand, his forehead furrowed and eyes so dark they looked like crushed up jade. "I'm sorry."

"You keep saying that, but if you were sorry, you'd let me go."

"Thank you for eating." He placed the empty plate aside and picked up the glass. "Please drink."

I held my head away, my gaze searching his. "Tell me why."

He struggled to reply. The truth stayed shuttered behind his anguish, but finally, he looked at my lap and whispered, "You need to eat so you have something in your system. If you're left out there for a while…the better hydrated and fed you are…the longer you'll survive."

"That wasn't what I was asking." I'd wanted to know *why*.

Why he'd chosen the easy way out. Yes, his daughter was captive, and he'd been dealing with this alone, but surely, having me help him rather than just sacrificing me was a better option?

When he didn't answer, I sighed heavily. "You think a sandwich will keep me alive? That it will prevent me from becoming yet another dead girl in a newspaper?"

His eyes squeezed shut; a single tear rolled down his ashen face. Opening them again, he held the glass to my lips. "Please."

My heart kicked at his brokenness, even now wishing to heal him.

I locked any emotion away and opened my mouth, allowing him to pour cool water down my throat.

I drank every drop.

I will survive this.

I will.

When the glass was empty, he lowered it slowly, studying the fracturing light as a droplet danced inside. That creative spark struck a match in his gaze, turning tortured into artist. He drowned in the colour spectrum, begging the flickering rainbow to fix everything.

I was envious of him. Envious that he could still practice his talent. Jealous he had a religion that could help him, even while discussing the murder of his childhood sweetheart.

His gaze met mine, and in the green depths, he showed me how endless he truly was. How long he'd fought this battle. How I was just collateral damage in a war I could never comprehend.

And I pitied him.

Pitied the struggle that had torn away his soul. Pitied the hardships he'd had to face on his own.

But I couldn't forgive him.

I couldn't absolve him for putting a price on my life and finding it less valuable than another's. Even if it was his daughter. Even if she was...*family.*

"Justin knows I'm here." I studied him with defiance. "He'll visit soon, I'm sure."

"He won't." Gil stood and carried the empty dishes to his side table where an airgun, brushes, vials, and everything else he needed for his work waited, prepped and mixed.

I sucked in a breath, my heart once again winging. "Why won't he?"

"Because I told him not to."

"He knows something is going on with you."

Gil laughed, but nothing was jovial about it, merely black and miserable. "He should. I've been hiding this nightmare for a while."

"What's a while?"

He kept his back to me, unlocking the wheels on the trolley and rolling the supply table toward me. "Over a year."

"A year?" I squirmed on the stage, my wrists and ankles sore from the tightness of his binds. "Why didn't you go to the police? Tell them—"

"Tell them that I'm a madman's puppet? That I've tried to keep so many women from death and only succeeded if my bank account was flush?"

I stiffened. "You could have. They might have believed you."

His eyes cast back to the past, to a time I wasn't there. "They wouldn't. It's always my word against someone else's."

That statement rippled with such stark truth, I wished I could dissect it and pull free every fact, but I kept my questioning focused, determined to solve this riddle. "How many women did your money save?" I tested the ropes again, a futile attempt, but instinct demanded I keep checking.

"Not enough." He shuddered visibly, his face turning grey as a corpse. "It doesn't matter."

"*Don't.*" My voice hissed like a python. "Don't *ever* say that to me again. Don't you think I deserve to know?" I held up my bound wrists. "You've turned me into a sacrifice, Gilbert Clark. The least you can do is—"

"You're right." His back stiffened as he pulled open a drawer and selected a pair of sharp scissors. "Ask me anything. I'll answer as honestly as I can." Coming toward me, he eyed my skirt and blouse. "I'm sorry to ruin yet another outfit of yours."

I scuttled backward, doing my best to avoid the silver flashes of his weapon. I asked again, "Ho-How many did you manage to save?"

His eyes met mine. This time he didn't deflect. "Seven. Seven girls before my finances ran dry."

"And he kept asking for more?"

He nodded as another well of rage and helplessness glossed his gaze. "I sold what I could. I worked every job possible. I gave him every penny. But it still wasn't enough."

"Enough for what?"

"To keep her safe."

"To keep Olive safe," I whispered his daughter's name.

"Yes." His fingers grabbed my ankle, pulling me back to the edge of the podium. With trembling hands, he cut my skirt along my thigh, right to the pretty faux croc-skin belt. With a snip, he cut that too, switching my skirt to a ruined piece of material now draped uselessly on his stage.

My garter belt decorated my black lace knickers; my stockings unable to shield me from the cold air.

He sniffed as if he couldn't hold back his emotion. Couldn't believe he did this to me. "Fuck, I'm so, so sorry."

"Then stop." I did my best to stay strong.

"I can't."

I flinched as he slowly cut my blouse, peeling it away from my skin. It fluttered lifelessly to join my skirt, revealing my bra.

"I need you to know." Gil cupped my chin with snowy fingertips. "I need you to understand." Tears strangled his voice. "Without Olive, I don't know what I would've become. Sh-She saved my life." His thumb stroked my cheekbone. "After I lost you, I barely survived. I was on a slippery slope of grief and heartache, but thanks to Olive…I had someone who needed me. I had someone to fight for—"

"*I* needed you!" My pain bled through my control as a sob caught in my throat. "I missed you so much. Why did you leave if you still wanted me? Why didn't you fight for me, Gil? Why don't you fight now?"

His tears flowed freely, glittering on his ghostly cheeks, tracking through his five o'clock shadow. "I had to stay away. Otherwise, she was going to destroy your life."

I struggled to breathe. "Who? Who was going to destroy my life?"

"It doesn't—"

"Gil!"

"Fine. It was Tallup." His teeth snapped the word in half, thick with disgust and heavy with loathing. "She blackmailed me." He pressed his forehead to mine, breathing hard. "I was stupid and gullible and way out of my depth. I should've told you. Should've told the authorities, but I was too afraid." He let out an agony-drenched laugh. "I was too afraid of losing you. Of being locked up. Of my life becoming a total screw-up. I thought I could protect you and fix what I'd broken. But I failed, and I lost it all anyway."

My mind scrambled to untangle the pieces. "Ms Tallup? Jane Tallup? Our *teacher*?" I frowned. "Why would she want to hurt me?"

"Because of me."

"What? Why?"

"She went after you to get to me." His gaze shot black with hatred and unresolved torment.

"I don't understand."

"It doesn't ma—"

"Gil." I ripped my face from his touch. "I swear I'll—"

His lips crashed on mine as if he couldn't stop himself. As if the whole deranged evening was just a role-play and I'd had every choice to participate. His tongue licked at the seam of my mouth. His groan vibrated in his chest with black-edged sorrow.

I didn't kiss him back.

In that, I had a choice.

He pulled away, resting his forehead on mine as he breathed hard. "Fuck." He trembled as if he had hypothermia and only had seconds to live. He kissed me again, quick and hard, his breath catching. *"Fuck."*

Falling away from me, he punched the stage.

He punched it so hard, the vibration ricocheted beneath me and made him groan with agony. He punched it again, punishing his knuckles, ruining his painting hand all because he couldn't stand the prison we were locked in.

Part of me wanted to soothe him. To tell him it was okay. That I understood his pain.

But I *didn't* understand.

This was my life he was using to pay a debt.

This wasn't his choice to make.

"What did Tallup do to you, Gil?" My question was achingly soft after such violence.

His shoulders hunched, grief crippling him. His eyes were wet as they met mine. "She wanted me." He shrugged helplessly. "So…she took me."

"What does that—"

No.

I wanted to be sick.

A rush of heat and nausea raced up my throat.

My cheeks burned. My body throbbed with injustice. "You *slept* with her?"

He swiped at the liquid on his face and looked away.

He didn't answer as he reached for my bra and snipped it with the scissors. Cutting the straps, he let it fall to the graveyard of my clothing before slicing up my stockings and leaving me in just my knickers. A single piece of protection against so many things I didn't know.

"You slept with her." Tears I didn't want to cry spilled over my cheeks. "Why would you do that? Why didn't you *say* something? I was waiting for you. I was *saving* myself for you. I was a virgin, Gil. I wanted you to have that. No one else. You were supposed to be my first...and my only."

His voice was dangerously low. "You think I didn't want that too?"

"I don't know what to think." My heart bruised with agony. "Did she proposition you? Why didn't you tell the principal? He would've fired her immediately for even looking at you wrong."

His jaw gritted. "Like I said...I was trapped."

"Trapped because you secretly wanted her?"

His head snapped up. *"What?"* His eyes narrowed. "Why the fuck would you ask something like that?"

"Why wouldn't I?" Anger flickered through me. "You're a guy. She was small. You could've fought her off. I mean...if you didn't want it, you wouldn't have been able to get hard—"

"Fucking hell." He swooped up, dragging hands through his hair. "I know you hate me. I know you're currently tied up and cursing the very air I breathe, but do you truly think I wanted her? Wanted her over you? Do you honestly think I went to her willingly?"

My chest rose and fell with quickened breaths. "You broke up with me in front of her. How am I supposed to know if you did that because you two were playing some twisted game—"

He bent and grabbed my face, his fingers digging into my flesh. "I deserve your doubt. I deserve you thinking the worst of me...after all, look at what I'm fucking doing. But...O, you couldn't have hurt me more if you'd tried."

My chin arched in his hold. "Well, good. I'm *glad* you're hurt. Maybe now you'll understand how I feel." Yet more cursed tears welled. "I *trusted* you, Gil. I gave you everything I had, and instead of telling me how I could help you, you went behind my back and decided for me. Twice!" I sniffed coldly. "You did it at school. And you're doing it now. We were family. We made a deal to be there for each other—"

"I was trying to keep you safe!"

"Safe by sleeping with her?"

"Yes!"

"All because she threatened my future."

"Yes, okay?! I was an idiot. I—"

"You're a walking disaster for blackmail." I wanted to laugh at the absurdity, to cry at the tragedy. "I could've handled my own future, you know! My grades were good. She couldn't have stopped me."

"You're right." He let me go, pacing in front of me. "I'm fucking pathetic. I try to do the right thing, but I always fail. She told me she'd destroy your hopes of university and dance. She said I could never talk to you again. That I had to give her my virginity and—"

"You—" I choked. "You were a virgin?"

His boots stuck to the floor as his body sagged with crippling confession. "My virginity was yours. I was waiting to make sure you were in love with me." He looked away, unable to hold my stare. "Because once I took you, there was no going back. I was going to marry you and move you away from that shitty place. I had it all planned—"

"Wait." Fury tangled with my sadness, making me tremble in my ropes. "You're telling me…that all this time…you saw a future together? You were going to *marry* me…?" A wash of tiredness crashed over me, scrambling my thoughts. I struggled to pull them back into comprehension. "You let her ruin us, all because you were too afraid to stand up to her!"

"It was my word against hers." He pinched the bridge of his nose. "There was no way I could've won."

"The *truth* would have won." I blinked back another tug of tiredness.

"The *truth* was I was the son of an alcoholic pimp who beat me. My upbringing wasn't with siblings but with whores. Tallup was a Christian teacher who lived with her mother and did charity work. Do you honestly think I stood a chance? That her word against mine wouldn't win? She could do whatever she fucking liked, and there was nothing I could do."

I swallowed hard. "And what exactly…did she do to you?"

Shutters came down over his eyes. His hands balled as pure rage dripped over him. "I already told you."

I shook my head from yet another lick of lethargy. "You slept with her."

His teeth bared. "Yes."

"How exactly? If you didn't want it, how—"

"She tricked me into taking Viagra."

"Oh…"

Time froze.

Everything stopped.

And I saw this from an outsider's point of view. I heard my judgement. I saw my dread. And I despised myself.

This isn't me.

I wasn't a woman bound and trapped by a man willing to kill me. I was just a girl, judging a boy for sexual molestation. I did what chauvinistic society did to girls who were raped. I blamed him. I believed it must've been his fault.

But it *wasn't* his fault.

And it wasn't fair to use my hurt against him.

The truth stabbed me right in the chest. "You didn't sleep with her, Gil. She raped you."

God.

She raped him and cut him off from everyone.

She—

I want to kill her.

Rip out her heart and burn it on a pyre.

My fingers turned numb along with my tongue, shutting down piece by piece. "She abused you. God, Gil, she took everything from you—"

He held up a hand, his entire frame shaking. "Don't feel sorry for me. Don't you fucking *dare* feel sorry for me. Do not be that good. Do not be that fucking kind!"

"But you were just a child. And she was our teach—"

"Stop it. I want you to hate me. You *need* to hate me." He howled at the ceiling. "I need you to resent me with everything you have. Be disgusted with me. Curse me. Fuck, please." He fell to his knees. "I can't do this if you forgive all my sins. I can't do this if you still love me — no matter what I fucking do to you."

Another lash of heaviness slithered through my brain, scattering my thoughts before realigning. I blinked back the increasing lethargy. "You dealt with that…on your own." I cried tears for the boy I'd lost. "You didn't tell me. You didn't trust me to help you. You were all alone."

He rocked with his hands clasped in prayer, bowing to me, placing me in position of a goddess. A goddess of death and destruction. An offering to a bigger, more malignant power. "I thought I could keep you safe."

"Instead, you cut me out." My voice was silk-wrapped daggers. "You ruined both of us." I longed to touch him, to hug him. If I touched him now, I might be able to stop him from doing this. I finally knew what'd twisted him up so badly. "It's okay. It's over now."

My roped hands reached for his face to grant him absolution. To let him know, I might hate his actions tonight, but I didn't hate him—no matter how much trust he'd shattered. "Gil…it's over. Untie me. It's not just your word against hers. I'll stand beside you. We'll ask for help together. We'll save Olive some other way."

"Olin." His tears fell openly now. "Goddammit, I—"

My fingers grazed his five o'clock shadow. He reared backward, terror filling his gaze. "Don't. I'll break if you touch me. I'm breaking already."

"Let me go."

"I *can't.*"

"You're not alone anymore." Another crush of exhaustion pressed into me, forcing me into haziness. My eyes unfocused on the rope around my wrists. My mind flickered on and off. I licked my lips, clawing my way back to lucidity. "I forgive you for this, Gilbert Clark. I forgive you for everything. Just let me go and…" Reality checked out for a second, my brain tiptoeing into sleep. I opened my eyes with a jerk, raising my heavy head. "What…what's going on? Why am I so tired?"

He ignored me.

"Did you…drug me?" I licked my lips, the numbness spreading.

"I can't do this anymore." Scrambling to his feet, he grabbed something from his trestle. He placed a bottle of paint beside me while holding his palm open by my face. I couldn't make sense of the small black dot in the centre. "I can't keep making you believe the worst."

I struggled to focus.

"I wasn't going to tell you this." His voice stayed low as if afraid monsters would hear. "You need to believe this is real…just like you believed the breakup at school was real."

I laughed coldly. "That *was* real. You broke up with me and never spoke to me again."

He shook his head, his hair a wild, untamed mop. "I meant to apologise that night and fix us. But you never went home, and then…I couldn't." He cleared his throat. "But this is different. I won't keep you in the dark like I did that day. I need you to know, so I have the strength to finish this."

"If the breakup wasn't real…but it ended up being true…why do you think this will be any different? You think by telling me you have a plan, it will stop me from getting killed?" My thoughts scrambled again, unable to stay cohesive. I swam in question-filled quicksand. "Wait…why did you break up with me if it wasn't real? I don't understand."

His jaw worked. "It was for her. I thought she'd back off if she saw I was no longer into you."

"Yet it only left you wide open to be pulled into her bed."

He winced. "She knew I loved you regardless that I broke your heart. It was *because* I loved you that she managed to keep me on a leash."

My eyes unfocused again. "That sounds like you're blaming me."

"Fuck no." His hands shook, still holding up the black dot. "I know I'm to blame. For all of this. I know I've broken everything between us. I know you'll never love me after—"

"I'll be dead. How can I love you?" My tongue tried to slur, battling whatever thickness swam in my blood.

"You won't be. I won't let you die." He once again shoved the dot into my vision. "This must stay secret. You can't let him know this is on you. Act as terrified and as enraged as you were before."

I couldn't keep up with his tricks. "What are you saying?"

"I'm saying I'm going to paint you, deliver you, sacrifice you, but it was never my intention to abandon you. Not again. *Never* again." He nudged my chin up with his knuckles. "I'll be with you every step, O. I'm not leaving you.

"What do you mean?"

Bending, he very gently pulled the waistband of my lacy knickers until a small gap formed between lingerie and skin. Placing the black dot against my hip, he let the tightness hug it close.

It burned my flesh with iciness.

"That's a GPS tracker. It's synced to my phone." His voice cracked again, a fresh tear trickled over thick eyelashes. "I love you, O. With all my goddamn heart. I can't bear to risk you, but I also can't leave Olive in his control. This is my last chance." He swiped at his nose with the back of his hand. "He's asked me to drop you off…painted in camouflage. I'll do what he's requested. He thinks that by taking you—by taking the only other person I love—it will make me far more obedient than I have been. But…what he doesn't get is, this has pushed me to my limit." His fists curled. "He can't have you both. He can't keep hurting those I love. This ends…tonight."

The warehouse no longer acted like steel and concrete but

liquid and air, loose and floating. My mind was drunk on fatigue. My tongue twisted into knots, making conversation harder. "Wha-What are you going to do?"

He tucked a curtain of hair behind my ear. I didn't have the energy to swat him away. His lips caressed my cheek. "I'm going to kill him."

My heart picked up a panicked beat, shooing away the sleepiness. "How?"

Gil let me go, turning to his paints and brushes. Placing more on the stage around me, his mouth remained grim and resolute. "I'll follow where he takes you. He'll take you to Olive. Once I know where she is, I'll kill him."

My mouth turned dry. There were so many holes in that plan. So many things that could go wrong. "What if…he doesn't…" I blinked, fighting harder against the urge to snooze. "…take me to Olive?"

He dropped a glass jar holding sponges. It clanged on the stage, making both of us flinch. "He will." His teeth sank into his bottom lip. "He has to."

"What if he kills me first?"

"He won't."

"What if he kills us all?"

Gil unwound the hose for his airgun. "I won't let that happen."

My head was too heavy to hold up. I sagged forward, my spine rolling. "You might not have a choice."

His warmth settled into me as he sat beside me on the stage. His arm wrapped around me in both comfort and threats. "Sleep now, O. It's better that way."

Dreams dragged me down. Dreams of darkness and torment.

A single green olive in a martini glass appeared in the blackness, crystal liquid sloshing with rainbows. A cocktail stick speared the olive.

It screamed.

"Wait…" My fingers grew claws as I fought back to the surface. "I need to know something." A question danced out of reach, frolicking with sheep, begging to be counted. There was something about Olive that was important. Something about Olive that I didn't understand.

Olive…

"Hush." His lips pressed against my temple. "Don't worry. Everything will be over soon."

Tallup…

A blackboard with chalk.

A teacher with evil eyes.

Olive and Tallup.

A little girl in front of class.

A child who looked like our teacher.

His daughter!

"No!" I shot upright, blinking slow, my mind a black cloak of exhaustion. "Olive…she-she's your daughter."

Gil went statue stiff beside me, understanding the rabbit I chased. "O…don't. Please don't ask things I can't answer."

"Tallup raped you."

He trembled. "Go to sleep now, I beg you."

"Please tell me…" I forced my bowling ball of a head up, searching for his eyes. I met them. I held them. I knew. "Olive—"

"Don't." Gil's entire face cracked and crumpled. The lines around his eyes deepened. The crags in his forehead shadowed. He looked as if I'd killed him just by guessing the biggest secret he'd been hiding. The only secret that mattered. "Don't."

Our gazes tangled.

His denial blazed against my unspoken conclusion but the truth burned brighter.

Sleep tried to claim me again. "Olive…she's hers."

Gil shuddered as if he begged for any other solution than my life as currency. Any way to stop me from figuring out what he'd kept hidden. His head hung. His breath caught. He was trapped. "Olive is hers. But she's mine too. I named her…for you."

Tears beyond my control rained heavy and hard down my cheeks. I was allowed to hate him. I was meant to curse his very existence. I had no trust where he was concerned. No obligation in any form.

Yet, I cried for him and for me.

I cried for both of us because it wasn't fake breakups, molesting teachers, or blackmailing murderers who'd broken us.

It'd been the lies.

The tricks.

The shadows that'd always surrounded Gilbert Clark and the ones he retreated to rather than staying in the light with me.

No matter what happened.

No matter if I died tonight, he died, we all died, *this* had died.

Us.

There is no more us.

His arms wrapped me in a cage, his love imprisoning me.
I tried to stop crying. To put aside my grief and *wake up*.
But slowly, stealthily, finality crept over me.
My eyelids no longer opened.
My brain no longer operated.
My head lay on Gil's shoulder, needing support.

He clutched me closer as the final dregs of energy siphoned out of me. He stroked my hair and kissed my ear as I gave in to the cloud of unconsciousness. "Hopefully, by the time you wake up…this will all be over. You'll be free. You'll never have to see me again." He angled my chin, his lips claiming mine.

I tried to pull back, to stop the kiss, to study his godforsaken eyes, but he caged me closer. He pulled heat and hunger from deep within, sending me into lullabies with his taste on my lips and his grief on my tongue. "I'm so sorry, O. So sorry for ever thinking I could make you happy. You deserve so much more. I love you. I love you with every fucking part of me, but I can't stop this. At least sleep is a gift I can give you. The only thing I can give you."

Voices were far away and not of my dream world as he lowered me down until I lay on the stage. My eyelids fluttered as he turned on the air compressor and the first lick of unwanted paint landed upon my skin.

But I couldn't move.
Couldn't fight.
Gil was an artist.
Art was his drug.
The creation of beauty helped him cope in the depths of his despair. He needed art to function, to survive.
And with his talent, he stole my function.
Brush by brush, he destroyed me.
Colour by colour, he sentenced me to die.
He snuffed out my survival.
He'd poisoned me so I'd sleep.
So I wouldn't be awake when my purpose as his masterpiece was over.

Chapter Three

Gil

-The Past-

"SO…."

I looked up from my untouched beer. My eyes met Justin Miller's curious ones, and I wondered all over again what the fuck I was doing in a bar with him two weeks after the worst thing in my life had happened.

Olive had been taken from me.

Taken by someone I trusted.

I'd paid the first ransom.

The second had arrived this morning.

I'd been in my head, plotting and scheming, doing my best to figure out how to snatch Olive back when I'd bumped into my past on the street.

"So…" I gritted my teeth, tipping the pint to my lips and sipping wet froth.

Gross.

"This is random, huh?" Justin chuckled, glancing around the darkened pub that'd survived the days of witch trials, Saxon sieges, and sooty open fireplaces. The low ceilings made the dingy booths and low beams cocoon us like a cavern, while the stained glass windows refused to let twilight perk up the place.

The entire establishment matched my mood. My heart. My aching, useless soul.

I sipped again—despite my hatred of liquor—struggling to hold small talk when all I could think about was my daughter in the hands of my goddamn uncle. Why did I not see it coming? Why didn't I do something before it was too fucking late?

Goddammit, Olive.

My chest spasmed as if a grenade had exploded and shrapnel dug into my insides, poisoning me, killing me.

How could I let this happen?

Sweet little Olive who'd I'd named after Olin. Adorable little Olive who'd named herself thanks to a children's book I'd found on the bus in the first few weeks of parenthood. A dog-eared, well-loved edition of *Popeye The Sailor Man.*

I'd flicked through the pages, my heart aching at the images of Popeye in love with a feisty, perfect woman named Olive Oyl.

All he cared about was making her his.

Just like I'd done with O.

I'd read the tattered book to my nameless daughter as she'd cooed on my lap. She'd wriggled and blown bubbles each time I said Olive Oyl.

By the time the story was over, I knew what her name was.

Justin cleared his throat, dragging me back to the present. "So…are you a house painter or an artist…or something else?"

I scowled at my colour-stained hands. The clues of my trade. The signs of my failure. "Uh-huh."

"What do you paint? Houses? Canvases?"

"Doesn't matter." I shrugged, my eyes trailing to the door and the street beyond. I had twenty-four hours to come up with the second payment. I had the cash. I had more than enough. Ever since I hit success with body painting, I'd squirrelled away every penny to pave a golden path for whatever Olive wanted to do when she was older.

Those funds had been for her college, travel, or passion dreams. Not to pay a fucking bastard not to kill her.

My mind once again lashed tight to my daughter. I couldn't do much else these days apart from think about her, worry about her, stare at my goddamn ceiling at night and hate myself for failing her.

"Not very talkative, are you?" Justin chuckled, taking another sip. "How about we start with easy questions?"

I resented him for dragging me back. I hated this. I refused to live in this world where Olive wasn't with me. I'd rather live in my memories where she was safe and happy.

My memories also held moments of another girl I'd loved.

O.

I growled under my breath.

Two loves of my life.

Both stolen.

"What did you get up to after school?" Justin asked, successfully breaking me from my past.

I forced myself to sit there, to give a generic answer of ex-schoolmates. "Nothing of interest."

How could I tell him that I'd run from school and never graduated? That the weeks following my disappearance with a baby hadn't been easy. That I'd managed to find a small studio apartment by paying cash and three months' rent in advance—almost all my father's ill-gotten money gone, just like that.

I spent the next week educating myself on how to feed, burb, clean, and soothe a newborn.

I kept her alive by some crazy miracle.

"Well, I went on to get my master's in accounting. Loved math enough to make it my career."

I grimaced. "Good for you." I didn't bother pretending to be interested in my beer. Alcohol repulsed me. The taste and smell were utterly repugnant after the beatings Dad gave me thanks to the violence found in a bottle.

"So…I'm going to say you're an artist not a decorator. That fair to assume?"

"Assume away."

"Okay then…how did you start making money with your art?"

I doubted the truth would be a good answer. To admit that while Olive slept, I painted. That I created a few original pieces, while others I copied previous masters, doing my best to have something worthwhile to sell on street corners for coins. Olive had rested in the satchel I'd stolen, and I'd swallowed my morals as I used her as a tool to open the wallets of dog walkers and women with their own children.

That was how I began.

But not how I became rich.

"Lucky break."

"Yeah, I'd say." Justin grinned. "You're living the dream that most never get to achieve."

I coughed on a morbid laugh. I stifled the urge to fucking cry. "Yep, living the dream. That's me."

The worst kind of nightmare.

Olive…I'll figure this out.

Somehow.

My daughter had eclipsed everything in my life.

If something ever happened to her…

I'd die.

Plain and simple.

Her place in my life was absolute. She'd been the only reason I'd survived after walking away from O. If I didn't have her, I would've slipped so deep and dark into the shadows, I wouldn't have cared about anything.

She was the reason I was still functional as a human being.

Take her away for much longer and…*I don't know what I'll become.*

"When you left school suddenly, I figured you'd been given an opportunity you couldn't refuse." Justin clinked his beer glass to mine on the bar. "Scored a deal before even graduating, huh?"

My hands clung to my pint glass, squeezing to the point of pain.

Fuck, what am I doing?

I shouldn't be here.

I should be at my warehouse painting another commission to keep idle hands busy and broken minds out of trouble.

Then why did you say yes to a beer?

Justin must've heard my thoughts as he asked, "Look, mate, if you don't want to catch up, then why are we here?"

I stiffened.

O.

O and Justin.

I need to know.

A crest of history and heartbreak crashed over me, and honesty that I could no longer hide spilled out in a snarl. "How's Olin, Miller?"

His eyes widened, eyebrows shot up as he shifted uncomfortably on the barstool. I held his stare, not giving him any reprieve.

That was the reason I'd said yes to catching up for old time's sake.

She was the reason.

The only fucking reason.

I'd lost Olive just like I'd lost O.

The pain of that was brutal…two bleeding wounds in one.

Turned out, I enjoyed torturing myself with unfixable things.

"Olin and I…" It was his turn to swill a mouthful of beer. He was older with weathered lines and age that no longer graced us with teenage youth, but his voice stayed genuine and truthful. "We broke up pretty much the week you vanished from school."

I froze.

Questions roared for answers. I had no right to ask. She wasn't mine. But all this time, I'd soothed my agony by convincing myself O was with a guy who would protect and love her—even if it wasn't me. All the days and nights that I gave my all being a father to a kid who would *never* have the upbringing I did, I promised myself that Olin was better off without me.

That she was happy…with Justin.

"What happened?" I swallowed hard, fighting to get my voice into some semblance of calm.

Justin rounded his shoulders. "Well, eh, I knew she still had feelings for you. I mean…that was what drew me to her. To help her get over you."

"Gee, you're a real saint, Miller. A goddamn hero."

He held up a hand. "Look, you knew what O was like. She was so sweet to everyone. So kind and helpful. She helped me once when I locked my keys, wallet, phone—all my shit basically—in my car. Everyone else had gone home, and I was stuck like an idiot. She called a locksmith and waited with me until he'd popped the lock. I offered to drive her home but she said you'd be waiting for her. That you'd make sure she was safe." He whistled under his breath. "Even then, I knew she was head over heels for you. And she deserved to be happy. Not that I understood it. The sweetest girl in school with the meanest boy?" He drank again, rolling his eyes. "Didn't get that at all. But we were friends, and I was there for her when you made her cry." His gaze flashed bright blue. "I hated you for that by the way. Thought you were a right git."

I yanked my hands off the bar, curling them into fists between my legs. "I broke her heart, but you took advantage of her. You jumped straight into her bed."

True anger highlighted his normally rational face. "Fuck you, Clark. It wasn't like that. I offered to be her friend, that's all. To be there for her, seeing as you refused to be."

My eyes narrowed. "Don't give me that bullshit. I caught you two kissing. I saw your goddamn hand up her top."

His gaze filled with calculation, doing math on our past and forming conclusions he shouldn't have. "You sound as if you're not over her."

"It was years ago." I looked away, wishing everything was different. Wishing O was mine, and Olive was safe, and I'd never made such a fucking mess of everything.

Justin muttered, "Yeah, but time doesn't matter when hearts are involved."

My eyes flickered to the exit again, weighing up the options of running. Olin wasn't with him. He couldn't provide me with any comfort knowing she was happy or safe. She was out there. Alone. Somewhere.

My back tensed. "Why did you break up? If you were such good friends, what went wrong?" My voice had way too much bite, but Justin ignored my temper, being gracious with his reply.

"She was hurting. I'm not going to deny that we kissed a few times or that I asked her out for real. I seem to like damsels in distress. It makes me feel good to help them." He shrugged. "Still does if I'm honest. I'm with a girl right now, Colleen, who I found crying at a bus stop after her twat of an ex broke up with her at the movies and drove off with her handbag. I took her home, gave her a shoulder to cry on, and asked her out the next day. I dunno how it happens. I see someone hurting, and I have to help."

"You get off on helping?"

He scowled. "It's not sexual. It just…makes me feel like I have purpose. Like life isn't all about me."

I had no reply to that. How could I respond to someone who I'd nursed a teenage hatred for? I couldn't hate him because of how genuine he was. I couldn't despise him for taking O away from me when I'd been the one who pushed her into his arms. They were similar. They were both *good people*. And I was the bad guy all over again.

I wanted to punch him in the jaw. "O was never a damsel in distress, you idiot. If you think that, then you didn't know her at all."

Justin blinked. "Yeah, you're right." He took another swig, his beer rapidly vanishing. "After we broke up, O threw herself into dance. Became obsessed with it. You know her parents weren't really in her life, and the moment school finished, she left and joined a troupe in London. I didn't see her again."

London?

Had our paths crossed when I'd lived there with my infant daughter? Had we walked the same streets and not even known it? Had I brushed past her and not realised my soul-mate had been right there?

Fuck.

The gnawing, clawing pain of missing Olive tangled with the

hot poker of loss from O. I grabbed my untouched beer and shot it down my throat. Alcohol wasn't welcome in my world. But my world had become unbearable.

The nights were the hardest while I lay unable to sleep in Olive's bed, smelling her favourite strawberry body wash, hugging a pair of her small pyjamas, wondering if she'd been fed and hugged, showered and tucked into bed.

I needed something to numb that pain. To slam a door on the horrors and grant silence from the nightmares.

Maybe beer could grant that peace.

Maybe that was why alcoholics abandoned their life for the numbing prostration that liquor provided.

I struggled for something to say. Justin kept looking at me far too intently—almost as if I was his next victim in his 'gotta help someone in need' crusade.

"Well, I'm glad she followed her dreams." I pushed away my empty glass, feeling sick to my stomach. I had ransoms to pay. Daughters to save. Ex-girlfriends to forget.

I couldn't fucking afford to drink.

Justin nodded slowly. "How about you, Clark? Everything okay with you? You don't look so good."

I couldn't hold back the cold snort. *"Me?"* Fuck, what a loaded question. My life was completely out of bounds. No one must know that I'd failed my daughter. The child who was born of rape and threats.

"Yeah, what have you been up to? Getting much sleep?"

"Ah, you know." My eyes once again trailed to the exit. My legs bunched to get up and leave. He'd told me all I needed to know. He wasn't with O. He hadn't married her and given her a family in some white picketed home where she would never be lonely again.

Instead, he was with a girl called Colleen, and O was off dancing in London.

There was no connection between the three of us anymore.

And I was done.

Standing, I worked out the crick in my neck. The past two weeks of no sleep, barely any food, and the stress of Olive's kidnapping had turned every fist and kick from my youth into a delayed injury. I should've been too young to suffer arthritis, but I swore every joint and muscle had crept past eighty and no longer knew how to work. "I've got to go."

"Busy night painting?"

"Something like that."

Justin stood too. "I'll walk you out." Throwing a tenner onto the bar, he waved his arm, waiting for me to stride ahead first.

Hiding my annoyance, I stalked to the exit and bowled into twilight.

Justin crossed his arms against the slight chill in the air. "Who do you paint for?"

I'd hoped he'd quit with the questions the moment we'd left the bar, but he didn't. "Myself."

"Do you have a business name?"

I narrowed my eyes. "Why?"

"I'd like to pop by sometime. See your work."

"My work is different. My canvases are…not what you're used to."

"I'd still like to come by."

"Why? To check up on me?"

"Maybe." He smirked. "What do you paint?"

I looked down the street, past the milling pedestrians and smiling shoppers, and only saw a world that didn't care that my daughter was in the hands of a monster or that I was screaming inside for goddamn help.

I couldn't enlist the police.

I couldn't go to the media.

I had no family or friends to help me make decisions.

All I had was a fat bank balance that was waiting for me to withdraw a hefty amount for ransom number two.

"Come on, tell me." He laughed. "I'm a boring accountant. O has her dance and you have your art. Both of you followed your passions, not a paycheque. Share a piece with me, so I can live vicariously through you."

I sighed, wanting this meeting to be over. "I paint women."

His eyes lit up. "Naked women?"

"Knickers on but breasts mostly bare, yes."

"Wow, that's a career choice they don't mention at school." He punched me lightly in the shoulder. "Good for you, mate."

I stepped out of his reach. "I have to go."

"Fine. But we should do this again sometime. Soon."

"Why would we bother doing this awkward attempt at conversation again?"

For a second, he paused, no doubt annoyed that I'd spoken the truth about this farce, but then he nodded with sincerity. "Don't get mad at me, Clark, but…I think you need someone you can have an awkward attempt at conversation with every now and again."

"What the fuck does that mean?"

"It means you look half-starved and the black circles under your eyes are either from working way too many hours or worrying about way too many things. Problems are better shared, mate."

I bared my teeth. "Keep your guesswork to yourself, all right, Miller? I'm fine. I don't need you or anyone—"

"We all need company at some point in our lives." Pulling his phone from his pocket, he quickly typed in something before scrolling through lines of text that appeared. It only took him a second before looking up with a triumphant, almost pitying look. "Master of Trickery. Cool name."

"How…how did you find that?"

"I googled man who paints naked women in Birmingham. You're on the first page."

Shit.

Was Olive mentioned on there?

Was my past and what'd happened with Tallup printed for the world to see?

Snatching my phone, I did the same search, relaxing when only business-related stuff and my website popped up. Reviews of my work and chatter on Facebook feeds about my time-lapse videos cluttered the search results, but there was no mention of my personal life, who I was, and what I'd lost.

Justin put his phone away and turned to leave. "I'll be seeing ya, Clark. I'll pop by with a takeaway sometime. Make sure you're not a starving artist and eating something occasionally."

"I don't need your charity, okay? Just back the fuck—"

"Who said anything about charity?"

"I don't need you sticking your nose in at my warehouse when I—"

"Cool, you have a warehouse? Definitely popping round now."

"Don't want you there, Miller."

"Too bad. I'm a nosy git and already issued myself an invitation."

I crossed my arms. "Don't you have some other helpless stray to smother with good intentions?"

"Nope." He smiled. "Just you for now. Colleen is getting a bit annoyed with my mother hen routine, so I need someone else to bug."

"Count yourself successful."

He laughed. "I will when you've lost that tortured, haunted look."

That won't happen until I get my daughter back.

Until I can stop thinking about O.

Until I'm no longer such a fuck-up.

I backed away. "Like I said, I don't do pity. This is where this ends. Got it?"

He just smirked. "I don't call it pity. I call it being a friend. See ya next week, Clark." Waving goodbye, he vanished in a sea of tourists and pedestrians, his threat lingering on the air.

Chapter Four

Gil

-The Present-

I WAS A bastard.

I knew that.

I'd known it since I was born: a self-centred, down-to-his-core *bastard*.

But being a bastard was necessary when raising a little girl on your own. I had to suspect everyone, protect her from everything, and be on my guard at all times.

Because if I didn't treat the world as if it was my enemy, it wasn't me who would get hurt.

It was Olive Oyl.

It's almost over, little spinach.

I promise.

I stopped the car.

The engine idled as I stared into the dense blackness of Lickey Hills Country Park. Rugged and wild, the trees silent and savage. He'd brought me to this forest when he'd first taken her. It'd been the only information he'd given me—taunting me with her safety every day of my godforsaken life since she'd been stolen.

And it was all my fucking fault.

I should have stayed true to my rules.

I should never have trusted him.

The past seven years, everything I'd done was for my daughter.

I'd learned how to paint with every medium to give me the best chance at employment. I'd accepted small commissions and badly paid work to get noticed. I'd slowly gone from penniless to middle-class, earning enough to keep Olive warm and fed.

And then what had I done?

I'd failed her.

In the worst possible way a father could fail his child.

My scratchy eyes landed on my hands strangling the steering wheel. They still held colour-splatters from painting O while she'd lain unconscious in my warehouse.

I wanted to cut out my heart for drugging her.

I'd rather give up my life instead of hers.

Who knows…you might.

He'd told me to paint her with the shadows of bracken: greys and greens, blacks and browns. The perfect camouflage to make her disappear in a woodland, leaving her to die alone and unprotected.

I'd disobeyed.

Instead of nondescript concealment, I'd painted every inch of beautiful skin in a personal punishment.

Punishment for me.

I'd used the colour palette he'd requested…but the symbolism airbrushed into her skin reminded me that tonight…it all ended.

One way or another.

Turning to study O, a suffocating wave of guilt wrapped around my chest. She lay sprawled and sleeping in the back seat, her eyes closed, lips slack, her beauty even more radiant thanks to the earthy colours she wore.

She looked as if she was the queen of an olive grove. Crowned with a wreath of silvery leaves, her arms and legs entwined with the supple branches of an olive tree. Thousands of olives. Black and green, brown and purple hung heavy on the interlocking, protecting foliage that crisscrossed and hugged her chest and stomach.

It'd been the worst commission of my life.

Painting a lifeless lover with the emblem of my daughter's name, all because if I didn't have the blatant reminder of who I was doing this for…I wouldn't have the guts to go through with it.

My daughter came first.

That was how it should be.

But O…*fuck*.

The urge to vomit rose again.

The back of my throat was raw. The taste in my mouth

disgusting. I hadn't eaten properly in days and couldn't keep anything down.

I was fighting for both of them…but there was a chance this might not work.

I might lose my daughter or my soul-mate.

I might lose both.

I would rather lose my own life than allow that to happen.

You're late.

Turning off the engine, I climbed achy and beaten from the shitty hatchback I'd bought after selling my expensive 4WD when the bribes kept coming and I no longer had disposal cash to pay them. I opened the back door and bent to untie the ropes around her wrists and ankles so they were looser.

Rubbing away the redness my knots had caused her, I swallowed down another avalanche of guilt as I re-tied them, looser and not nearly as imprisoning.

Hopefully, she'd be able to wriggle out of them and run if this all went to shit.

I'm sorry.

Gritting my teeth, I slipped my arms under her legs and back, pulling her from the car and into my embrace.

She remained unconscious. Her paint had dried enough not to smudge. The weight of her in my arms made me suffocate and stumble in horror.

Fuck!

I couldn't do this.

I have to do this.

Hoisting her higher into my arms, I carried her paint-naked body from the small glade I'd parked in and entered the midnight wilderness.

My boots—that had been witness to my many crimes—once again squelched through mud and forest debris. The number of hours I'd trekked through woods trying to find Olive couldn't be calculated. Days at a time, midnight to dawn…always coming home empty, drowning my sorrows in liquor—the medicinal vodka burning my throat with hypocrisy.

I'd walked the entire length of England and back, searching, searching, always searching. Hoping I could find her before the next ransom came in. Before the next murder. Before the next threat.

O stirred in my arms.

Her eyelids fluttered upward, fuzzy and hazed pupils meeting mine as I carried her through the dark.

"Gil…" She swallowed. Her face scrunched up, fighting the nitrazepam the doctor had given me for my insomnia.

Ever since Olive had been taken, I'd turned into a total insomniac. The only sleep I snatched was filled with nightmares of chasing after Olive, promising her I'd find her, protect her, save her, only to slam me back into loneliness.

I'd crushed a few into O's sandwich, knowing the punch they delivered when they kicked in.

"Shush. I got you." Tears scalded my eyes as Olin shivered.

"I'm c-cold."

"Go back to sleep. It's warmer in your dreams."

She shook her head, sluggish and slow. "I don't wan—" Her eyelids drooped closed again, sucking her back into false hibernation.

"I'm so sorry, O," I murmured while silhouettes of trees swayed around us, spectators at a funeral.

Her funeral.

My funeral.

His funeral.

Anyone's but Olive's.

I had a long walk in front of me, off the marked trail and hidden from hiker's knowledge. My heart ached with grief that I couldn't stop this. My body trembled with every step. And the rotten bastard inside me couldn't just let Olin rest peacefully in my arms.

I treated her as my confessional. A priestess who had the power to absolve me.

Looking down at her lovely face, I whispered, "I have no excuse for what I'm doing, but…I was broken when I left you, O. Damaged beyond repair. If it hadn't been for Olive—" I slipped on a wet section of decomposing leaves. "I've been such a traitor to you. The worst kind of monster. You trusted me. You tried to help me. And this is how I repay you."

She murmured sleepily; her slumbering, gentle face ripped my heart out. Lax and young, innocent and pure. Her dancing dreams had been stolen. Now, thanks to me, the rest of her life might be too.

Nausea swarmed, prickling sweat under my shirt and making sourness coat my tongue. "I won't let him have you. I promise this will all work out." I raised my arms, bringing her close enough to kiss her cheek—the softness of her painted olive grove skin.

"Once you're safe and Olive is safe…I'm going to kill him. And once he's dead, I'm going to confess everything to the police. I can't live with this anymore. I deserve to be punished for what I've done." I laughed hollowly. "After all, I've always been destined to go to prison. I've avoided it longer than I expected. I was born to a pimp, whore to a teacher, and now, I'm a collector for a murderer. The first two crimes weren't my fault. But the third…I'm guilty."

My voice thickened. "I'm guilty, O. Those girl's deaths smear my hands, and I'm done. Tonight is the last time he'll ask me to kill."

Olin mumbled something in her sleep, her lips working with mysterious words.

I needed to believe she'd heard me and understood.

In reality, if she had heard, she'd condemn me to the devil and rightfully so.

My fingers feathered over her hip where her painted-lacy underwear ruined the perfection of smooth branches and tiny, silver olive leaves. Inside the seam rested the GPS tracker. I prayed to everything holy that it worked and didn't fail me.

I was placing all my faith in its accuracy.

I was gambling my daughter's life as well as O's that Jeffrey would return to his unfindable location with Olin and keep her alive long enough for me to hunt.

The small piece of technology hadn't warmed from her body; it didn't feel like a friend…merely another foe I couldn't trust.

"I'm a bastard, O, but I'm not giving up. He's bled me dry of everything. I hate what I've become. But he can't have Olive, and he can't have you. It's over. It's time for *him* to feel what it's like to die."

My hands curled into fists, tasting the black satisfaction of murdering a murderer. I had the perfect weapon to do it. It sat quiet and unassuming in my left pocket, ready to steal his life.

Once he was dead, I'd gather my daughter and soul-mate and walk back into the light.

And if he kills them before you get to him?

My rage once again became brittle with fear.

My plan was flimsy and chaotic, but it was the best I had.

I'd been backed into a corner and was willing to do whatever it took.

Including sacrificing myself if it comes to it.

My eyes continued to trace O's prettily painted face while I shifted her weight into one arm. Stopping for a moment, I pulled my phone free from my right pocket.

It was time to send plan B.

Bringing up the message I'd typed to Justin moments before O arrived at my warehouse, I fought the urge to be sick all over again.

To see what I'd become in black and white...to re-read my crimes.

Fuck.

This sort of message wasn't meant to be sent. Justin and I didn't exactly have the sort of relationship where any of this was acceptable.

We'd just bumped into each other by chance, and instead of him walking away like he should have, he'd barged into my world and refused to take no for an answer. Our 'friendship' consisted of him being far too forgiving and me being a fucking asshole.

He reminded me too much of O's kindness—constantly tormenting me with memories of them together...kissing.

But each time he'd turned up at my warehouse, his presence somehow gave me the energy to keep going. To paint another commission. To pay another bribe. To keep my secrets hidden because, despite my outward unwelcome, he'd become *needed.*

Needed to keep me human so I wasn't a total monster when I finally rescued my daughter.

I owed him so fucking much.

And this message...well, it sold me into debt that I would never be able to repay.

Miller,
I have so many things to say, but I don't know how to say any of them.
I'll begin with the simplest one.
Thank you.
You're a better man than I'll ever be. You've had my back. You've helped me book commissions. You've nodded when I've snarled at you. And you never once asked why I was such a twat.
This message should end here. It should be a simple thank you.
Unfortunately...I have a favour to ask.
I've named you executor of my estate.
Why?
Because I'm involved in the painted murders.
I've helped take lives to save a life.
The life of my daughter.

Olive.
*The story of her origin isn't important, but what is important is, I will do
whatever it takes to save her.*
And this is the part where you'll hate me all the more.
I know you cared for O.
I love her with all my fucking heart, but…I need you to help her.
*Along with this message is a link to a GPS tracker. The device is hidden on
Olin. She is the next victim, and I'm doing everything I can to keep her alive.*
But…if I fail.
If I die.
I need you to find her before it's too late.
Call the police. Tell them everything.
Find her, rescue her, keep her.
And…when you find her, please find my daughter too.
My heart belongs to both of them.
If I've failed…please take care of them.
I name you godfather.
Keep my loved ones as your own.
Tell O I'm sorry.
Tell my daughter that I tried.

Chapter Five

Olin

-The Present-

"YOU'RE LATE."

My eyes struggled against the heavy curtains pulling them down. A cloak of sleepiness and weighted imprisonment.

Gil's arms twitched around me, his deep rumble of a voice threatening and soothing all at once. "It's a long walk."

"Long walk or not, you took your time on this one, Gilbert. Dangerous time." The man's tone changed, speaking to someone younger and innocent. "Look who decided to join us, sweetheart. Told you he'd turn up."

I squirmed to focus on whoever he spoke to. A camping light hung in a tree, illuminating the small clearing. My eyes closed again, my muscles ignoring my commands in favour of exhaustion.

But this time, I fought back.

I fought hard.

I moaned and clawed my way to the surface.

This is important.

It was imperative I had wits and wisdom, flight and fight.

I couldn't quite remember why, but...

Killers.

Painters.

I'm next.

Standing in the gloom of the false moon lashed to the tree, a man stood with a calculating grin on his face. Beside him stood a child. A girl with long sooty hair, her pretty eyes huge as a nocturnal creature better suited for darkness, not light.

"Get your fucking hands off her." Gil's entire body stiffened as his gaze landed on the child. His chest heaved against me, his heart thundering painfully. "Hey, Olive Oyl. You okay?" His voice echoed with grief and the gravity of seeing a little girl with an older man's paw resting on her shoulders in the woods.

My own stomach churned at the picture.

Olive?

Olive!

His dream, his nightmare, the love of his life.

Olive…the consequence of rape.

"Hey, Daddy…." Her face scrunched up with worry. "I missed you."

"Oh, God. I missed you too, little spinach." Gil's legs gave out, forcing him to stumble forward and place me as gently as he could on the ground. His voice cracked. "Wow…you've grown so big."

She smiled cautiously. "Uncle Jeffrey said I could come see you."

"That's great." Gil dared look at the guy holding her captive. His entire body trembled to rush forward and grab her. "You finally brought her? After a goddamn year of keeping her from me?"

"Be grateful I was feeling generous." The guy chuckled quietly, his hand waving permission to continue conversation.

Gil cleared his throat, doing his best to find strength I feared he no longer had. His eyes drank in his daughter as if he was drowning. "You okay? God, I've missed you *so* much."

Olive cried quietly. "You don't look so good. Are *you* okay?"

"I am now that I'm with you." Gil strangled a laugh. "Missing you is hard work." He forced a wink, his face twisting with relief and terror. "I haven't had anyone to help me cook spinach lately." He added wobbly humour into his tone. "Know anywhere I can get some out here? Could do with a shot of strength right about now."

Olive kicked her dirty sneaker into the earth, no longer willing to talk. "Are you not strong like Popeye anymore?"

Gil flinched. "I am now you're here."

Olive sniffed. "Daddy, I want to go home."

The love in her voice. The yearning and need. She adored Gil. Totally in love with her father just like he was in love with her.

I wanted to hate her.

I wanted something to direct my rage at Gil's molestation. Jane Tallup deserved to be publicly shamed and then shot...but her daughter? The little girl who stood in the darkness wasn't her awful mother.

She was afraid and small and trapped.

And she needed her father.

Desperately.

Another wash of tiredness tried to suck me under.

Something hurt me deep, deep inside.

My heart cried for this small family who'd been ripped apart by greed. My head pounded for freedom for all of us.

Gil's entire fight vanished; he left me lying on the bracken, raking both hands through his hair as he stood upright on exhausted legs. "I want that too. And we're going home. Tonight we're going—"

"Ah, ah, ah, making promises you can't keep again, Gilbert?"

Whatever drugs Gil had fed me fractured at the man's tone.

Him.

The black van.

The asshole who beat up Gil all because I'd used the word *us.*

Gil stiffened; his face turned black. "I'm done playing this pathetic game, Jeffery." His voice dripped with menace. No more distress, only danger. "I've given you everything I have. I have nothing left. You hear me? Nothing. You've made damn sure of that. Just let me take my daughter and—"

"Not so fast."

The little girl shot forward, spying an opportunity to run. "Daddy!" She bowled toward Gil, her arms outstretched, her face afraid. "Please—"

She didn't get very far.

Jeffrey swiped at her, catching the hood of the lemon jacket she wore. Wrenching her back, he tutted under his breath. "That's rude, sweetheart." Ducking to his haunches, he yanked the girl into the cage made by his legs. "Living with me hasn't been so bad, has it? You've enjoyed the toys I gave you. You said you did." He shook her. "Be a grateful little girl, sweetheart. Go on."

Olive sniffed back tears, nodding bravely. "Yes, Uncle Jeffrey. Thank you for the toys."

"And?"

"And for taking care of me when Daddy couldn't."

Gil roared with fury. "Leave her the hell alone."

"There's a good girl." Jeffrey spoke to Olive before rising to his feet. "I see you brought me a gift, Gilbert." He acted as if he hadn't heard Gil bellow at him. He behaved as if this meeting in the woods was perfectly rational behaviour.

"Name your price," Gil snarled. "Any figure. I'll give it to you. A million? Ten? I'll do whatever it takes to pay you. Just let it be about the money and forget about O and Olive."

He bartered for my life.

He begged for Olive's.

My brain short-circuited, unable to accept such wrongness.

The drugs snatched me back.

My world went dark and silent.

I slipped.

Slipped from chilly forest to soft clouds.

Blackness.

Blankness.

A void.

* * * * *

I came to, being collected gently from the forest floor, only to be placed at the feet of the man who'd destroyed Gil's life.

I was cold.

The ground was prickly and painful on my bare, painted skin.

Gil's face hovered above mine as my eyes shot wide.

I was coherent and blazingly aware, if only for a moment.

His eyes held lines only old men who'd buried loved ones and survived holocausts should carry. His lips were bitten and cheeks sunken. He barely looked alive, sucked dry by the devil keeping his daughter as collateral.

"It's always been you, O. Always." He kissed me softly; his voice sullied with despair. "But...I never had a choice." His lips skated over mine again, shivering with apologetic misery.

"D Don't..." I blinked madly, fighting the binds of tiredness, wishing my tongue worked as well as my vision.

But it was too late.

Gil placed me tenderly at the feet of a murderer.

"Now, get back." Jeffrey pointed a finger at Gil as if he was an unruly wolf. "You know what we agreed."

What did they agree?

What did I miss while I'd been sucked back into sleep?

Gil tripped backward. "Please."

I struggled to sit up, to dig my palms into the dirt and stop this madness. My mind might be awake, but my body definitely wasn't. It was loose and languid, powerless and prone.

It took every bit of energy I had to twist my head to keep Gil insight.

He looked as if he wanted to rip Jeffery into pieces all while he slowly fell to his knees and prepared to beg. He might have resorted to pleading, but there was nothing pathetic about him. Nothing useless or inadequate about a man willing to lower himself to dirt for those he loved.

He was regal, a legend, a father who knew where his loyalties lay and what love demanded.

He was the reason I was here.

His paint on my skin, and my death on his hands.

He didn't deserve my forgiveness, but he did have my understanding.

I had no choice but to understand the depths of his pain and desperation whenever he looked at his daughter. It blazed all over him like a physical entity. A power he couldn't deny.

His hands banded together in prayer as his gaze flickered from me to Olive. His throat worked as he swallowed hard, his voice strangled and dying. "Name it, Jeffrey. What do I have to do—"

"Keep delivering what we agreed."

"I have. Thousands of times over."

"Yes, but retirement is expensive."

"I'll pay your every bill and whim until the day you die, just let me take them home."

Jeffrey chuckled coldly, wrapping his fist in Olive's hair.

She cried out, flinching as he pulled her cruelly into his side. "You think I'd trust you to pay without incentive?"

"I give you my word." Gil swallowed again, his face white and strained. "You'll always be rich. I'll give everything I have—"

"Enough," Jeffrey shouted. "Get out of my sight before you humiliate yourself further."

"You can't take her again." Gil scrambled to his feet, his fists curled and shaking by his sides. "Keep your side of the bargain." He winced, looking at me bound and drugged on a bed of twigs and leaves. "Olin for Olive. I've paid your price." His hand came up, waiting for a smaller one to fit into his. "Give me my daughter."

"Popeye," Olive whimpered.

Jeffrey snickered, yanking her against his leg. "Change of plans."

Gil's face lost any sign of vulnerability. His eyes shuttered, his lips thinned. Aggression rippled over him. "Give her to me. I won't ask again."

My heart picked up, filtering the drug and granting a tiny trickle of strength to limbs tingling and tight from being tethered.

"I like how you think you're in the position to threaten me." Jeffrey snaked his arm around Olive's shoulders, hugging her close. "Maybe I'll keep both of them, tighten your leash a little more."

Olive winced, curling into herself.

Jeffrey sighed dramatically. "And you used to be so obedient."

Gil bared his teeth, his entire body vibrating with pure hatred. "A deal is a deal."

I wanted him to win.

I wanted his daughter to be saved and no longer living with a madman.

But if he won, that meant I lost.

I would die in her place, and my survival instinct wouldn't let that happen.

Flexing my fingers and toes, I willed more blood to circulate, to wash me clean, to give me power.

Slowly, my body shed the garment of lethargy, answering my commands.

Gil stormed forward, all negotiations and pleasantries over. He looked as if he'd tear Jeffrey's head right off his shoulders.

I wanted him to.

Kill him

Save us both.

But it only took Jeffrey the smallest move to halt Gil mid-step. His hand vanished behind him, whipping forward with a gun. "Decide. Here and now." The black weapon glinted in the lamplight, morbid and menacing. He swung the muzzle to face me. "The woman you love?" Almost lazily, he tracked the weapon to wedge against Olive's temple. "Or your daughter?"

She froze like a tiny rabbit. Teeth locked on her bottom lip. Her shivers pure fear.

Gil struggled to breathe. His eyes shot black, cursing Jeffrey to purgatory for even pointing a gun at his child. "I promise you, you motherfucker, if you shoot either of them, you'll be dead a second after."

The two men's eyes locked.

A silent war passed between them.

Finally, Jeffrey nodded and waved the gun at the dense blackness just out of reach of the lamp. "I think I'll keep both alive…for now. Higher incentive for you to pad my retirement a little more, don't you think?"

"I'm not painting any more girls."

"So you don't agree with my little hobby?"

Gil couldn't hide the growl in his chest. "Killing for sport is—"

"A recognised pastime," Jeffrey sneered. "Hunters shoot deer. Humans eat animals. Anything with a heartbeat is killable." He grinned darkly. "I just happen to like the two-legged variety."

Gil spat on the ground. "I'll kill you, you son of a bitch."

"Perhaps." He laughed, way too confident and assured. "But as long as I have your daughter, you're my puppet. So…I expect you to keep dancing on your strings." He waved the gun again. "Now, run along, Mr. Popeye, and don't forget to eat some spinach. Olive Oyl is right; you aren't looking so good."

Gil didn't move.

For the longest second, he stared at me, then Olive and shook his head as if he couldn't believe the trap he'd been caught in.

He hated himself.

His self-loathing permeated the air until he choked on it.

I waited for him to walk away.

To leave both of us to our fate.

But something triggered in him. Some base instinct that didn't bow to rules or threats, not anymore. He couldn't walk away. I knew that in my bones.

I didn't know how long it'd been since he'd seen Olive.

I didn't know anything about his life anymore.

But the building outrage on his face spoke of a man who'd reached his limit. A man who would no longer kneel to another—not when those he loved were in danger and within grabbing distance—ready to be saved if he could only kill the monster in the middle.

He stalked toward Jeffrey with his gaze locked on his daughter. "Olive, come here."

Olive squirmed and fought, kicking and scratching at Jeffrey as he struggled to hold her.

I played my part in the distraction, kicking my tied legs and wriggling on the slippery bracken.

Jeffrey witnessed his carefully choreographed meeting

dissolve into anarchy.

Gil leaped forward.

One hand reached for Olive, and the other punched Jeffrey in the jaw.

The three of them tumbled in a pile of body parts while Gil tried to murder his enemy with nothing more than fists and fury.

I tried to scream. To activate a voice that stayed dormant with drugs.

But then a gunshot rang out.

A swarm of crows exploded from the treetops. Pigeons and sparrows, finches and thrushes all soaring for the sky thanks to violence.

I squirmed and gasped, trying to sit up to see. To know if the bullet had missed or…

Tears pricked as Gil fell backward, his hands high above his head in surrender, his eyes frantic as he searched Olive for injury. "You okay?" His breath caught and voice scratched with gravel. "Please tell me you're not hurt."

Thank God, he wasn't shot.

Fierce hope filled me that the rogue bullet had lodged inside Jeffrey.

Olive cried, crystal tears glittering on pretty cheeks. "I'm all right." She stayed sitting in the dirt, shoulders rolled and grief overtaking, knowing that Gil's attempt at rescue had failed, and she was about to pay the consequences.

Just like me.

With his gun high, Jeffrey clambered to his feet, brushing off leaf matter and curling his nose at the mud stain on his knee. The flutter of disgruntled birds still flapped around us.

He wasn't shot.

He wasn't defeated.

"That was stupid, Gilbert. Very, *very* stupid." He aimed the gun directly at Gil's heart. "I suggest you start walking before I change my mind."

Gil shook his head, furious despair painting his features. "I can't leave them."

"But you will if you want to live another day."

Gil looked at me, apology and uselessness blazing bright. He looked at Olive, desolation and failure crippling him.

He came to the same conclusion I did.

He didn't have a choice.

Fight now.

Die now.

Or walk away and hope to save us later.

Olive cried harder, understanding that the family reunion was about to end. "No! Take me with you. Don't—" She stood and tried to run to Gil, only to be cornered in Jeffrey's arms. "Don't go. Please!"

Gil squeezed his eyes shut, a tear licking down his cheek. "Olive. I love you. Forever and ever." His gaze opened, locking onto his flesh and blood. A family he'd created not borrowed. A little girl who idolized him. A child who believed he could fix this when he couldn't. "Please don't hate me for failing you. I'm not leaving you, okay? I'll never, *ever* leave you. I just…this is temporary. We'll be together again soon. I promise."

Olive cried harder. "*When?* When is soon?"

He shuddered. "As soon as I can. I promise we'll be together. I *promise.*"

Olive somehow managed to sniff up her sadness and nod bravely. "Okay. I'll be good. Maybe Uncle Jeffrey will let me go home if I behave better."

Gil vibrated with hate toward the man holding her captive. He couldn't stop his boots crunching forward, taking him toward the gun aimed in his direction and his young daughter. "Jeffrey, please…for fuck's sake, you have O. I'll continue to paint and deliver on your demands. Just give me Olive. Let me take her home. Accept the trade."

I winced at the urgency in his voice. The utmost dedication to his child while using me as collateral.

He'd already destroyed all my trust. Now, he destroyed all my hope.

Destroyed any hope that I was as important to him as Olive was. I was only valuable if I could be traded for what he truly wanted.

Once again, I wanted to hate.

I wanted to hate him and her and the man they called uncle.

But…no matter what he'd done to me—no matter the drugs he'd fed me and the bargains he begged for, I didn't have the strength to hate.

Hate demanded such a lot. It needed energy and emotion and a deep, dark heat that *burned.* Mostly naked and shivering on the forest floor, I had no energy. I'd used up all my emotion. The only thing I felt was tired.

Tired and resigned and sad.

So, so *sad*.

I'd lost everything.

I thought I'd lost it the moment I couldn't dance anymore.

But I'd been naïve.

A tattoo couldn't fix this.

Scars couldn't repair this.

This truly was the end.

I closed my eyes, willing the drugs to whisk me away.

But they didn't. They kept me awake and at their mercy as Gil whispered, "O…I'm so fucking sorry."

My eyelashes opened, filling my vision with his misery.

"I love you." His lips turned down as he drank me in. His gaze travelled over my skin painted with his mark, my love left as his sacrifice. For the longest moment, he stared, pouring love and apology into me, and begging me to understand, all while knowing he'd lost me forever.

There was no coming back from this.

No way of repairing what was broken.

With the heaviest of nods and most reluctant acceptance, he blew Olive a kiss, gave me one last look, then turned and walked away.

He tripped as if exhausted. He stumbled as if wounded. He moved like a man who'd forfeited everything.

A cresting, debilitating wave of terror cracked my ribs, one by one. My lungs sipped air rather than inhaled it. Fear vised my skull with pressure. Grief mushroom clouded until it filled me.

I hadn't had a panic attack since the first day I'd woken and found my body restricted by pins and pain.

I couldn't afford to have one now.

Steadying my breathing, I kept my eyes locked on Gil as he slowly left us behind.

The crunch of his boots sounded as horrid as cannon fire.

The sniff of his sadness as damning as death.

As the night swallowed him, Jeffrey bent to speak to Olive, his voice just loud enough for my enjoyment too. "Daddy isn't being a good boy these days." He stroked her hair even as she squirmed to get away. "He's not a very good painter anymore." He tapped her on the nose. "You know what? I think we've had enough of boring old Popeye, don't you?"

Olive gasped, clinging to Jeffrey's arm. "He just needs some spinach—"

"No…he needs a harsher lesson." He shook her off him,

standing tall. He raised his hand, pointing the gun at Gil's back.

Olive bounced on the spot, trying to grab his wrist. "No. *Don't—*"

"Shush, he'll hear you." Jeffrey snatched her and wrapped his free hand around her mouth. "Be quiet, sweetheart."

She moaned and mumbled behind his palm while he chuckled quietly, keeping his tone low so Gil would never know. "Let's shoot him and say bye-bye." He closed one eye, scoping out his prey. "Bye, pathetic nephew."

It happened in slow motion.

I couldn't believe he'd do it.

But then, it became real.

So unbelievably real.

No!

I opened my mouth to scream. To shout. To warn.

I jack-knifed as high as I could with rope and tiredness and yelled into the night. *"Gil!"*

But…just like before…it was too late.

The gunshot ripped my voice apart.

The bullet flashed through the dark.

Somewhere in the blackness, Gil grunted.

A vague shadow cartwheeled forward.

His arms flew backward.

Birds squawked.

Twigs snapped.

Death lodged in his spine.

Gil landed face first in the dirt.

"No!"

Oh, my God.

"No!" I rolled onto my stomach, trying to wriggle with my hands bound behind my back to get to him.

"Gil!"

I fought harder, the ropes slipping a little.

But strong fingers plucked me from the earth. Harsh breath slithered over my nape, and brute strength whipped me around to face him. "Hello again."

I had no time for him. I didn't care about him. He was nothing. *No one.*

"Gil!"

Looking over my shoulder, I willed him to be okay.

But…he didn't get up.

Didn't move.

Didn't react.

"Daddy!" Olive tried to run past Jeffrey, only to be jerked to a stop by her jacket hood again.

"You two, fuck, you have some manners to learn." Pulling a length of rope from his pocket, he managed to catch Olive's flying fists and block his ears from her terrible screams as he tied her tight.

Slapping her cheek, he snarled, "Quiet. He's dead. It's over. I'm your father now."

Olive just cried harder.

I had so many things I wanted to say.

So many curses to slur and promises to decree, but the awful, clinging sleep still hadn't freed me entirely. I opened my mouth, but only tears fell.

He shot him.

He shot him!

"Gil...*please* wake up!"

Jeffrey slapped me, just as he'd slapped Olive. "You shut up, too." Bending a little, he wedged his shoulder into my belly and hoisted me over his back. The air crushed out of my lungs. My ribcage bruised as he slung me like a carcass.

Jerking Olive forward, he looked back one last time at Gil's corpse as he stole us away. "Say goodbye to that useless body painter. You won't be seeing him again."

Chapter Six

Olin

HE'S GONE.

Gone.

Gone.

I didn't dare voice the other word. The more permanent word.

Dead.

He's dead.

He might not be.

I saw him fall.

I watched the bullet.

But I didn't see the wound.

Didn't see the blood.

Too far away to feel his pulse or check his breath.

Gone or dead…they were both the same.

The GPS tracker dug into my hip as I swung over Jeffrey's shoulder. The bones of his arm burrowed into me, compounding agony on top of agony. If Gil was alive, I was grateful. If he was dead, I was distraught.

But it didn't matter because I'd never see him again.

The GPS coordinates wouldn't save us as there was no one coming. The little blinking location on Gil's phone was utterly pointless.

Gil might still be alive.

But…I was dead.

Olive was dead.

Every heartbeat on borrowed time.

Olive hadn't stopped crying. I'd lost track of how long Jeffrey had dragged us through the dark. The paint on my skin tugged the fine hairs beneath. The bite in the air dressed me in chills. And Olive's hiccups and distress sent empathy digging deep into my soul.

Her grief consumed the entire forest.

Her belief that her father was dead absolute.

I wanted to comfort her.

To tell her he might be okay. He might live. He might still come and save us.

But I had no air in my lungs from being hung upside down. I had no freedom from pounding temples or slithering tiredness that still threatened to drag me under.

Jeffrey snapped a curse, hauling Olive into a walk as she tripped mid-cry.

She'd just witnessed her father being shot, and he didn't care at all.

Numbness spread over my stomach, doing its best to protect me from the pain of being carted like a kill. My ears strained for sounds of someone chasing us. Of Gil barrelling through the darkness, healthy and very much alive.

But there was nothing.

No one.

Just my terrified thoughts jumping from topic to topic.

Of freedom.

Of fighting.

Of forgiveness.

Gil hadn't wanted to do this to me. He'd thought he could win by gambling two lives in order to save one.

But he'd lost.

Three lives in one.

His family…his true blood…his child.

A child that couldn't stop sobbing.

Jeffrey snarled again, hushing Olive so that only the hoots of owls and scratchings of foxes serenaded us as we travelled the final way.

His footsteps slowed as we reached a small clearing. I tried to see around the upside-down view of his butt but could only make out a lumbering shape in the gloom.

Olive tripped again, only to be hauled to her feet thanks to the rope around her wrists and a harsh jerk from Jeffrey. A clink of keys sounded as he shoved them at her. "Run ahead and unlock, sweetheart. You know the rules now, don't you?"

She sniffed loudly. The keys stopped singing as her fist clutched them, and she shot forward away from Jeffrey's abuse. The rope wrapped around her wrists slithered after her in the bracken like a venomous snake.

She moved as if she knew this place well. As if this was her home, all while Gil had done his best to save her. Jeffrey chuckled as he jostled me higher, carrying me to where Olive sniffed and struggled to unzip a large tent.

Bending his knees, my captor groaned as he slid me from his shoulder and plonked me onto the forest floor. For a moment, I couldn't breathe. The release of pressure from my ribcage was too much, and my lungs no longer knew how to operate.

My head pounded as blood whooshed from my ears and back into my legs. Grey and black spots danced over my vision as I shook my head, doing my best to clear the remaining fogginess.

Whatever this place was, I couldn't afford to stay a victim. Jeffrey had shot Gil after telling him he'd keep us alive for better motivation. He'd ended his retirement pay-out by shooting him, so why would he need to keep us breathing?

We were merely a nuisance now and not an incentive.

Time was running out.

Jeffrey checked the rope around my wrists and ankles, re-tightened the knots Gil had done around my wrists, undid the ones around my legs, and hauled me to my feet.

He grunted as I wobbled. "For fuck's sake, I've carried you for long enough. Walk the final distance." Shoving me forward, he chuckled as I plummeted to my knees. With my hands tied and balance still compromised, I face-planted into a rotten pile of leaves and muck.

"Don't know what he saw in you." He nudged me with his boot as I pushed up and did my best to stand. His gentle kick was enough to land me in the dirt again. "Come on, Bambi, don't have all day."

I threw him a glower over my shoulder. "Stop it."

"Stop what?"

"This. Whatever you're doing. Let us go."

I fought for the child of the woman who'd ruined Gil's life. A child of her creation. But Olive was Gil's, not Tallup's.

And this bastard shot him.

My heart squeezed, allowing the word 'death' to sink past my fortress. I didn't have time to grieve.

Sticking my chin up, I forced myself to picture Gil alive. I stood, working out the tightness in my muscles as my body came alive after being hung like drying meat, and focused on freeing myself and Olive.

Jeffrey grinned. "Didn't learn your lesson from last time, huh? You're still using that dangerous little word." His face shot close to mine. "Us."

"Fine. Release Olive and me."

"Nope." He laughed. "Why would I do a stupid thing like that?"

"You shot Gil. What other use do you have with us if he's not around to pay your demands?"

"Oh, I have other ideas." He tapped his nose with airs and graces of a secret. "He did a good job padding my retirement. He kept his mouth shut and his wallet open. It'll be sad not to have such a lucrative nephew, but…" His hand shot out, arching my chin up with his knuckle, bringing the whiff of old cigarettes. "You two can fetch me a pretty penny in other ways."

I wanted to spit in his face. "We're not for sale."

"Sweetheart, everything is for sale." He smirked coldly. "Gilbert knew that lesson very well."

My teeth clenched together, hate rolling over me like a wave.

Jeffrey pulled me through the tent's entrance, revealing it wasn't a tent but an awning attached to a caravan. A three-seater couch sat beneath an outdoor heater along with a coffee table, TV, and two plastic boxes of household supplies. A threadbare rug covered most of the bracken and twigs, creating the illusion that this was a cheery cabin in some safe woodland. The caravan door hung open, spilling light into the awning.

"Gil was born to whores and became a whore. Their shelf life isn't the longest—just like any merchandise." Jeffrey looked me up and down, licking his lips. "He was at the end of his use-by-date. But you…you're just getting started. I'll probably sample you before I sell you. Write a review for prospective buyers—that'll be a laugh. Are you worth one star or five?" He snickered to himself, dragging me up the caravan steps.

Olive whimpered as we entered the cramped space. She huddled against a window, wedged between a long table with bench seats on either side. She pulled her legs up, scrunching them against her chest. She hugged herself tight, while her chin rested on her knees.

Colouring books scattered the narrow table, revealing vibrant doodles and designs outside of the printed mandalas. She was Gil's daughter all right: she had his talent with colour.

I gave her a smile. A smile that I hoped said I was there for her and I wouldn't let anything happen to her. A smile that most likely said the same things her face did: that we were screwed and all on our own.

She gave me a watery smile back, tears still falling silently down her cheeks.

Jeffrey pushed me until I slammed into a bench seat opposite Olive. My bound wrists throbbed as they smashed against the table. Pencils jumped at the impact.

Jeffrey rolled his eyes as if I couldn't do anything right. Closing the caravan door, he locked it, then marched to the kitchen and fridge in the middle of the tiny home. Ripping open the door, he pulled out a beer. Twisting off the cap, he drank the entire thing in one go.

I supposed shooting his nephew and kidnapping was thirsty work.

Gil.

He's dead.

My heart skipped a beat.

You don't know that.

He tied me up and left me to die.

Stop it.

My hands balled as I focused on Olive.

Her eyes skated away from mine, wet and full of sadness. I studied her cute button nose and petite forehead—two features that came from Tallup. I traced the thick unruly dark hair and cutting cheekbones—two inheritances that came from Gil.

She was a beautiful child.

Dainty and delicate, long-legged and sweet.

She looked as if she'd been born to these woods. As if she'd had a fawn for a father and a fairy for a mother.

Her eyes met mine again.

Grey.

Not green. Not blue. Not brown.

Grey.

Gil doesn't have grey eyes.

Didn't *have grey eyes.*

Stop that.

He's alive.

My stomach clenched as I fought off black thoughts, recognising the identical stare of the woman who'd been our teacher.

Years existed between that time and this yet, watching Olive, I saw similarities. The quick movements as Olive swiped at her damp cheeks. The intelligent gaze as she glanced at Jeffrey.

She had a lot of Gil running in her blood, but she also had a lot of her mother.

My heart fissured with hurt.

The pang of jealousy didn't make sense.

The rush of confusion and pain was a luxury I couldn't afford.

The GPS tracker in my underwear pinched against my side, giving false promise that someone would find us before unspeakable things happened, but all I could do was stare at the sweetest girl born from assault on a teenage boy.

A boy who'd given up all his dreams to love and protect her.

Another tiptoe of tiredness hit me.

I didn't want to think or worry or hurt anymore.

I wanted to sleep.

And then wake from this nightmare.

Olive sucked in a shaky breath, her tears still flowing. Looking at her uncle, she whispered brokenly, "Ca-Can we go back?"

Jeffrey tossed the empty beer bottle into the sink. "Go back where?"

"To see Daddy. He was hurt." Her fists curled. "You hurt him."

With a threatening swoop, Jeffrey squeezed onto the bench beside Olive and crowded her against the wall. Her shoulder bumped the lacy tieback on the cream curtains. She didn't whimper when he gathered her into his side and wrapped a reptilian arm around her fragile shoulders. She had courage. She'd lived with this monster a while.

"I didn't hurt him," Jeffrey muttered. "He hurt himself by not being a good boy and following the rules." He tapped her on the nose. "Unlike you, sweetheart. You're very obedient, aren't you?"

I squirmed on my side of the table, my body writhing in denial of this grotesque human being tormenting a young girl. "Don't touch her."

Jeffrey chuckled, cuddling Olive closer to spite me. "You, meanwhile, have a lot to learn."

Olive's cheek squished against his chest, her eyes closed while evermore tears fell. I didn't know how such a young girl could be so brave and quiet.

It hurt me to see her so manhandled and alone.

Ignoring Jeffrey, I spoke to the little girl who desperately needed a friend. "Olive...I'm Olin. Our names are so similar. So...that means I like you straight away."

Olive stiffened, her eyes flashing to mine.

Grey as a winter's day. Endless as infinity.

Her grief over Gil's shooting twisted into shock. "You're...you're Olin, too?"

It was my turn to stiffen. I didn't like the way she looked at me. As if she knew me. As if we hadn't just met and she knew my deepest, darkest secrets.

Jeffrey narrowed his eyes, waiting for me to reply. I hated that he shared in this conversation but at least it bought me time to figure out how to escape. "I am. Do you know another?"

Olive sniffed, wriggling in Jeffrey's hold to rub her nose with the back of her hand. "Daddy has an owl called Olin." Her eyes filled with more liquid. "I bought it for him with my pocket money."

My heart slowed and raced at the same time. "A nice name for an owl."

She cried quietly, her sorrow consuming her. "He told me he had an owl as a friend when he was younger. It was called Olin. It was my favourite story. He always seemed sad, so I bought him a stuffed one to try to make him happy."

Something hot stabbed me in the chest. "That was very nice of you."

My mind raced back to the second night Gil was drunk. When we kissed in his bed and he clutched a fluffy owl beneath his pillow. An owl that represented me, given to him by his daughter.

Tears welled and overflowed. I couldn't stop them.

The secrets.

The pain.

It hurt too much, firing through my insides, leaving a vast, aching emptiness behind.

"He's a good liar, my nephew," Jeffrey said. "Promised there was no connection between you two. Yet I find out that you were the one telling the truth. There was an 'us'." He smiled cruelly. "Although...not anymore."

I swallowed back my hate and tears. "You're a bastard."

He chuckled. "No swearing in front of the kid."

"Age doesn't stop her from knowing exactly what you are."

Jeffrey soared upright. The caravan wobbled from his momentum, shuddering like an earthquake. His fist connected with Olive's colouring books, scattering pencils.

Olive quickly snatched them before they rolled to the floor. Scooping them into a pile, she nursed them as if they were alive and in need of soothing.

Leaning toward me, he growled. "You're lucky you're worth more to me alive. Otherwise, you'd be tied to a fucking tree, dying." Without looking at Olive, his tone switched to syrup. "Sweetheart, can you tell our guest what happens if you speak out of turn?"

Olive gulped. Grabbing a sky blue pencil, she coloured furiously, keeping her gaze on the paper. "You don't get any food for a full day and have to sleep tied to a tree outside in only your nightie." She licked her lips, obviously reliving a similar sentence. "It's scary and cold, and you don't sleep much. And then, in the morning, you have to wash your mouth out with the dishwashing brush while Uncle Jeffrey helps clean your dirty tongue with vinegar."

"Thank you, Olive. You remembered your lesson very well."

She shivered and switched her blue pencil for a red one, digging the pigment into the paper all while tears dripped onto her design.

I held back my own shiver and kept my spine locked. "You think you're special for torturing a child? You're nothing more than a mons—"

His hand lashed out, all five fingers squeezing tight around my throat. The smear of paint on my skin felt oily against his touch, all while dried parts flaked away.

My roped wrists swooped up, trying to scratch him for breath. But he merely caught the rope and kept my hands away.

I held his stare, doing my best not to panic or struggle.

He smirked, leaning into me to whisper in my ear. At least he had the decency to keep diabolical plans for adult ears only. "Listen up, Olin Moss. And yes, I know who you are. I know about you and Gil at high-school. I know about your failed dancing. I know everything there is to know about your pathetic little life."

His fingers relaxed a little, granting a much-needed gush of air. His nose tickled my throat as he dragged his lips along my painted skin. "You want to know what's going to happen? I'll tell you. We're about to hit the road. I've had a long day. I wanted to sleep before we began our long journey, but you're just so eager to get started that I'll be a good host and do what you want."

His sour breath sent goosebumps all over me. He angled my head toward Olive, his thumb pressing hard on my pulse. "And that little girl is going to come for the ride. We're heading to Italy. There's a market there in a few weeks. A market for men who want exclusive, pretty things. That gives me plenty of time to train you up for whoever is stupid enough to buy you. And it gives you time to stare at that cute kid and know what her fate will be. Every time she plays, you'll know that in a few short days she'll belong to some man who will pay a fortune to fuck a child. You'll know that her time of innocence and freedom is ticking away, hour by hour, and there is nothing, *nothing* you can do about it."

Bringing his lips to mine, he forced words into my mouth even as I struggled to get away. "You'll do your best not to get attached to her. You'll try to save her. To be her friend. To promise her you'll both get free. But you can't stop what's going to happen. You'll hope that each day will bring rescue, and each day it won't happen. That's what will kill you. Not the fact that this rope will never leave your wrists. Not the fact that you'll be chained to this caravan until your new master takes control. Not the fact that I will fuck you daily until some other bastard pays for the privilege."

He kissed me harshly, pulling away with a feral gleam in his eyes. "The thing that will kill you, Olin Moss, is hope. Idiotic hope that this is all a crazy mistake and will be over soon."

Letting me go, he stepped out from the bench seat and towered over me. "Do you know what I loved about letting dehydration and exposure kill those painted girls?" He sighed with contentment. "I never got my hands dirty—apart from the last one—but the thrill was just the same as if I'd been the one to snuff out their lives."

I couldn't unlock my jaw to be human and speak words. If I opened my mouth now, I'd snarl and spit and howl like a trapped animal that held nothing but loathing for its captor.

"It was the anticipation. The journey of watching them fight; their eyes bright with hope and expectation of being found in time. Then slowly, minute by minute, that hope vanished all while their bodies gave out."

Olive bit her bottom lip, acting as if she couldn't hear her uncle talk about murder.

He clapped his hands. "Olive. What time is it?"

Olive leaped to her feet, scurried around him, and bolted to the bunk beds at the other end of the caravan. In a flash, she dove beneath covers with pink ponies on them and stared back at us with big, grey eyes. The obedience and quickness in which she moved broke something inside me. She didn't smile or seek reward for her good behaviour. She didn't obey him out of respect.

Just fear.

"Bedtime, Uncle Jeffrey."

He beamed like a proud gorilla. "Good girl. You stay there until I come get you."

Snatching me, Jeffrey unlocked the caravan door and hauled me from the couch. His fingers wrapped around the rope on my wrists.

Light-headedness made me sway while I blinked back residual drugs.

"We're going for some private time."

Stark fear clogged my veins. "No."

He didn't reply, just dragged me down the caravan steps and into the chilly awning. His yellow teeth glistened in the hanging lantern by the boxes of belongings. Wrapping his arm around my waist, he pressed himself against me, rolling his hips into mine, revealing the horrid hardness in his dirty jeans. "Time to learn what my nephew saw in you."

"Take your fucking hands off me." I squirmed and tried to knee him in the balls, but his hold was too tight. My wrists burned as I fought to get free. My heart raced faster than it ever had before.

Jeffrey let me wriggle, unfazed and gloating, knowing he'd won. "Let's see why he never got over you, shall we?" Throwing me onto the threadbare couch, he cupped my jaw and held me down. His knee landed on my belly, pinning me onto my back. "I'm telling you now, I'm more experienced than my nephew. I also have different needs." His rancid lips landed on mine. "You'll find that out soon enough."

I bit his bottom lip, spitting onto the floor as metallic copper hinted I'd broken his skin.

I braced for a fist or retaliation. However, he just chuckled as if my rage was mere melodramatics. His hand landed on my naked, painted breast and squeezed so hard white light exploded behind my eyes.

I gasped and bucked, trying to run from the painful whip of

hot agony.

He stopped.

He shoved my arms up and looped my roped wrists around a hook holding the metal framework of the awning.

My shoulders screamed for release.

My soul bellowed for salvation.

Jeffrey climbed off me and pulled the gun he'd shot Gil with from his waistband. He stroked it as if it were alive and a very good friend of his. "I didn't like guns before tonight, did you know that?" He placed the heavy weapon onto the chipped coffee table reverently. "I'm more of a fist and blade kinda guy." He smiled. "That's changed. I'd rather enjoy another excuse to use it, so by all means, fight. I'm sure whoever bids on you won't mind an extra hole somewhere on your body."

"You're deranged."

"Maybe." He unbuckled his trousers, his belt buckle dangling as he winked. "Deranged or not…you're mine now. And I'm ready to play."

Chapter Seven

Gil

I'D WITNESSED MANY things children shouldn't see.

Things *any* person—young or old—shouldn't see.

I'd watched men beat whores. I'd heard whores scream behind walls. I'd lived in hell where the devil constantly drank and slurred and punched his only son.

I'd dealt with all of it.

I'd blocked out what I couldn't process and focused on a future that he could never touch.

Before Tallup put her claws in me, before I lost O, before Olive was stolen, I still believed in hope.

But now, I didn't have much left.

My boots crunched and tripped as I followed the flashing dot on my cell phone. My vision faded around the edges, my breath shallow, my blood decorating the forest floor like a cookie crumb trail back to freedom.

The pain had become unbearable.

The urge to drop to the ground and die a sinister whisper in my veins.

Keep fighting.

I texted Justin, willing my fingers to move over the tiny screen.

Call police. I fucked up.

I could barely see to send it, falling to my knees as another lick of agony lashed down my back.

With a groan, I climbed to my feet.

And kept going.

* * * * *

I was too late.

O would never forgive me.

Not for any of my sins.

Especially this one.

I couldn't see my daughter, but I knew she was here.

The camouflaged painted caravan and its long-stay awning was where that bastard had kept her from me.

I would've killed him for that alone.

But watching him tear off his shirt and unbuckle his jeans added a whole new homicidal rage to my already flaming hate.

O lay trapped on her back on the couch, glowering at him, her lips pulled back in a snarl. She didn't beg or reason; she just waited for his attack as if ready to fight until death rather than let him touch her.

My vision flickered again as my hand slipped into my jeans pocket where my weapon of choice still waited. The violence that I'd always pushed aside roared through me. It heated my blood and deleted my agony.

I stepped silently into the awning.

The darkness kept me hidden. The lantern too weak to throw illumination my way. O fought my uncle as he grabbed her thighs and tried to spread them.

Both of them preoccupied.

Both of them unaware as I sneaked on shaky legs.

My fingers ached to steal his gun, discarded and lonely on the coffee table. To point it at his head and pull the trigger like he'd done to me. He deserved to feel the fire it left behind. The punch. The shove. The heat.

But he also deserved to feel how his victims had felt.

The helplessness.

The awful, terrible sensation of dying from passing time.

Pulling the syringe from my pocket, I carefully uncapped the needle while O screamed a curse and Jeffrey threw himself on top of her.

The deadly sharpness of the needle made my heart pound.

I couldn't fuck this up.

If I did…

O's gaze wrenched to mine as I took the final step toward my uncle.

Her mouth fell open, her fight vanished, disbelief pinning her to the couch.

Jeffrey froze, twisting on top of her to look behind him.

I couldn't let him grab his gun.

I couldn't second-guess.

Without a word, I lunged forward and jabbed the needle into his naked ass.

The entire length vanished into him, earning a howl and violent fist swinging in my direction.

But it was too late.

My thumb pressed on the plunger, and I shot the entire contents into him. I didn't know if it would work, not going directly into a vein, but I had to hope.

He roared upright just as I stumbled backward and snatched his gun from the coffee table. My back roared from his previous bullet. My vision grey and black. I levelled the muzzle at his chest. "Don't move."

His boxer-briefs clung to the top of his thighs. His disgusting erection made me want to vomit.

If I'd been any longer…

O squirmed and kicked on the couch, doing her best to remove her binds. I would've given anything to free her, but it wasn't over yet.

Soon.

Soon it would be and I could rest.

Wedging one arm against my bleeding side, I struggled to keep the gun raised and ready. "Pull your pants up, you fucking bastard. Don't want to die with them around your ankles, do you?"

His lips pulled into a snarl as he hoisted the material up. "Die? The only person dying here is you, my boy."

I shook my head. "Not tonight."

That might be a lie or the truth. I couldn't tell anymore.

I was mentally and physically exhausted.

The trek through the forest. The worry over what I'd done. The warm blood cascading down my legs.

My body didn't feel right anymore.

Pieces of it shutting down.

I didn't have much time.

Jeffrey lunged toward me. I feathered my finger on the trigger. I'd put a bullet in his face if need be. I wouldn't hesitate. But he was already dead. He just didn't know it yet.

"Daddy?" Olive appeared at the door of the caravan. She had a blanket around her shoulders and her long hair static from a pillow.

"Hey, little spinach." I grimaced, doing my best to smile.

"Stay in the caravan, okay?"

"You're alive!" She leaped down the three steps and launched toward me. "I knew you were okay. I knew—"

Jeffrey grabbed her, yanking her by the hair and jerking her into his side. "He's a ghost, sweetheart. A dead man walking."

"No!" She struggled, her cheeks wet with tears.

"Let her go!" O kicked the air and cursed.

And I just smiled at my daughter, relief slowly overtaking my panic. I'd kept my promise. I'd found her. "It's okay. Don't struggle."

Tears spilled down her cheeks. "You're here to take me home, right?"

"Right." I nodded, the gun growing heavy in my hand. My arm shuddered with the weight as another wash of lacerating agony slashed at my back.

Jeffrey's hand curled around Olive's throat. She went deathly still. "Give me the gun and I won't kill your daughter."

Just like I'd been over the dramatics and threats with Tallup, I was over this too.

I let my arm fall. The gun clattered to the leaf-strewn carpet.

Olive whimpered, thinking I'd given up.

I hadn't.

I'd won.

Jeffrey coughed and stumbled.

Olive squeaked as he pulled her with him. I shadowed them, ready to grab Olive the moment he dropped.

It wouldn't take long.

His eyes widened as things started dying in his body.

"Wha-What did you give me?"

My voice was cold as stone. "Succinylcholine."

He swallowed hard, his throat blocking breath. "What the fuck is that?"

"It's as close as I could get to showing you how your victims felt."

His knees gave out, plummeting him to the floor. Olive cried as he clutched her for support. But I was done letting that monster control my daughter.

My side snarled as I leaped forward and scooped Olive out of his grip. He didn't fight me. He couldn't. His muscles and bones no longer obeyed him.

Already his eyes struggled to stay open. His mouth hung lax. He tumbled onto his side, bound in a prison of his own making.

Olive clung to me as Jeffrey drooled. I kissed the top of her head and let her stay plastered to me while I skirted Jeffrey and unhooked O's rope.

She glared unforgivingly as I grabbed a knife from my back pocket and sliced through the final restraint.

She rubbed the rawness on her skin, embracing freedom. She looked me up and down, no sign of trust or affection, just relief that I wasn't dead. "You're alive."

"I'm alive." I bowed my head, unable to stomach the blood ringing her wrists from where she'd struggled against the rope.

Fuck, I'd let her down so much.

Backing away, understanding she wouldn't want me close to her, I twisted Olive around so her face pressed into my stomach. I didn't worry that her arms would get sticky with my blood. I didn't have any idea how much this would traumatise her or how I could ever make it up to her.

Olive moved with me as I crouched beside him. His eyes stayed half-hooded and crazed with confusion.

I murmured, "You're dying, Jeffrey. The drug is used to paralyse. It's part of what surgeons use in local anaesthesia. Administered like this with no breathing apparatus or doctors nearby, it's fatal." I sighed, reliving the utter despair I'd felt one night. The inability to sleep. The failure of losing Olive. The destitution at paying blackmail. I'd walked the streets, seeking help.

I didn't know what I wanted. I wasn't weak enough to kill myself, but I was weak enough to dabble with the idea of forgetting for a night.

The drug dealer I'd spoken to had a range of pharmaceuticals. His sister was a nurse. Underpaid and overworked, she helped stock his street store with things otherwise impossible to get hold of.

He'd described the deadly drug with a strange kind of fondness. Said he'd watched a *Forensic Files* from America and how it'd been used in a killing where the murderer got away as the drug left no trace behind.

He'd told me the method of death.

How the nervous system shut down, followed by respiratory failure, and every other pump and flow that kept us humans alive. The victim suffocated to death, all while their body lay paralysed. Unable to scream. Unable to move. Locked inside a form that no longer belonged to them.

I didn't know why I'd bought it.

I used up money I didn't have.

But I was angry.

I was broken-hearted for the girls who'd lived such similar fates, tied to trees and hidden under bushes, bound by ropes and silenced by gags.

Jeffrey deserved to feel a fraction of what they went through.

And even though I'd researched it—read studies on other killings involving the drug that said science and forensics had gotten too advanced to no longer be the invisible killer—I didn't care.

I would go to prison for murder.

But so what?

I'd been avoiding jail my entire life.

I'd managed to stay out of the system even though my childhood was primed for me to become a pickpocket and delinquent. I'd managed to raise a daughter on my own after a teacher molested me and threatened to have me thrown in jail for rape.

Jail for me was always a shadow, stalking me, waiting for me, playing roulette with which crime I'd be imprisoned for.

At least this one was justified.

Patting Jeffrey's cheek, I said, "Thank you for teaching me the most important lesson of all, uncle. Thank you for showing me that trust isn't something I can afford. I'll make sure to teach my daughter, so she's never as gullible as me."

His lips didn't move even though his eyes begged for breath. His stare was full of panic and pleas, desperate to live. He didn't even have the luxury of gasping for air or thrashing around for help.

He was silent.

Still.

A corpse already.

He'd taught me how to use my painting talent. He'd also taught me that I'd come from a lineage of bastards.

I was the last one left.

And who knew, maybe I'd die with him tonight.

The adrenaline keeping me awake finally gave way under an icy cloak of shock. The blood that'd steadily been pumping down my legs was no longer warm but chilly.

I was cold.

And very, very tired.

My eyes met O's as she hugged herself, dabbled in painted

olives, crowned in silver-leafed twigs, she was so beautiful she could pass as the angel that would guide me to heaven.

But I didn't deserve heaven.

I knew where I was heading, and I clung to my daughter one last time.

"I'm sorry, Olive Oyl. So, so sorry." Her hair smelled wrong. No scent of strawberry or home. She felt bigger than last year. Her arms stronger and hair longer. I'd missed her growing. I'd failed her for far too long.

She wriggled closer as my head swam and I no longer had the strength to fight.

Olive was free.

O was safe.

That was all that mattered.

I fell to the floor and blacked out.

Chapter Eight

Olin

THE AWNING HAD become a tomb.

My hands were soaked in Gil's blood from trying to stem his bleeding. Olive had helped me grab kitchen scissors and cut up one of Jeffrey's shirts to wrap around his wounded waist.

We'd both tried to revive him, yelling, touching, even throwing a glass of cold water on his face.

I couldn't carry him out of here on my own and I had no idea where we were.

My skin had turned to frost from the bitter night and Olive couldn't stop whimpering beside her unconscious father. My gaze kept crawling to Jeffrey, open-eyed and slack mouthed, dead and silent on the floor.

Forcing myself to stay focused and not give in to shock, I patted Gil's pockets, searching for a phone. I cringed against the tackiness caused by his cooling blood, refusing to look at the red pool beneath him.

I couldn't carry him to help. Therefore, help would have to come to him.

I cried out in relief as I found his mobile.

Olive huddled close to me as I swiped it on. No password, which was good. A black screen with a red dot and a dark forest glowed. The GPS had worked.

Gil had chased us.

He hadn't given up.

I won't give up on him either.

Typing in the emergency number, I pressed connect, only for the device to leap in my hands with an incoming call, interrupting the outbound attempt.

I recognised the name.

I answered with a shockwave of relief.

"Justin." My voice cracked. Heat flashed up my spine.

I sticky-taped my emotions together for Olive and Gil's sake.

"O? Oh, my God. Is that you?" Justin's panic filled the awning, cutting through Olive's fresh sobs. Poor girl had witnessed her dad being shot and had his blood all over her innocent hands. And now she shared space with a cadaver. What sort of psychological issues would she battle?

"Yes, it's me, but I'll have to talk to you later. I need to call the police."

His voice lowered with authority. "I already did. I called them forty minutes ago when Gil sent his second message. What the fuck is going on, O? Where's Gil? Are you okay?"

I looked down at the taupes, silvers, and blacks decorating my mostly naked body. I couldn't make out what foliage pattern he'd covered me with, but I had no injuries of my own—just Gil's blood painting me in a morbid hue.

"He…he said he has a daughter. Is she…with you?" Justin's tone held disbelief. "Tell me what the hell is happening."

I looked at Olive. She curled beside Gil, nuzzling into his side, crying softly for him to wake up. Inching closer, I stroked her back, doing my best to offer comfort when I had none to give.

"Yes, she's with me. We're fine. But Gil's been shot. He needs medical attention urgently."

Something rustled outside. Twigs snapped. Leaves crunched. My skin pebbled with fear as I stood and braced for yet more predators.

Jeffrey had been a predator and had been put down for his violent tendencies. What new evil had found us?

"The police shouldn't be too far away. They'll be able—"

"Police! Don't move." A bright spotlight suddenly shone from the deep darkness beyond the awning. I raised one arm, keeping the phone by my ear with the other. "They're already here." My eyes squinted against the brightness, shivering in the cold.

"Hands up!" More boots, more footsteps, more officers.

Letting the phone fall to the floor, I raised both arms and stood as close as I could to Olive and Gil. Nudging him with my toe, I wished he'd wake up and tell them exactly what'd happened.

But he stayed unconscious. His blood was a dark stain on the dirty carpet. Three officers flooded into the awning, their shrewd gazes bouncing from my painted nakedness, Olive's tears, Gil's blood, and Jeffrey's corpse.

A cop ducked to Gil's side, tending to him, checking for a pulse.

A wave of utter exhaustion swept through me. Most likely from the drugs but also from the chaos that would come from this. The fear of Gil's survival. The worry over Olive's trauma. The total upheaval of my own life going forward.

Tomorrow lurked largely with the unknown.

If Gil died…my future would unfold one way.

If he didn't…it would unfold another.

Either way, I would never be the same.

A young male cop with a black beanie and bright blue eyes came toward me. "You can put your arms down, miss."

I nodded, lowering them gratefully. They automatically wrapped around myself, seeking warmth after being naked for so long.

Another officer with a matching black beanie and grey beard appeared behind me after checking the coast was clear in the caravan. He draped a woollen blanket over me from one of the bunk beds.

I gave him a weak smile, tugging the scratchy material closer, glancing at the officer still checking on Gil.

A female agent with her blonde hair wrapped in a knot at the base of her nape went toward Olive. "Hey, you okay? Not hurt anywhere?"

Olive scrambled to her feet, Gil's blood all over her from where she'd hugged and pleaded with him. "It's my dad. Please help him."

The woman nodded. "We'll take care of him. But right now, I need you to come with me. All right?"

Olive scowled. "No. Dad needs me." Tears wobbled on her bottom lashes. A tantrum made up of horror and heartbreak quickly scrunched up her face.

I scooted next to her, wrapping half my blanket around her tiny shoulders. "It's okay, officer. I'll stay with her."

Olive looked up, her huge eyes blinking and distrustful. "Do you know how to fix Dad?"

Shaking my head, I whispered, "No, but these nice people do. They need to take him in an ambulance to the hospital. The doctors there will help."

Olive bit her lip. "I don't want him to leave. He can't leave me again."

How many fears would she have to overcome after the tragic year she'd suffered? The separation and threats?

Two officers squatted by Jeffrey's body, their voices low while checking vitals. Finding none, they spoke curtly into a walkie-talkie, hinting they'd just elevated this crime scene from worried caller to homicide.

A young male agent asked me, "What happened here?" He gaze travelled over my painted legs poking from the bottom of the blanket.

Where did I begin?

What could I say?

I would never be able to lie, but I also couldn't tell the truth.

Gil killed him.

I wanted him to do it.

Another wave of tiredness caught me, making me wobble. I overacted the effects, purely to get out of unanswerable questions.

An older man appeared. He'd taken his beanie off and his dark hair stood up in disarray. He spoke into a walkie-talkie stuck on his shoulder. "Three for an ambulance. One critical." Giving me a smile, he said, "Questions will come later. For now, let's get you help."

Chapter Nine

Gil

"YOU GOOD FOR *nothing son of a bitch!*"

I ducked my father's swing, missing the full brunt of his fist. I wanted to shout back that he would know. Only he knew which of his whores I'd been born to, seeing as when I asked them, they never answered me. Never hinted who I belonged to.

But even at seven years old, I knew better than to answer back.

Dad chased me, quick for a man drowning in booze.

I bolted from the lounge and into the dingy kitchen. "Come here, you little runt."

Breathing fast, I tried to charge around the table piled high with dirty dishes, only to be yanked back with his fist in my hair. He threw me to the ground. He loomed over me like a bear. He kicked me so hard in the side, I almost blacked out.

The world went slow and sluggish as pain overtook every perception.

I curled around the dull throb from his boot, swallowing back silent tears, refusing to let them fall.

"There. That's your punishment for not picking up my pack of smokes like I told you to."

The pain didn't diminish.

It only spread.

When I didn't get up and scurry away like I normally did when he beat me, he crouched and nudged me with his cigarette-stained finger. "Winded, boy?"

I gritted my teeth and didn't move.

I couldn't move.

The agony in my lower back stole everything.

Bored of my injuries, he stood and chuckled. "Ah well, learned ya lesson. Next time do what I tell you and you won't get hurt."

He strolled from the kitchen with a drunken whistle, leaving me to watch

daylight switch to midnight. Whores came in and stepped over me. Paying
customers rolled their eyes as they chose which woman to use.
  And I waited until I felt better again.
* * * * *

I woke to heaviness.

To false numbness.

To terrifying strangeness.

My limbs were connected to my body, but they were stretched and knotted, utterly useless against the softness I lay upon. Just like so many times in my youth, I lay still, waiting to heal so I could be free from overwhelming agony.

My throat was the first thing to trigger an avalanche of pain. I swallowed, trying to push away the sensation of underwater sluggishness, but it seemed to give permission for every injury to roar alive, every cell determined to destroy me first.

I gasped, crashing fully awake, wishing I could reverse the process and fall back into the numbing blackness once again.

The heart-rate monitor attached to my chest beeped as my pulse increased. A door opened and closed, delivering a middle-age female with brown hair and silver-framed glasses to my bedside. Her blue slacks were covered with a white coat and the pink sneakers she wore squeaked a little on the linoleum. "You're awake."

Turning a few dials on the machine beside me, she stayed busy for a moment, administering something with a push of a button. "I've just given you another dose of morphine. It will take the edge off."

I didn't have chance to thank her before the door opened and another visitor arrived. Not a white coat of medical personal but a stern uniform with important buttons and emblems.

Police.

He marched to the bottom of my bed, his arms crossed and face cold. "You're under arrest, Gilbert Clark, for the murder of Jeffrey Clark and accessory before the fact in four other cases."

I winced as a flare of heat lashed around my back.

So this was what it felt like to finally be held accountable for your crimes.

His chin arched, delivering the rest of my fate. "While in the care of Birmingham Medical, you are not to leave this room under any circumstance. You are allowed an attorney and have the right to remain silent—"

"Can't that spiel wait?" The female doctor scowled. "He's just woken up from surgery. He won't be walking anywhere."

I swallowed again against the wildfire in my throat. I didn't care about me. I was irrelevant. "My daughter. Where's Olive?"

The doctor patted my hand, careful not to bump the IV line disappearing into my vein. "Your daughter is fine. She was kept overnight for observation. You can see her later."

"No visitors." The cop frowned.

"He can see his daughter, for crying out loud. She's screaming blue murder to make sure he's okay. If you won't let him see her for his sake, then do it for the child's. She's been through enough."

I didn't know who this woman was, but I liked her immensely.

A flood of gratefulness and fresh agony gushed through me. "Is...is Olin Moss okay?"

The woman nodded. "Fine. Both are fine."

I had so many questions, but they scattered the moment I tried to move and my side felt like hungry wolves shredding my innards. "Holy—"

"Ah, yes. Don't move if you don't have to." She lowered her voice, shooting a look at the lurking cop before focusing on me. "You sustained a gunshot wound to the back. The bullet didn't cause excessive damage, going in clean and causing a large but manageable puncture wound upon exit. The good news is, it didn't hit anything vital. Far enough away from your organs to go clean through you."

I blinked. "I bled a lot."

"You did. You needed a transfusion." Turning to the cop, she snipped. "Can my patient have some privacy please?"

His eyes narrowed. "He's under arrest. He doesn't get privacy."

"What happened to innocent until proven guilty?"

"He's guilty of murder."

I flinched.

Before, I'd been willing to pay the price, but now sick worry filled me.

Will they take Olive away?

How could I be such a fucking idiot not to think of that?

Fear landed like a landslide on my chest.

I'd only just gotten her back.

I wouldn't survive losing her again.

Losing Olin again.

You lost O a long time ago.

The doctor's tone softened as she did her best to ignore the unwanted visitor in the room. "Do you remember arriving in the emergency room? We did a CT scan before surgery to ensure there were no internal injuries."

I frowned. "I don't remember."

"That's okay." She smiled. "The complicated jargon can wait. For now, the abbreviated version is, you'll live. You've been stitched up and responded well to treatment. You'll be in a fair amount of pain for a few days, but then it will ease, and healing will accelerate."

Days?

I didn't want to be in here for days.

I wanted to be with Olive.

I needed to talk to O.

You leave this bed, and you're in prison.

Either way, I would be kept away from the people I needed the most.

Shit.

A lash of agony ripped up my back. I sucked in a breath, shifting on the bed.

"We'll leave you to rest." The doctor patted my hand again. "Sleep. Heal. I'll answer any questions you may have when you're a little more comfortable."

I resisted the urge to capture her wrist, asking, "Can I see my daughter?" I needed to see her with my own eyes. To touch her. Kiss her. To never let her go again.

"Soon." She backed away from the bed, eyeballing the cop to leave too. "Rest first. I'll bring her to you in a bit."

I wanted to argue, but sudden tiredness hung off my eyelashes, dragging them down. I felt cold and strange—as if the foreign blood in my veins poisoned me from the inside out.

I couldn't fight the sinking.

I lost the fight.

I slept.

* * * * *

"No! I want to see him. I need to make sure he's okay. Daddy! Dad! Popeye!"

My eyes wrenched open, my heart galloping at the sound of Olive's shout. Jack-knifing upright, I forgot too late about my stitched together side.

I groaned in pain as I lay back down, a prickle of sweat

breaking out all over me.

The heart-rate monitor went berserk, and the sounds of angry officers threaded with the melodic calm of O's gentle tone. I couldn't hear what she said, but after a minute of whispered argument, the door cracked open and Olive bowled inside.

"Dad!"

I braced myself for her hug. Ready to hide my agony from her at all costs. My arms spread as she launched against the bed, her face landing on my stomach and arms around my hips. "You're alive!"

It fucking hurt.

Everything fucking hurt.

My body screamed to push her away, but my heart would never do such a thing. My heart hurt worse than any physical form.

I'd failed this perfect creature.

I could never fix what'd happened.

I clutched her so damn close, suffocating her into me. I stroked her soft, silky hair, squeezing my eyes from suspicious, stupid tears.

The luxury of touching her.

The privilege of having her back in my embrace.

Fuck.

I didn't care I was bankrupt, full of holes, and other people's blood.

I didn't even care I wasn't a free man anymore.

All that mattered was Olive was safe.

Finally.

Swallowing back heavy gratitude, I pulled her away so I could see her pretty face. "Hey, Olive Oyl. You okay?" Nudging her chin up, I smiled as her huge, gorgeous grey eyes met mine. I'd long ago stopped comparing her eyes to her mother's. In Jane Tallup, the grey had been evil and flat. In Olive, the colour was pure and wholesome. I loved the soft shade. I loved how serene and endless they were.

The greyness suddenly glossed with tears. Her mouth wobbled, and she pressed her cheek into my palm as I raised my hand to touch her. "You were lying in the forest. Not moving."

"I know. I'm sorry I scared you."

"I wanted to come back to get you. But Uncle Jeffrey wouldn't let me."

"It's not your fault, little spinach. None of this is your fault."

She bit her lip, doing her best to stem her sadness. "I missed you so much."

"I missed you more."

She threw herself onto me again. Her face pressing into the blankets covering my wounded side. I hid my pain, wrapping my arm around her fragile back.

I didn't think about the future.

I didn't worry about how much time I had with her.

I just closed my eyes and hugged my daughter.

Chapter Ten

Olin

STARING AT MYSELF in the hospital bathroom mirror, I did my best to clutch to the resolve I'd made last night. The oath I had no choice but to follow.

I didn't like hospitals—they reminded me too much of what I'd lost after my accident. I hadn't wanted to come back.

But I had to see Gil.

To convince myself he would be okay…before I left.

You know what you promised, O.

I pointed a finger in my face, waggling it at my reflection.

Stand by it.

I nodded.

Today, my skin was its normal colour. My hair clean and brushed. My pink jumper and tight jeans my only decoration. I was just a simple girl visiting an old friend from school.

Yesterday had been a different matter.

I'd showered at the hospital so they could apply creams to my rope-burned wrists and ankles and check me over. They'd given me a hospital gown to dress into and guided me to a room to wash. I'd closed the door on the nurse helping me and seen my painted flesh for the first time.

I hadn't known what Gil had painted me with.

But there, standing under the bright neon, I found out.

Olives.

Thousands and thousands of olives.

He'd cried while forcing me to eat a sandwich laced with sleeping tablets. He'd apologised while he'd carried me deep into the forest. And he'd painted me in the namesake of the only girl who would ever own his heart.

That had been the moment.

The moment.

Where all my misery and patience just…stopped.

It was like a switch flicked from forgiving to done.

Gilbert Clark had been through a lot. He'd dealt with things no one should have to deal with. He'd never had anyone to rely on and kept far too much sorrow to himself. He'd pushed me away out of some broken chivalry to protect me.

And by trying to protect me, he'd forced me to face his demons and risk being sold by his uncle.

I'd believed I could save him with kindness. I'd hoped compassion could set him free.

It's time to stop being so idealistic and blind.

He'd broken my trust while painting me that night.

He'd saved my life by killing Jeffrey before collapsing at my feet.

The wrongdoing he'd done by sacrificing me was paid in full by stopping a terrible fate. I could forgive him for what he'd done. I forgave him for everything he'd put me through.

But…that was where my tolerance ended.

He might have had a rough upbringing and allowed society to carve him into something he wasn't, but I'd had my own share of nightmares.

I'd coped with a lonely childhood, a life-changing accident, and loving a boy who would always grant more pain than happiness. I'd endured trials and sacrifices and managed to retain the goodness that I valued over anything.

That was where we differed.

I fought for what hid beneath the lies.

Gil pushed away what was in front of him.

And…it was over.

I would be nice and gentle. I would be his friend.

But I would also pick me from now on because I'd given him everything I had.

I'm leaving.

Starting afresh.

I had to.

As I'd stepped into the shower, a calm sense of relief filled me. Relief to finally have a decision that felt binding. I would always be Gil's friend. I would answer his calls and accept his messages if he wanted to stay in touch, but that was where my loyalty had to end. Where I had to choose not to be the tragic wallflower, wilting in a sad little vase, waiting for him to choose me.

He could never choose me because he'd chosen Olive.

As it should be.

That night, I'd done my best to sleep in an uncomfortable hospital bed, tossing and turning, knowing Gil was in surgery and his daughter was in the care of strangers.

I'd been released in the morning and gone home to my apartment.

Everything had felt in a different dimension. A strange new planet.

My key still fit in my lock. My kitchen still held my dishes. My bed still smelled of me. But none of it seemed real anymore. I'd distanced myself from it and needed to leave.

To leave and start again…for me.

Shannon had called from Status Enterprises, and I'd apologised yet again for not turning up for work. She assured me it was fine. She'd heard the news about what'd happened. That the company would give me two weeks fully paid to recover before returning.

I hadn't had the heart to tell her I no longer wanted to live in my home city.

I didn't have the courage to go online and read the news articles about what'd happened.

Instead, I dressed and ate a muesli bar before catching public transport back to the hospital.

To say goodbye.

My hand dropped. My reflection showed a girl far older than she was. Dark circles painted under my eyes; my lips permanently sad.

I didn't want to be that girl anymore.

I wanted more.

I deserved more.

You deserve to be happy.

I nodded at the mirror, brushed a few stray hairs from my forehead, and left the bathroom.

* * * * *

I stood outside Gil's room, listening to the low rumble of his voice and the high-pitched tone of Olive's. The two cops guarding his door stared at me with annoyance. Pissed off that I'd stood up to them when they'd tried to deny Olive from seeing her dad.

It'd been serendipitous timing.

I'd arrived at the barricaded room just as Olive came flying down the corridor, no longer willing to wait for a nurse to take her to her father.

I'd argued on her behalf.

I'd won her entry.

And now, I wanted to give them time to say hello, before I said goodbye.

Focusing on the older cop with his handlebar moustache, I asked, "Why are you guarding Gil's door?"

His eyebrows drew together. "He's a prisoner."

My heart kicked, not wanting to accept that Gil's problems weren't over. "For what?"

"For killing Jeffrey Clark."

I scowled. "But Jeffrey kidnapped us and murdered at least four women. He took me and would've raped and killed me if Gil hadn't—"

"Murder is murder, miss." He crossed his arms. "And Gilbert Clark was involved."

My temper rose. "He didn't kill those girls."

"He was an accessory. Caught with his hands dirty."

I gritted my teeth, unwilling to argue the painted murders but needing to justify Jeffrey's. "Did you not hear me? Jeffrey Clark was seconds away from raping me. Gil killed him in my defense. He killed him because he kept his daughter for over a year. He was *justified.*"

The cop didn't react.

It wasn't fair.

Gil had done many wrong things, but killing his uncle was not one of them. I still didn't understand if they were related or if it was just a term of speech, but his death was the only good thing to come out of all of this.

Footsteps sounded on the bleached linoleum. Wrenching my head up, I expected to see a doctor. Instead, the air in my lungs vanished as Justin spotted me and increased his speed until his arms wrapped tight around me. "O. Thank God, you're okay."

I squeezed him back, drinking in the familiarity, no longer cringing against it. "Thanks to you."

He pulled away, shaking his head. "Thanks to Gil." He glanced at the cops watching us closely and cupped my elbow to guide me away. Keeping his voice low, he said, "He told me he's involved in the painted murders. Is that why the police are outside his room?"

My heart turned to stone. "He told you that? How…how is he involved?"

He painted them…didn't he?

He painted them for his uncle.

He has their blood on his hands.

I didn't want to believe it, but the thought had been growing ever since I'd seen my photo wedged in his door.

He frowned. "He said….you know what? It doesn't matter. We'll talk about it later." His gaze flashed with pain. "I need to see the bastard. To see with my own eyes he's still alive. That text he sent sounded too full of death for my liking."

I arched my chin back at the two police. "We can ask to see him, but I'm not holding my breath. They barely let Olive in."

"Olive…his daughter?"

I nodded.

"Did you know he had a daughter?"

"Not until recently."

"Who's the mother?"

Looking away, I whispered, "You'll have to ask him that."

"Fine. I will." Straightening his spine, he took my hand and led me back to the law enforcers. "We want to see our friend."

The guy shook his head. "No visitors."

"He has his daughter in there right now."

The younger cop with his sleek dark hair glowered at me. "Only because someone wouldn't accept no for an answer."

Justin narrowed his gaze. "Just like I won't accept no for an answer." He sighed. "Look, the bloke isn't going anywhere. He's in a hospital, for God's sake."

The older cop sighed, his resolve weakening.

I jumped in. "Please let us in. I'm leaving and want to say goodbye before I do."

Justin froze beside me, blue eyes trapping mine. "What? You're leaving? Since when?"

I shrugged. "Since I decided."

"Because of Gil?"

"Because of me." I didn't want to discuss this in front of uniforms. Smiling at the older officer, I did my best to appease him. "We'll only be fifteen minutes. I just really need to say goodbye before…"

His hand rested on his baton before he sighed again, heavy and annoyed. "Fine. Fifteen minutes. But no longer." Turning the doorknob, he opened it enough for me to slip through.

Justin followed, pushing the door closed behind him.

Olive looked up from where she stood beside Gil's bed hugging him. Her eyes were red and cheeks damp but she smiled for the first time since I met her. "Hi, Olin. Thanks for helping me sneak in to see my dad."

I nodded with a soft smile. "You're welcome."

My gaze travelled to Gil.

The world once again stopped and spun in the opposite direction.

He looked wrung out and pale. His hair a diabolical mess, his body cocooned in white blankets while a needle punctured the back of his hand and fed necessary antibiotics and painkillers.

His mouth opened to speak.

My heart begged to retreat.

And Justin broke the tense connection, striding in front of me to embrace his friend. "Good to see you're still alive."

Gil winced, his gaze struggling to leave mine as he focused on Justin. "At least I get to say thank you in person now."

Justin nodded. "You owe me. Owe me huge."

Gil nodded, his tone deadly serious. "I know I do. And I'll pay you back somehow. Some day."

"You do know I expect to be told everything." Justin's eyes narrowed. "And I do mean everything, Clark. You can't leave anything out."

"I know."

Olive's attention danced between her dad and the man she'd never met. Her curiosity practically burst out of her. The scared girl from the caravan gave way to a feisty little thing, almost as if having her father back erased the badness of before. She drank strength from him. She trusted that things were okay now—that the past year of entrapment was over because she was with her dad and the world was righted.

She's the bravest little thing I've ever seen.

I envied her ability to ignore history and live purely in the present.

It made me feel weak for wanting to leave, guilty for choosing myself over Gil when he lay sore in a hospital bed.

I should stay.

I should help.

But how much is enough?

After everything…when was it okay to say no more?

My heart beat strangely, confused and afraid as I stayed on the outskirts of their conversation.

Gil cleared his throat, smiling at his friend. "Justin, I'd like you to meet Olive. My daughter." His body melted as he looked at Olive, his eyes so proud and grateful. "Spinach, I want you to meet your godfather, Justin."

"Yeah, about the godfather thing." Justin coughed quietly. "You do know I have no experience with kids right, Clark?"

Gil nodded. "I know. And it's not fair of me to nominate you without telling you, but for now…while I deal with this aftermath, do you think—" His eyes caught mine, wincing. He seemed almost apologetic, as if he didn't know if he should've asked me if I wanted that role instead.

I approved of his choice.

Justin was stable.

I was not.

Justin was staying.

I'm…not.

"It's fine." Justin grinned. "All good. You know that."

"I know you're a goddamn saint, and it pisses me off no end," Gil muttered wryly. "But it also makes me a lucky SOB to have a mate like you."

"Aww, I'm blushing." Justin laughed. "Seems getting shot took that stick out of your arse."

Gil's gaze narrowed. "Don't use bad language in front of—"

"What's a godfather?" Olive's nose wrinkled, her eyes volleying between the two men as they spoke.

Gil seemed different. Lighter, even while heavier. Happier, even while hurt. Just like Olive, he took support and strength from his bond with her, drinking the same medicine she did just from being around him.

They couldn't survive without each other. Couldn't be whole while apart. The true sense of connection and family.

I rubbed at the ache in my chest as Justin bent to Olive's level, offering his hand in polite introduction. "A godfather means I get to keep you if your dad here ever has enough."

I cringed.

Justin meant it in a relaxed, soothing way, but after a year of forced custody with her uncle—

Olive looked at him warily, obviously thinking the same thing I did. "I don't want anyone to keep me who isn't my dad."

Justin dropped his hand, noticing his mistake. "Of course. I only meant that—"

"You can trust him, Olive," Gil gruffed. "He's not like Jeffrey."

"You were wrong to trust him, Daddy." Olive stuck out her bottom lip. "I told you something wasn't right about him, didn't I?"

Gil flinched but nodded. "You were right. He was a bad man."

"He was mean." She scuffed her blue sneaker into the floor. "I-I'm glad he's not alive anymore."

"Me too." Gil squeezed his eyes shut for a second before opening them again. "I agree that Uncle Jeffrey was bad, but Justin is one of the good guys. Look at him. You'll see."

Olive pursed her lips suspiciously, eyeing up Justin. "I dunno." She traced his face, his chest, his legs, and back to his eyes. Her head cocked as if deliberating. "I don't think I want you as my weird godfather, but you can be my friend…I guess."

Justin chuckled. "Gee, thanks." He bent down again, whispering, "I promise I'll be a trustworthy friend who doesn't kidnap you."

"You better not." Her fist shot up in a laughable but totally serious threat. "I only want to live with Daddy from now on."

Gil froze in bed. His gaze lost the pride and adoration, filling with torture and the familiar unhappiness of before. He pinched the bridge of his nose with a hiss, doing his best to shove aside whatever had terrified him before Olive noticed.

His head turned, his gaze caught mine.

The electrical current that refused to be cut hummed with honesty.

He's afraid.

Afraid of being arrested and imprisoned.

Afraid of having Olive taken from him.

My chest filled with painful pressure. He'd only just been reunited with his daughter. They deserved their happily ever after, but this was just an intermission. A brief, sweet interlude before real-life wedged between them again.

Gil had promised Olive that it was all over.

He'd lied.

It's only just beginning.

"O…" Gil's eyes tightened, pain etching into his skin. "Can…can we talk?"

Justin twisted to look at me, his eyes narrowing. He rocked

his head in a come-hither gesture, moving away from Gil's beside. "Here, take my spot."

I couldn't move.

Talking was too dangerous.

I'd made my decision.

I couldn't take it back.

No matter if Gil might face prison and Olive's future was uncertain. No matter if this little family was once again split up.

They weren't mine to care for or worry over. I shouldn't fear what would happen to the tiny girl I'd just met, or the boy I would never forget. I should pick me.

I will pick me.

I will walk away.

I will say goodbye.

Gil's energy wrapped around mine as physical as a hug, as brutal as a fist, as sharp as claws. We didn't need words to talk. We communicated right there, in our silence.

He shouted apologies.

I shielded my intentions.

He begged me to move closer.

I stood my ground.

This was safe.

Distance was safe.

Gil's forehead furrowed, accepting the mess between us, and knowing, without a shadow of a doubt, that whatever we'd been, whatever we'd had, whatever we could have been...was over.

The tension between us thickened with clouds, a rumble of thunder was the sounds of hearts breaking.

Justin shifted by Gil, his hand skating on the bedspread.

Olive immediately pushed him away, her voice high and worried. "Don't hurt him. He has a hole in his tummy. Things might fall out."

Justin coughed. "A hole?"

I fought my smile, amazed that I found Gil's injury humorous thanks to his adorable child.

Gil groaned, struggling with his own grim grin. "I told you, little spinach. It's not a hole anymore. Things won't fall out of me."

"But I saw it. Back at Uncle Jeffrey's. Blood fell out of you. Lots and lots of blood." She looked as if she fought tears and a tiny bit of rage. "You said that if I ever hurt myself that bleeding wasn't good, and I should get help straight away. But you were sleeping and didn't get help, so you still have a hole where blood can slip out."

Gil twisted in bed, swallowed his grunt of pain, and scooped his daughter into a side hug. Pressing his lips to her hair, he murmured, "I love you so, *so* much." His smile glowed with affection. "You're very sweet to worry about me, but I did get help. I'm in the hospital, and the doctors sewed up the hole inside me. I'm all better now. See?" He raised his arm, showing no blood stained the white sheets around him. "No more bleeding."

"I dunno." Olive wrinkled her nose in distrust. "Are you sure you're okay?"

"Never better."

"But you said it hurt when I hugged you there." She pointed at his side. "You shouldn't be in pain. I don't want you in pain. If the doctors can't fix you, I can. I know I can." She wriggled in Gil's embrace. "Tell me what to do, and I'll do it."

Gil kissed her nose before letting her go and reclining against the pillows. "You do make it better. Just having you here takes all my pain away."

Olive pouted. "No, it doesn't. I'm not magic, you know."

Justin chuckled, catching Gil's eye, sharing the vibrancy of the little girl willing to stand up to agony for daring to hurt her father.

Gil gave me a quick look, his face unguarded for the first time since I'd answered his job advertisement. No hidden secrets, no diabolical blackmails, just him in a hospital bed with his daughter from another woman fussing over him, and my heart healed a little. It let go of its own pain and sense of betrayal, repairing a tiny piece of friendship.

My feet drifted toward Gil without my permission. I joined their group, not in touching distance, but no longer ready to bolt out the door.

Gil sighed heavily, his gaze tangling with mine. His head tipped down in a silent thank you.

My voice scratched as I asked, "Are you sure you're all right?"

He grimaced. "I should be the one asking you that." His eyes flashed. "O...God, I'm so sorry."

"It's fine."

"It's not fine. And it won't ever be, but I need you to know how grateful I am. I took far more than you were willing to give. I'll never forgive myself, but you're the reason I found Olive—"

"Don't." I held up my hand. "I understand."

Justin cleared his throat, moving away a little, giving us

privacy.

This wasn't the place to discuss.

Not with Gil fresh out of surgery, cops barricading the door, and his daughter who listened to every word.

"But how can you stand there and—"

"Because it's my choice what to forgive and what not to. It's over." I sighed, signalling an end to airing dirty laundry. "It's okay, Gil. Truly."

He snorted as if he couldn't believe me. His mouth opened as if to argue but I shot my attention to Olive instead. "You're wrong, you know."

Olive pinned me with her grey stare. "Wrong? About what?"

"About not being magic."

"I don't get it."

I nudged my chin at Gil, smiling gently. "You do take his pain away. I knew your dad before you existed, and I knew him while he was searching for you, and I can say you are definitely magic. Want to know how I know?"

Olive licked her lips, her gaze so eager to learn. "How?"

"You make him happy." I looked at Gil, unable to ignore the pull. To ignore the truth of what I said. "You make him whole. You take away all his pain, internal and external." I dropped my attention back to her. "You truly are magic…to him."

"Am I, Popeye? Do I really do that?" Olive sidled closer to Gil.

He wrapped an arm around her tiny shoulders. "Definitely. All the time. Without you, there's something missing deep inside me."

"Me too." She pressed her face into his chest. When she pulled away, tears shone on her cherub cheeks. "I'll make sure I make extra magic, so you can get better super-fast and can come home with me."

"Sounds like a great plan."

Justin's phone beeped. "Sorry, guys." Pulling it from his pocket, he withdrew from the tender family moment and went to stand by the window, typing quickly on his phone.

Gil caught my eyes over Olive's embrace.

A vortex sucked us into the same undeniable depth we'd always shared. Tension appeared from nowhere. The air became heavy. The possibilities of so many futures and fates waiting for us to decide.

Gil broke the unbearable quietness. "I know it isn't worth

much, and for some reason you don't want to hear it, but I truly am sorry, O. From the depths of my soul. I'm forever in your debt."

"Enough."

But he didn't stop. "I need you to know I will *always* love you. I will always adore you for what you've done for me—both willingly and unwillingly. I don't expect to ever hear you love me back. I know that's something I lost and the price I had to pay."

I dared meet his green gaze; my spine threaded with steel.

He wasn't supposed to talk of love.

He wasn't supposed to be so open or genuine.

I wasn't protected against this new Gilbert Clark. This honest, hurting, hopeful version who no longer believed in silence but in truth.

How could I tell him I'd come for closure? That I'd emptied my hope of ever having more with this man and now only wanted a farewell?

"I had to see you…one last time."

His body stiffened, fear licked into his eyes. "One last time?"

"I'm very glad you're okay. That you survived…for Olive's sake."

And for mine.

I might not be able to be with him but I didn't want him dead.

Gil was sweet with a heart full of affection and protection to give. He'd just never really been given the opportunity without monsters tearing that heart to pieces.

In a way, I was failing him at the worst possible time.

But time never did play fair when it came to us.

"He…he didn't hurt you, did he?" He swallowed hard. "Please tell me I arrived before he—" His voice cut off, unable to verbalize what could've happened if he'd been five minutes longer.

I wouldn't have just had rope-burned wrists to treat but a whole host of other ailments. Rape kits and counselling. Stopping those thoughts, I shook my head. "He didn't hurt me."

"He yelled at her," Olive said, popping into the conversation. "And then he whispered some things that made her go all white and strange-looking, like she'd be sick."

I winced, studying Olive and what Jeffrey had threatened. How he'd planned on selling both of us. How Gil might never have known the fate his daughter was sold to. "He wasn't a nice man, was he?"

Olive narrowed her eyes. "Nope. Not one bit."

I smiled, shaking away that night all over again. "But you're with your dad now and things will be better."

Gil flinched, knowing as well as I did that things might be about to get worse.

"Yep. I'm never leaving him again," Olive vowed. "Ever, ever, ever."

"I'm glad. He needs you."

"What aren't you saying, O?" Gil asked gently, his eyes roving over my face. "Are you truly all right?"

Bracing myself, I prepared to say the hardest thing. "I'm fine. And I came…I came to see you because…" I sighed, forcing myself to finish. "I came to say goodbye."

The flash of agony glowed and fired in his eyes. He cleared his throat, nodding fast, accepting there was no other choice. "I understand."

"I'm moving."

His body twitched on the bed. "Where?"

"I don't know yet. I-I guess I'll figure that out when I'm there."

"You'll travel?" His voice gruffed and thickened.

"Perhaps. I'm not sure."

Our awful conversation petered out. There was *so* much to say, but it wouldn't make a damn bit of difference to the way we'd ended.

Olive reached out to take my hand, her shoulders still wrapped up in Gil's embrace. By accepting her touch, she united us. An unlikely trio all bound in complicated ways. My skin tingled as I allowed her hold, a similar curse to what her father made me feel.

There was something about this girl that snatched me around the heart just as much as Gil did. Probably because she was half his. Half his blood. Half his soul.

And my soul reacted to both of them.

"You can't leave." Her pretty face cast upward to look at me. Her plea reached into my chest and squeezed. "I don't want you to go."

"O has a destiny to follow, Olive Oyl. We can't stop her from being happy." Gil pulled her closer to him, doing his best to dislodge her hold on me. "She has to go."

He smiled at me, but his eyes didn't look happy. They looked sad and lonely and breaking. "Don't let her guilt trip you, O. She's mastered the art of that unfortunately."

I laughed quietly, feeling endlessly sad. "I'll do my best."

"But you *can't* go." Pinpricks of colour highlighted Olive's cheeks. "You're the owl from the stories. You're his friend. Friends don't leave."

Gil groaned. "God, did she tell you about the owl?" He blushed like his daughter. "I'd run out of bedtime stories and was sick of reading *Popeye The Sailor Man*. I told her about a dancer who—"

"Turned into an owl at night and danced with feathers in the moonlight." Olive nodded furiously. "The owl was called Olin— which is a crazy weird name—but was kinda cool too. And you're called Olin, so you *have* to stay."

I struggled with how to reply.

Justin re-joined us, tucking his phone into his pocket. "What did I miss?"

Gil shot his friend a grim look while I tried to untangle my hand from Olive's. "Not much."

Olive let her hand fall, her shoulders slouching as if the past year had caught up to her. "Can we go home yet, Dad? I want to sleep in my room." Her face shadowed, showing signs of the trauma that would take a while to cure. "I miss my room. I didn't like sleeping in Uncle Jeffrey's caravan."

"Yes, we can go home—" Gil froze, halting his lie. His eyes rose to mine, pleading for a way to break the news to her. That he couldn't go home until he'd healed. And even then...it might not happen.

"Your dad has to stay here another couple of nights." I reached out and stroked her dark, glossy hair. "The doctors are magic too, and they're making him better."

"But...what about me? Where do I sleep then? Will you take me back home and stay with me?"

My heart flipped at the thought of returning to the warehouse where Gil had drugged and painted me.

Gil jumped in. "You'll have to stay here with me in the hospital, little spinach. Just for a couple of days." He looked at Justin. "They allow that, right? Single parents are allowed to have their kid stay?"

Justin shrugged. "I can find out."

Olive stuck out her tongue as if she was gagging. "I don't want to stay here. It stinks and I don't like sick people."

"I know," Gil muttered. "I don't want to stay either, but—"

The door opened with no knock or request for entry.

Two women entered, stern and prim. Their matching black suits strict with discipline and an official-looking badge over their breasts.

"This is a private meeting," Justin said, striding forward to intercept them. "You can't just barge in——"

"Mr. Clark?" The younger of the two with red hair in a sleek ponytail held up a piece of paper. "We're here to discuss the accommodation and care of your only offspring, Olive Clark."

Justin continued acting as bodyguard. "And you are?"

"Child Protective Services."

I sucked in a huge breath.

Oh, no.

Tension in the room wound tight.

I moved closer to Olive, shielding her.

The woman cast her stare on all of us, saying, "The police informed us of the incapacitation of Mr. Clark, along with the impending trial for the events over the past few months. We were asked to arrange appropriate care for Olive Clark, and to discuss the fact that she hasn't been attending school for over a year. As far as we're concerned, it's in the best interest of the child that she be placed with a foster family who will ensure her wellbeing and education is——"

"You are not taking my daughter." Gil sat straight up in bed, his face blanching with agony. "No way."

The redhead bypassed Justin, coming far too close for comfort. "Do you have relatives who could take the child?"

"The child's name is Olive," Gil snarled. "And she's standing right in front of you."

Olive kept her shoulders squared, her little body brave but trembling. "I don't want to leave my dad."

"I know," the other CPS agent said, coming toward us with her satchel swinging by her side. "But you need structure, sweetie. You need a family who——"

"Don't call me sweetie!" Olive slammed hands over her ears. "Uncle Jeffrey called me sweetheart and I *hated* it!" She turned into me, and my arms automatically wrapped around her.

"I think you better leave," I snapped.

"Get out." Gil tried to climb free from the tight bed sheets, but the monitors beeped and accused him of movement not recommended for someone in his wounded state.

Justin came to my side, forming a barrier, a family unit where all of us stood up to the law. "I'm Olive's godfather. She can stay with me while Gil is in the hospital."

The redhead scowled. "Have you had experience with children before? Will you ensure she attends school, seeing as Mr. Clark failed on that account?"

"She was fucking kidnapped," Gil snarled, finally ripping off the sheet even though his face shone with sweat and a bloom of red appeared on his side. "I've been trying to find her for a year. Do you honestly think the kidnapper would take her to goddamn school?"

I reached out, resting my hand on his quaking arm. "Calm down, they're only here for Olive's best interest."

I did my best to stay rational, even though I wanted nothing more than to dump the carafe of water on their head and kick them out the door.

"Thank you." The woman with dark hair sniffed in my direction. "Like your friend said, Mr. Clark, we're only here for the best interest of—"

"Her best interest is to stay with her father." Gil panted, raking a hand through his hair and dislodging my hold. "I have no intention of letting her out of my sight again."

"You're in a hospital. She can't stay—"

"I can take her to my place," Justin interrupted. "I'll care for her."

Olive scrunched up her face. "No, I want to stay with Dad!"

The agents looked triumphant. "It seems you are unsuitable. We believe the child needs to undergo extensive therapy after her ordeal. She needs to be placed with a family capable of nurturing troubled—"

"She's not troubled," Gil roared. "She's loved and she's back home with me. You're not having her." His finger soared to the door. "Leave. Before I do something I'll regret."

The redhead stood up to his temper. "You're about to go through a lengthy trial for your involvement in the painted murders, Mr. Clark. Do you really believe you're in a position to care for a child who needs psychological—"

Get out!" Gil tripped from the bed, his IV line catching on the railing. Justin swooped toward him, supporting his weight as his legs gave out. More blood saturated the side of his hospital gown.

Olive began to cry, silent and sorrowful.

It broke my heart.

All of this…

It broke my stupid, foolish heart.

"I can look after her."

Everyone froze. All eyes locked on me.

I trapped a lock of Olive's hair and pulled gently. "Would that be okay? Would you be all right staying with me while your dad heals?"

Olive blinked, her eyelashes dewy with tears. "Stay? With…you?"

I nodded, bending to her level. "You don't have to. You're the bravest girl I've ever met, so I know you can face anything, but while your dad gets better, you can stay with me…if you want."

Gil made a noise in his chest.

A noise that wrapped around me and made tears prick my own eyes. Even now, I wasn't immune to him. Even after everything.

"You don't have to do that, O," Gil strangled. "You're leaving, remember?"

"I know."

I wasn't a martyr or a sacrifice.

But I was a person who tried her best to be good.

This offer wasn't for him.

It was for her.

This little girl who'd captured me from the moment I'd seen her blinking like a woodland creature in the dark.

Olive's shoulders fell, her hand slipped into mine. She held onto me while she turned and faced her father. "Can't I stay here with you?"

Gil's throat worked hard as he swallowed. "I wish you could, little spinach, but it seems that option has been taken away." He threw a glower at the women. His gaze tracked to mine with a shake of his head. "You don't have to do this, O. Truly. I'm not trapping you into yet another mess of mine."

"I can help," Justin murmured. "I don't mind."

Gil shot him a grateful look even as pain blended. He'd only just found his daughter, yet he had to relinquish her all over again. To watch others care for her the way he wanted. "Do you think you could stay with her at my warehouse? Instead of taking her to yours?" His voice lowered. "I don't want her to think she's been kidnapped twice."

Olive sniffed, her energy levels quickly slipping into sadness, knowing her happily-ever-after of going home with her father wouldn't come true. "I don't want to go home with him. I want to go home with *you*." Her grey eyes snapped fiercely to Gil, her hand squeezing hard around mine.

Gil sighed sadly. "And I want to go home with you. And we will." His attention shot to the CPS agents watching us with suspicion. He dared them to refute his claim about going home.

Gil might've saved Olive but he'd lost any right to keep her.

I thought he'd have more time before they tried to take her away from him.

It wasn't fair.

What would happen now?

Who would have custody while he was arrested and put on trial for a murder that he *did* commit? A murder that would come with prison time.

I froze as the future unravelled before me. Gil in jail. Olive with foster parents. A lifetime of broken families. We weren't just talking about a few days here; we were talking about Olive's entire livelihood.

She can't be allowed to leave with them.

Justin followed the same path I did. His harsh inhale wrenched everyone's attention to him. He looked at Olive with a pained expression, wanting to talk frankly but aware that word selection had to be careful.

"Clark…" He cleared his throat. "Um, seeing as your hospital stay might be longer than a few days…" His hand shook as he rubbed his mouth. "And we all know how slow doctors can be…" He looked at me, seeking support, refusing to look at the agents. "Perhaps we should arrange a longer-term arrangement for Olive than just a few days."

The agents crossed their arms, tapping their feet.

Olive narrowed her eyes, trying to follow the cryptic conversation.

I deciphered it and my heart sank further. *Seeing as you're arrested and we all know how slow court dates and hearings can take, Olive needs a caregiver for the next few weeks at least. And longer if you're convicted. These CPS agents can't be allowed to take her. Who knows if you'll ever get her back.*

Gil's whitewashed face turned a greenish hue. He rested on the edge of the bed as he buried his hands in his hair, tugging hard as the ramifications crashed into him. "Oh, God." He looked as if he'd be sick.

I wanted to go to him. To rub his back. To assure him he

wouldn't lose her for the second time.

But if I did, I'd fall into the same pattern.

The pattern I was trying to break.

The pattern you're stuck in now that you've offered to care for Olive.

"What? What is it?" Olive asked.

I pulled her into my side. "Nothing. Your father is just sad he can't come home with you for a while." Turning her to face me, I added, giving her options, giving myself options where I could still leave and not be linked to Gil, "Justin has the coolest place, and you can stay with him for a bit. It's probably best if you stay with him." I smiled as wide as I could. "He's your godfather, after all. He's kind of like an angel who will look after you. It will be fun. A little holiday."

Olive's eyes welled with fresh tears. "But I don't want a holiday. I want to go home."

"How about I come stay at your place then?" Justin offered. "It will be a holiday for me, instead."

She cried harder. "I just want to go home with my dad."

I hugged her close, my heart a bleeding ruin.

Gil looked into me, his stare piercing and full of so many troubled, hurting things. He nodded in thanks while I rocked his most precious belonging.

My stomach knotted.

My heart pounded in answer to his gratefulness, his sorrow.

God, what a mess.

"Look, we can discuss the fine print in a few days when emotions aren't running so high." The redhead tried to pry Olive out of my arms. "Just give us Olive, and we'll ensure she's well taken care of—"

"No!" Olive's little hand slipped into mine again, deepening the bond between us that'd formed from dark forests and her father's blood. "I'm not going anywhere with you!"

I stood, keeping Olive's hand tight in mine. "I think it's best if you come back later."

"We can't leave until we're sure Olive's living arrangements are satisfactory."

"Can...can you look after me?"

I looked down as Olive tugged on my hand. Her face seemed older, alive with understanding that I was the lesser of the evils. She couldn't have her father. She didn't want Justin. She definitely didn't want to be given to strangers.

She'd chosen me.

And her choice sentenced me to yet another cycle of not being able to say no.

"Can you? Please? Can you come stay until Daddy can come home?"

Justin stiffened.

Gil groaned, putting my welfare above Olive's in a way that made me feel both cherished and utterly guilty. "No, little spinach. Let her go. O has already done far too much. She's going away—"

"Please?" Olive looked up, her fingers so perfect and trusting in mine. "I'll be good, I promise." She practically climbed up my body with her panic. "I'll go to bed when you tell me. You won't have to tie me to a tree outside for being naughty. I'll be super quiet and good, you'll see."

My eyes flew to the CPS agents.

Shit.

The dark-haired one narrowed her eyes, hearing what I did. That Olive had been subject to abuse that needed to be repaired. Abuse that I wasn't qualified to deal with.

Gil made a broken noise, forgetting our unwanted audience. "God, he tied you to a tree?" His hands curled. "What else did he—"

"Gil." I flashed him a warning look. "Now is not the time."

He choked, his face white and hospital gown bright red. A crimson trickle ran down his naked calf, licking through leg hair and plopping onto the disinfected floor.

He shouldn't be vertical. He shouldn't be fighting such fear.

This wasn't fair on either father or daughter, and I'd had enough.

No wonder I despised hospitals.

They were the steppingstone to hell.

A stopping place where those injured had to get better and those waiting had to hope their loved ones returned. It was purgatory and I wouldn't let them suffer anymore.

I looked down at a little girl who'd somehow replaced my desire to run with unbreakable loyalty.

Olive's tears were fast and fat, heavy with hurt. "Please! I don't want to go with them—"

"You're not going anywhere." My vow hissed with promise. "Ever."

She burrowed into me, trusting me. She trembled; the brave, curious girl who I thought was resilient to what she'd gone through buckled in my arms. She was fragile beneath her courageous exterior. She was hurting beneath her spirited exterior.

She's like Gil.

A perfect chameleon, hiding her true feelings until she couldn't hide them anymore.

This promise would break me all over again.

But I also couldn't deny her.

Glaring at the agents, I clipped, "I'll take care of Olive. She can stay at my apartment with me until Gilbert Clark is released from hospital. I'll ensure she attends school and any other requirements you have. I'll fill in any reports and do what you ask as long as you don't take her away from her father."

I could care for her in my home, as long as she didn't want to return to the warehouse.

I couldn't go back there.

Not yet.

"And when he goes on trial?" The redhead crossed her arms. "Who's going to look after her then?"

"I will." Justin puffed up his chest. "We all will. We'll make it work."

"She has family," I said. "She doesn't need strangers."

"O," Gil groaned, his voice deepening. He couldn't stop looking at me, his body rigid. Love that he could no longer hide poured from his gaze, wrapping around me, drowning me. "O, you don't have to—"

"I do." My voice was bold and determined. "I am." Wrenching my gaze from his, I focused on his daughter. The daughter I'd been sacrificed to find. The daughter who'd been the reason Gil had left me.

Her creation drove us apart.

Her desperation kept us together.

There was no other option but to protect her like Gil had.

Pausing all my plans, allowing love to trap me further, and kindness to make me powerless, I arched my chin at the agents. "Is that satisfactory enough for you?"

The redhead pursed her lips, looking at her colleague. "I suppose that would be okay, for now. We will monitor the situation."

"Fine." I nodded. "Now, please leave."

In a tense standoff, the women looked one last time at all of us, turned around, and vanished out the door.

The moment they'd gone, Gil almost crashed off the bed.

The monitors screamed.

A doctor flew in.

The chaos that followed ensured everyone focused on Gil's recovery and not the future where he might have wished he'd died in that forest instead.

I wished I could stop what was coming for him.

I wished I had the capacity to slay monsters and defeat court dates and stop murder trials, because it wouldn't be a disgruntled, greedy family member who would tear him apart this time, but the law.

A monster no one could win against.

Chapter Eleven

Olin

POLICE RELEASED A statement today, assuring the public that the killer responsible for the body painting murderers has been arrested. Currently, it is believed there were two men involved. Jeffrey Clark was killed the night a fifth girl went missing. Olin Moss was to be the next victim and was already painted before the police found them. The second man, Gilbert Clark, is in hospital. The families of the deceased are demanding swift and severe justice for their loved ones and have taken to online petitions and GoFundMe requests to ensure Gilbert Clark receives life imprisonment.
More details to come.

I trembled on my couch, phone in hand, internet searches giving me nightmares.

Darkness rained all around me, hissing with horrors, while Olive was in my room, asleep.

It'd been a long day.

After leaving the hospital, Justin kindly dropped Olive and me off at my place. He'd offered to stay, to run errands with us. But Olive had withdrawn and I sensed female company would be better for her fragile state. Once Justin had gone, I'd shown her around, changed the sheets on my bed, then taken her grocery shopping.

She'd perked up toward the end, asking if I could take her to Gil's warehouse to grab her things as she literally had nothing. No toothbrush, no nightie, no clothes.

But I'd rather use the money from Status Enterprises that'd been earmarked for rent and bills to replace her things rather than go back to the warehouse so soon. I bought her what she needed, doing my best to buy her happiness as well as staples.

The strawberry scent I'd caught in Gil's apartment now laced mine from her shower. The sweet pull of maple syrup and pancakes lingered from the unhealthy dinner I'd made, cooking Olive pancakes like I'd once cooked for her father, hoping it would fix her troubles and knowing nothing had that much power.

Exhaustion had sat on my shoulders all day—a whisper in my ear to fall asleep and hide, but I waited until Olive collapsed beside me watching Netflix before carrying her into my bed and returning to the little nest of blankets and pillow I'd made on the couch.

I got comfy.

I closed my eyes.

And images of paintbrushes and caravans and blood, blood, blood surrounded me.

Gil followed on such gruesome thoughts, fisting my heart and making me fear he'd died after all. That the blood he'd lost at the hospital would push him the final way into a grave.

He won't die.

He can't.

Even though his future was bleak, he had to stay alive for Olive's sake.

Heart winging, I sat up, peering into the darkness. I checked the door was locked for the third time, and grabbed a glass of water from the kitchen.

My pulse stayed too high to rest, so I made the terrible decision of googling information on the most recent body painting murder case.

I hated that my name was printed for everyone to see.

I hated that Gil sounded like a blood-thirsty beast.

They hadn't given any facts, just vague accusations that would lead to a witch hunt.

Returning to the page results, I braced myself all over again and clicked on a link for a petition set up by the parents of Moira Jonston, one of the murdered girls.

Sign the petition below to ensure this doesn't happen to any other English girls. Gilbert Clark, the renowned body painting artist and owner of the company Master of Trickery, used his stature as an artist to lure unsuspecting women into his lair to kill them.

He is a despicable human being and we boycott all his work.

We want Facebook to delete his Master of Trickery page.

We want the police to provide clear justice.
We want compensation for the families he's torn apart.
We want him to pay to the highest degree.
Sign now to ensure he doesn't get away with it.
#deathsentenceforthebodypainter

I tossed my phone away, closing my eyes from the screen's glare.

Could they do that? Could they take away his business and force the law to lock him away indefinitely? There was no mention of his arrest for killing his uncle. But they'd pinned the girl's murders on him instead.

Gil hadn't killed them.

He might have painted them, but he didn't actively kill them. Jeffrey had gloated that he'd done that.

Their deaths coated his hands, and Jeffrey's demise coated Gil's.

He'd done the world a favour by removing him from society, yet he might end up serving a life sentence because of the power of social media and the pressure of people with a voice.

And Olive…what will happen to Olive?

I rubbed my eyes.

God, this is such a catastrophe.

My phone illuminated the gloom as it vibrated across the couch. An unknown number flashed across the screen.

Who the hell is calling me at two in the morning?

My heart kicked.

Gil?

Could he call me from his room in the hospital? Had something worse happened?

Scooping up the phone, I answered with a whisper, doing my best not to wake up Olive. "Hello?"

"Olin, is that you?"

I stiffened against the cushions. "Mum. Wow, hi." I hadn't heard from my parents in months. The last time was via email because phone data was expensive and international calling daylight robbery according to my father.

"We just heard the news. Are you okay? What on earth is going on?"

"I'm fine."

What could I tell them? We'd never had a close relationship, and I'd never learned the art of assuring them I was happy and healthy while hiding things I didn't want them to know.

"Did someone try to *kill* you?" my father bellowed. "Are you in protective services? I hope you're taking this seriously and listening to authorities."

I sat taller, scrambling for things I could admit while censoring so many others. "It's all over. I'm safe. The murderer is dead and—"

"He's not dead. He's in hospital. He could get out at any moment and come and finish the job." My mother lamented.

Dad jumped in. "We'll send you a plane ticket. Come join us in Argentina. Get away from that place until he's in a cell and some inmate with big arms and lots of tattoos rips him into pieces."

The mental image of Gil being abused and killed in prison made me rub the sudden ache in my chest.

God, I hadn't even thought about that.

What if he was killed behind bars?

What if he was found guilty and—

Gil can't go to jail.

His personality wouldn't survive. He'd either shut down and give up or he'd join the ranks of merciless criminals and never look back.

Or he'll die.

I swallowed away my parent-induced panic. "I'm fine here, Dad. I don't need to fly—"

"Are you traumatised?" Mum asked.

"No, I'm good."

"You don't sound good."

"Well, I don't know how I'm supposed to sound at two in the morning."

"Why are you up so early?"

I held back my frustrated laugh. "You called me. Remember?"

"Humph." Mum huffed. "Well, are you working? You're not dancing, so where are you working?"

I gritted my teeth. They knew about my accident, but they hadn't really understood, nor cared what the lack of dancing did to my soul. It was an open wound, and this phone call was not the time to tell them how callous such comments made me feel. "I got an admin job. It's enough to get by."

"Do you need more money?" Dad asked.

I balled my hands. I'd never taken money from them. Not

once. Not even when I'd been in hospital with my surgery. They'd offered. Fairly regularly in fact. The guilt probably made them offer me at least something. They couldn't provide love or companionship but they could provide cash.

"No, it's fine. I can manage."

"It's not about managing, Olin; it's about being honest if you need help," Dad snipped. "I'll send you something anyway. In case you're not up for work with what happened. Shock can be delayed, you know. Don't want you to end up homeless."

I slouched into the couch, drained beyond belief. I was grateful for the money. Of course, I was. But I was also devalued and left with a sour taste in my mouth. "You don't have to do that, Dad."

"Already done." He snorted down the line as if he'd fixed world peace. "Anything else we need to know?"

A two-minute conversation and they were ready to go back to their lives. They'd been good parents and checked on their offspring who hadn't been murdered, they were free again.

I shook my head. "No, everything is fine."

Fine.

Fine.

That word echoed around empty and meaningless.

"You guys all good?" I added, being the dutiful daughter.

Mum mumbled something in the background while Dad replied, "Brilliant, honey. Time of our lives."

"I'm glad you're having such a great adventure."

"You too, honey," Mum said as if completely forgetting the circumstances of why they'd called me in the first place. "Love you."

"Love you guys, too."

Kisses were blown down the line before they hung up, and I clutched dead air and a cell phone that judged me.

Throwing it away for the second time, I slid sideways onto the couch and closed my eyes.

Chapter Twelve

Gil

SEVEN DAYS PASSED excruciatingly slowly.

I might not have been in prison yet, but I was trapped against my will. I wasn't allowed to leave my room. I couldn't care for my daughter. I had police watching my every move and listening to every doctor's visit.

The only spots of happiness in my long, lonely days of healing were when O brought Olive to visit. Without fail, the woman who'd I'd treated so badly and done so many unforgivable things to, arrived at lunchtime with my daughter.

The first day, Olive looked tired and timid. She'd clung to O's hand as if sleeping in a strange bed in a strange apartment had regressed her to living with Jeffrey. I'd held her close, kissed her glossy hair as she admitted that O had made her pancakes. I'd told her how jealous I was after sharing my gross hospital lunch with her, all while O made an excuse to go to the gift shop to buy me a book so boredom didn't kill me.

I did my best to stay light-hearted and normal, asking Olive lots of questions to assess her mental health. Overall, she seemed resilient. The same adorable kid I'd been lucky enough to share my life with until a year ago.

She was older.

A little more cynical, a lot more distrusting, and wise beyond her young years, but she wasn't too messed up from her year-long ordeal.

Thank God.

Despite her seemingly okay exterior, I did my best to pry what'd happened without asking directly, trying to determine if she truly *was* okay or if a psychiatrist was needed.

Olive was too like me. Too clever at hiding her real emotions behind fake ones.

If I hadn't killed Jeffrey, I would kill him all over again for what he'd done.

Each day, I was grateful to O for bringing my child and the time alone she gave us, but I hated that, once again, I was adding more stress on her.

I wanted to talk to her.

To tell her she should leave and forget about me.

That I didn't deserve her help.

And it fucking tore me up that she was *still* helping me.

After everything I'd done.

I was draining her, breaking her, taking things I wasn't allowed to take.

It didn't matter that I loved her.

That now I had Olive safe, my heart no longer felt guilty for wanting her. All I could think about was the closeness we'd once shared, the ease between us, and the intensity of connection.

I'd always loved her.

I would *continue* to love her.

And that was why she had to get as far away from me as she could because I couldn't offer her what she deserved. Olive and I were just another accident that O had to heal from and move onto better things.

By the end of the week and seven visits of O and Olive, my body had healed enough that the painkillers had been reduced. My stitched together side no longer stabbed me each time I took a breath, and my desire to escape the hospital became undeniable.

I still hadn't been able to talk to O alone. Olive was always by my side, listening to every word O and I said to one another. My desire to set O free dwindled with every hour we spent together because how was I supposed to say goodbye to her? How was I supposed to face what I was about to face without her?

But how could I keep her after everything that I'd done?

My heart waged war against itself, wanting to be selfish all while knowing it had to do the right thing.

O had kindly brought a sketchpad and watercolours two days ago, along with magazines and a fully stocked e-reader. However, the distractions weren't enough to stop me from watching the news and seeing how many people wanted my head on a spike for the girls my uncle had killed.

My future was undetermined.

My freedom no longer guaranteed.

And it all came to an end at eleven a.m. on the eighth day in hospital.

I looked up as the door opened, a smile already on my face in anticipation of my favourite visitors popping by. My heart pounded harder just at the thought of seeing O. My arms empty to hug both of them, even though O never came in touching distance.

But my smile fell as the kind doctor came in, her professional nod and gentle eyes familiar now. "How you feeling today?"

Sitting in the chair by the window, I sat taller. I didn't hiss in pain anymore. Considering they'd stitched a big chunk of my side back together again, my body was miraculous with fast healing. The black threads holding my flesh together no longer looked morbid. My skin no longer swollen or infected. "Better."

"That's good."

She read something on her iPad, skimming my notes and updates. "Your blood work looks fine and you're healing better than I expected." She looked up and smiled. "The good news is you'll be fine. No long-term complications. Just listen to your body as you continue healing, and you should have no issues."

"Okay, will do."

Her face fell as she looked at the door then back to me. "Unfortunately, I do have some bad news."

My pulse quickened. "They're sick of waiting?"

She clutched the iPad to her chest. "Yes."

"When?"

"Today. Now."

My heart rate exploded. "Shit."

I still accepted the consequences of my actions. I would be honest and take whatever punishment they deemed fit. But it didn't stop the rush of panic or cold sweat at the thought of never having a private conversation with O again. Of never kissing my daughter or tucking her into bed.

Of never being free.

I wasn't under any illusion that I was a saint. My chances of having a light sentence were slim…especially with the hate threats online and screams for justice on the news.

The doctor came closer. "If you tell me you're not feeling well, I can ask to keep you here for another few days."

I half-smiled. "I'm grateful, and believe me, I'm extremely tempted. I don't want to go to jail, but I also can't sit in limbo. I might as well get it over with."

"Fine, but we'll need to see you for check-ups every other day for the next week, so they'll have to bring you back. And if you go home, please take it easy. Don't ruin your progress by overdoing it."

I thought of Olive and O. I thought about my warehouse that I'd sold to pay yet another ransom. I thought about paying rent on something I used to own and the mess I'd left my paint supplies in.

I thought about all of it in a terror-coloured blur.

Would I be released to sort out my life before I was jailed?

Or was this it?

Maybe I should feign sickness to stay a little longer.

My thoughts blackened as she backed toward the door. "I guess there's nothing left to do apart from say you're ready."

Bracing myself on the armchair, I stood.

My body stayed upright. My pain stayed low.

I'd lived through worse.

I'd survived worse.

I'll survive this.

"Thanks for fixing me," I said, smiling gratefully as she reached the door.

She stared into me, stern and worried. "Good luck, Mr. Clark. For the record, I believe you're a good person and not what they're painting you out to be online." Turning the handle, she gave me one last look before slipping into the corridor just as two uniformed officers barged in.

Their legs spread, their arms crossed, their pleasure in finally arresting me glowed bright. "Mr. Clark. Please come with us."

"Give me two minutes." Grabbing the bag that Justin had brought me from my warehouse with a pair of jeans, a t-shirt, and boxer-briefs, I stepped into the bathroom. Slipping from the god-awful hospital gown, I dressed slowly, favouring my right side. I cleaned my teeth and stared into the mirror, trying to come to terms with no longer being a free man.

When I returned to the room, the police looked me up and down, then moved aside to the now open door. "After you."

"Can I call my daughter? She's only eight. I can't just—"

"That will be sorted later."

"I can't be locked up without figuring out her safety." My voice vibrated with anger. "She's my responsibility—"

"Should've thought of that before you committed a crime."

My hands balled. "I killed Jeffrey Clark because he'd kidnapped her. I did what I could to save her."

"And your excuse for killing those other girls?" The older one glowered.

"I didn't kill them."

He chuckled. "How about you hold off on your unbelievable explanations until you have a lawyer present."

"But my daughter—"

"Can wait," the younger clean-shaven one said. "Now, do you need a wheelchair?"

Temper raged through me, but I managed to stay controlled. Just. "No. I'm fine."

"Good."

The older one narrowed his eyes. He pulled out a pair of handcuffs.

I stiffened.

He chewed his cheek, eyeballing me. "Do I need to handcuff you?"

"No." I held his stare. "I won't run. And even if I did, I wouldn't get far. All I care about is ensuring my daughter has someone to—"

"Fine. Don't have time for this." He pursed his lips. "Let's go. All that nonsense can be taken care of at the station."

My anger flared hotter. "You're calling my daughter nonsense?"

"I'm calling you thinking you have any special privileges nonsense." The older one rubbed his nose and cocked his head toward the exit. "No cuffs is your one and only privilege. Now, no more delays. Out."

The younger officer moved first, expecting me to follow.

Swallowing back my rage, I fell into line and did my best not to shiver as the older one positioned himself behind me.

A sandwich of law and criminal.

I wished I'd been able to call O and tell her.

I didn't want her to come here with Olive and find me missing.

I couldn't expect her to figure out Olive's living arrangements.

She was only supposed to look after my daughter until I was released from hospital.

But now my custody included police instead of doctors.

This whole fucking mess was on me.

No one spoke as I did the walk of shame through the hospital, down the elevator, and out into the bright sunshine. England looked practically cheerful even though my freedom was ending.

The older officer stayed with me, his hand resting on my elbow while his partner went to collect the patrol car.

No lights, no sirens, just a smooth glide to the curb and a door opening wide to welcome me.

I winced, holding my side as pain flashed. Ducking to climb inside wasn't as easy as I hoped. The internal pain of healing organs and stitched together muscle grumbled at the movement.

The second I was inside, the door locked me in, and the older officer joined his colleague in the front. They drove me away from the hospital just as I spotted O walking from the visitor's car park, holding Olive's hand.

Her gaze caught mine.

A brief, violent moment.

Our connection snapped tight.

My heart crashed hard.

I twisted to keep both girls in my sights as the car turned the corner and she vanished.

* * * * *

"Mr. Clark. You've been arrested for the murder of Jeffrey Clark by use of succinylcholine." The judge read the file on her desk, her half-moon glasses sliding down her nose. "You've also been charged with accessory before the fact and second-degree manslaughter for the four women who lost their lives while covered in the same pigment found in your paint supplies."

She pinned me to the spot, her brown stare severe and unyielding. "How do you plead?"

"Guilty for the murder of Jeffrey Clark. Not guilty for the women, your honour." My voice stayed stable, but my heart was a fucking mess.

"You don't have a lawyer present. Are you sure you'd like to submit those pleas?"

I nodded.

The sooner this was over, the better.

The past few hours had been mayhem.

Thanks to the eight days I'd already technically served being arrested in my hospital room, the moment I'd arrived at the station, they booked me, fingerprinted me, asked for any personal items, which I did not have, and placed me in a holding cell with a few other men who looked as shell-shocked as I did.

I didn't know how the justice system worked and figured the cell I was in was the cell I'd be living and sleeping in for the next unknown while. However, a few hours later, an officer appeared, called my name, and hurried me down a concrete corridor and into a room with heavy wood panelling.

The judge eyed me up and down. "Murder charges are serious, Mr. Clark. Ordinarily, I would hold you without bail until your trial." Her gaze went to my pale blue t-shirt and the small bloodstain that'd appeared from my stitches. I'd twisted too far in the squad car, trying to see Olive and O. I'd ruptured something.

"As you've come here directly from hospital and still have at least a month of recovery, I will permit you to post bail with the strictest instructions not to leave Birmingham or even the street where you live. You will wear an ankle bracelet at all times. Do you understand?"

I nodded again. "Yes, your honour."

Bail sounded great. I could go home. I could be a father. I could cram in as much normalcy as humanly possible before I couldn't anymore.

But I had zero equity. I had no cash. No assets to use as collateral.

It didn't matter if bail was ten pounds or a million, I couldn't afford it.

My shoulders rounded, my pain level magnifying as she muttered, "Bail is set at two hundred thousand pounds, and your hearing date will be advised." Her gavel smashed down with finality, and the next unlucky schmuck was shuffled forward.

I had no time to question or let shock trickle through my bloodstream.

I'd been processed.

It was done.

I was guided to a small room where more paperwork was presented and signed, a monitoring anklet was locked around my leg, and the terms and conditions of my bail advised even though I had no way of taking them up on their offer.

With the condemning device strapped to my ankle, the guard guided me back to the holding cell. This time, the icy depressing space was empty.

"In." The officer pushed me forward.

I hissed as my wound twinged. I sat on the metal bench and rested my head in my hands.

Now what?

If I couldn't post bail, would I have to stay here until my trial?

Would they at least give me a blanket because I was fucking cold?

Would they let me see my doctor tomorrow like she requested?

I didn't even know O's cell phone number to call and tell her what happened. To make arrangements for Olive. To advise her that Justin would once again have to pick up my fucking pieces so O could run far away from the mess I'd caused.

Fuck, poor Olive.

She wouldn't understand.

She'd hate me for failing her all over again.

My grey sneakers would soon be traded for prison shoes. My jeans would become a jumpsuit. My business no longer operational. I would never paint again. Never watch TV with Olive again. Never tell O every answer to her every biting question.

It's over.

I couldn't catch a proper breath as I accepted that fate had once again fucked me over.

I'd lost my freedom, daughter, and the love of my life all over again.

And this time, I only had myself to blame.

* * * * *

"Clark, you made bail." A guard banged his hand on the bars, wrenching my eyes open.

I hissed between my teeth as I moved too fast, hurting my side. I would kill Jeffrey all over again for some painkillers and a hoodie.

The guard opened the cell, waiting for me to exit.

The prison vanished for a moment as my blood pressure dropped. The goosebumps that had permanently decorated my skin increased as my bones complained of being so cold.

I hauled myself to my feet, fighting a body that craved rest.

I'd been stupid to think I was cured.

I wasn't nearly as healed as I'd hoped.

Clearing my throat, I moved into the corridor and waited for the guard to lock up. "Who paid my bail?"

He shrugged. "No one tells me nothing." Striding forward, he looked back at me. "Come on. I don't have all night."

Following him as fast as I could, I kept my hand on my wound as we entered the foyer of the precinct and I signed yet more paperwork that they shoved under my nose.

My back prickled as someone came up behind me.

Someone I knew.

Someone I owed more than I could ever repay.

Turning slowly, I held out my hand to shake Justin's. Half of me wanted to punch him while the other wanted to bow in defeat. "You didn't have to do that."

"I know." He nodded, his dark blond hair neat and body encased in a suit from work. "But I couldn't let you rot in there awaiting trial. Besides, I know you won't run, so it's not like I'm going to lose my investment in you."

We broke contact. "I won't cost you bail." I frowned. "How did you find out about it? No way should you have had to part with two hundred grand for my sorry arse."

He smiled, heading toward the exit and waiting until I fell into step with him. "You've listed me as next of kin. They called and asked if I wanted to post your bail or knew of someone who would."

"Why did you do it?"

"It's either free your sorry arse or become surrogate father to your child."

"I wouldn't expect you to do that." I winced. "I've already asked so fucking much of you."

"So you're okay with O looking after your kid?"

"O needs to be free of me. I've already hurt her too much."

"So your plan is to let O run away and Olive to be packed into foster care?"

My heart stopped beating. "Fuck, no. But I refuse to put my fuck-ups on others anymore. None of you deserve this. I should've handled the situation better. I should've—"

"Look, I'm going to be black and white here, all right?" His eyes flashed. "You don't have a choice. You need us, mate. Me and O. You need our help. There is nothing wrong with that. It doesn't make you weak. It doesn't make us hate you for asking for help. But it does get old when you constantly fight the help we're trying to give you."

I had no reply. I stared at him dumbfounded.

The first time Justin had shown a spark of temper and he'd put me in my place like a kick to a barking dog.

He sighed, shrugging. "Sorry, but that's the reality of the situation. You have no choice but to lean on us, all right? The other shit? It doesn't matter. It's all in the past." His long legs ate up the pavement, his back ramrod straight. "Just focus on getting better. The rest we'll figure out."

I wanted to argue. To tell him I would figure this out without him, but fresh air licked over my skin as we strode through the door and into the night sky, and reality smashed me in the face.

I was lucky.

So fucking lucky to have people who hadn't given up on me, no matter what sort of bastard I'd been.

Relief tried to worm under my overwhelming guilt.

I would never take freedom for granted. I would forever be in Justin's debt. But I also couldn't justify his sacrifice.

Why had he put so much on the line after only a troubled year of friendship?

Who did that?

Who was that selfless?

O.

O is that selfless…and so is Justin.

Two similar people who'd been lumped with the unlucky job of looking after me.

My teeth ground as self-hatred wormed through my chest. "You've given me time, Miller, and for that I'm terribly grateful. I will cherish every moment I have with Olive, I'll do my best to repair what I did to O, and I'll figure out a way to pay you back, but you can't keep doing this. I'm not your responsibility. I know I listed you as Olive's godfather but I don't expect you to adopt her if this all turns to shit. Don't feel like you're trapped just because I am."

He closed the gap between him and his parked car. Resting his hand on the roof, he scowled. "You're a friend, Gil. Friends help out."

"There's helping out and then there's being too fucking generous."

"Look, I put myself in your shoes. I thought about how shit I'd feel being locked up when my daughter is too young to take care of herself. I don't know a hell of a lot of what you've been going through, but I know it hasn't been easy." He unlocked the black sedan, cracking open the door. "I'm still waiting for that explanation, by the way. But in the meantime, just accept it for what it is. Despite all your efforts, you actually have two friends who care about you. You should be with them until…" His eyes flickered away.

"Until I'm sentenced."

"Pretty much. Yeah." He waited until we'd both slipped inside, and I'd puffed with pain to fasten my seatbelt.

He asked softly, "Do you know when they'll call you to court?"

I shook my head. "They didn't say."

He started the car and shoved it into gear. "It can sometimes take months for a hearing."

Staring out the window, I didn't reply as my gaze landed on a small group of people with placards walking down the road to the police station in the dark. Streetlights highlighted a banner linked between the two women walking in front.

A banner that said, *'Gilbert Clark deserves the death sentence.'*

My heart stopped beating.

The placards all depicted paint splashes and pictures of the girls who'd worn my colours and who'd died because of it.

The family of the murdered.

"Shit," Justin muttered as he stomped on the accelerator and shot in the opposite direction.

Yep, shit.

The world was out for blood.

And I was at their mercy.

Chapter Thirteen

Olin

UNKNOWN NUMBER: *O, it's Gil. I've typed, deleted, and retyped so many messages to you, but none of them sound right. No amount of apologies will be enough. No number of thank yous will ever come close. So…I'll keep it simple. I'm back home. I saw you arrive at the hospital today with Olive as I was driven away by the police. I tried to get in touch but was refused. I don't know what the staff told you, but I was officially arrested, booked, and granted bail. Anyway, I just wanted to say, you're free to travel now. I can look after Olive and figure out another scenario for her before my court date. I'm desperate to see her. Tomorrow, I can pick her up or you can drop her off. Either way, I'm extremely grateful to you for looking after her.*

I re-read Gil's message ten times, sipping on a glass of cheap supermarket wine, glancing at my bedroom door to make sure Olive stayed asleep and none the wiser.

I'd never had a message from Gil before.

The novelty sent shivers down my spine.

A teenage reaction to flirting and fun when neither of those options was real.

The wine was to settle my fear over what'd happened to him. After seeing him being driven away in a police car and being turned away at the hospital because he'd been discharged, I'd hid my own concern to protect Olive. I'd taken her to the library and checked out whatever books she wanted—mainly sketching and painting workbooks—and done what I could to distract her.

After a week of living with her, I'd grown used to her triggers.

Her bravery was sometimes far too good. She could laugh and joke and seem like any normal child her age. However, there'd be a moment. A fleeting second when her guard would drop and I'd see the truth. The worry over being in public if I'd gotten too far away from her. The bitten lip if a man walked toward us on the street. The jumpiness if someone came up behind us unannounced.

The fact she could hide her true fears as well as Gil drained me because my instincts took over—just like they had when doing my best to help Gil through his secrets.

My brain told me to give her space—to watch but not hover, to accept that time would heal her from the worst of being held hostage—but my heart wasn't interested in giving her space or letting time heal her. My heart wanted to cure her. It wanted her laughter to be true and not some carbon copy of joy. It wanted her to be able to stroll down a supermarket aisle and not freeze in panic if I wasn't there.

I sighed.

Poor thing.

But at least, she had her father back.

She could go home now.

She could bask in normalcy until Gil was summoned for trial.

Saving his number into my phone, I typed a reply.

Olin: *I'm glad you're back at home. Did everything go okay with the police? I can drop Olive off tomorrow around mid-morning if that works. She'll be beyond happy to be home with you. She's really missing you.*

I inhaled sharply as I pressed send. I didn't want to go to his warehouse. I still wasn't prepared to enter the place where Gil had painted me. But I equally didn't want him in my space, either.

Dropping Olive off was the best choice because I could leave straight away. If he came here, he might stay...he might try to talk.

Gil: *Okay, great. Thanks. By the way, don't feel like you can't keep using my car if it makes your life easier. I'll figure out an alternative.*

Olin: *It was kind of you to let me borrow it to drive Olive around, but it's yours. I'll just catch the bus back after I've driven her to you.*

He took a long time to reply, as if he was once again typing and deleting multiple responses. My heart flurried as words flashed over my screen.

Gil: *I know it's over between us but...if you want answers, I can give them to you. I'm done with lies and hiding. I'll tell you all of it...if you ask.*

My eyes flashed to my bedroom door as it cracked open. Olive rubbed her eyes sleepily, her forehead furrowed with exhaustion. "Oh, good. You're still there."

I tossed my phone onto the couch, climbing to my feet and

going to her. She walked into my embrace, squishing her face into my chest. "Of course, I'm still here. I told you I'd keep you safe."

She pulled away, looking up at me. "You're the best, O. My second favourite person after my daddy."

"Wow, that's a great honour." I smiled, pressing a kiss to her forehead. "And you're the greatest little girl I know." Holding her shoulders, I pushed her away until I could study her face clearly. "What woke you? Another nightmare?"

She dug her barefoot into the carpet. "I thought I heard something. A man."

"Nope. Just us."

"That's good."

She'd grown used to Justin but not to the degree of our bond. Justin had come over a couple of times with pizza and Thai takeaway. He told kid jokes, brought dessert, and braved through a Netflix program for little girls. He was allowed to touch her shoulder in goodbye and take her dishes into the kitchen, but that was where her comfort level ended.

If Gil did get sentenced, who would care for her? Who would step up to be the parent she needed—the protector, the artist, and the disciplinarian?

"Want to know something awesome?" I made my voice bubbly and light.

Her eyes widened in excitement. "What?"

My phone vibrated on the couch behind me, signalling a new message had been delivered.

Gil.

God, why couldn't we have messaged each other before? It would've made a lot of his secrets easier to share via a faceless text.

"You're going home tomorrow. Your dad healed enough to leave the hospital. How freaking cool is that?"

Olive froze, then pure joy rippled through her. She clapped her hands and spun in place with the biggest grin. "Oh, wow, *really*?!" She bounced on the spot. "Yay! *Yay!*"

I pointed at my bedroom door. "It's going to be super fun tomorrow, so you better get some sleep. You don't want to be tired, do you?"

She turned deadly serious. "You're right. I don't want to be tired. I get cranky when I'm tired."

"Yeah, me too. Should we go to sleep, and when we wake up, we'll go see your father?"

She threw herself at me, planting a wet kiss on my cheek.

"Yes, please!" Pulling away, a frown stole her smile. "Wait…you'll stay with us, right? You'll come live at the warehouse?"

I stiffened. "That's your home. This is mine."

"But I like living with you."

"You'll love living with your dad more."

Her face fell. "But…I'll miss you."

I hid the dagger she stabbed me with. The dagger of kindness and affection. After living a lonely life, being told you're wanted was the worst kind of drug because you could swiftly become addicted to it.

Smiling broadly, I turned her around and marched her back into my bedroom. "You won't miss me, silly. You won't even notice I'm not there the moment you're back with your dad. Now, go to sleep so you have lots of energy tomorrow."

Closing the door, I returned to the couch and let out the tangled breath I'd been holding.

What was it about Gil and his daughter that turned me inside out? How did both of them have the power to reach inside my chest and claim what wasn't theirs to claim?

The sooner I leave, the better.

My phone revealed the newest message that'd come in, flashing in warning as I clicked on it.

Gil: *I have no right to say this after what I've done, but I love you, O. I always have. I always will. I know I don't stand a chance to fix what I've broken, and I'm not asking you to forgive me. I guess…I just wanted to be honest. To finally be honest how it's always been you. I was in love with you for two years before we even officially talked. I was in love with you the entire time we were apart. And I'm still in love with you, even though I know I will never deserve you. I guess that's my true punishment. I won't bring it up again. I won't make you uncomfortable. But I had to say it.*

Anyway, goodnight.

Thank you from the bottom of my heart for looking after my daughter. If I know her as well as I think I do, I know she'll miss you. She'll ask you to move in with us. She'll be as in love with you as am I.

And I don't blame her.

I slouched against the pillow, my heart racing, my blood gushing. Tears glazed my vision as I read and re-read his message. A text like that had the power to drop my guard and give me permission to forgive anything and everything.

It reeked of a promise of love and togetherness and home.

It made me want to type that I loved him too. That I always had and probably always would. To accept his proposal to become a part of his life, to possibly become his wife, and mother to his child.

I could have my very own family.

No.

Stop it.

You can't.

Our foundations were rotten and full of holes.

Our walls were riddled with secrets and lies.

Our trust was torn apart.

There is no us anymore.

And it's for the best.

Swiping away a tear, I clung to my resolution of being stronger this time. Of not letting my need for company and closeness belittle my own self-worth. Gil had taken and taken from me.

The small part that was left had to remain mine.

Olin: *Goodnight, Gil. I'll see you tomorrow.*

My hands shook as I sent the polite message back.

A message that didn't just give a generic goodbye but an entire fistful of honesty.

An ending hidden behind the simple phrase.

It's too little.

It's too late.

We're friends.

And nothing more.

Chapter Fourteen

Olin

"IT LOOKS WEIRD," Olive muttered as I parked the car in front of warehouse twenty-five. The Master of Trickery graffiti and gravel frontage hissed with memories of Gil being beaten by his uncle, of Jeffrey trying to drag me into his van, of Gil pulling me inside to paint and deliver me.

I swallowed hard, scolding my pounding heart.

I could do this.

It's just a building.

He's just a man.

It's all in the past.

"How did it used to look?" I unbuckled my seatbelt, climbing from the car as Olive hurled herself outside.

She squinted in the watery sunlight. "Not sure. It's just…different."

"Maybe the paint has faded since you last saw it? It has been a year."

"Maybe." She didn't look convinced. Slamming the passenger door, she skipped eagerly to the pedestrian access in the large roller door. "Dad? Daddy?" Her tiny fist rapped on the metal, echoing down the driveway of warehouses.

I flinched.

Needing to stay occupied, I reached into the backseat for Olive's backpack full of newly purchased clothes and toiletries. I didn't need them anymore.

She was home.

Hopefully indefinitely.

The door swung wide, and Gil appeared. His face immediately turned lighter, younger, *happy*. The seriousness in his gaze became playful. The worry in his jaw relaxed. I'd never seen him so enamoured and carefree. "Spinach!" He bent down and swung her into his arms.

Immediately, he groaned and plopped her back on her feet. "Sorry, kiddo. I forgot I still have a few weeks of healing until I can lift you. You've gotten big."

She pouted but buried her face in his belly, wrapping her arms tight around him. "It's okay. I can wait." She jiggled in his embrace, her joy at finally being home overflowing as she looked up. "Can I go see my room? I missed this place so much!"

Gil nodded, sidestepping out of the way so she could bolt inside. "Of course. Go ahead and get reacquainted." He chuckled as she took off, vanishing into the cavernous warehouse.

His head tipped up, his gaze caught mine, and instantly the dreary English day became alive with electricity. My skin sparked as I clutched her backpack closer, forcing myself to delete the distance between us. "Hello."

He wiped his mouth with a rough hand. "Hello." His green gaze once again became weapons. Only this time, they weren't weapons of annihilation—determined to scare me away and hurt me—but pools of regret and love.

Love...the most terrible weapon of all.

He didn't try to hide it.

He didn't care his guard was down.

He acted as if showing his true colours was a relief after a lifetime of hiding.

"Thanks so much for looking after her, O."

"Not a problem." I held out the backpack. "Here, this is hers. I bought her a few things."

"I'll pay you back."

"It's fine." I backed away. I'd completed my task. I'd delivered his daughter and returned his borrowed hatchback. I was free now. Free to pack up my life and run far, far away like a coward.

"Will you come in? Olive will want to say goodbye."

"Um, I might go if—"

"Daaaaaad!" Olive's high-pitched voice travelled through the space and erupted outside.

Gil looked over his shoulder, his body already turning to go to her. He grimaced. "Look, don't go. I have to...I better go check on her." Striding deeper into the warehouse, he waved for me to follow. "Please, O. Stay…for a moment."

I really didn't want to, but some invisible force tugged me.

Stepping inside, I braced myself as my attention fell on the podium where I'd eaten a drugged sandwich, found out about Gil's past, and fallen asleep while he'd painted me.

He'd tidied up the equipment and hidden away the brushes, but goosebumps spread over my arms. I hugged myself, keeping my chin high and spine straight.

I wasn't afraid of this place.

I wasn't afraid of him.

I was just wary of falling into the same trap of being caught up in the pain of others. Of wanting to fix what I couldn't fix and believing I could be happy if I could make others happy.

I'd learned a valuable lesson that giving too much of yourself never ended well. Generosity with feelings was a must in a relationship, but endless forgiving was a recipe for disaster.

Gil made his way to the office leading toward the small apartment. Olive bowled right into his arms from the opposite direction. Her eyes wide and mouth parted as she pointed around the space suspiciously. "Where is everything?"

Gil hid his wince, his hand pressing to his wounded side as he steadied her. "What do you mean?"

He let her go as she darted toward me, pointing like a crazy thing at the empty walls, cupboards, and floor. "The paintings, the furniture. It's all gone." She spun to face her father with a helpless shrug. "Where'd it go?"

Gil looked at me, fibs forming in his eyes. Fibs to protect her from the truth. But almost as if he didn't have the strength to tell another lie, or because he valued his daughter far too much to keep things from her, he said, "I sold most of it."

"Sold your *paintings*?" She soared around and shoved her finger toward the sky where a bare hook hung between two windows. "Even that one? The one we did together?" Olive marched toward me, stealing my hand as if this was very important. "I liked that painting. It wasn't all that nice 'cause I wasn't as good as I am now, but I liked the turtle. It was huge and scaly and its shell had lots and lots of little creatures painted on it." She nudged her chin at Gil. "Daddy did the smaller animals. He also had the turtle eating spinach 'cause apparently they like that and said it would always be a joke that I'm so fast and speedy, but the giant turtle ate me."

Gil came toward us, looking at the blank spot on the wall. "Someone paid big money for your turtle, Olive Oyl. It's gone to a good home."

"But it belongs here."

"You belong here more."

"I don't get it."

Gil bent forward, bringing his stare in line with hers. "I sold things to get you back. Some things I didn't want to get rid of, but I wanted you more, so I found them new homes." He cupped her cheek with a soft smile. "And it worked because you're back here. We can paint together again. We can go shopping and replace what I sold. It will be fun. You'll see."

Her eyes lit up, already her mourning for missing things replaced by the idea of new. "Can you take me to Kohls...like before? Is it still there?" She looked up at me, pinpricks of excitement on her cheeks. "Daddy used to take me to Kohls once a week if I did my chores and helped him tidy up his paints after he worked. He let me buy one thing each visit. Last time, I bought a pencil case to keep my crayons in." She frowned, facing her father with a strict expression. "You didn't sell my pencil case too, did you?"

Gil chuckled. "No, that I kept. Go and see for yourself."

Olive sniffed, flashed him a grin, and bolted back through the office. A second later, she called, "My room is locked! Why is my room locked?"

Gil groaned. "I forgot what a little tornado she is."

"She's definitely bouncy." I smiled, sucked into Olive's purity and infectious energy.

"She's always kept me on my toes."

"You probably need it." I scanned the sparse place, trying to see it from Olive's point of view. Imagining it full of artwork and couches and chairs and *life*. I'd been so used to Gil's melancholy and his unattachment to physical items that the bareness of his home didn't ring alarm bells. However, in the short interactions I'd watched him with Olive, I uncovered a totally different version of him.

A man who found peace in the chaos of parenthood.

A man who decorated and nested because his little daughter demanded vibrancy and colour.

His lies fell apart while standing in that barren room, the truth blazing hotly in the emptiness, the forlornness. The plastic cups in the cupboards weren't for his painting but his daughter. The room he kept locked a shrine to the little girl he'd lost.

He'd been dying day by day, pushing me away for my safety and jerking me back for his next breath. My soul wanted to chase that path, to vindicate him and give me permission to give in, but my mind focused on something trivial but vitally important.

He takes her to Kohls.

My heart squeezed, condemning myself for my spat of jealousy in the Kohls changing room. The huge store where we'd fought and my jealousy had reached critical, and Gil had turned me green (in more ways than one) to match their logo.

He'd seemed uncomfortable talking about visiting the place when I'd called him out on his familiarity. I'd assumed it was because he didn't want to admit he'd taken prior girlfriends.

Now, a whole new meaning arose.

"You took her to Kohls. It was her you were talking about when you said you went there often. Not with other women."

He massaged the back of his neck, embarrassment etching his cheeks. "I wanted to tell you then about her. I wanted to tell you so many times. But…it wasn't as if I could say… 'oh, by the way. I have a daughter. Want to meet her?' She was a product of a night that should never have happened, and I'd failed to protect her from being taken. The guilt just wouldn't allow me to tell you."

I nodded. "I understand."

"Do you?" His forehead furrowed. "*Do* you understand, or are you just being nice again?"

My back straightened; my temper bristled. "I'm done being nice when it's not deserved."

"Good. I'm glad."

"And I do understand. I know why you kept her secret. I follow your reasoning. I just don't agree with it."

"So you would've enlisted the police and told everyone what a fuck-up you were?"

"No. I would've enlisted the help of those I trusted and asked for their advice."

"What if you'd never had anyone to trust and those you *did* trust turned out to be the worst?"

I frowned. "You're saying I'm the worst?"

"Fuck no." His face darkened with horror. "I'm saying my uncle was."

My temper refused to be pacified. "Well, regardless, I'm not just anyone, Gil."

"No, you're *everything.*"

"And you destroyed any trust between us by—"

"Dad. Hey, *Dad!*" Olive came bowling out, grabbing Gil's hands and yanking. "Key. Is there a key? Why can't I get into my room?"

Gil wrenched his gaze from mine, the heat from our almost-argument hissing with hope of a bigger blow-up.

I hadn't noticed it before.

I hadn't allowed myself to feel it.

But now I did.

Now I felt the burn to shout, the urge to yell, the undeniable need to tell him exactly what I thought about everything.

That was what was missing.

A fight.

A cleansing, healing good-old-fashioned *fight*.

But the luxury of frank conversation—of raised voices and angry shouts couldn't happen in front of a girl who'd already been through so much.

I knew it.

Gil knew it.

We allowed the moment to ease and the tension to fade between us.

Gil sighed, his skin a little whiter than usual thanks to his healing side. He stroked Olive's hair as he pushed her back the way she came. "I've got the key. Come on." Following her into the apartment, he fished out a key ring and selected the right one. Inserting it into the door, he stepped back as it cracked open.

The door that'd always been barricaded next to his in the graffiti rainforest wall. The room he'd consumed a lonely bottle of vodka in, the room I'd glimpsed inside and began to wonder if Gil wasn't as safe as I thought.

Olive ran in.

Curiosity got the better of me, and I drifted forward until her room came into view. Olive bounced from her pillow-stocked bed to the rattan rocking chair to the wardrobe to the pink tallboy. Touching everything, examining anything, getting reacquainted with her old belongings.

Her face glowed with relief. "You didn't sell anything in here."

Gil slouched against the doorframe, his hand touching his wounded side as if pain snuck up on him. "This room was off-limits. It's yours."

Olive threw herself at him, squishing him in a hug. "I love

you, Popeye."

He tripped backward, deep pain and endless gratitude radiating in his eyes. He crushed her close, bowing over to press a kiss to the top of her silken hair. "I love you too. More than you'll ever know."

"Oh, I know." She grinned up at him. "I know you love me loads and loads."

He nodded, releasing her with a grimace. "I do."

"And I know you love Olin loads and loads, too." She gave me a sneaky look. "You told me so in the stories."

Gil groaned, trying to laugh but tangling up a tortured noise instead. "Sometimes stories don't have happy endings."

"Ours does," she said with utmost conviction.

His skin turned ashen. "Ours will, eventually. However, just like other stories, there will be new trials ahead."

My heart skipped a beat.

He's trying to prepare her for the possibility of him going to jail.

"Nothing bad will happen now we're together, silly." Olive patted his waist, still smiling at me. "And nothing bad could ever happen if O moves in with us. We can be safe together."

I coughed, shaking my head. "You guys have each other. You don't need me."

"Yes, we do. I don't want you to go." Her voice slipped into a plea. "Please...can you stay?"

"O has her own life, little spinach. Don't make her sad by asking for things that can't come true."

Her shoulders fell. "I didn't mean to make anyone sad."

I held out my hand. She immediately flew to my side and took it, blinking huge grey eyes, wrapping her little spell around my soul all over again. She made it sound so easy—nullifying a lifetime of complication into one stupidly simple conclusion.

Love had the power to heal, start afresh, move on.

Pity I didn't have the strength to do such things.

"I'll always be your friend, just like I'm your dad's friend. We've been friends for ages."

"Can you be our friend while living with us?"

I chuckled. "Stubborn little thing, aren't you?"

"Yep. Dad said I'm worse than a donkey."

"A donkey?"

"A stubborn arse." Gil chuckled. "I shouldn't call her an arse, but...if the description fits." He smiled, slightly embarrassed, mostly proud.

"I'm an arse." Olive snickered, alive and happy as if she'd been asleep for the past year and just woken up to her father's protective kiss.

"The prettiest arse I've ever seen." I pressed her nose.

She wrinkled it, tossing her head. "I want to draw a donkey now. Wait here." Dashing away, she barrelled to her dresser, ripping open drawers and finding stationery and pencils.

I smiled, entranced by her innocence and total faith that in this moment, nothing could be more perfect.

Gil came toward me, sucking all the air from my lungs.

He stopped within touching distance, his eyes firing, lips parted. For the longest moment, he stared at me. His intensity was bright and fierce. His shields fell, revealing every emotion I'd never been allowed to see. "I shouldn't have messaged you what I did last night. I shouldn't have told you I've always been in love with you. That even now I want you, all while knowing I've ensured I'll never have you."

I shivered, needing to back away, unable to move. "It's fine."

His hand came up, cupping my cheek as if he couldn't control himself. "Fuck, I'm so fucking sorry."

My skin blistered beneath his touch. My stomach bottomed out. My heart cried. I backed up, forcing his hand to drop and my skin to scream in denial.

"Don't." I did my best to keep my stupid heart in its iron-clad box.

This was one promise I wouldn't break.

He'd broken my faith.

My confidence.

Me.

And with that came a distance I wasn't prepared to cross.

I was struggling, I would admit.

I came here offering condolences and concern but nothing more.

But standing there? *God*, every part of me wanted to be touched. Every cell wanted to combust with lust and lunacy. I wanted to scratch him, scar him, and show him just what he'd thrown away. But I shook my head, forbidding both of us from thinking there was any chance to repair this.

He sighed and raked a hand through his hair. The strands were unkempt and wild, as usual. "I'm so deeply indebted to you...for everything."

"You don't need to keep saying that, Gil. You don't have to

repay me…for anything."

He licked his lips. "Are you sure? There's nothing I can do to fix this?"

Kiss me.

Fight for me.

Prove that I'm wrong to leave.

It was time to go.

Time to walk out of Olive's life after falling headfirst into it the past week. Loss kicked me in the stomach. I would miss her. I would miss watching her come alive again.

I could understand why she'd helped Gil so much. She was a natural cure to the hardships of life.

"I…I better go."

He tried to hide his flinch but wasn't successful. "Of course."

"Will…will you be okay? Do you have arrangements made for Olive if you're…"

He swallowed. "I'll figure it out. It's my problem, not yours."

"If you need help…"

"I'll manage. You've done far too much already." His face twisted. "I'll never be able to apologise enough for what I did."

"Stop. Honestly, you don't have to mention it again." I tripped backward, instincts ordering me to leave now, before more memories of murdered girls and body painting sprang anew. "You killed your uncle…for that I'm grateful. But…"

I couldn't ask.

I couldn't *not* ask.

My voice abandoned me.

"What? What do you want to know?" His eyebrows tugged over his gaze, shadowing him. "I'll answer anything you want."

My heart raced. "What part of this did you play, Gil? Did you…did you hurt those girls?" My question fell like unexploded dynamite, dangerous and volatile.

Silence stole the carnage before Gil shifted and sucked in a breath. His stare smoked with apology. "I painted them." He shrugged, holding up his palms. "It was my paint on their skin."

I trembled. "I don't want to believe that."

"It's true."

"I can't believe you could paint someone knowing they would die."

His face fell. "I painted you."

Silence fell.

Truth fell.

Despair fell.

My insides collapsed into one another.

He'd painted me in olives. He'd prepared to sacrifice me.

If he could do that to someone who'd been in his bed and in his heart…what made strangers any different?

The chilly warehouse prickled my arms. "Those people online and the ones on the street…they want you dead."

"I know." He no longer glittered with the ice he'd used to keep me at bay but wore a cape of desolation. Of acceptance that everything had gone wrong and the only thing he could do now was pay the price. "I'm aware that I've fucked everything up all over again. And Olive will pay the most."

"What if they put you away for decades?"

"I'll find her a family worthy of having her love before it's too late."

"And you? What will you do?"

He gave me the saddest, rawest smile. "I'll tell the truth. I'm done hiding, O. When they come for me, I'm going to tell them…everything."

Chapter Fifteen

Olin

"THANK YOU FOR seeing us, Miss Moss."

I nodded, cupping my warm cup of tea with icy hands. "You're welcome."

They weren't welcome, but it wasn't like I had a choice. I'd woken to a rude knock at seven a.m. I'd made the mistake of opening it. I now stood in my pyjamas and dressing gown in an apartment that felt even more lonely and oppressive now that Olive had gone home, and did my best to shake away the nightmares.

Nightmares of Gil being given the death sentence. Of him being fried in an electric chair. Of Olive going to live in a whorehouse with a backpack stained in dumpster dirt. Of Ms Tallup selling her off to the highest bidder.

It'd been three days since I'd dropped Olive off.

And I was going out of my mind.

I needed to do something.

Go somewhere.

Figure out what the hell I should do from here.

"Are you okay? Healthwise?" Two new officers interrogated me today. Two women. One plump with her uniform neatly pressed and her name tag, Gloria, proudly pinned to her breast, and the other as skinny as a pen with her hair tied tight at the base of her nape.

"I'm fine. I wasn't hurt."

"You were found naked in a forest, on a cold evening in England. It's lucky you didn't have hypothermia."

"The adrenaline kept me warm." I stared into my milky tea, wishing I'd never opened my door. What did they want? What could I tell them that would benefit anyone?

Almost as if they sensed my unwillingness, they jumped straight to their point. "Can you tell us, in your own words, what happened the night Gilbert Clark painted you and took you into Lickey Hills Country Park?"

I looked up. "I already told the officers who found me."

"Yes, but we'd like to hear it again."

"There isn't anything to add."

Gloria scowled. "Just in your own words, please give us an account of the evening in question."

I paused, going over the facts and wondering if lies were necessary to protect Gil. A fabrication to perhaps grant a shorter sentence. But lies hadn't saved him, and lies wouldn't save me. The truth was the only option.

My voice stayed monotone as I gave as much information as I could in as few sentences as possible. "Gilbert Clark painted me at his warehouse, drugged me so I'd stay asleep, planted a GPS tracker on me so he could follow, and took me to the location his uncle had advised. The plan was to trade me for his daughter and then chase after me and set me free. He was shot in the back after his uncle decided to keep both me and Gilbert's daughter. Jeffrey then took both of us deeper into the forest where he'd been living for a while in a camouflaged caravan. He said he planned on selling us into the sex trade. He took me outside to rape me, Gilbert arrived just in time, he passed out once Jeffrey was dead. That's it."

The skinny officer looked up from scribbling notes. "You said he put a GPS tracker on you? So he had hope that you wouldn't die?"

"Of course. His intention was always to keep both of us alive...if he could achieve it."

"Yet he painted those other women and allowed them to be murdered?"

I still couldn't believe he'd been guilty of that.

I looked into my tea again, wishing it had the answers.

"Do you think Gilbert Clark is a good person?" Gloria asked, pen poised over paper.

I nodded fiercely. "Yes. He's a good person."

"Is he a killer?"

I don't know.

"I don't believe so."

"But he did paint them?"

I swallowed hard. I didn't want to answer because Gil had told me the truth. The same truth he'd provide in court. I stood taller. "Yes. He painted them."

Flicking back through her notes, Gloria asked, "In your previous statement, when you first called the police about the attempted kidnapping outside Gilbert Clark's warehouse, you said the van used was white with blue stripes. Do you still wish to stand by that statement?"

I slouched, knowing I'd been caught in that fib. "I lied to protect Gil. It was a black van."

The skinny cop sniffed. "Do you think, if you'd told the truth about the van, we might've been able to prevent what happened to you and ensured both Gilbert and Jeffrey were in prison?"

"I have thought about it, and I agree that lying prevented Jeffrey from being found. However, I lied because Gil asked me to, and I would lie again, knowing what I know now."

"And what is that?"

"Olive would've died in that caravan if Jeffrey had been caught. She wouldn't have been found until it was too late."

"And the life of one girl is worth the lives of others?"

I tipped my tea down the sink. "I can't answer that." Striding to the door, I opened it. "I need to go to work. I'm sorry, but I have to ask you to leave."

They stood, tucked their notebooks away and walked in heavy boots across my threshold. "We'll be in touch, Miss Moss."

I nodded, smiled goodbye, then closed the door in their faces.

The moment their boots sounded on the staircase, I grabbed my phone and called Shannon at Status Enterprises.

"Hello?"

"Shannon, I've had enough time off. I'm ready to return to work."

"Oh, that's great! We're short-staffed so we'd super appreciate it. You can come in tomorrow."

"Today? I'm free today."

"Today is great! See you soon."

I hung up and padded toward my bathroom and the shower.

I couldn't save Gil from what was coming for him.

I couldn't protect Olive from having her family torn apart.

I couldn't figure out what I needed to do to put this behind me.

But I couldn't sit at home anymore.

I had to do something productive.

Before I did something wrong.

Something like catching a bus to Gil's and demanding the entire sordid story so I knew what he would face in court, so I knew how long he would be imprisoned, so I knew how this sorry tale would end.

Chapter Sixteen

Gil

I UPLOADED ANOTHER time-lapse video of a girl I'd transformed from human into a lush, dew-misted strawberry last year. My Facebook page no longer acted as a positive beacon for my business. Instead, it granted a platform for people to comment on how vile I was, how they wished I was dead, how they planned on killing me if I wasn't dealt life imprisonment.

My star rating had plummeted from five stars to one, effectively blacklisting me from any future commissions.

I'd done my best to keep uploading previous videos and pieces of art, hoping my inbox would fill with a request for work rather than death threats. But no company contacted me for ad work. No campaign or business dared hire me with the bad press surrounding my name.

It fucking sucked because yes, I was involved, and yes, I had taken a life, but no one knew the full story, and they'd stolen my livelihood. I only had a finite amount of time to pay off my debts, squirrel away enough cash for Olive, and figure out a way to keep her happy and safe before the police summoned me to trial.

I even considered getting a job as a house painter or some other labourer, but I couldn't leave Olive. I knew I should enrol her back into school and set up a routine so she had something familiar and trustworthy in her life, but I wasn't prepared to miss out on huge chunks of time together.

Not now.

Not when every moment was precious and our time together unknown.

Two weeks had passed since I'd seen O.

Two weeks since I'd had my daughter back and pretended things were normal. I'd taken her to Kohls and bought her a new outfit to replace the ones she no longer fitted. I'd sold my car so I had some disposable cash for food and incidentals. And Justin had become a regular dinner guest. Some nights we ordered in. Some nights I cooked. Most times he fucking paid.

My guilt and self-hatred at him picking up the bill and delivering groceries because I couldn't leave ensured I diligently kept note of what I owed him. I had a little notebook now, full of numbers, the tally growing bigger and my debt growing heavier each time he popped round.

I'd warned him that he wasn't welcome if he continued to bring small gifts for Olive and found some unsubtle way of ensuring we ate. He'd jokingly said 'I'll put it on your tab' when I'd tried to force the entire three-thousand-pound pay-out I got for my car into his hand.

He'd been kidding.

I hadn't.

I took it literally, and my notebook had become my tab.

One that I had every intention of wiping clean one day.

I wanted to banish him from popping around so much, but yet again, I was fucking selfish.

I knew why he made the effort after a long day in the office to swing by my place and watch TV with Olive. Why he learned the names of silly cartoon characters and sat on the floor and submitted himself to a painting lesson that ended up speckling his suit with colours.

I'd catch his eye mid stupid joke with Olive and my heart would squeeze in agony.

This bloke, who'd been more like a brother to me than any other family, went out of his way to make sure Olive was comfortable with him. To prove to her that he was trustworthy. To prove to himself, and to me, that when the day came for me to be locked up, he could cope being a godfather and Olive could cope being raised by yet another man who wasn't her dad.

Fuck.

Slamming my laptop closed, I eyed it. Perhaps I should sell it too. After all, the uploaded content didn't seem to be resurrecting my career, and I didn't need the expensive Photoshop software to edit my painted canvases.

My career was dead.

The public had officially murdered any chance I had of

climbing my way out of the hole I was in. Not to mention, O hadn't messaged me or emailed or attempted to get in touch in any way.

I checked my phone for the billionth time today.

She'd gone from coming around when she wasn't invited to avoiding me at all costs.

The amount of times I'd stared at her number on my phone, willing myself to call her, even while knowing I never could was pathetic.

In her mind, we were over.

In my mind, I couldn't allow us to be.

Not like this.

Not without confessing everything.

"Hey, mate."

I jolted as Justin appeared behind me, slapping a hand on my shoulder and eyeing my phone. O's contact details blazed on my screen, condemning me to a life I'd totally destroyed.

"Still not got the balls to call her, huh?" He tutted under his breath. "Two weeks is a long time. She might've moved out and flown overseas for all you know."

I stood, shoving my phone into my pocket and marching past all my paint supplies that no longer had a purpose and into the small apartment.

"Hey, Dad." Olive waved with her tiny paintbrush as I brushed past her and planted a kiss on her crown.

"Wow, that's amazing, little spinach."

And I wasn't just saying that.

My daughter was fucking talented.

Her eye for shading. Her patience with detail. Her skill at intricacies. I'd like to think she inherited all that talent from me, but the reality was, she got some from Jeffrey too.

God rot his soul.

"It's a toucan to go in the rainforest." She pointed behind her at the rainforest graffiti on the wall. "It needs more animals in there."

"Good idea. Perhaps do an otter next."

The word turned to ash on my tongue.

Otter.

O.

Fucking hell.

I couldn't stop thinking about her.

I'd always carried her in my heart since I'd walked away from school, but now the memories of her, the thoughts of her, were a hundred times stronger.

I couldn't stop them. I had no peace from them. Every part of me craved to see her. To touch her. Kiss her. Slip inside her and erase all the badness between us.

Carrying on into the kitchen, I tore open the pantry and grabbed a box of risotto. Tonight, I'd cook creamy mushroom risotto because it was filling and cheap and the leftovers could make a pasta bake tomorrow night.

I'd make every penny stretch as much as I could, so Olive at least had some cash to take with her when I was incarcerated.

Justin unbuttoned his blazer and sat on the wooden barstool. His hands rested on the same counter where O had cornered me, stolen my vodka bottle, and I'd consumed her instead of alcohol.

My gaze fell to the floor where I'd thrust inside her for the first time. The rush of lust and the cloak of shame at being so rough with her after only wanting to be gentle. My healing side twinged a little, jerking me back to the present.

"You're thinking about her again," Justin muttered under his breath. "Why don't you do what I said and *talk* to her?"

"Shut up." Opening the fridge, I pulled out an IPA and shoved the cold bottle at him. "Here. Sip your beverage, let me cook, and then you're leaving."

Unscrewing the lid, he smirked. "How about I'll drink my beer and harass you while you cook? I like that plan better."

"I just won't listen to you." I tapped my ears. "Selective hearing, Miller. And tonight, I don't want to hear what you say every fucking time you come here."

"What? That I think you're giving her too much space and should go over there before it's too late?"

My heart kicked. "You keep threatening me that she might have gone. But…has she left yet?"

"No, but that's beside the point. The longer you leave it, the harder it will be."

Hard, definitely.

Hard emotionally and physically.

My body tortured me on a daily basis. I almost had a fucking wet dream the other night. I woke to an orgasm threatening to crash over me, her scent in my nose and her touch on my skin. I'd finished myself off in the dark, drowning in the fantasy that I hadn't destroyed us.

"I'm honouring her wishes, Miller. She wants nothing more

to do with me. And I can't fucking blame her."

Justin swigged his beer, settling in to give me the lecture he'd given almost every night he'd visited. "Yes, you fucked up. Yes, you used her to find Olive. You didn't tell her—or me, I might add—what you were going through. You pretended you hated her, when really, you've always loved her. You sent out so many mixed signals and made up so many lies that she has no idea what part of you is real."

"Exactly. That's exactly why she wants nothing to do with me." I dumped the risotto into a pan and scooped some butter into it.

"So...why don't you go and tell her the truth? Why don't you show her what part is real so she knows for sure that leaving is the right choice."

"She deserves better."

"Ugh, don't start this martyr bullshit again, Clark. You know as well as I do that if she'd truly been afraid of you, if she truly never wanted to see you again, she would've booked a ticket anywhere in the world to run away from you. She would've vanished by now." He pinned me with a stare. "But she hasn't. She's still here. She's waiting for closure or hope—just as much as you are. So...you should go to her."

"She probably wouldn't even open the door if I knocked on it."

"Don't you owe it to both of you to find that out instead of making up bullshit excuses?"

I scowled. "Just stay out of it."

He looked over his shoulder at Olive still engrossed in her painting. "Answer me one question. If the answer is honest, I won't bring this up again." He drew an x over his chest. "Cross my heart."

I rolled my eyes, ignoring the itch of healing from my wound. "No chance."

He lowered his voice, not giving me an option. "That teacher bitch you told me about. She took your virginity, right?"

Tearing open vegetable stock and pouring it over the risotto was suddenly fascinating. I kept my gaze well away from Justin's. I'd told him where Olive had come from a week ago. I'd skimmed the details but gave enough that he looked even more fondly at Olive. As if being abandoned by her mother after raping her father made her even more worthy of being protected at all costs.

It so happened I agreed with him.

Olive didn't have an evil bone in her body. She was my little firecracker. My tiny tornado angel. The fact that I'd soon be torn away from her brought as many sleepless nights as I'd suffered when she'd been torn away from me.

Life could stop being a bastard.

I just wanted simple.

A job, some money, and freedom to keep my daughter happy.

If I could have O to fix my broken heart, then that would be a dream come true, but if I couldn't, I'd always been satisfied to put my needs aside and focus on Olive's.

"Answer me, Clark," Justin muttered. "It's the first and last time I'll bring this up."

Spinning to face him, I closed the distance between us so I could keep my voice as low as possible. Olive didn't know about her mother.

I'd lied on that front.

Again.

I'd told her her mother had given her to me because she was sick and loved Olive far too much to put her at risk. That she'd moved to Japan to get treatment and could never come back.

In a roundabout way, it wasn't a lie. Jane Tallup had been sick…in the head. And she had gone to Japan for treatment…teaching other kids. Who I hoped to fucking God she hadn't molested.

"Fine, I'll answer you. Yes, she took my virginity. What's the problem?"

He shook his head, asking me another question. "And have you been with any other women since her?"

I froze.

Where was he going with this?

What was the point?

"Just answer it, douche-bag." He raised an eyebrow. "Any other women between you being raped as a kid and then falling into bed with the love of your life?"

My hands balled.

There'd been one other girl.

Not that it could be classified as sex.

I'd been lonely.

Olive had been about three years old.

Her tiny hugs kept my pieces together, but one night, it wasn't enough. I'd missed O with every fucking fibre. I'd gone to a bar. I'd watched men and women drink while I'd stayed stone-cold sober. A tipsy chick flirted with me. She touched me. She laughed with me. She asked me back to her place.

I went.

I tried to be with her.

I really fucking did.

But I just…couldn't. It wasn't the fact she was tipsy—by the time we fooled around she was coherent and fully aware of her choices. It wasn't the fact that I didn't trust my babysitter to keep Olive safe—I'd used my elderly neighbour before when I'd stayed up all night painting.

I just couldn't move past being forced by Tallup.

I couldn't stop thinking about O.

I sighed, my shoulders slouching. "What's your fucking point, Miller?"

Justin smirked, the beer bottle dangling from his fingers as he took a smug sip. "My point, Gilbert Clark, is you're fucked if you don't go and at least try to talk to O. You fell in love with her before the bullshit with your teacher. You don't associate her with forced assault. You *trust* her. You don't stand a chance with anyone else but her."

The stock started to boil, overflowing the pan.

Giving him the finger, I returned to my job as chef, doing my best to ignore his twisted logic. I didn't necessarily believe in the phenomenon of soul-mates. But I did believe that O was the only woman who fixed me. The only woman I could ever adore with all my being.

But if I couldn't have her, a life of celibacy and singledom was fine.

I had Olive.

I'd live through her.

She would grow, fall in love, and have a family of her own.

And I'd be there, on the outskirts, a desperate father begging for scraps of attention, pleading for them to come round for Christmases and holidays, slipping further alone as the years wedged us apart.

Or you'll just be in jail.

A sad old convict with no one.

Goddammit.

Justin chuckled. "Once Olive's in bed, I'll stay and catch up on a bit of work while you go and see if you can fix at least one thing before you're thrown in jail."

He meant it as encouragement.

But it only made me hyperaware that even if I told O everything. Even if she forgave me. Even if we could *somehow* make it work, I would still let her down the moment I was sentenced and locked away.

The monitor bracelet around my ankle said I couldn't leave the street where I lived.

The promise of fixing what I'd broken with O overrode the consequences.

I should ignore Justin's advice.

I should let O continue to live without me.

But I'd never been very good at doing the right thing.

Chapter Seventeen

Olin

TWO WEEKS HAD passed.

By day, I returned to work and kept to myself.

By night, I went home to an empty apartment and surfed the internet for news about the upcoming trial.

Justin had popped round a few times to check on me, delivering little notes and paintings that Olive had done. She still wanted me to move in with them. Her hints with her drawings of happy owl families made that totally obvious.

I missed her.

I missed Gil.

But he kept his distance.

He respected my need for space, even though I tormented myself each night with thoughts and dreams of him. It didn't help that each day there was a new article or slur about him. A new claim that he'd killed a hundred women. That he'd killed puppies and kittens and even had his eye on children.

Two new GoFundMe campaigns had sprung up asking for money to hire a hitman to kill him before the justice system gave too soft a punishment.

The amount of hate was insane.

It sickened me.

It worried me.

Social media had so many positive applications, but where Gil was concerned, it was worse than a witch hunt. They didn't care about the true story, only about blood. They didn't want facts, only carnage.

Even Gil's Facebook page dripped with venom. The hostility in the comments on his posts gave me nightmares that he truly might be hurt before he could face trial and the truth could protect him.

He needed to address it.

He needed to douse the flames of malevolence with honesty before it got dangerous.

I shivered and pulled the fake-mink blanket tighter around my shoulders. The TV mumbled in the background, and a library book of the best places to live in the world rested on my lap. The edition was from the 1990s so I was sceptical about some of the claims like Australia's cheap housing and Thailand's low taxes. If I had skills in finances or trades, I could've travelled and found it relatively easy to relocate overseas, but with nothing more than menial labour and a failed dancing career, I doubted I could settle anywhere long-term.

And I didn't know if I had the gumption to waitress in foreign places or live in backpackers with travellers far younger than me.

Why couldn't I make a decision?

Why couldn't I just book something?

Why couldn't I stop researching Gil and worrying about his future?

Because you're a sucker, that's why.

A spineless, stupid fool who still wants the boy she shouldn't have.

A fist hammered on my door, wrenching my head up.

Who on earth?

I cuddled deeper into my blankets. I hated unannounced visitors, especially late at night. Justin had made a habit of popping by, and I'd grown used to it, but tonight, I wasn't in the mood.

It might be those awful police again.

The knock came a second time.

Dammit.

Hauling myself from the couch, I placed the heavy book on the coffee table and padded across the small apartment to open the door. I didn't have a peephole, so risked unlocking and opening it a crack.

"Gil." My heart hammered against my ribs. "Wh-What are you doing here?"

He rubbed his face with a shaky hand. "I'm not here to hurt you." The tormented vow in his voice made my stomach squeeze.

"I know you won't hurt me."

"I'll stay out here if you're more comfortable."

"You don't have to do that." I opened the door wider. "I

know you won't hurt me now that you have Olive back. Is she okay? Do you need anything?"

He grimaced. "You're still so kind, even after everything I've put you through."

My fingers latched tighter around the handle. "It's not kindness, Gil. It's concern. How are you…and her? You guys safe?"

"Safe?" He scowled. "Why wouldn't we be safe? Jeffrey is dead."

"I mean the online stuff. I don't know if you've looked, but it's getting scary. For me at least."

His green gaze searched mine. "You've been reading up about me?" His tone stayed carefully neutral.

I'd never been one to play games or pretend I didn't care when I did. I knew I should tell him to leave, close my door, and book that damn plane ticket out of here. Instead, I fell into old patterns and backed into my apartment in invitation. "We haven't been in touch. I research a little at night to see if you've been granted a court date."

His black sneakers crept over my threshold as if he couldn't believe I'd invited him in. Where were his paint-spattered timberlands? Had the police confiscated them as evidence?

Most likely, yes.

They were the same size as those found by the body of the last girl.

A clue to the crimes committed.

"I haven't heard when I'll go to trial."

"I can imagine the not knowing is driving you crazy." I closed the door. "Have you got things arranged…for Olive?"

He shrugged helplessly. "How can I have another home ready when I can't bear the thought of not being the one to take care of her?"

I nodded, backing away for my sanity.

It was so, *so* hard not to reach out and comfort him. Not to honour old promises to always be there in times of trouble.

I was his friend.

But that friendship now came with uncrossable boundaries and restrictions. "I'm so sorry, Gil."

He sighed, raking a hand through his messy hair. "It's nothing I don't deserve." His head tipped down as he followed me into the kitchen. His teeth sank into his bottom lip before he blurted, "I shouldn't have fucking come. I know that. I've done my best not to contact you, even though I think about you every damn day. I know I have no right to be here…but I need to talk to you. I can't end it like this."

Goosebumps exploded all over me. "End it like what?"

"Like this." He spread his arms as if incorporating our twisted, tangled lives. "Not able to have an honest conversation because Olive is there. Not able to be truthful and finally have the guts to give you answers to your questions." He held up his hands in surrender, looking healthier than the last time I'd seen him. His colour was back and his wound no longer draining his energy. He looked ready to tear open his secrets and purge.

And as much as I wanted to finally understand, I didn't trust what I'd do if I finally knew.

I shook my head, pulling the blanket that still caped my shoulders tighter around me. "It's fine. We don't need to—"

"We do." He stormed right into me, shoving me back and pressing me against the countertop. His hands clamped on my hips, his forehead nudged mine, and my entire world combusted in a rain of comets.

I couldn't swallow.

Couldn't breathe.

Couldn't blink.

"Gil…"

His fingers dug harder into my hipbones in denial of touching me. His nose brushed mine, his eyes closed, his lips came so, so close to kissing me.

We stood like that for an endless trembling second.

A second where our hearts *pounded* against each other. Where cymbals and castanets replaced my ribcage and stomach. Where we fought fate and battled with decorum.

"I can't stop myself," he groaned. "Not anymore." With a belly twisting growl, he stumbled away from me, shaking out his hands, no doubt suffering the same surge of heat and chemistry I did. "Fuck."

I shuddered, desperate for him to deliver on his threat, but grateful that he'd pulled away before he did.

My blanket lay abandoned on the floor.

My hands shook and body quaked, and I tripped to the fridge for something to do.

With my back facing him, he confessed, "I can't sleep at night with wanting you, O. I'm fucking hard just at a single memory of you. I feel sick that I'm so goddamn hungry for you, because what sort of monster thinks about sex after he willingly betrayed your trust and prepared to trade your life for another?"

He laughed coldly. "I don't know why you haven't tried to shoot me yourself. Why you're still standing there, listening to my bullshit, when you should call the police and have me arrested for intruding on your life all over again."

Grabbing the cheap supermarket wine that was my guilty pleasure, I poured two generous glasses. "I know that's the logical reaction. And I know I'm being stupid by not doing those things. But…I've asked myself the same questions, and I don't have any answers. Why can't I move on after what you did? Why can't I just forget about you? God only knows, I should."

Gil shook his head gently as I tried to pass him the glass. "I can't drink alcohol." He pointed at his stitched-up side with a self-conscious sigh. "Not while I'm healing. And now I have Olive back, I doubt I'll ever turn to liquor again. It didn't solve my problems; it only made them worse." His eyes shadowed. "If I hadn't been drinking that night, I would never have fucked you on my living room floor, and we might not be in this mess."

My insides clenched at the crudeness. And the barbarity and the fact that my heart might be bruised and my common-sense in tatters, but my body most definitely had its priorities.

And it wanted rough.

It wanted anger, violence, passion.

It still craved a fight.

A rough, dirty, hot-as-hell fight.

Swallowing a big mouthful of tart courage, I whispered, "Maybe that was the only honest thing we did."

"What?" His voice turned dangerous. His body went loose and rigid all at once. "What do you mean?"

My skin blazed with fire. I didn't recognise myself. I didn't know this demoness who thirsted at the thought of tearing at his body, scratching his scars, and taking from him like he'd taken from me.

I was hungry.

Hungry, hungry, hungry for the blunt, basic truth that came from wild inhibited sex.

"You let down your walls that night. You gave in to the years of build-up between us. Maybe you should get drunk again and see what else happens."

He made a strangled noise. "If I got drunk again, I'd probably have you spread-eagled on the floor and so far deep inside you we'd both die of pleasure."

I shivered. I grew wet. "Do it then."

He choked. "Do what?"

"Fuck me."

He groaned long and low. "O…what are you doing?"

"I'm avoiding facing what has to happen."

"What? What has to happen?" He stepped toward me almost unwillingly. His hands opening and closing, his body tight and predatory.

"We need to walk away. There is no future for us. There can't be. Not after everything that's happened." I drank back the rest of my wine, welcoming the buzz, the lightheaded recklessness. "Words can only do so much. Conversation can grant sentences and paragraphs and finish this mess with a full stop, but only sex can grant us an ending."

"You want us to end?"

My heart wanted to shake its head.

My soul screamed for him to call me out on my lies.

I nodded instead. "Yes."

He crowded me against the countertop again, bringing fire and regret and the deliciousness of the forbidden. His eyes blazed with lust and love. "I came here trying to prevent an end."

This was wrong.

This was dangerous.

But I was through being good and safe.

I *wanted* this.

I wanted a clean, corruptible goodbye.

"It's inevitable."

"It's salvageable." His hand cupped my chin, jerking my head to the side so his mouth could latch onto my throat. His teeth unsheathed and sank into my skin, sharp and unforgiving; his tongue lapped at me a second later, soft and pleading. "It has to be."

I moaned and puddled into his chest, wanting my brain to turn off and my body to take full control. I wanted to be used, abused, and then I wanted him gone.

I wanted him gone for my sake and for his.

We were toxic to one another.

He'd always screw up and I'd always forgive him.

He's going to jail.

Even if I did agree to try, our futures had already been decided.

"Shut up and kiss me." I arched for his mouth, desperate to stop talking.

"Don't command me, O." He bit me again, yanking at my cotton pyjama top, popping the buttons holding the cute pink umbrella fabric together. My bare breasts ached to be bitten, squeezed, claimed. "Don't force me to do something I don't want to do." His voice rippled with history. Of another time when sex had been used against him.

A flush of guilt made me lucid, but then vindictiveness made me nasty.

Perhaps, by using Gil's demons against him, I could sever this infernal link between us. Maybe by pushing him too far, I could push him into admitting that we just couldn't work.

I could break us both so we could finally walk away without constantly looking back.

"God, you taste amazing." His tongue lashed against my throat, his arms banded tight around me.

For someone saying no, his body screamed yes.

I wriggled against him, rocking my hips into his. "You know as well as I do that we're powerless against each other."

He groaned, his hips answering mine with a slow, heavy grind that sent heat and wetness between my legs. "I'll always be powerless when it comes to you."

"That's why we're not good for one another."

"You're the best thing to ever happen to me." His fingers latched onto my hipbones, jerking me harder against his erection. He winced a little from his still tender wound. "I've never wanted anyone else but you. Never loved anyone else—"

"Stop." I cupped his cheeks, yanking his lips down to mine.

He growled low in his throat as I kissed him, stealing from him, all while offering him to take. This was war. This was a white flag of surrender even while I desperately tried to survive.

His tongue plunged deep; his body crowded mine. We rocked and clawed, slipping down the slippery slope of foggy desire.

Our lips crashed, teeth clacked, tongues danced a fiery battle.

Our bodies understood the goal, rocking and thrusting, seeking space to join.

I was too far gone to care.

Too drunk on lust to worry about consequences.

Too stressed and spiteful to stop trying to hurt both of us, all because I wasn't strong enough to admit that there would never be anyone else like him, never be another boy I loved so deeply.

"Fuck me, Gil." I kissed and licked him. "I need you."

"Don't do this, O." He growled again, ripping his lips away and ducking to suck my nipple into his mouth. "I want to talk. This isn't what I came here for."

His voice said no. His touch already agreed.

My head fell back as he branded me with his teeth.

I clutched his head to my chest, crying out as he bit harder; he suckled, making wetness gush between my legs. "Finish it, Gil. We need to finish this."

"I want to *save* this." His hand dove between my legs, finding me drenched. "Goddammit, O. We can figure out a way to fix this."

Yes, my heart screamed.

No, my mind cautioned.

I embraced sex to protect myself.

"It's over, Gil. It has to be."

"Don't fucking say that. It's not." Even as he begged, he shoved my night shorts down and plunged two fingers inside me. "Don't ask me to give you up."

"God." I buckled in his arms, my hips thrusting forward unashamedly.

"Fuck, you're driving me insane." His fingers pulsed inside me; his gaze shot black with need. "You're pushing me too far." His eyes closed tight, his brow furrowed and lips thin. "I'm losing control. I won't be responsible for—"

"For fucking me?" I licked my lips, moaning as his fingers dove deeper. "I want you to. I *need* you to."

"And I need to earn your forgiveness. Not fuck you like you mean nothing."

That sounded delicious to my current delirious state.

I didn't want sonnets or softness.

I wanted fast and brutal.

I need this over.

"Do it. Please." I clawed at his shoulders, not caring I was naked and he was fully dressed. My eyes hazed as my hands dropped down his front and unbuckled his jeans. "Gil…"

"O." He snarled as I shoved the denim down along with his boxer-briefs. "Fuck, stop."

His cock leapt out and I pumped him.

His back bowed. His legs buckled. He drove his fingers deep inside me. "Goddammit." His forehead crushed on mine, both of us stroking the other, punishing the other. "I'll never be free of you." He thrust into my hand as his fingers rocked against my G-spot.

"Me either." I trembled, moaning, "And that's the problem."

"That's our curse."

I arched up to kiss him. "I don't have the strength anymore."

His lips slammed down to kiss me. "I never had the strength."

Our tongues knotted.

Our bodies battled.

And he lost.

I lost.

We destroyed each other with a violent kind of lust that incinerated right and wrong, past and present.

All I wanted was him.

All he needed was me.

Sex.

The rawest link that could come with the strongest of love or the most painful of hate.

Gil had suffered both.

His body had been used against him. My heart had been used against me.

I was in the wrong to do this, but he followed me into despair because that was all our future held. Despair and complication.

Our kiss turned far too hungry.

Our patience snapped.

"Fuck, O." Breathing hard, he tore his fingers out of me. "You're trying to make me hate you. But you're only making me want you more." He hauled me up, imprisoning me against the cupboards. "You're it for me. Always were." The tip of his cock nudged my entrance.

I sucked in a breath as he swallowed a curse. Pain etched his features, his healing side adding another element of torture.

Our eyes locked and held.

Glowing and wild. Hungry and hurting.

"You're mine. You always will be." His voice sucked shadows from the room, a vow of irrefutable possessiveness.

And then, he thrust.

One.

Thick.

Long.

Blistering *thrust*.

One second, we were separate, the next, we were joined.

We froze.

Panting and moaning, stripped to our most basic core.

We looked at each other as if we couldn't quite believe what'd happened. Shaking against the crack of our hearts and the thunder of our souls.

Every joining felt like this.

Like the earth shattered and the skies cried and the only place we belonged was with each other.

He was right.

We are a curse.

Softness slipped between our passion, covering me with goosebumps and the poems I hadn't wanted. His gaze whispered that he would never let me go, even though he would always do what I asked. His cock throbbed with fury that I belonged to him, even while he accepted that he'd lost me.

All of that emotion. All of that pain.

It punched us in the chest and we buckled beneath it.

His hips rocked.

He broke the spell.

And I was immensely grateful.

Clinging to his shoulders, I bowed into his control.

And he began to move.

To fuck me.

To eradicate the agonising moment we'd shared.

His mouth captured mine, his hands held me prisoner, his hips were the polar opposite of his lovesick gaze, punishing me, pistoning quick and deep inside.

Wordlessly, he fucked me exactly like I wanted.

He ignored his injury and showed no mercy.

He treated me with no kindness.

The countertop wedged into my spine.

My breasts bounced.

My core clenched.

And an orgasm spindled out of nowhere.

I kissed him violently.

He kissed me brokenly.

We rode each other as if the world would end in twenty-eight heartbeats.

I didn't try to slow it down.

I didn't nurse the idea that this was it.

That I'd made this happen because I wasn't strong enough to hear his secrets after weeks of begging to know.

I was weak.

But this made me strong.

This is goodbye.

"More. Gil, more. More!" I dug my nails into his neck, riding him as he rode me, our skin slicked with sweat. Pain radiated in his eyes. Agony lived in his kisses. And the finality of farewell added a sharper, sinister flavour to our release.

Thrust.

Thrust.

Thrust.

I exploded.

My insides ricocheted with broken bliss.

He roared into my mouth with fractured feeling.

We shivered and convulsed in each other's arms.

And then, his phone rang.

Ring.

Ring.

Ring.

A sense of déjà vu struck me. Whenever something momentous happened between us, the phone always managed to ruin it.

At least this time, there was nothing to ruin.

I'd done that.

And it was over.

Gil winced as he pulled out of me, his cock glistening and angry. Hoisting his jeans up, he pressed a hand against his injured side, and ripped his phone from his back pocket. Breathing hard, his face lined with fear. "Shit." Pressing accept, he held it to his ear, his eyes locking onto mine. "Justin. What's up?" His breathing was tattered and torn.

The faint voice of Justin echoed in the silence.

Gil's cum trickled down my inner thigh.

I made no move to dress. No move to hide.

"Okay, I'll rush back straight away. Tell her I'm coming. I'll be as fast as I can." Gil hung up, shoving his phone where it belonged and buckling his belt. "I have to go."

"I understand."

"Olive woke up. She expected to see me but found Justin instead. She's broken down and barricaded herself in her room crying." He backed toward the door. "I'm so sorry."

"It's fine. Go to her. I hope she's okay."

"Will *you* be okay?" His eyes cast down my nakedness,

focusing on the remnants of the explosive, hurried sex we'd shared.

I nodded, forcing a smile. "I'll be fine."

Unlocking the door, he paused as he opened it. "I don't feel right leaving you like this."

"You don't have a choice."

"But…this. What happened between us—"

"Was closure."

He winced. "Closure? That wasn't fucking closure, O. That was…I don't know what that was." He raked a hand through his hair. "Most of it was way too fast and sudden, and I feel guilty as fuck for taking you when we should've talked, but it's far from over. We're not done here. Not by a long shot."

"We are. We have to be."

He stalked toward me, his hands fisting by his sides. "And if I don't want this to be over?"

I hugged my breasts, cursing the goosebumps covering me. "It's already happened."

"It hasn't. Nothing's happened apart from the realisation that I was wrong to stay away. I thought I was doing the right thing letting you walk out of my life, but fuck, it was totally the *wrong* thing. I'll do whatever you need to make you trust in this, trust in me. I'm not going to quit, O. I'm going to fight to keep you—"

"I don't belong to you, Gil." I rested my hand on the door handle, growing weaker by the second.

This was what I wanted.

This was what I *needed*.

I needed him to fight for me.

To prove he cared above everything.

Above court dates and murder trials and a life he might have to abandon.

But just because I was cruel to need his undying declarations didn't mean they'd throw me back into his arms.

He wasn't mine.

He was Olive's.

And soon he'd be locked out of my reach.

If we didn't choose for this to end now, his prison sentence would do it for us.

His face waged battle between calm and furious. "I'll come back. We'll talk about this. Talk about everything."

"No." I locked my knees from trembling. His body still summoned mine. The crackle of electricity, the sharp serenade of desire. Even though we'd just had sex, the lust between us never died.

And that was why this had to end.

Now.

Here.

Forever.

Because…I couldn't be his friend.

And I couldn't be his lover.

Because I would give everything, over and over again, and I would never have enough left over for me.

He backed over the threshold. "I'll come back. Once Olive is settled, I'll come back and we can try this again."

"I think it's best if you didn't."

Frustration etched his face. "This isn't over."

"It has to be."

"Stop saying that. It doesn't have to be. If you feel anything for me then we can talk and—"

"I do feel something for you." I allowed brutal truth to break us. "I love you, Gil."

His eyes flared, he moved to touch me. "Then let me fucking fix this."

I held up a hand, praying my voice stayed steady. "I love you, but I can't be with you."

"But—"

"Please…don't make this any harder than it is." I clutched the door, ready to close it. "It's done. It's over. We just ended it."

"So…that's it? You don't want to know? You no longer care?"

I shook my head, fighting the sudden tsunami of tears. "I no longer want to know. I no longer care."

Pain that I'd never witnessed burned deep in his gaze. "What the hell is that supposed to mean? For weeks you wouldn't stop badgering me to tell you what I kept hidden, and now that I'm finally free to tell you everything, you suddenly have no interest to hear me out?"

I locked my fingers together, keeping my curiosity buried.

I wanted to know.

I wanted to know *all of it*.

But…if I knew, I wouldn't have the power to put myself first. I would risk everything because I wouldn't have the strength to walk away.

"I wanted to know so I could protect you." I shrugged sadly.

"Now, I don't want to know to protect myself."

Our gaze caught.

My heart hiccupped.

He froze as he finally heard what I said. Finally accepted what I wanted. "You truly mean it, don't you?" His voice roughened. "You've had enough of me."

"I've had enough of lies and deceit and feeling as if I'm cheating myself out of happiness by being too weak."

"You were never weak."

"*You* make me weak."

He swayed on my doorstep. Anger and hurt blazed in his green gaze.

A loud beeping noise came from his ankle, dragging his attention to his foot.

He growled like a beast.

He nodded.

He stared at me one last time, trying to figure out a way to stop my stubbornness.

His ankle beeped again.

His shoulders fell. "If that's what you want." Looking at me one last time, he whispered, Goodbye, O."

He turned and vanished down the staircase.

Chapter Eighteen

Olin

A WEEK PASSED.

Every day, I struggled not to hand in my notice at work.

Every night, I struggled to sleep.

Every time I went into the kitchen, I stared at the spot where we'd had sex, and a wash of regret and relief filled me.

The regret was the hardest—full of tears and heartache and the overwhelming sensation that I'd made a massive mistake.

The relief was a gentle balm—doing its best to heal me and remind me I did the right thing.

I'd done the *only* thing.

No matter how hard it'd been.

But it did mean I could no longer stay here and postpone my decision.

The money my parents had deposited into my bank account remained untouched, even though my salary wasn't enough to carry my weekly bills and pay off the debt I'd accumulated while looking after Olive.

I didn't want to owe them anything, even though their funds would be greatly appreciated right about now.

They'd tried calling again two days ago. I'd ignored it, unable to discuss the latest news articles and the ever-growing unrest about Gil's involvement in the body painting murders.

Maybe I'd go visit them on their travels.

Maybe I'd vanish like they had.

Either way, tonight, I had a plan.

Placing a spinach and feta pizza into the oven—unable to

stop my mind from thinking of Gil calling Olive his little spinach—I carried my decrepit laptop to the dining room table and turned it on.

This time, I wasn't looking at job sites.

Clicking on the website I'd found last week that compared international airfares and found the cheapest, I hovered my fingers over the keyboard.

Birmingham to…

I bit my lip.

Hong Kong?

Vietnam?

New Zealand?

America?

Where could I find a fresh start?

Where could my mind find peace from Gil?

I deliberated while my pizza cooked and made a list of pros and cons while I ate.

I finished two glasses of wine—very aware I had the potential of becoming an alcoholic if I kept up my alone-time drinking—and decided to let fate choose for me.

Fate had messed up my life, so perhaps, it could fix it too.

Clicking on the icon that listed last-minute sales, I held my breath as one for Brisbane, Australia popped up. Warm, friendly, lots of beaches, and tanned locals. They spoke English so I could get a job. The temperate weather would be good for my ruined back, and it was too far to rush home if I feared I'd made yet another mistake.

I inputted the parameters, chose a date two weeks in the future to give me time to end my lease, hand in my notice, and sell my few pieces of furniture, and pulled my tired and battered credit card from my purse.

I peered at the faded number.

My phone vibrated across the table.

Not again.

No.

I refused to let a phone destroy every big moment of my life.

I locked my attention back onto entering my credit card details.

It vibrated again.

And again.

God!

How was I supposed to move on if so many things kept

yanking me back?

Snatching my phone, I swiped it on.

Justin: *When was the last time you saw Gil?*

I sighed heavily, remembering all over again what we'd done when we'd last seen each other. The way he'd been inside me. The way he'd grown angry when denied a second chance. The way I couldn't stop thinking about him even though I made a vow to move on.

Me: *A week ago. Why?*

Justin: *He was attacked two nights ago.*

My heart crawled into my throat.

Me: *Attacked? How?*

Justin: *Two men who knew one of the murdered girls. They waited for him outside his warehouse. Beat him up pretty good.*

Me: *Was Olive there?*

Justin: *She was inside. Gil called me before she found him. Got most of the blood off but he's stiff. I've just been with him for a check-up to make sure they didn't injure his side or rupture anything internally.*

Why didn't he contact me?

You ended it, remember?

I'd given no room for negotiation, even when Gil had begged for a single conversation.

Guilt slithered through me.

Worry followed on its tail.

I'd been so *selfish*.

I'd chosen myself over him.

I'd acted as if I had the worst deal just because he'd lied and tied me up and carried me unconscious into the woods.

He was facing prison.

His life was threatened thanks to a mob of enraged people.

His daughter had a high possibility of growing up without having him as her father.

Oh, God.

What had I been thinking?

Me: *Thanks for being a good friend, Justin. He's lucky to have you. I haven't exactly been there for him lately.*

Justin: *Yeah, he's been pretty low ever since I loaned him my car and offered to babysit so he could come talk to you. He didn't tell me what happened between you guys, but I'm guessing it wasn't anything good.*

I didn't know how to respond. Admit that I'd forced him to find closure through sex or pretend things were a work-in-progress?

Before I could fib or confess, Justin messaged again.

Justin: *O...I have another piece of news that I don't know how to tell you. I'm not expecting anything. I'm not asking for something you can't give it. I'm just...telling you.*

I went ice cold.

Me: *What is it?*

Justin: *Gil sold his warehouse to pay the blackmail on Olive a few months ago. He's been renting it back from the new owner ever since.*

I waited for him to continue, terrified of the conclusion.

Justin: *The owner has just given Gil notice. With all the shit happening online, he doesn't want a murderer living there. He's given him five days to move out.*

Me: *Oh, no.*

Oh, God.

Justin: *I've offered him to move in with me, but Olive hasn't gotten over what happened last week. She's relapsing. Doesn't want to be near other men apart from Gil. I know he'd never ask this himself but...is there any way you can put them up for a night or two? While I figure something out? Gil has to stay in Birmingham so he doesn't void his bail agreement—he already got in trouble going to see you. If they think he's a flight risk, they'll revoke his bail, and Olive isn't ready to cope with that shit.*

I sat frozen in my chair.

Why hadn't Gil told me he'd get in trouble for visiting me?

Why had he put his freedom on the line, knowing there'd be repercussions when the cops figured out he'd left his home?

I stared at my phone.

My blood raced in my veins.

The last time Gil had stayed the night in my apartment, we'd been in a much better place than our current one. Even with his secrets, I could handle him being near. We'd had Thai and I'd woken to him talking to his uncle, agreeing to yet another blackmail to protect Olive. He'd unsettled and confused me but at least we'd been civil.

I'd gladly let Olive stay again.

She'd been a perfect little house guest but my apartment was too small for the three of us.

Far too small for the tension and complications that would curdle.

You don't have a choice.

Could you honestly turn him away when the entire world is turning its back on him?

Olive was too important and sweet to let her suffer.

And Gil…well, Gil was also far too important.

I was fighting an unwinnable battle. I was lying to myself and only causing pain.

I couldn't abandon Gil while he faced incarceration. Just like I couldn't abandon Olive.

I should've known I could never be so self-centred not to put anyone else first.

I can't leave.

Not yet.

No matter how much I needed to.

Once I knew how his trial went, maybe then I'd be free to move on.

Once I knew Olive was safe, hopefully then I could leave and never look back.

Until that happened, I was stuck in limbo.

We all were.

Me: *Of course. Goes without saying.*

Justin: *You're a saint, Olin Moss. I know how hard this is going to be for you. I also know how worthless Gil is going to feel being such an imposition.*

Me: *It's fine. We'll work it out.*

Somehow.

Justin: *I wish it could've been different for you guys. I really do.*

Tears rushed up my spine.

Yeah…me too.

Justin: *I'll help him pack and see you in a couple of days with your new tenants.*

Chapter Nineteen

Gil

"I CAN'T FUCKING move into her space, Miller. Goddammit, stop trying to be a fairy fucking godmother. I can figure this shit out on my own."

"First, I'm a godfather, not a mother. And second, excuse me for doing what any good godfather would do and think of Olive's livelihood instead of her stubborn mule of a relative."

"You're taking your role as her guardian far too fucking seriously."

His face tensed. He marched closer so Olive, who was packing the final things into her backpack in her room, didn't overhear. "Aren't you glad about that? I didn't ask to be a dad, Clark. But you assigned that possibility to me and then went and got arrested. For *murder.*" His eyes narrowed. "I don't know how it's going to work. She tolerates me, but she's still uncomfortable around me. She had that crazy meltdown that's left me totally wary of what other crap might happen. And if you're called to trial tomorrow, what then, huh? Isn't her protection better than your sorry excuses of why you can't couch surf at O's for a few days?"

I rubbed my face, wanting to punch him but knowing he was right. "I can't impose—"

"It's either my place or O's. Unless you have some money you want to tell me about and you're planning on staying at the four fucking seasons?"

My temper blazed. "You're really getting on my nerves, Miller."

"Yeah, well. You too."

I blinked. "I'm sorry my shitty life is ruining yours. I didn't ask you to take over. I'm perfectly capable of arranging accommodation for myself and my daughter. I've done it many times before you barged in."

Justin crossed his arms. "Yeah, but have you done it while healing from a bullet wound, suffering a mild concussion from being beaten up, and an anklet that reports your every fucking move to the cops?"

I froze, breathing hard.

He had a point.

I'd had a visit the morning after sleeping with O from two uniforms. They'd given me a warning: leave a pre-approved location again and my freedom would be replaced with bars until I faced court.

After dealing with a broken heart from O kicking me out, worry over Olive breaking down just because Justin had babysat, and now being served notice that my home had been snatched away...I didn't know what problem to tackle first.

I wanted to see O. I *needed* to see her. But I'd been blocked from visiting. A phone call or text wouldn't cut it. I didn't know how to say what I needed to without seeing her face. And now, Justin expected clearance from the cops for me to couch surf and Olive's mental health to cope with being homeless, all while the goddamn bruises on my body reminded me all over again that I sucked at life.

I rubbed my face, trying to get my anger under control. "Look, I'll figure something out. You're not responsible for us. Just let me deal with this."

Justin rolled his eyes. "Do you honestly expect me to just let you be kicked out onto the street?" His voice lowered. "Come on, mate. Don't be such a stubborn ass. Let me help."

"I'm not accepting charity."

"For the last fucking time, it's not charity. It's what friends do."

"And you've already done far too much. So has O. Where does it end, huh? How many favours do you both have to give before enough is enough?"

Justin shrugged. "Until you're back on your feet."

"And if I'm never back on my feet?"

"Then we figure it out."

"No. *I'll* figure it out. This is on me. Not you."

"You made it personal when you said I was her damn godfather, Clark! Just accept it and stop being a twat, all right?"

175

I wanted to tell him to get the hell out but…I couldn't.

He had every right to yell at me.

Had every concern about how I'd fix this shitty situation.

I'd sold my warehouse and in turn ran the risk of renting.

I'd put Olive's future at risk all because I hadn't kept her safe to begin with.

I had no money for a hotel.

No other friends to impose on.

I couldn't stay at Justin's 'cause I didn't want to risk Olive having another meltdown so soon—which only added to the stress of who would look after her if I was imprisoned if she never got over her fear.

And just because no commissions had come in didn't mean I wasn't actively trying to find work. Temporary, menial—I'd accept anything if it meant I could at least leave something for Olive.

My temper faded. "O doesn't want to see me again. Even if I was okay with imposing, *yet again*, I can't."

Olive appeared from her bedroom. Her backpack slung over her shoulder.

The past four days had been an awful whirlwind of trying to explain that we could no longer live in our home, that the few pieces of furniture we had left had to be sold, and I didn't entirely know what the future held.

Olive had hugged me tight and whispered she didn't care where we lived, as long as we were together.

I'd been both proud and horrified.

Proud that she was such a brave little thing not to worry about material things. And horrified that I was about to fail her all over again when the summons came.

"Eep, are we moving into O's?" she asked, her eyes sparkling with hope. "Yay! I miss her. I sent her notes and drawings asking her to visit, but now we get to visit her!" She spun in front of me. "Her bed is super comfy. Do you think she'll share with me, or I'll have to share the couch with you, Dad?"

I choked. The thought of being in O's space, of wanting her, craving her, only for her to look at me in that dead-eyed, all-hope-ended way was unthinkable.

I'd gone to her place hoping to explain myself. To finally share the secrets she'd begged to know. Only for her to push me until I'd pinned her against the kitchen bench and taken her fast and ruthlessly. I hadn't wanted to do that. I'd never wanted to touch her so violently. Yet, each time we slept together, softness wasn't part of the equation.

She'd made me take her, use her, and then she'd told me goodbye.

My heart fisted at the thought of living through that torture, day after day.

"Can we go now? I want to see her." Olive took my hand, tugging me toward the exit. Not caring this would be the last time she'd be allowed in this place.

I held her back, stopping her momentum. "O is too busy to have us stay right now, little spinach. We can visit her, though. You guys could have lunch next week."

"But Justin said we're staying."

"Justin was mistaken."

"Justin already cleared it with O, and she's agreed," Justin interrupted.

"You what?" I spun on him. "What the fu—" I cut myself off, not wanting to swear in front of Olive.

"I asked her a few days ago. She said no problem."

"Of *course*, she said no problem." I raked a hand through my hair. "She's the sweetest person on the goddamn *planet*."

"It's only for a few days, Gil. Until we can sort something else—"

"A few days is too long, don't you see?" I wanted to punch him. How dare he fucking meddle? My still healing side twinged. My insides felt hollow. Pain lashed through me. "I can't expect her to do this."

"It's already done." He strode past me, heading to his sedan and the meagre amount of belongings I'd packed. I wasn't attached to clothes, and with a totally different living arrangement in my future, I hadn't bothered keeping crockery and other life requirements. I'd sold everything in a flash sale, earned another few thousand pounds, and budgeted each penny to its maximum.

The only items I couldn't sell had been my paint supplies. Boxes of brushes, sponges, and airbrush attachments would travel with me. The bottles of pigments would also come. Along with rhinestones, metallics, and a few prosthetics that made fantasy into reality.

One day, I would use those mediums to make another fortune.

Until then, I had to pay the taxes on my life choices.

Jeffrey popped into my head. He'd fucked me over while he was alive, and he still fucked me over even when he was dead.

Would I choose differently if I could redo the night I killed him?

I'd asked myself that question a lot.

And the answer was…complicated.

I would've spared his life if it meant I didn't have to let Olive down by going to jail.

I would've still killed him because he deserved to know what those girls felt as he watched them fade into death.

There was no right or wrong answer.

Unlike now.

It was wrong to go to O's. Wrong to encroach on her space. Wrong to not honour her wish to end things permanently between us.

But what other choice do you have?

"Come on, Popeye." Olive pulled her hand from mine, skipping after Justin as he continued stomping through the warehouse to the pedestrian access. "Time to go see, O."

* * * * *

"O!" Olive bowled through the door the moment it cracked open. "Hi! Yay, I'm so happy to see you. Did you get my notes? Did Justin give you my drawings?" She squished her face into O's chest, hugging her fiercely. "I missed you!"

O froze in almost comical shock. Unprepared for a hurricane to smother her with conversation and cuddles. Her eyes met mine, then skated away almost immediately. "Hi, Justin. Hi, Gil."

"Olin." I nodded.

The moment polite greetings were done, O dropped her arms and squeezed Olive back with just as much affection. "Hi, little Olive Pip. Man, I swear you've grown since I last saw you." She pressed her hand on Olive's glossy dark hair. "Yep, you've definitely sprouted another inch at least."

Olive Pip?

O had given my daughter a nickname?

Yet another fist reached into my chest and punched a bigger hole into my heart. If I wasn't careful, the hole would soon be big enough to bleed me dry.

Olive snickered. "Probably been eating too much spinach. Dad makes sure we eat lots of veggies."

"That'll do it for sure. You'll be taller than him soon."

"Eww, no." She wrinkled her nose. "I don't want to be that tall. I want to be dainty, like you." Looking past her, she asked, "Can we come in? We don't have much stuff. We promise not to take up too much room."

O backed up, welcoming us. "Of course. Come in. It seems my home is now your home."

"Only for tonight." I cleared my throat. "I won't put you out any longer than that."

O nodded. "One night, one week. It's fine." Her smile was genuine, but her eyes remained guarded. She'd returned to the sympathetic sweet friend who always put others first. No sign of the explosive heat from the week before. No hint of the heart-breaking farewell.

Goddammit, the agony was more than I could bear.

My back prickled as Justin practically shoved me inside, moving to give O a kiss on the cheek. "Olin. You're looking gorgeous as always." He winked, making her chuckle.

"Yeah, jeans and old t-shirt totally deserve compliments like that."

"They do if they fit you that well."

"If you like them so much, you wear them. Let's see if the t-shirt becomes a bra on you or a crop top."

Justin laughed. "God, no one wants to see that."

"Seriously, no one." O smiled.

Their friendship was no longer stilted with history but smooth with familiarity.

For the first time, I wondered.

Wondered if Justin still had feelings for O. If O still had feelings for him.

I shut those thoughts off straight away. There was only so much torture I could tolerate.

"Come in. Come in." O backed up, catching my eye again with a hurried glance. The second we locked gazes, the world faded, noise silenced, and that damn connection that would destroy me until my dying day hissed like wildfire.

I couldn't take my eyes off the girl I'd loved since I was a teenager. I couldn't stop looking at the smudges under her pretty hazel eyes or the tense strain I'd put there. The strain of being a good friend while never wanting to see me again.

Justin pushed past, breaking our moment.

I followed, lugging in the two duffels of paint and work equipment. O's apartment wasn't exactly big enough to expect her to store my shit as well as put us up as house guests, but I couldn't exist without the ability to paint.

Just like when I was younger, it was the only thing that cured me of the constant chatter in my head. The worries, the guesses, the failures.

Moving forward, my arm brushed against O's.

She stiffened and backed away. That slight movement was as sharp and as deadly as a blade to my chest. My shoulders sank. "Can't get rid of me, huh."

"Seems as though destiny has other plans."

"Destiny can take a hike. She only seems to screw things up."

Her nose wrinkled. "Or it's just us who does the screwing."

My heart pounded the longer we stared. Images of screwing her in her kitchen exploded in my mind. It'd happened so fast. It'd been explosive and raw. It'd also been the last time I would ever be with her.

She blushed, no doubt thinking the same thing as me. "Anyway…like I said, it's fine for you guys to stay." She closed and locked the door.

Ignoring my heated stare, she moved forward, pointing at the new additions in her small space. "Gil, you'll have the couch. It's not much, but I bought a new pillow and washed the blankets. Olive, you'll have the blow-up mattress behind the couch. Again, it's not much, but I got you a cute flower comforter and hot water bottle in case you're cold." She sighed, shrugging. "I'm sorry I can't offer you your own rooms. It's frustratingly small this place."

Olive zoomed to the mattress behind the couch. Back there she had privacy and her own little world.

"You kidding? This is awesome!" Olive threw herself on the air mattress, only to bounce far higher than I expected. "Wow, it's like a trampoline."

Justin chuckled. "I don't think the manufacturers were going for that. But hey…looks fun."

"It's better than any of the hard bunk beds in Jeffrey's nasty caravan." Olive sat cross-legged in contentment. "Thank you so much, O."

"You're very welcome."

I cleared my throat. "Seriously, Olin. This is better than any five-star hotel. You shouldn't have gone to so much trouble."

She smiled self-consciously. "It's not luxury, but that's nice of you to say."

Our eyes locked all over again, imprisoning each other—two elements that always joined whenever close.

I couldn't break the spell, and neither could she.

Justin cleared his throat. "Look, I…eh, I'm gonna get going. Have to go back to the office. You guys all good?"

Shivering at the overwhelming need to touch O—to pull her into me and drop down all my barriers, I forced myself to look at my friend. A friend who sometimes I wanted to kill but a friend I trusted to look after my daughter when I couldn't.

"Thanks, Miller." I held out my hand. "Thanks for the lift over here and for arranging this."

O came closer, smiling gently. "You're a good man, Justin Miller."

Justin actually blushed, backing toward the door as if he couldn't wait to run from honest compliments. "Just don't kill each other, okay?" He pinned me with a stare. "I'll call tomorrow. Maybe you guys should go out for dinner. The three of you. Celebrate your new living arrangements."

Any tender thoughts toward him evaporated.

Dinner?

Fuck, I would rather inject myself with succinylcholine than go out for dinner. To a restaurant with the woman I loved and the daughter I'd do anything to protect. To eat food that O would have to pay for because I couldn't afford it.

No way.

No fucking way.

O deserved so, *so* much. I owed far too much to ever pay back.

I wouldn't add yet more debt to my pile of worthlessness.

My pride was bruised.

My ego destroyed.

If I let O pay for dinner—when I knew how tight her own finances were—I'd never forgive myself.

And I couldn't go out anyway.

The move here had been cleared with the police, but that was as far as my new boundaries went according to my anklet.

"That won't be necessary. I brought the rest of my groceries. I'll cook something," I muttered. I couldn't take her out, but I could at least prepare something. "A tiny thank you for having us."

"Sure, that sounds nice." She gave me a wary smile. "Appreciate it."

"Dad makes a yummy pasta," Olive piped up from the bouncy bed, her hands already rummaging in her backpack for crayons and paper.

O grinned, forcing lightness into her face when only heaviness existed between us. "Look forward to it then."

My thoughts tripped backward to a time when O had made

me lunch. When she'd pulled me into her house and made me fall head over heels for her.

Pancakes and syrup.

We'd vowed to be each other's family.

I doubted a simple bolognese could reinstate family bonds that were long gone.

"Okay, guys, have fun playing happy families." Justin waved, opening the door. "See ya soon."

The door closed.

The apartment seemed to shrink around us.

O made an excuse to disappear into her bedroom.

And I stood like an idiot in her living room, so fucking aware of everything that I'd lost.

Chapter Twenty

Gil

I COULDN'T SLEEP.

The ceiling offered no salvation from reliving the most awkward evening of my life.

I'd cooked in O's tiny kitchen while Olive and her played scrabble at the coffee table.

We'd eaten in relative ease, both of us using Olive as the ice breaker. Talking to her instead of each other, overly attentive to her every need.

O's smiles had been reserved and her voice measured whenever she'd had to speak to me directly. Her eyes hid so many things. She was angry with me. Annoyed. Pissed off. All of the above. So many painful things bubbled beneath the surface, and the longer we spent together, the more the tension increased.

I shook while doing the dishes.

I fought with ways of ending this nightmarish situation.

But then, O retired early with the excuse of a headache, and Olive and I stayed up a little longer watching TV on low.

By the time Olive passed out on her mattress and I slipped beneath the blankets on the couch, my entire system felt jacked up and on edge.

We needed to talk.

O and me.

Truly, *really* talk.

No sex.

No swearing.

Just frank conversation that might have some chance at clearing the air.

But O had made it obvious she wasn't open to speaking.

That she'd pulled away from me—accepting my presence while waiting until I was out of her life for good. She didn't need to tell me she'd locked her heart to me.

I felt it.

I felt the emptiness when she looked at me.

I tasted the sourness of obligation.

This was goodbye in a terribly drawn-out way.

Checking my phone, I cursed under my breath.

Two a.m. and I was fucking wired.

I couldn't stay here.

I needed to expel some of my tension before I marched into O's bedroom and demanded she listen to me. Listen to my apologies, explanations, and every dark, dirty confession I'd collected over the years.

Hauling my arse from the covers—ignoring the stiffness and new bruises from being beaten up a few days ago—I pulled on a pair of tatty jeans and t-shirt from my packed duffel. The one saving grace of having to sell off your possessions for blackmail meant when you got kicked out of home you didn't have much to pack. Another blessing in disguise was being kicked out of the place where angry society knew you lived and planned an attack when you stepped out the damn door.

Even if we hadn't been evicted, Olive wouldn't have been safe to stay there.

Because of me.

It's always because of fucking me.

At least thanks to the punishment I'd received, the police had approved my address change. Allowing me to travel and stay at O's without revoking my bail.

Checking on Olive and finding her fast asleep, I slipped from the door and jogged down the communal stairs.

With the stars and crescent moon for company, I stood outside O's building and watched night turn to dawn.

I couldn't walk away because of my anklet.

I couldn't prowl the alleyways and find salvation in graffiti.

I couldn't head back inside and slip into O's bed and delete this awfulness between us.

All I could do was watch the world wake up and count down the moments I had left.

Chapter Twenty-One

Olin

"OH, WOW, I love that."

I spun around, holding the towel tighter around myself. Olive stood in my doorway; her gaze transfixed on my tattoo-covered scars.

I'd just had a shower after being unable to sleep. Dawn crested ten minutes ago and I figured I'd get ready for work early, so I could sneak out and not have to deal with Gil this morning.

However, when I'd tiptoed to the bathroom, there'd been no sign of him sleeping on the couch. Olive had been tucked up in bed, but I guessed the creaky pipes and running water had woken her.

I shivered a little as my damp hair clung to my shoulders. I craved clothing for both protection and warmth, but Olive drifted into my room, her hand up as if to touch my back.

Turning to face her, I said gently, "You should still be sleeping."

"I woke up and I'm not tired anymore." She skirted around me, looking at my ink again. "That's so cool. Is it a tattoo? It doesn't look real."

I caught a glimpse of what she saw in my wardrobe mirror. The huge geometric owl bleeding into realism. The many animals beginning with O hidden in its feathers. "Yes, it's a tattoo. And no, you can't have one." I laughed. "I don't think Gil would ever forgive me if I'm the reason you get ink before you're eighteen."

Her nose wrinkled. "It's my body. I can draw on it if I want."

"Your dad called it scribbling when he first saw it."

"It's not scribbling. It's amazing!" Her tiny hand reached out, stroking the ridges and ugliness of my patched together wounds. "Did it hurt?"

I guessed she asked about the ink rather than the injury hidden beneath. Unless you knew what to look for, the tattoo did what I intended and camouflaged the mess.

Striding away, I turned my back on her and pulled on a sports bra and black blouse. "No, it wasn't too bad."

"Do you have any more?"

"No." Feeling strange dressing in front of her, I stepped into a pair of knickers before dropping my towel and wriggling into a skirt. "That piece is enough."

And you can't tattoo over emotional wounds, so I'll just have to cope.

Making my way to my small dressing table by the window, I grabbed my hairbrush. Olive followed me, her cute hummingbird pyjamas revealing Gil didn't worry about masculinity when he obviously doted and bought his daughter the most girlish, prettiest things.

"Are you going somewhere?" Her happiness level dropped. "Can I come?"

Quickly taming my dark blonde hair, I smiled. "I have to go to work. Believe me, you don't want to come. It's boring being in an office all day."

"But you didn't work when I stayed here with you last time. It was so awesome spending the entire day with you." She leapt onto my bed. "I wanted to go to that park again and the library and that place you took me to that sells those yummy muffins."

Adding a lashing of mascara and some peach lip-gloss, I looked at her in the mirror. "I'd love that too, but I need to work to pay the bills. Being an adult sucks sometimes." Placing my makeup down, I spun to face her. "But you don't need to spend the day with me. You have your dad. You guys will have a great day together. Maybe paint or—"

"He won't have time. He's trying to get work too." She pouted, plucking at my bedspread. "I want him to paint those women canvases again instead of being stressed about money. At least at the warehouse, I could watch him work. I helped him clean up when I wasn't at school."

"Do you miss school?"

She shrugged. "Kinda. But not really 'cause I missed my dad more and all my friends won't care about me anymore."

"They will care." I sat on my haunches in front of her,

grabbing her ankles as she kicked her legs off the edge of my bed. "They'll have missed going to school with you."

"But I won't even be with them in class. Won't I be held back a year? Seeing as Uncle Jeffrey kept me out of school for so long?"

Damn.

Gil had been held back because a teacher had her own diabolical reasons.

Olive might be held back because of her uncle's.

Life truly isn't fair.

"Maybe you can be in the same grade and just have some extra coaching at home, so you can catch up fast. I'm guessing you're a very fast learner."

She perked up. "I am. I love books and things. I don't want to be with younger kids."

"Okay then, well if we enrol you back in school, I'll do my best to find you a good tutor."

We enrol you?

What are you saying, O?

You can't promise such things. You won't be in her life. You're leaving, remember?

"Could *you* teach me?" Her grey eyes searched mine. "That would be so much fun."

Standing, I shook my head. "I don't know enough to teach you, Olive Pip, but I have no doubt you'll be the smartest girl in class."

The front door opened and closed, wrenching both our attentions to it.

Gil appeared in the living room, his eyes catching mine and then Olive's. Lines etched around his mouth, and his hair was once again messy from being outside, but he looked calmer than last night.

Moving slowly toward us, he cleared the gravel in his throat. "Seems everyone is up early this morning."

"Daddy!" Olive leaped off my bed and ran straight into his arms.

Gil dropped to one knee, wrapping her tight in his embrace. "Morning, tiny spinach. How did you sleep?"

"Fine. The mattress was super comfy. But then I woke up, and you weren't here." Her head tilted. "Where'd you go?"

Gil gave me a guilty glance, climbing back to his feet. "I watched the sun rise."

Raking a hand through his hair, he looked my office attire up and down. "Heading in this early?"

I nodded. "Duty calls."

"It always does."

His face filled with love, ruining me all over again. I wasn't used to this respectful version of him. The one who accepted my boundaries and didn't scale my fences to talk to me.

I didn't know if I liked it. If I was honest, I hated the distance between us even while we stood so close.

"O…I—" Raking a hand through his hair, he sighed. "Thank you for letting us stay the night."

"You're welcome." Something lodged in my throat, a stone heavy with hurt and honesty.

Olive piped up, "Have you seen Olin's tattoo? It's amazing! Like amazing, amazing. Can I have one, Dad?"

The tension evaporated as Gil snapped into father mode. His eyes gleamed with strictness even as his lips quirked in a grin. "Any drawings you do, missy, are to end up on paper only."

"What about on people? Can I paint naked people?"

"When you're older, fine."

"So when I'm older, I can get a tattoo like O's?"

"No. Absolutely not."

Olive pouted, hanging on Gil's hand. "I'll make you say yes. I always make you say yes."

Gil chuckled painfully. "That's entirely true." He looked at me, his eyes clear and smile simple. A simple smile of frustration and pride for his child. "She's a master at getting anything she wants."

I laughed quietly. "Maybe you're just a soft touch."

His simpleness vanished under a cloak of awareness. "Maybe I am. Maybe I'm being too soft on you, too."

My heart pattered quickly. "What do you mean?"

"I mean…I still want to talk." Patting Olive on the butt, he said kindly, "You. Shower. Now."

"Aww, but I don't—"

"Shower and I'll cook you pancakes for breakfast, and then, we'll spend the day together. Just you and me."

Olive's adorable face lit up. "All day? Really?" She wriggled in place. "No job searching? No working?"

"Nope. Just you." He bowed to kiss her, covering her with unconditional love. "I want to spend the day with my favourite girl. Job hunting can wait. Maybe we'll go apartment searching instead, so we don't impose on O any longer than we have to."

"I like living with O, but I can't wait to spend the day together. Yay!" Olive sped toward the bathroom, throwing a wave in my direction. "Bye, O. Have a good day working."

"See ya." I waved to a closed bathroom door, laughing quietly. "She certainly adores the ground you walk on."

"And I can't imagine my life without her." His tone slipped into despair. "Shit, I can't leave." He scowled at his ankle. "I'm under house arrest. Is it okay if I hang here with her? I'll do my best to find alternative arrangements online."

My heart squeezed. I'd opened my home to him because it was the right thing to do, yet I couldn't deny I'd been selfish too. Selfish and dishonest because as much as I didn't have the strength to deal with the mess between us, I wasn't ready to never see him again.

"Of course."

He rubbed the back of his nape. "You must think I'm pathetic. Unemployed. Locked in one place. A single dad who can't do anything right."

I stepped toward him. "I don't think you're pathetic, Gil. I never have."

"But you've had enough of dealing with my nonsense."

"No. I just…" I held up my hands in surrender. "I don't know anymore. I don't know about anything. I don't know about you or me or what I should do…it's terrifying."

He stormed toward me, grabbing my cheeks and holding me firm. "All of this is fucking terrifying. Knowing I've lost you. Knowing I'm about to lose Olive. My freedom. My future." His thumbs ran over my cheekbones, his hands shaking. "Knowing I'm one of the reasons you're afraid." His forehead pressed against mine. "It fucking butchers me, O. I never meant to hurt you. I'll never forgive myself for painting you, drugging you. I could apologise every damn day of my life, but…it's not going to change anything."

I swayed in his touch, suffering heat and hunger.

The same violence that clawed for a fight returned, and I didn't entirely know why. Gil had apologised. I'd forgiven him. We should be able to move on.

And yet…we couldn't.

We kept clinging to each other in unhealthy ways, making us weak and wanting.

My lips throbbed for his.

His body stepped into mine until no space existed between us and his head tipped down. His mouth descended, and we both jerked at the connection.

Hot.

Painful.

Unforgiving.

I sighed.

He groaned.

His hands fell from my cheeks to wrap around my hips, pulling me into him, making my stomach flip.

The kiss wasn't planned.

Our confessions messy and dangerous.

But as his tongue touched mine, and we began a dance that twisted me up and made me fly, I didn't care.

I hugged him back.

I kissed him back.

And then it was over as he pulled away.

The early morning sunshine shone through the window, highlighting a shadowy bruise on his jaw and the discolouration under his eye, reminding me violence had found him once again.

That his troubles weren't over.

"Are you okay?" My question was breathy, my heart out of control.

He chuckled darkly. "No, I'm not fucking okay. I miss you, O. I've missed you my entire goddamn life."

My knees wobbled. "I meant your incident with whoever hurt you."

"Oh, that." His forehead furrowed. The connection between us faltered as he took a step back. "Yeah, I'm fine."

His departure wrenched deep inside me but my question had done what I'd intended. I'd popped the bubble we'd been in. The bubble we had a habit of creating. The precious, perfect moment where it was just us and kisses and nothing else mattered.

If we could live in that illusion, we could be happy.

But we couldn't because real life wasn't that easy.

"Justin said a few men surprised you outside your warehouse. That they were friends and family of one of the painted girls."

Gil stroked his jaw where a bruise hinted he'd been punched pretty hard. "They got a few strikes in, but I didn't let them use me as a punching bag like I did my uncle, if that's what you're worried about. I fought back."

"I'm just worried that society is lynching you."

"They don't know I didn't kill those girls."

"No, but vigilante justice is dangerous."

He shrugged. "Nothing I don't deserve."

"Don't. Don't keep saying that."

He didn't argue. Instead, he stared at me the way he'd stared at Olive. With undying affection and unconditional love. "Feel free to throw a punch too, O. A fist would hurt far less than you cutting me out of your heart."

Tension once again detonated around us.

My heart flurried.

My stomach knotted.

I couldn't look away from him.

This was another blistering moment.

A moment that could fix all other moments.

A fragile moment where we could break the ice, talk, and find happier ground than this precarious plateau we currently navigated.

But I didn't know how.

Gil raised his hand as if to touch me. He licked his lips as my name fell with a whisper, "O...I—"

I shook my head. I backed away.

Gil honoured my wishes.

Barely.

His body bristled with explosive need. The sudden softness of before vanished as he clipped, "If you don't leave to go to work now, I won't be responsible for what I'll do. I won't care my daughter is the bathroom. I won't care that I hurt you beyond anything. I'll grab you and fuck you, and I won't let you out of bed until you forgive me."

I stood rooted to the spot.

Unable to move.

Unable to stay.

It was my turn to struggle with a sentence. "Gil...I—"

He pinched the bridge of his nose, his hand trembling. "Go, O. I don't want to hurt you any more than I have." He looked up, his eyes blazing emerald desire. "And I will hurt you. That's why you're keeping your distance, isn't it? Because you know that soon I'm going away. And no one knows for how long. I could be an old man before they let me out. I might die in there. What sort of bastard would I be to fight for you to love me, only to abandon you all over again?"

He gave me the saddest smile. "Fuck, I wish I'd never let you go when we were younger."

I tripped backward.

I'd waited so, *so* long to hear that.

It sucker-punched me in the chest. It ripped out my soul. It brought tears to my eyes.

Olive darted from the bathroom with toothpaste dripping all over her pyjamas and her toothbrush in her hand. "Dad, I don't like O's toothpaste. Do you have the stuff we use?"

And just like that, another moment was gone.

Again.

I sucked in a breath, jittery and lost.

Gil swallowed back the hurt between us and ducked to scoop his dirty daughter from the floor. "Sure, it's in my bag."

Life once again carried us in different directions as he performed fatherly duties, and I grabbed my handbag, looked at him one last time, and slipped out the door.

I was two hours early for work.

I was trembling like a fool.

I was in so much more trouble than I feared.

Chapter Twenty-Two

Gil

I LASTED THREE days.

Three long, terribly excruciating days of loving O, wanting O, knowing I couldn't have O.

We'd both come to the same painful conclusion.

This was all we could afford.

This tentative friendship.

This tense flatmate arrangement.

After that first day when O went to work and I did my best to come to terms with letting her go, I looked for apartments so I didn't have to destroy any more of her life.

But the market held no decent rentals and the ones viable required a one-year lease. I had no idea when I'd be called to trial, and frankly, I couldn't fucking afford anywhere anyway.

Not with my business in ruin and hate still vicious online.

I had to accept that for now, I had no choice.

No choice but to stop cursing Justin for his charity and stop hating myself for taking O's generosity. This was my life right now...no matter how I wished it wasn't.

Life slipped into a routine.

O would go to the office, and I'd spend the day with Olive, all while doing my best to find work. I allowed the necessity of earning money and the needs of life to drive me, but I also permitted myself space to enjoy my daughter. To make up for lost time. To learn all about her and the growth she'd done in the year that I hadn't been part of her life.

I did it for her.

I did it for me.

We made memories that hopefully would sustain me through

whatever was coming.

By the time O returned in the evenings, I'd already have dinner cooking and conversation carefully stayed on Olive and her increasing excitement of returning to school.

O's idea of a tutor was great but just added yet another financial strain.

I made a note to see about taking out a loan, so I could make Olive's hopes a reality. Not that I held my breath with my current shitty situation.

When bedtime came around, O would vanish into her room, and I would lie on her couch doing my best not to get hard or burst through her door and force her to listen to me. To tell her I was wrong in staying away. That I needed her to fight beside me...like she always had.

I missed her.

I wanted her.

But I wouldn't do that to her.

At least having Olive between us gave us safe harbour and prevented any chance of breaking our strange, brittle truce.

Our voices had to stay light and civil for innocent ears. Our interactions had to be upbeat and chipper, all while we acted our arses off for my daughter's sake.

It physically crippled me watching O laugh with Olive and Olive fall in love with O. They'd been thrown together by a mad man—two, including me—and that bond only grew stronger the longer we stayed in O's tiny apartment.

I knew I couldn't let them get any closer. I was only setting Olive up for yet more heartbreak if I did. O was leaving on a jet plane, and Olive would soon have to face my disappearance for a second time. Plus, O couldn't be expected to share her heart with a child created by our old teacher and me.

But knowing all that didn't mean I could stop the inevitable connection they shared. The sweetness when Olive showed O how to blend watercolours, and the pride when O showed Olive how to dance.

Fuck, it would've been so perfect if O was mine.

We could've been a family.

A true, happy, *perfect* family.

Instead of this pretend pocket of time, both of just waiting for it to end, preparing how to tell Olive that life wasn't fucking fair and her hardships weren't over yet.

"Dad....*Dad*! You're not painting."

I snapped out of my thoughts, slamming back into the present where I hung with Olive across the street from O's apartment. I hoped the distance from the approved flat and this park wouldn't set off the sensor in my anklet.

Poor Olive had cabin fever.

We'd come to the tiny square between four busy roads to paint the fountain splashing over marble swans and lilypads.

I'd carried my portable easel, a selection of paints, and a packed strawberry jam sandwich—her favourite—and spent the afternoon while O was at work painting the sun-glittering structure with my daughter.

"Sorry." I held up my paintbrush. To be fair, I wasn't doing much. The sketch and slowly-coming-to-life painting was all Olive's, and once again, I was blown away by her young talent.

She had the scale nailed. The shadows perfected. The bend of the swan's neck lifelike.

"What'cha thinking about?" she asked.

I smiled, nudging her small shoulder with mine. I didn't have chairs, so we'd set the easel low so we could sprawl on a blanket. "Nothing much. Just how talented you are."

"Nah, I'm not nearly as good as you."

"You're getting close." I eyed up the way she blended white, blue, and black to make a shade of grey so similar to her eyes. "I'm very proud of you."

She blushed. "You're a good teacher."

"Nope. It's all you, kiddo."

Her tongue stuck between her teeth as she shaded the swan's neck. "O said she was proud of me too. She showed me another dance move this morning while you were still sleeping."

"She did?"

How the hell did I not hear them?

"Yep. In her room. She said I have good balance."

I pretended to shove her, jerking her back into place before she fell. "You do. Look how stable you are."

She snickered. "Do you think we can stay with O? I really like living with her. She's super nice." Her sweet gaze met mine. "I like her and you like her. I know you do. You more than like her. But you're sad too." Her head cocked, sending shiny hair over her shoulder. "Why are you sad? Don't you like living with O and me? Do you want to go back to the warehouse?"

I swallowed the sudden obstruction in my throat. I'd long ago learned not to be shocked at the intuition of children and their perception of the truth, but it still punched me in the chest. "I'm not sad. I'm so happy we're together again." Dropping my paintbrush into the water jar, I added, "And you know we can't stay with O for much longer, right? This is only temporary. She has her own life to live, little spinach. And we're not part of it."

"We could be. She likes you too, even though she's mad at you right now."

I froze. "How do you know she's mad at me?"

Had O talked to her?

She wouldn't.

Would she?

Our drama was our own fault—*my* fault—and shouldn't be dumped on a kid.

Olive scowled as if I was an idiot—which I was, so I couldn't argue. "I know the way she talks to you. She really likes you, but you did something, and she's mad." She pinned me with a ruthless stare. "Whatever you did, you should apologise and then we can all move into a bigger place where we all have bedrooms and can be happy forever and ever."

Shit.

This was getting bad.

Olive had attached herself way too much to O.

I should've taken her to Justin's so she could bond to him instead. How the hell was I supposed to dump her on him when I got sentenced and expect her to be comfortable living with yet another strange man?

Fuck.

My phone rang, vibrating in my pocket.

I didn't want to answer it.

Nothing good ever came from answering my goddamn phone, but I pulled it out and climbed to my feet. "I'll be a sec, okay?"

Olive nodded, pinning all her attention on her painting again. "Okey-dokey."

Pressing accept, I walked away, answering the unknown number suspiciously. "Hello?"

"Gilbert Clark?"

"Who's this?"

"This is Brad Scott from Scott, Smith, and Grampton. I'm calling to inform you that a court date has been set, and you're expected to be at the crown court in six days' time at nine a.m. sharp. Please be presentable and prepared. I request we meet tomorrow to go over your testimony and explain in detail what to expect."

Shit.

Shit.

Shit.

"Six days?" My heart sank to my toes. "That soon?"

"They've hurried your trial. These things happen with high-profile murder cases, especially when pressure is put on the system by the public."

I rubbed my mouth, spinning to face Olive who sat innocently on the blanket. "How long with the trial take?"

"Not sure. Depends how much evidence there is to present. You'll be subjected to a jury trial. Your verdict might be given that day or it might take a week or a month, who knows. I'll be able to advise more once we've sat down, and you've answered my questions."

"Questions?"

"We'll run through a fake trial. I'll pretend to examine you, you answer, we get our ducks in a row, and you'll be prepared for the real thing. Sitting in a courtroom can be scary business, Mr. Clark. It's my job to ensure you're ready and nothing goes wrong."

I couldn't stop looking at my daughter.

I wanted to be fucking sick.

"What if I'm found guilty? Will I be sent to prison straight away?"

Brad made a noise; paper shuffled in the background. "I'm afraid so. It's best to get your affairs in order and prepare your family, just in case."

Pacing the soft grass, blanketed by warm sun, I asked as quietly as my nerves would allow. "Do you think I have a chance of walking out of there?"

After a long pause, Brad muttered, "You killed a man, Mr. Clark. It might've been in defense of Olin Moss being assaulted, but the fact remains, you took a life."

"He held my daughter hostage for over a year."

"He was your family."

"He was a liar and a traitor."

"So you say."

My hands curled. "What are you implying?"

"I'm implying nothing. Just showing you how the court will be. No one will be on your side, Mr. Clark. Except me."

"So you believe I deserve to go to jail?"

He sighed with exasperation, as if he'd had this conversation with so many criminals. "It's not about what I believe. It's about what the facts prove. I'll do my best to ensure they work in your favour. But you confessed to the murder. You are being lynched online. The possibility of this all blowing over and you remaining a free man are slim to none."

Silence filled in the gaps.

I had nothing more to say.

He cleared his throat. "Tomorrow at my office. We'll go through everything and I'll make sure you're prepared. Until then, enjoy today, Mr. Clark. Enjoy all your days because you might only have six free ones left."

He hung up.

I stared at the traffic surrounding us.

I tripped back to Olive and collapsed beside my daughter just as a stopwatch started a countdown to the end.

Tick.

Tock.

It's over.

Chapter Twenty-Three

Olin

I DIDN'T KNOW how much longer I could take it.

Seeing Gil every day.

Having him in my house.

Watching the incredible way he loved his daughter.

Suffering a stupid heart that still wanted what it couldn't have.

It was too much.

I needed space.

Time alone.

I needed to rein in my rapidly fraying life before I was left with tattered pieces and no hope of ever sewing myself back together again.

The civility between us was worse than fighting.

The fakeness between us far more draining than being honest.

But we couldn't have a fight, and we couldn't be honest because Olive was there.

Every night.

Every meal.

Every morning.

That sweet, adorable little girl who watched me and Gil with far too much understanding in her grey gaze. She saw what we were trying to hide. She heard what we weren't saying. And it worried me because the longer we skirted around each other, pretending we could be friends when it was obvious that we couldn't, the more Olive watched with a plan gleaming in her eyes.

A plan that little girls make up when they think they can play matchmaker to two people who are stubborn and broken and successfully ruining any chance of happiness.

I couldn't let her do that.

I had made my choice.

I've made it.

I have.

I won't fall into the same patterns.

Not this time.

Yes, being a supportive friend and offering free accommodation was harder than I thought. Yes, being kind wasn't nearly as rewarding as it used to be. But at least I had my work. I could lose myself in the repetitive routine and find salvation from an unsolvable complication until five p.m.

Unfortunately, the moment I climbed on the bus and travelled home, all those jumpy, itchy needs swarmed me, and by the time I walked in the door, I was exhausted, frustrated, and just plain twisted up with barbwire-filled knots.

Tonight, I honestly didn't know if I could walk through the door and do it all over again. To smile and laugh and let Gil cook me and his daughter a simple but tasty dinner.

It was far too domesticated.

Way too dangerous for my heart.

Sighing, I fished my keys from my handbag and sucked in a deep breath.

Unlocking the door, I braced myself, schooled my features from tortured to serene, and stepped into my apartment.

"Oh, hi." I stopped on the threshold, finding more people than I expected.

Justin immediately got to his feet where he sat at the dining room table with Gil and Olive. A tower of pizza boxes rested in the middle of the table, along with wedges and garlic bread. "Great, you're back. We've been staring at this food like slobbering hyenas for twenty minutes but didn't want to start until you were here."

Olive giggled. "I wasn't slobbering."

"You were too." Justin stuck out his tongue at her. "I saw drool on your chin and your tiny fangs."

"Did not." She crossed her arms, a cross between a smirk and a pout on her face.

Gil just sprawled in his chair, his gaze once again pinned on me, his body wound tight despite his relaxed pose. I didn't know how I knew, but something had happened today.

Something bad.

I read it in the way he studied me as if he'd never see me

again.

I felt it in the electrified air between us.

I grew wet despite myself.

I grew angry because my body kept betraying me.

Ripping my gaze from his, I kissed Justin on the cheek as he kissed me. Gil stiffened in his chair.

I smiled. "You could've started without me, you know."

"Nah, that wouldn't be fair." Justin took my handbag, tossed it on the couch, then escorted me to the table. "Gil called and asked me round. Hope you don't mind me imposing." Sitting down, he divided up the boxes and opened them.

A punch of cheese, barbecue sauce, and grease filled my nose.

"I don't mind. You're welcome anytime."

"I bought pizza as a guest tax." Justin grabbed a piece of veggie-something-or-other and plopped it onto Olive's plate. "After you, tiny one."

Olive plucked a piece of onion off, then took a dainty bite. "Yummy."

"Great. I'm glad it's approved." Justin chuckled, placing a piece onto my plate then onto his. He didn't serve Gil, just shoved the box his way. "All yours, mate."

"Cheers." Gil took one and ate quietly. Once again, that intensity, that wrongness scratched down my spine.

What'd happened?

Why was Justin here?

How could I ask when it wasn't my place?

Conversation was few and far between as we ate unhealthy but delicious takeout. Olive managed two pieces and a handful of wedges. I ate three pieces. And the guys managed to devour almost an entire pizza each.

By the time everyone had their fill, Olive looked ready to pass out and threw herself on the couch amongst Gil's blankets and turned on the TV.

Justin passed out napkins for greasy fingers.

Gil raised an eyebrow, catching Justin's attention.

"Yeah, yeah." He grinned, hiding the scary urgency in his tone. "Prove to her I'm trustworthy before it's too late."

"Appreciate it." Gil sat forward in his chair as Justin went to Olive and struck up a conversation about whatever show she'd selected. He perched next to her on the couch, his gaze on the screen but his attention entirely on her.

"What are you watching?" he asked gently.

"Dunno. What do you want to watch?"

Justin grinned. "Anything you want to watch." The strain in his shoulders relaxed. He'd successfully proven not to be the monster she'd feared just a few weeks ago.

Once again prickles shot down my back, suddenly understanding why Justin was here. Gil had invited him to bond with Olive. To ensure they could live harmoniously when the time came.

Oh, no.

My eyes shot to his. "Did something happen today?" My pulse pounded in worry.

Gil stiffened and stood from the table. "Can I talk to you, please?"

I looked up, frowning. "Sure…please tell me—"

"Not here." He arched his chin at my bedroom. "In there."

I instantly shook my head.

Him and me in a room with a closed door?

No way.

I wouldn't have the strength to stop whatever would happen. And it would happen.

Each stare was a touch.

Each word was a lick.

Living together and not acknowledging the flying, raging need between us had ensured we'd been pouring gunpowder directly onto open wounds. If we had a single opportunity to even say a fraction of something that wasn't controlled and civil, I didn't know what would happen.

You do know.

You know exactly what would happen.

The rough, quick sex we'd had in my kitchen would be *nothing* compared to the explosive aggression we'd indulge in.

"It's probably best if we stay—"

"It's important." His head tipped down, shadowing his gaze. "Please?"

Olive giggled at something Justin said.

He beamed as if he'd solved complex math.

Just because Olive was distracted didn't mean we were free to become animals behind my bedroom door. The walls were paper thin. Justin was right there. There was safety in that—knowing we still had boundaries and rules in place.

"Okay." Brushing off pizza crumbs, I didn't say a word as I followed Gil through the small living room and entered my bedroom.

The moment we were inside, he closed the door.

He took a deep breath.

I spun to face him, crossing my arms, doing my best to hold myself together. "What is it? What's happened?"

He rubbed his face with both hands, the mask he'd kept in place the past few days slipping to the floor. "Fuck, do you know how hard it is not to kiss you? It's all I ever fucking think about." He moved toward me, only to pace away before he could touch me. "Fuck, if I kiss you, I won't be able to stop."

He headed to my window, raking hands through his hair. "Night after night, I battle myself not to come in here and take you. To see if there's any way we can fix us. To stop our inevitable separation."

"Gil, don't—"

He held up a hand. "It's okay, O. I'm not going to force myself on you. I'm not going to kiss you. I'm not going to do anything apart from say…it's all too fucking late."

The hair on the back of my neck stood up. I stepped toward him instead of away. "What do you mean, too late?"

"I had a phone call today."

"From who?"

"The lawyer who's been put in charge of my case." He pinched the bridge of his nose before looking up. "I'll be sentenced in six days."

My heart stopped beating. "*What?* That's so soon. How can they—?"

"Six days before I have to say goodbye to Olive for who knows how long. Six days to make sure she's comfortable with living with Justin, even though she's fallen madly in love with you. Six fucking days to find some way of making even the smallest amount of money so she's not destitute like me." His voice cracked with rage and impotency. "Fuck!"

His shout was heartfelt and passionate, but also quiet, staying below the decibel guaranteed to reach Olive's small ears.

I didn't know what to say or how to comfort him.

I was petrified for him. I couldn't imagine how it would feel to know your freedom was about to be stolen, and there was nothing you could do about it.

He'd committed the crime.

He wouldn't run.

He wouldn't lie.

Whatever sentence he was given would be served with honour, and his daughter would miss him every day of her life without him.

The urge to hug him overwhelmed me. I moved toward him. "What can I do?"

He held up his hand, his eyes flashing with a mixture of helplessness and violence. "Don't touch me, O. Not when I'm like this." His voice turned dangerously dark. "You touch me and I'm inside you. I won't be able to stop myself."

I stopped.

Pain crashed over his features.

"Tell me what you need," I whispered.

"I owe you so much already."

"Tell me what you need, Gil."

He glowered at my carpet, unable to meet my eyes. "I need money. To pay you for the days we've stayed here. To pay Justin for Olive's upkeep. To give Olive some pocket money for while I'm gone."

"I don't see how I can—"

His head tipped up, the heat and hardness back in his stare. "Be my canvas. Let me paint you...one last time."

I stumbled backward. "Excuse me?"

What about the petitions online chanting for his business closure and death?

What about the absolute hate bleeding through the keyboard?

"I know my business is dead. No one wants to be associated with a murderer. My visibility and ratings are in the gutter. I have no new content to share, which means algorithms aren't delivering to new people." He paced again, driving yet another hand into his hair. "I'm aware it probably won't work. I know what I'm asking. It's a huge gamble that any commissions will arrive in time before my court date, but...I have to try."

He chuckled blackly. "I've really fucked up this time, O. I should never have killed him. I should've let the police deal with him. But...I did it and I won't apologise for it nor regret it; he needed to die. I'm okay paying that price. I just don't want Olive to pay with me."

Old habits were so hard to break.

I wanted to grab him close and tell him that yes, I would be his canvas. That I had the strength to help him all over again after I'd used up every ounce of help I had to give.

I was so close to doing exactly that.

So reckless to touch him, knowing what would happen if I did.

His warning was real.

The desire rampant between us.

One touch would lead to him attacking me, taking me, destroying the final weak pieces of me.

I was prepared to do all that...but one thing stopped me.

A single memory.

A tiny piece of the past.

I swallowed hard and prepared to say the hardest thing in my life. "I can't help you, Gil. I'm so sorry."

He locked in place. His urgency slipped into despondency. His need into acceptance. "I understand."

"I'll help you find money some other way, but...I can't let you paint me again."

He froze. His nostrils flared. He slouched with self-hatred. "Of course. What a fucking arsehole thing to even ask." He paced again, shaking his head as if he could punch himself for being so clueless. "The last time I painted you, I drugged you and—"

"I know what you did." I held up my hand, trying to figure out how to say what was needed. "Gil, the fact that you're asking for help is...healing. You didn't lock things inside this time and make mistakes because it." I licked my lips, stalling for a second. "I don't want you to take my refusal as a sign to never ask for help again. You should be able to trust that sharing your burdens with others is beneficial...for everyone involved. I'm honoured. Truly. I'm grateful you came to me. And I'm eternally sorry that I have to say no."

His hands fisted by his sides, struggling to control whatever he felt. With jerky steps, he came toward me.

I stiffened and sucked in a breath as he placed a chaste kiss on my cheek. "Don't ever apologise to me, O. Ever." His lips trailed to my mouth, hovering over me in punishment and prayer.

I swayed into him, swept up and unable to fight.

But he closed his eyes and backed up, physically putting space between us while emotional space was that much harder. "I was wrong to ask. Wrong to stay here. Wrong about so many fucking things."

Shivering, I hugged myself. Whatever fragile moment we'd shared was ending and I had to know. Had to ask. "When you face the courtroom...what are you going to tell them?"

He smiled sadly. "The only thing I can. The only thing I have left." He strode to the door and wrapped his hand around the handle. "I'm going to tell the truth. I'm sick of lying. I'm done running. I'll tell the truth and accept the consequences."

A tear escaped my control as he stepped through the door and went to sit on the couch with his friend and daughter.

Scooping Olive up, he dragged her onto his lap, rocked into her, and pressed a kiss to her hair.

He didn't say a word.

But all around them echoed goodbye.

Chapter Twenty-Four

Gil

WHILE O WAS at work, I moved my daughter and meagre belongings into Justin's place.

I didn't tell O we were leaving. I didn't give any hint that we wouldn't be there when she returned home. Once Olive was settled, I would visit O one last time to explain, to thank her, to apologise, to say...goodbye.

I'd called the cops and asked for yet another address change, gaining permission to travel between the two locations. They gave me twenty-four hours to complete the move before warning I'd be under house arrest again.

Justin took the day off from the office and spent every moment with us. He showed Olive the spare bedroom, which used to be sterile and bland but now held purple curtains, lacy pink pillows, and a massive artwork of a field filled with wildflowers on the wall.

I'd caught his eye as Olive shot to the bed, the white desk, and the cute little dresser he'd arranged.

Fuck, I owed this man a lot.

Bumping into him on the street after so many years had been one of the best things to happen to me. He hadn't been a curious sod—only there while times had been normal. He hadn't bailed when I finally accepted his help and kept requesting more.

He'd proven himself to be loyal and generous, and I would be grateful for the rest of my godforsaken life.

After Olive explored her new space, still suspicious about why she got a room and I got the couch, I whispered into her ear to hug Justin. To push them together and create that trusting bond so I could be locked away next week and not worry that Olive would have a breakdown, that Justin could handle her, and that there was no chance of this falling apart.

No one knew how long I'd be in jail for.

A year, a decade, forever?

Justin was taking on so fucking much without asking for anything in return.

There is something *you can give him.*

The thought appeared and ran away, as if too scared to stick around and find out how I truly felt about offering him something that meant more to me than my own life.

But as Olive tentatively shuffled to Justin and hugged him at my request, I balled my hands and made a promise.

Once I knew my punishment.

Once Olive was no longer mine to care for.

I would tell him what I was willing to sacrifice for all his support.

* * * * *

"You sure you got this?" I muttered as Justin grabbed a beer from the fridge and I stacked the dishwasher from the plates we'd used with Thai takeout.

"I'm sure." He twisted off the cap and tossed it into the bin. "If Olive and I can't hang out on our own for a few hours, then I don't see how living together is going to work out. You need to do this, and we need time alone to figure out the ground rules." He patted me on the shoulder, leaving the kitchen and returning to the living room where his black couches faced the TV and Olive sat snuggled in one watching Disney's *Mulan.*

Drying my hands on a dishtowel, I followed and kept my distance while he collapsed next to her and tapped his beer bottle to her glass of apple juice. "What are we watching, tiny pipsqueak?"

She grinned. "I'm not a pipsqueak."

Justin smirked. "See, to me, you're smaller than a pipsqueak. You look like a mouse. An itty-bitty, teensy-weensy mouse. So pipsqueak fits you well."

"Well, you're just a…a…you're a hippopotamus."

"You calling me fat?" Justin scowled dramatically. "Is it because I had two beef curries?"

"Yep!" Olive giggled, sipping her juice as her attention fell back on the TV.

Justin gave me a wink. "All good, mate. I got this."

Nodding, I made my way to the exit. "Olive? I'm heading out for a few hours. Justin will keep you company."

I didn't ask if she was okay with that.

I didn't make her doubt her comfort level.

She didn't really have a choice in the matter anymore.

She nibbled on her bottom lip. "Will you be back in time to say goodnight?"

I braced myself. "Probably not. But Justin can help, and I'll be back later. I'll definitely see you in the morning, though, okay?" Unable to leave without touching her, I strode over and bent to kiss her forehead. Keeping my lips on her sweet-smelling skin, I murmured, "You're safe with him, little spinach. Jeffrey is gone. You were right that he was bad, but Justin isn't. I need you to be okay with having him as your friend, all right?"

She gave a side-eye to Justin before nodding slowly. "I like him as a friend. We can hang out."

"Great. Good girl."

"But I miss O. Can we go back to see her tomorrow?"

"Maybe." Backing away, I imprinted the image of my friend watching cartoons with my daughter then turned around and walked out the door. I'd keep that image safe. I'd pull it up when I got sentenced and I was alone in some goddamn cell, missing Olive with every fucking fibre of my being.

Not for the first time, the urge to pick up my daughter and run hijacked my nervous system.

I wanted to fly away and hide on some secluded island where I would never have to be torn away from her again.

But that was selfish.

That would backfire on Olive as she got older.

I meant what I told O.

I was done running.

I'd been running since Tallup blackmailed me into sleeping with her—always wondering when I'd be arrested for sexual assault.

Well, I wouldn't have to wonder anymore.

Consequences were almost here.

I'd done what I could to protect Olive from the worst of it.

But tonight…tonight I *was* going to be selfish. So fucking selfish.

Tonight was for me.

My last shred of happiness.

Tonight…O was mine.

Chapter Twenty-Five

Olin

"WHAT ON EARTH?" I froze on the threshold, confused. Did I walk into the wrong apartment?

Where my couch and dining table used to be, a black sheet now hung from the window and draped on the floor, creating a void of darkness, a backdrop to nothingness.

"You're later than I planned."

My attention shot to the kitchen where Gil stood, mixing paints. He'd lined his bottles and tools up neatly, pigments from gold and taupe right through to aqua and obsidian waited to be used. He tested the airbrush, wiping the nozzle with a paper towel all while I gawked like an idiot.

"Eh…" Closing the door behind me, I slung my handbag onto the floor, kicked off my heels, and padded toward him. "What are you doing?"

"I came to say thank you." His green eyes met mine. "And to say goodbye."

My heart fisted tight. "What do you mean?"

"I mean Olive and I moved out today. I thought you'd be home before I could come back but you weren't…and…" He looked at the black sheet and his takeover of my place, adding. "I had some spare time on my hands."

"You moved out? Without telling me?"

"It was for the best." He gave a sad smile. "My daughter is attached to you. She needs to bond with Justin, so she's comfortable for when I—" He groaned low, cutting himself off.

I nodded, hating the way my chest squeezed. "That makes sense."

He cleared his throat. "I hope you don't mind me, eh,

redecorating."

Grasping at the change of subject and latching onto a less painful conversation, I said, "Depends what you're planning on doing." I crossed my arms, keeping the breakfast bar and my body language between us. "Do you have a canvas coming here to be painted? Did you get a commission?"

Gil winced, shaking his head. "No…no canvas." Placing the airgun down, he pinned me with his stare. "Only you."

Goosebumps scattered over my arms. "Gil…I told you I can't be painted again. Not yet."

"I know." He stared hard, his gaze deep and deliberate. "But I can't accept no for an answer, O."

I backed up, goosebumps turning into trembles. "Why are you looking at me like that?"

"Like what?" He tipped his head down, watching me beneath shadowed eyes.

"Like you don't care if I give consent or not."

He shrugged. "I love you. I want you. And now…you're here."

I gulped, grasping to say something normal and not laced in lust.

I failed.

I swallowed.

Gil placed his palms on either side of the sink, bracing against the countertop. The same countertop where we'd had a furious quickie. Where we'd chased fast pleasure. Where our hearts had once again become tangled.

His voice was decadent and dangerous as he murmured, "I've had a lot of time to decide if I should do this or not."

"Do what?"

"Take something from you that you undoubtedly don't want to give."

I swallowed again. Hard. "I don't know what you mean."

"You do know." His gaze turned brittle. "You know exactly what I mean. Leaving me alone for so long wasn't a good idea, O. It's not been good for my self-control." He looked down at his ankle where the monitoring device kept him leashed. "This is the last time I can be here. I've changed my address with the authorities to Justin's apartment. I won't be able to come and see you before I go to court." His fingers clutched against the counter. "This is the last time I'll have you alone. And I'm done."

"You're done?"

He nodded once. "I'm done. Done pretending I can cope without you in my life. Done lying to myself that I don't need you. Done accepting your choice to break my fucking heart."

Heat filled my cheeks as his gaze travelled over my cream blouse and pinstripe skirt. "You should probably strip, O. I don't want to ruin any more of your clothes."

I coughed. "Excuse me?"

"Have you eaten? Are you hungry?" His voice stayed smoky and deep, even though he'd just sent me into a free-fall.

"Hungry? No, I'm..."

"Okay then." Pushing off from the countertop, he exited the kitchen and stalked me. He stopped within touching distance but kept his hands fisted by his sides. His energy wrapped around me. Energy that used to match mine. A synergy of auras and souls.

Tonight, his energy was treacherous, precarious.

I shivered with premonition. "Gil...what are you doing?"

"I'm going to paint you."

"But I told you—"

"That it brings bad memories." He nodded. "I understand. But it doesn't change the fact that tonight, my brush is touching your body and my paint is staining your skin."

"It does if I don't say yes."

His brow tugged over turbulent eyes. "But you will."

"Why? Why would I agree to let you paint me after the last time?"

"Because this is the last time we'll ever have."

"When you painted and drugged me and prepared to sacrifice me for Olive, I believed *that* was the last time we'd ever have. That I was about to die because of you."

"I was never going to kill you." His body twitched with pain. "I would've killed myself before he was able to do what he threatened. You have to know that."

"You almost *did* die, remember?" My temper crackled into awareness, remembering that night, the fear of him dead on the forest floor, the promise from Jeffrey of sex slavery and child molestation. "You left us both unprotected, all because you didn't ask anyone for help."

"You're right. Just like you were right last night. I asked for help too late and I paid for it. Who knows how our lives would've turned out if I'd told you back at school what Tallup threatened me with. We might be married. We might have our own family. But...I didn't ask. And I lost you. Twice."

His hand cupped my cheek, digging the pads of his fingers into my softness as I tried to back away. "Tonight, I'm not asking anymore. I'm *telling* you what I need. I'm being honest for the first time in my godforsaken life. I'm about to be locked up like an animal, O. I've done my best to ensure Olive will be okay, I've accepted way too much support from Justin, and I've stayed in your home without telling you exactly how I feel. I should walk out that door. I should pay you the pittance I have for the days you let us stay, and I should accept that I will never see you again."

His arm slithered around my waist, jerking me into him. "But I don't accept. I *can't* accept. And tonight, I'm done doing what I *think* I should. Everything I do is wrong. My natural instincts are fucked. So…I'm ignoring them. I'm ignoring the fact that you're trembling and want me to back the fuck off. I'm ignoring the part that this is yet another assault. For once, I'm going to be selfish."

"Gil…stop."

His hand left my cheek and captured the back of my head. His other arm crushed me to him, bending me, imprisoning me. "I can't stop."

My palms smacked against his chest, fighting his control. "Let me go."

"No." His lips smashed on mine. His tongue broke into my mouth. And the ferocity of his kiss was precisely what he said.

This was an assault.

Unwanted. Unprovoked. Assault.

His lips were warm and wonderful.

His body felt like home.

Every part of me screamed to give in. To rock with him, dance with him, explode with him.

But a final shred of common-sense made me squirm in his embrace.

You can't do this.

You're not strong enough.

My fingernails dug into his chest. I wriggled and fought to get free.

But he kept kissing me, holding me, forcing me to take what he gave.

He'd never been coldblooded before. Icy and impenetrable. Explosive and stubborn. But never violent against my wishes. Never tried to take something that wasn't his.

He groaned into my mouth, his tongue withdrawing, his lips leaving mine.

Our eyes locked and he showed me everything. The fear. The apology. The pain.

"Be my canvas."

"It's too late," I whispered.

His forehead pressed against mine. "It *is* too late. Everything is too fucking late. I'm too late to make any money. Too late to fix my business. Too late to save my daughter. Too late to repair everything broken between us. But it's not too late to say goodbye."

My heart jackhammered as he clutched my hair and tugged, forcing my neck back, kissing his way along the column of my exposed throat. "I'm running out of control. I'll ask one last time before I won't ask anymore. Be my canvas, O. Let me paint you, fuck you. I need to remember you for always."

I shivered at the naked beg in his voice. "I can't."

"You can." His lips were cool, but his tongue hot as he captured me in another kiss. He breathed against my mouth, "Fuck me one last time, O. You said your goodbyes the other night. You used me for closure. I pleaded with you not to make me do it. I begged you to stop. But you didn't. You took from me. And now, I'm taking from you."

I tried to push him away again, cursing how my blood bubbled and wetness gathered between my legs. "I didn't rape you, Gil. Don't you *dare* insinuate I'm anything like that bitch who—"

"You're not." Capturing my wrist, he jerked my hand down and pressed it over his erection. "I wouldn't be hard if I didn't want you. I've never been with anyone else. It's always been you. It will *always* be you. You'll move on after this. You'll travel the world and find a perfect ending, all while I rot in my jail cell. The only thing that will keep me going is my memories of you."

He rocked his hardness into my palm. "Let me have you, one last time. Let me paint you, love you, fuck you, imprint you." His lips trailed along my jaw until he found my mouth again, kissing me long and slow.

I did my best not to respond. Not to kiss him back. But a low moan echoed unwillingly in my throat.

"Let me try to forget you, Olin Moss, even though I know that's impossible." Stepping back, he let me go.

My hand fell from touching him. My lips tingled from his kiss. And we stood facing each other as if drawing the battle lines for war.

He acted as if he'd force me against my will, and I actually believed he would do it. But I also knew, he'd hate himself the entire time. He'd use me, but he'd ultimately suffer.

He was right.

We'd run out of time.

Everything was too late.

The end was here, and there was no right or wrong anymore.

I couldn't be with him. I shouldn't do this. But...it was all over anyway.

Another night together wouldn't change that.

Gil shuddered, his eyes dark. His erection wedged against his paint-splattered work jeans while the black hoodie he always wore in his time-lapse videos held colours from other canvases.

I might be the last one he ever painted.

All the rage inside me vanished.

He's losing everything.

Not just his freedom but also his art.

He'd stood in my apartment a few months ago and asked how I'd tolerated losing dance. He'd genuinely seemed perplexed that I'd survived having such an integral part of me stolen.

He'd told me he wouldn't survive if he couldn't paint.

I'd believed him then.

I believe him now.

Jail wasn't just an institution where he would be captive. It was the accident, the car, the restaurant window. Jail was going to strip him of his ability to paint. Possibly forever.

I sighed heavily, allowing my body to shed its terror and embrace lust.

Deep, deadly, unhealthy lust.

"Will Olive be okay if you're gone for a while?"

Gil stayed frozen, his hands balled by his sides. "She's with Justin. It's best they have time to figure their shit out before I can't be there."

"What happens after?"

His throat worked as he swallowed. "I walk away."

"And if this destroys us even more?"

"Then we're destroyed."

"This won't change anything."

He nodded. "I know."

"I can't be in love with you anymore, Gilbert Clark."

"I'm not asking you to be."

"I should curse you. I should hate you."

"You should."

Tears erupted out of frustration. *"So why can't I?"*

He stepped into me, cupping my cheeks with quaking hands. "Because I can't stop loving you either."

I couldn't *feel* anymore.

I didn't have the strength.

But I also couldn't *lie* anymore.

I didn't have the power.

"You're a walking gift of pain, Gilbert Clark."

"And you're the ultimate gift of redemption, Olin Moss." Brushing his thumbs over my cheekbones, he let me go to flip his black hood up and over his messy hair.

His mask in place. His face obscured.

I flinched. "You're going to record this?"

"Yes."

"Will you post it?"

"Yes."

"Why?"

He captured me again. "Because I deserve a lifetime of agony for what I did. This video will always be there. It will be waiting for me on the day that I'm free. It will be a constant reminder of my one and only canvas—my true work of art that I did nothing but try to destroy. You."

"I don't want to see it."

"Then you won't."

"I don't want to see you."

"But you're the only one who does."

I shuddered.

I didn't want to love him, need him, miss him.

The Master of Trickery.

The Wizard of Paint.

The Love Executioner.

But my head tipped up.

His tipped down.

We kissed.

And our denials were over.

Chapter Twenty-Six

Gil

O STOOD ON the centre of the black sheet.

Her breasts bare.

Her pussy covered by her black G-string.

Watching her strip had almost stolen everything I had left. My cock threatened to snap off. The tension between us hissed and crackled. And my lungs refused to deliver more than a few sips of oxygen.

I'd meant what I said.

Waiting for her to come home had given me far too much time to imagine what it would feel like to be with her one last time. If she hadn't agreed...I honestly didn't know what I would've done.

I'd like to think I would've had the strength to walk out the door.

But...

This was O.

This was the only woman I could be with without reliving the night Olive was created.

This was the other piece of my heart, and I couldn't go to jail without feeling whole one last time.

Keeping my distance, I brought my paints onto the sheet by her feet. I arranged my brushes and sponges, positioned my airbrush, and drank in every inch of her.

We didn't speak while I prepared.

Our silence only added pain to the quietness already torturing us.

With shaking hands, I turned on the small video camera I

used to capture my creations. I muted it so no sound was captured. I angled it so O took centre stage. And I made sure my hood tugged low over my face so I remained anonymous, even though mug shots and newspapers had shown the world who I was.

I wasn't a talented artist.

I was a murderer.

Forever and for always.

Moving toward O, I sucked in a useless breath as she trembled. I couldn't tear my eyes off her perfection. Off the scars on her back. Off the ink on her skin. Off her strength and femininity and broken dancer's grace.

"You've always been the most beautiful creature in the world to me." I ducked to my haunches, unscrewing a midnight blue vial, already diluted and ready for my airgun.

She bit her lip, keeping her gaze on the wall beyond. I hadn't asked her to hold a pose. She didn't need to. Just the way she stood echoed with angelic poise. Her wrists always delicate. Her fingers always curved. Her neck arched with royalty.

She looked as if she'd once had wings, weightless and balletic before a car crash stripped them from her, leaving her to the mercy of monsters like me.

"Wh-What design are you going to do?" her voice remained just above a whisper.

"I don't know yet."

"You don't have a concept?"

"I have a feeling."

"A feeling?" Her gaze snapped to mine, despite herself.

I loved watching her study me, bowed at her feet.

I wanted her to remember me like this, worshiping her, wanting her.

"Secrets."

She frowned. "Secrets?"

"The piece will be called Secrets."

Her eyes leapt from mine, fully aware of the connection binding us exquisitely tight together. I felt it. She felt it. Fate fucking felt it.

Her eyes glossed. "Secrets are always drenched in pain."

I nodded, testing the spray before standing in front of her. "They are. That's what you are." I kissed her softly. "Love painted in pain."

She swayed as I pulled back and pressed the button on my airgun. The spray of midnight shot from the muzzle, instantly changing skin to canvas.

I didn't normally cover a girl in one shade.

I didn't usually allow creativity to control me.

But this wasn't a commission.

This wasn't prepaid and scripted.

This was just us.

A canvas and a body painter.

Both in love.

Both in agony.

Both fighting goodbye.

Time slipped between the silence, blending the two until the world no longer existed. All I saw was O. All she felt was my paint. Slowly, I covered her from head to toe in deep, distressing blue.

The longer I painted, the tighter her muscles became. Her face strained and eyes full of memory. She was back in my warehouse the night I'd drugged and kidnapped her. She was back to cursing my existence.

"Jeffrey was my real uncle...did you know that?"

My voice snapped her from the past and did exactly what I hoped. Her eyes narrowed, locking onto me as I shaded the inside of her thigh. "What?"

"Jeffrey...I know you would've heard Olive call him uncle." I wiped the excess off, leaning in to spray again. "He was her great uncle. My father's brother."

"What are you doing?" She shifted a little, breaking the position she'd chosen.

Wrapping my hand around her ankle, I shook my head slowly. "Don't move."

She locked in place all while her voice rained from above. "Why are you telling me about Jeffrey? Why bring his name into this...when you're painting me?"

"To distract you."

"Distract me."

"To talk to you."

"To confess."

I nodded. "To confess."

She shivered as I added a final lashing over her kneecap and reared back. The whites of her eyes and teeth popped from the darkness of her face, body, and hair. She wasn't O anymore. She was a faceless secret with no substance. A white lie that hadn't been told yet.

As I added more depth and detail, the lie would grow, the

secret would swell, and the damage it reaped would magnify.

I no longer had frost around my heart. No icicles in my blood or snow within my voice. I was done freezing O out from my truth.

I wanted her to ask.

To know.

Unscrewing the empty vial from my airbrush, I reached for quicksilver.

She swayed as I added a splattering of stars on her leg. A twinkling galaxy over her stomach. The admission that secrets didn't just affect a single planet but the cosmos.

"Why did you sleep with her? You had to have known people would have helped you?" The question strangled in her throat. "Why did you throw us away?"

Finally.

Finally a question.

A question shooting a dagger straight into the heart of all our problems.

I looked up as I dipped a fine-tipped brush into blood-red pigment. "If we do this...no more secrets."

She held my stare, trembling beneath my colours. "No more secrets."

"Okay then." I cleared my throat again. "I threw us away because I was a fucking idiot. Tallup threatened your future. I kept it to myself because I was afraid." I drew a line over the top of her hipbone, tracing what felt right, but unsure what it would become. "I wanted to protect you, not ruin you."

"You ruined yourself."

I continued painting, half in the otherworld of creation where noise was muted and reality dulled and half with her in a dreamlike state of confession. "I was young and stupid."

"You were targeted and molested."

"I should've trusted someone." I drew my brush down her leg. "I should've trusted you."

She shivered as I continued staining midnight with blood. "Instead you broke up with me."

"I kept my distance because even though I'd done what she'd asked, my freedom came with consequences."

Her stomach tensed as I swapped red for black. Soaking up the ink, I sponged sinister shadows above her G-string and along her belly.

She breathed, "Consequences?"

"One of her conditions was that I could never talk to you or any other girl in school."

She gasped as I left her skin and pressed my sponge right between her legs. Hard. Hard enough to squeeze black paint and watch it dribble over her knickers-covered core.

"Why?"

"Because she knew I loved you."

"But why didn't you come to me when she left school? She wasn't there to terrorize you anymore."

I fought back the lashes of regret as I traded black for magenta. "I was going to."

"What?" She froze, her eyes locking onto mine.

"I had a plan. I waited to be sure she'd gone for good. I made up a script so I could talk to you without blurting nonsense. I had full intentions of finding you on Monday and begging your forgiveness."

Her face twisted; her eyes glazed with wetness. "But you ran away."

"Tallup visited me." I painted faster, my brush becoming an extension of my pain, using my secrets as its colour. "She brought Olive."

Silence once again whispered in as O stood still.

"The moment I saw her, O...I couldn't stop it. I fell in love." I painted harder, cursing the design that only now I recognised. "I fell in love and I knew, without a shadow of a doubt, that her life came before mine. I didn't have a choice."

O continued to shiver silently, giving me far too much space to fill. "I stole from my old man that night, and ran away. I didn't say goodbye. I made it work in London for a bit. Made enough cash with painting and selling my work to get by. Then I earned a few bigger jobs. I was hired to graffiti a local hostel and its dorm rooms with images of downtown. While Olive grew, I tried to find a more reliable income. However, time passed. Olive went to preschool. Then kindergarten. And I kept painting."

I looked up.

I ignored the scene I'd painted on her thigh.

A scene of a boy holding a fleece blanket, the blanket trying to escape on a kite string, hiding something priceless. "I'd already given you up, O. I couldn't give up my art too."

She trembled again. Her stomach fluttering as I once again traded brushes for the airgun. I didn't have control anymore. My body bypassed my mind and painted purely from my heart.

Whatever masterpiece O became tonight would have no input from me, just instinct, just hope, just pain.

"But you became the Master of Trickery."

"I did." My voice sounded rough, strangled. "Thanks to Jeffrey."

"What?"

"He appeared one night, knocking on my one-bedroom apartment. Olive was asleep. He claimed to be my dad's brother. He'd been looking for me and heard my name at a local market where a wholesaler sold my paintings."

"Why had he been looking for you?"

I continued painting, switching methods and mediums, trading pigment and metallic. "Dad died. Alcohol poisoning. He told me the whores left town, and the bank seized the house and sold it. Jeffrey was the one listed as next of kin."

"So…he came to give you an inheritance?" She sucked in a breath as I took her hand, painting a row of dying blackbirds up her arm.

"No. He'd already spent what pittance he got from the foreclosure." I swallowed, bowing my head over her shoulder as I traded birds for feathers, mimicking her tattoo, dressing her in a cape of them. "He tracked me down 'cause he thought I might have more money."

Her body swayed as I went behind her, tracing my brush over her scars, adding another picture to her ink. "He blackmailed you right from the start?"

My heart hurt. I didn't want to tell this part of my tale. It once again showed how gullible I was. How stupid. "No. To begin with, he was the perfect uncle. It took a very long time for me to drop my guard. To stop throwing the door in his face or walking across the street if he tried to talk to me. I kept Olive away from him at all costs. I told him to leave me alone."

I bent my knees, and my eyes became level with her gorgeous arse. The muscle definition and sexiness of her grace fogged my thoughts, conjuring more explicit designs. It was easier to tell her this way. Where she couldn't see me. Judge me. "A year passed, and he still stuck around. My resolve to continue hating him just because he was my father's brother faded a little. I let him buy me lunch. I actually listened to what he had to say. I began to *trust*."

My lips pulled back in a snarl. My brush slipped down her crack with temper.

She flinched and went to move away, but I grabbed her

hipbone, smudging my previous work. "Don't. Don't move."

It took a few heartbeats until I could uncurl my hand and continue. "I learned we were more similar than I wanted to admit. He painted cars for a living. Doing decals and pinstripe, special one-of-a-kind commissions on boy racer's wet dreams."

I made my way around to her side again, drawing a tiny car on her foot. "He let me set up an easel in the back. I painted there while Olive was at school. It was…nice."

My voice once again slipped into unbridled rage. "He was the one who taught me to paint other things than walls and paper. He showed me how to do bold lines on the panels of a jeep and airbrush wings on a Ferrari. Anything was paintable. Cups and plates. Glass and fabric."

"Women," O murmured.

I nodded. "Women."

"Is that how you got into painting girls?"

"Yes." I moved onto her calf, not caring what I painted just that I did. That I bled out the pain in purple and blue and grey. "He joked about it, showing me other artists who'd transformed human into landscape and animal. The moment I saw the pictures, I knew what I wanted to do. I wanted to create magic. To twist reality. To form an illusion just like others had."

I forced myself to chuckle rather than fucking cry. "The first few I did were terrible. The next were passable. Woman after woman. Night after night. I dabbled with camouflage and shadow. Olive was kept safe with a babysitter. I told myself I did this for our future. So I could afford to buy any dream she desired. I grew better. My skills improved. Until one night, I nailed the perfect illusion." I let my brush hypnotise me for a moment, needing a break.

O waited for several heartbeats before asking, "What illusion?"

"I made a girl vanish into a backdrop of vineyards and wine barrels. A huge movie poster for some rom-com that had been thrown out." I swallowed hard, chasing back the acid in my mouth. "Jeffrey congratulated me. Took me out. Praised me. And I let down my fucking guard. I told him about Olive. I offered to let him meet her. I invited him into our lives."

O stayed quiet but tangled up enough in my story to ask, "If he spent all that time helping you, why did he start hurting you?"

I shrugged. "Jealousy? Hatred? I never found out." Changing to my airbrush again, I went to her other side, allowing the vibrant aqua to highlight her skin. "Thanks to him, I started painting women all the time. Most of them for free, salvaging paints from second-hand suppliers, begging for finished tubes to do as much as I could on the cheap. One girl brought her friends to watch. They filmed me painting, and put it up on social media. The rest…is history."

I looked up for the first time in a while. I needed to see her now. "The post went viral. I can't even remember what I'd painted. But a few weeks later, I had a business profile, email account, and companies asking me to paint for them."

Rocking back on my heels, I shrugged again, helpless beneath the truth. "The money they offered, O? It was ten, twenty, forty, a *thousand* times more than what I could get for a hanging canvas. I accepted every gig. I gave half of everything I made to Jeffrey to say thank you. I introduced him to Olive, believing I'd finally found someone I could trust."

I dropped my eyes, unable to hold her stare. "I was lonely. I'd done my best to raise her as a single dad, but I knew I was lacking. I didn't know shit. I wasn't enough. She needed a bigger network to rely on so she didn't turn out like me."

"What happened?" she whispered.

"For a year or so, things were fine. He came round for dinners. He helped me source the warehouse. I offered to let him move in with us. But then, one day, I got a gig worth a fortune. Almost a hundred thousand pounds to do three girls camouflaged into a peacock. It took twenty-four hours, but it was one of my best pieces. Jeffrey popped by after his shift to see, and something switched in him. I felt it. I didn't know what it meant, but by the next week, he asked for a substantial loan."

I wiped my mouth with the back of my painted hand. "I gave it to him. Of course, I did. I was nothing without him. But the week after, he asked for more. And again, I gave it to him. I wanted to share everything because he was the reason I had such success."

"You were very generous."

"I was looking after family." I threw myself back into painting, my eyes glazed and colours finding homes upon her flesh. "I couldn't look after you, so I was determined to look after those I could."

I shook my head, rushing now, needing this over. "One night, he asked for everything I'd made on a recent commission. I'd already put it into a savings account for Olive's education and I couldn't withdraw it due to the terms of the account. He left in a rage. Came back drunk. I kicked him out and told him to return sober and tell me why he needed the money, then we'd talk."

Scowling at O's foot, I hunched into myself, finding it unbearable to admit. "The next day, he took Olive."

O sucked in a breath. "He took her because you refused to give him what you'd saved for her?"

I nodded, painting furiously up her leg, bringing to life little fishes of truth, swimming bright in a sea of secrets. I hadn't gone to the police because I didn't want them to know Olive's origins and risk having her taken from me. I'd stupidly thought I could handle it.

That this family spat would resolve itself without a fight.

I'd slowly fallen further and further.

Bankrupt.

Broken.

Until finally, an accessory for murder.

"How did blackmail turn into killing four young girls?" Olive asked, tears smudging her midnight cheeks.

I dared look up, embracing the agony. My hood cut out my peripheral, keeping my attention locked on her. "He was always a psychopath. I found out later that my father's whores hadn't left...he'd killed them. Jeffrey constantly moved because he couldn't restrain his thirst for death. And I introduced that fucking animal to my daughter."

"That's why you let him beat you up."

"Anything to keep his temper away from Olive."

"That's why you gave him every penny."

"Anything to keep her alive."

"That's why you were filthy the nights I came over."

"I was out looking for Olive, trying to stop another girl getting hurt."

O cried openly now. "And that's why you drank."

"To try to forget what I'd caused." My voice cracked. "It was my fault he took her in the first place."

Her entire body shuddered.

She collapsed to her knees beside me.

We were kissing before I realised a fucking tear ran down my cheek.

Chapter Twenty-Seven

Olin

HIS BODY CRASHED into mine.

His hands flew up, grabbing my cheeks and holding me firm. He didn't care about the paint, the art, or the confessions he'd strewn around my feet. He kissed me hard, tilting his head and licking me with twisted desire.

Dragging me closer, we bowed to each other, his body still towering over mine. We kissed savage and unforgiving. Gentle and tender weren't welcome here.

I'd had my dose of violence, and this was his. This was him doing his best to destroy me and remember me all at once.

This was a punishment.

Punishment for himself and the future he faced.

My hands shot to his face, skimming into his hair and pushing away the black hood. I tore off his mask, revealing the tortured painter, the broken lover, the boy I would always miss.

His teeth clacked on mine as he kissed me deeper, pushing me down until I sprawled on the black sheet on the floor. Bottles of paint spilled, oozing their vibrant contents into the fabric. A tub of rhinestones tipped over, scattering brilliant sparkles and sticking to my skin.

We didn't care about any of it.

He pressed himself on top of me the moment I lay on my back. His hand cupped my breast, squeezing and claiming, making them heavy and throbbing.

His touch smeared his art without a thought.

I arched my back, demanding more.

Needing more.

I moaned as he spread my legs and settled between them. Once again, he was fully clothed and I was gowned in just his creation. No words were exchanged. No soul-stealing stares. Just the urgency to connect.

He kissed me deeper, stealing our final shreds of sanity.

His taste erased everything. His touch deleted the outside world. It was just us. How it should've been. How it could never be.

His hand skated down my breast and over my waist to my hip. Tugging at the knickers he'd painted and pressed a black dripping sponge against my clit. With a savage kiss, he pulled them down until I kicked them away.

The minute I was bare, a slim piece of virgin skin amongst the colours he'd transformed me with, he fumbled with his belt.

I helped him, pushing his hand away and unbuckling the leather. He shuddered as I unbuttoned and unzipped his jeans, then arched his hips as I pushed down the barrier between us.

He groaned as he settled back between my legs. The warmth of his cock, belly, and thighs made me shiver with pleasure. He was heat and hope all at once.

"Fuck," he grunted as my fingers dived between our shared warmth and wrapped around his length. His teeth clamped on my bottom lip, sucking it into his mouth before kissing me roughly. Our lips never unlocked. We kissed violently but also slowly, devouring each other with ruthless determination. The glide of his tongue almost distracted me from the feather of his fingers over my core.

My back bowed as the feather became penetration.

I cried out as he drove two fingers deep.

He groaned as he found me wet.

His thumb rocked on my clit as his five o'clock shadow punished my skin; his kiss so deep, he smashed my head against the floor.

His fingers withdrew.

The soft nudge of his cock replaced them.

I froze in his arms, teetering on the precious knife-edge of anticipation.

His tongue swept into my mouth.

His cock thrust swift and thick into me.

God.

I was totally at his mercy.

Totally with him.

Totally his.

The final barrier Gil had always hid behind shattered. I felt everything he did. I felt his regret, his worry, his love. I felt his teeth and tongue as they left me hollow. I felt his thrusting hips and pounding cock as he stole me from any other thoughts.

He invaded me.

Consumed me.

Made sure that I would never, ever forget him.

"Please, Gil." I didn't know what I asked for. But he gave it to me. He thrust deeper, kissed harder. Grabbing the back of his nape, I forced our mouths together. I spread my legs shamelessly, granting him space to sink further, drive faster.

My body flushed with wetness and want.

"Shit you feel…" His forehead crashed on mine. He clutched the floor beside my ears, pulling himself up and into me, pinning me to the floor with his hips. "You're mine, O."

I didn't know how to reply.

I wasn't his.

I couldn't be.

But I nodded as his thrusts increased. His hips rolled. And his thumb found my clit again.

Fever sprang through my blood. Hot and hungry for the release he conjured. I purred, throwing my head back, scratching my nails on his hoodie.

Once again we fucked in the middle of blues and purples. Other paint bottles tipped over thanks to the sheet tangling beneath us.

We grew wild and furious.

The sensation of having him on top.

The hardness of him inside me.

The way his eyes sank into mine, begging access to my heart all while his body conquered my soul.

His paint had the magic to lie, hide sins, and camouflage flaws. He could create a masterpiece from imperfection. Too bad that tonight, our masterpiece was over, and the magic had to die.

"I love you, O." His voice resembled a colour, a dark broody copper. Something that had dulled with reality but could sparkle once again if polished.

Our eyes locked.

Gil paused inside me.

The moment stretched for far too long, turning this from goodbye to something unbearably complicated.

"Gil…I—"

"Don't." He shook his head. "Don't."

With our gazes still locked, he pushed harder, rocked deeper. He thrust so hard, I cried out, squirming under him. The pinching, consuming pressure of him. The delicious discomfort that followed.

My core rippled around him, welcoming and rebelling against his thrusts.

This was dangerous.

So, so dangerous.

Already I felt the crack in my heart, the tiny hairline fracture that would keep growing, continue to spread until it just tinkled apart.

I clutched him closer.

Our foreheads pressed together as he rode me with awe and dismay.

He kissed me again, joining our mouths as well as our bodies. Carnal and crude, pleasure spiralled from every cell.

We both became lost to it.

Lost to the cresting, lusting release.

I rocked my hips up, grinding myself onto his thick cock, seeking solace from the overbearing connection we shared. This wasn't fucking. This was something so much worse.

This was raw and bare. And it pushed me to the brink.

I wanted to surrender to him.

I wanted to give in to my heart and forgive and forget and promise I'd be there no matter what happened.

But then he shoved away the rawness, pulled curtains over the tenderness, and rutted into me. He deliberately shut down any feelings between us because feelings would ruin us.

His thumb rocked with single-minded determination to make me come.

My mind scrambled with the primitive instinct to mate.

I held onto his hoodie, throwing my head back and giving him utmost control.

Fireworks crackled in my blood.

I opened my legs wider, taking more of him. He sucked in a loud breath, stretching me, taking me. Our rhythm became wilder, brutally deep.

"Fuck, O. I need you to come." His hips rocked against me; his thumb pressed with pain.

Fireworks became comets.

Comets became a supernova.

My neck arched, rising off the sheet. "God—" Searing pleasure split me in two as he drove as hard as he could. My core squeezed around him, over and over and *over.*

I came and it brought a whole suitcase of fears.

I cried out as another wave caught me by surprise.

And Gil lost it.

His lips descended on mine, hips surged upward, and he fucked me with mind-numbing need.

He gave up part of his humanity. He traded decorum for death. The death of love between us. The sheet crashed down from the wall where it'd been pinned, floating over us as his hips slapped against mine.

I couldn't breathe. I couldn't think.

All I could do was hold onto him as he broke.

His heart thundered against mine.

He seemed possessed, entranced, utterly broken.

Another wave of paradise shot up my spine, hinting that one orgasm wasn't enough.

He felt it.

His green eyes gleamed, and his hips pounded unforgivingly into mine, punishing me all over again, dragging me up the mountain with him, coiling me, tightening me.

His cock grew bigger inside me, hardening, thickening.

And then, there was nowhere else to go.

We plummeted together.

Giving in to the rapture of release, knowing the minute it was over…we were too.

Chapter Twenty-Eight

Olin

I WOKE TO heart pangs and belly pain.

My core was bruised from the rough lovemaking we'd indulged in.

My skin still held stars and feathers and a school of fish swimming up my leg.

Smudges ruined perfection and fingerprints smeared crisp lines, I didn't need physical reminders that we'd had sex…my body shouted the truth in its painted defilement.

Along with my skin, my apartment had a paint-spattered sheet on the floor and evidence of emotional carnage.

But Gil had gone.

Along with his box of brushes, colours, and tricks.

We'd said physically what we couldn't say verbally, and he'd left the moment we'd untangled ourselves and our futures, then said a faint farewell at the door.

If I let myself think about him, agony was a sharp arrow waiting to stab me in the chest and deliver a bolt of poison. So, I did my best to keep him on the outskirts of my mind. To stretch out the kink in my spine and climb into the shower. To wash away the final body paint I would ever wear.

It didn't help that I stopped in front of the mirror before sluicing his art down the drain. Or that I traced the many images hidden upon my skin. Of a peach blanket with a baby tied to a kite string. Of a boy holding a bunch of wildflowers outside a house he couldn't enter. Of a man watching a woman through a window he couldn't open.

Of so many things that Gil treasured and couldn't have.

Other images were ruined beyond recognition, bruised from reality to muddy memory.

But through the smears, I noticed dead girls painted and hushed upon my thigh. Tombstones decorated my hipbones. A prison cell glowed beneath my ribs. And through it all, a calligraphy stroke of letters looped around my belly like jewellery.

Love is misery. Lust is loss. Family is my failure.

Tears fell and mixed with hot water as I stumbled into the shower.

I cried all over again for things I could no longer differentiate. Every incident had blended into one painful despair.

I did my best to stop my tears as I finished washing away Gil's confessions. I tried to reset my scattered thoughts and focus on the monotonous and uninspiring task of heading to work.

Once dressed, I straightened up my place, folded the ruined sheet, realigned the furniture, and found my phone abandoned on the kitchen bench.

It flashed with a message.

A dangerous, deadly message.

And I made the stupid mistake of clicking on it.

Gil: *O, I have so much to say about last night. So much that it's literally killing me that I no longer have the luxury of talking to you. I asked for closure. I got it. I have to be happy with what happened. I know you said you didn't want to see the video of me painting you, but it's attached below...just in case. And don't worry, I deleted the part where we slept together before uploading to a public internet page.*

The good news? The video garnered a few positive comments before the haters turned up, and I received an email about a commission. Obviously, it's too late to do, but it gives me hope that I might be able to resurrect my business when I'm free again.

I love you.

Thank you.

For everything.

Tears welled and spilled as I clicked on the video.

The emotion I'd been hiding from found me, slipping through my ribs with its tiny pitchforks of agony.

It's over.

How could it be over?

My tears ran faster.

I didn't have the strength to watch what we did last night. To witness Gil hood-obscured and in his element of painting while I stood stiff and vulnerable as his canvas.

But I also couldn't turn it off.

My knees gave out, buckling me into a chair as the video skipped forward, increasing minutes into a blur of brushes and colour.

I swiftly transformed from normal human to some midnight, galaxy wearing goddess with power over birds, fishes, and every other symbol of secrecy that Gil adorned me with. I popped against the black background, giving the watcher no hint of where we were.

We were in a black hole, utterly alone and unfindable.

My heart stopped beating as the video suddenly slowed to normal speed, and Gil kissed me.

I watched as I kissed him back. I couldn't tear my eyes away from my hands as I pushed off his hood, revealing the Master of Trickery to the world.

He looked regal.

He looked ruined.

Truth blazed with its own colour on the video. Vicious and vibrant, a hue far too bright to ignore.

How could I make anyone believe I wasn't in love with him   that I wouldn't do anything in my power still to help him—when the evidence bled from the screen?

It was so blisteringly obvious.

So painfully real.

No lie could hide it.

No paint could camouflage it.

I was in love with him.

He was in love with me.

There was no end or over for that kind of bond.

Gil had let me walk away because he didn't have a choice. In a couple of days, he was stepping into a courtroom and might not walk out as a free man for decades. He'd let me go because he felt it was the best thing for me, even with blatant evidence that we were made for each other.

That our bodies weren't the only thing joining last night.

That our souls had found each other as kids and had been claimed ever since.

I was an idiot.

A stupid, *stupid* fool to think I could find happiness overseas with new people, new places, new me.

Gil would always be the key to my happiness, no matter what he'd done.

And the fact that he'd set me free showed just how deeply he cared.

Showed that my happiness meant more to him than his own.

Showed that Gilbert Clark had grown up and shattered the ice that'd protected him since his childhood.

More tears rolled as our video kiss hissed with passion and heartbreak.

Everything we'd done last night replayed in crystal detail.

The pain.

The ecstasy.

The *realness.*

It hadn't been sex. It'd been a testament to soul-mates, consuming two hearts, knitting two bodies into one.

I trembled as Gil entered me.

Last night, it'd felt raw and violent. A claiming plunge that wrenched my back off the sheet and made me cling to him.

Now, I knew the truth.

I paused the video.

I froze time as Gil's body joined with mine, and our eyes locked onto each other's.

The way he mounted me *was* raw and violent, but it was also achingly vulnerable and intense. The way he curled over me in protection. The way he kissed me with devotion. The way his body worshipped mine with every apology and sweetness he could.

We'd made love last night.

We'd made promises we hadn't been aware of.

Promises that couldn't be broken.

Chapter Twenty-Nine

Gil

WALKING INTO THE courtroom seemed simple enough. Shoes on feet and suit on body, striding into a room just like any other day.

But it wasn't any other day.

It was judgement day, and I was fucking terrified.

For the rest of the week, after I'd painted O, I'd avoided all thoughts of her and focused entirely on my daughter.

O and I...we were over.

And soon, I would have to say goodbye to my child too.

Olive sensed my urgency for her to accept Justin's care. Her suspicious little nature turned into clingy need, wanting to be near me in ways she'd never done before.

And to be fair, I clung back.

I held on for all I was worth because I knew this day was coming.

My days were entirely Olive's. I did whatever she wanted. I set up a contract with Justin that I would pay back whatever he spent on Olive's care while I was gone. I even had an enquiry for a commission or two, thanks to the video I'd shared of painting O. I'd told her the truth that I hadn't shared the part where we'd had sex.

But I had shared the part where she pushed down my hood, revealing me to the online world, and the exquisite agony of our first kiss.

I wanted to show the people who wanted me dead that I was human too.

That yes, I'd made mistakes.

A fucking lot of mistakes.

And I would continue to make them, just like them.

But I was prepared to answer for those mistakes without needing death threats and pure hate.

"You all good?"

I looked across at my lawyer. Brad Scott was a typical lifer in a suit. I'd met him twice now, being open and honest in his office, learning his lesson on how I'd be torn to shreds on the stand. For a crown appointed counsel, he gave me confidence that I wasn't just another schmuck to half-heartedly fight for.

His face had switched from trying not to judge me for killing four women to curiosity in how it'd all fallen into place.

He trusted that I hadn't been the one to murder innocence and now had a thin vein of pride that I'd killed the bastard who'd done it.

I was under no illusion that today would not have a happy ending for me, but I hoped he could convince the jury that what I said was the truth.

I had no intention of lying, embellishing, or using tricks to avoid my punishment.

I just didn't want to have to pay more than what I owed.

"Yeah, I'm okay." My voice was rough and eyes gritty from refusing to break in front of Olive. Saying goodbye had bled my heart dry. I hadn't recovered from ending it with O. I'd fallen to my knees losing her, and now I'd collapsed into hell losing my daughter.

"You have things in place like we talked about?"

I nodded. "I filed my will—not that there's anything to bequeath—and signed that contract with my friend who is officially Olive's caregiver while I'm gone. Child Protective Services have been dealt with and are happy with the arrangement. I did what you said."

"Good."

Silence fell between us again.

I'd made Justin swear to stay away from court. To spend the day with Olive and focus on taking her to school for re-orientation. She'd officially start back next week, once my fate was decided.

Justin had once again proven to be a friend who deserved a seat on the council of heaven. He was so selfless that it sometimes seemed sinister. I caught myself searching for an ulterior motive, some sign he was evil and running a long game like my uncle.

I almost wanted him to turn out to be a bad guy because I

couldn't accept that there were people as good as him. As good as O. They were the same. Two generous, loyal people who shouldn't have to put up with the likes of me.

"Does your kid know what's happening?" Brad asked, shuffling his legal pad and pen into orderly fashion on the desk. We sat in court, waiting for everything to begin.

I cleared my throat. "I told her I would still be close and that she can visit but that I won't be living with her for a while."

"How did it go?"

I laughed painfully. "Awful."

"Always is." He gave me a pitiful look. "Just remember, nothing lasts forever. Good, bad, terrible—it all passes in the end."

I didn't reply.

Last night, while hugging Olive, I'd done my best not to suffocate her, knowing my allotment of hugs had come to an end. Justin had given us privacy, vowing he'd guard her while I could not.

I'd never felt more destitute as I had in that moment. Asking another man to look after my own flesh and blood. I didn't have shit in my bank account, and I didn't have shit in my human worth to ever pay him back.

My heart pounded as more people trickled into the courtroom. Brad Scott had fought many cases, representing low-level criminals and white-collar, but I doubted he'd dealt with a case where the public stood outside the courthouse, demanding justice by cutting off my hands so I could never paint and then tying me to a tree to bleed out.

The family of the girls who'd been killed sat silently on the benches, waiting to hear my fate. A few journalists with pens poised over notepads and recording devices also waited for the show. It wasn't a big audience—probably court requested so emotions didn't get out of hand—but I had no support or friends in the sea of people who wanted me to die.

Justin was elsewise occupied.

And I hadn't told O what time I would face judgement.

I didn't want her to see my end.

My gaze danced around the space, not making eye contact with anyone. The overall atmosphere was of death and decay, ready to send me to a coffin rather than a cell.

The jury hadn't come in yet. I didn't know how courts worked or what I was in for.

I would learn as it unfolded and then suffer the

consequences.

"How will this go?" I linked my hands together, thinking of the paint supplies and boxes that I'd put into storage that Justin had in his apartment building. I thought about Olive and her pretty smile and not being able to tuck her into bed tonight. I thought about the waste of a life all because I'd always been so fucking naïve and too proud to ask for help.

I wanted help today.

But I didn't know how to ask for it.

"Well, you're slightly different. The public have put pressure on the system which is why your court date has been rushed. You'll be judged by a twelve-person jury. Once they're sworn in, the prosecution will present the evidence. Call a few witnesses if they have any. Maybe call you to the stand. And then, it's my turn. The judge has already read the case files but we'll give our side of the story as candidly and as truthfully as you did when we rehearsed the other day. Okay?"

I nodded even though nausea ran through me. "Okay."

"Good." He brushed lint off his navy suit. "Once everything has been presented, the jury will deliberate, and the judge will oversee the verdict."

"And then I go to prison."

"Maybe."

"But the chances of me going home tonight are nil."

His eyes narrowed, not sugar-coating or making false promises. "You committed murder, Mr. Clark. You admitted to it. Unless a miracle happens today, you're serving time. The question is how much and in what form."

I settled back in the hard chair as more people dribbled in. Time took on a strange nightmare quality. My body felt as if quicksand sucked at me, sinking into the floor.

A loud clang sounded behind me as the double doors of the crown court were closed. An official clerk asked us to rise for the honourable judge, and the selected jury trickled in from the backroom to be sworn in to assess me fairly but harshly.

By the time the judge pinned me with her icy blue eyes, her age wearing lines around her lips and white wig sitting perfectly on her head, I'd died, revived, and waited for death all over again.

Shifting in the chair, I pulled out a picture of Olive that I'd tucked inside my wallet. A printed piece of normal paper where the colours were wish-wash and paper creased, the image snapped on my phone and printed on Justin's printer.

It was us two nights ago while we'd sat at Justin's dining room table with the views over the Birmingham skyline while I taught her yet another technique of bending paint to her will. She was so smart. So talented. She could scale any goal and crush any dream.

She'd survived a year without me.

She could survive more, especially now that she had Justin looking out for her.

My thumb traced over her lovely face as the prosecution began presenting the evidence. I didn't listen. I already knew what happened to the girls as they'd slipped into drawn-out death. I already knew how Jeffery took his last breath.

I just kept my eyes on my daughter and waited for my turn to tell a story.

* * * * *

"Mr. Clark, as you're aware, today has been a long day and we've seen and heard some disturbing things. It's public knowledge that the family of the deceased want you to pay for what happened to their daughters, as they should—as anyone should when a loved one is stolen from them." Brad Scott paused, walking around with his hands in his suit pockets, looking at the jury, judge, and audience. "I'm an upstander of justice, and I'm also sworn to represent you to the best of my ability. Since taking you on as a client, I've had emails and phone calls, death threats and curses if I get you off what you deserve."

I swallowed, risking a quick look at the jury. They sat stone-faced and already resolute on their verdict, thanks to the overwhelming evidence presented by the prosecution. Sitting in the box in front of court was a terrifying place to be. I was on display. I had nowhere to hide. No way to stop the inevitable.

For four hours, they'd thrown every fact and grotesque incident that'd happened, sticking it entirely to me. Even I couldn't deny the facts—the man who orchestrated those poor girls' deaths was a monster and deserved to rot in hell.

Only problem was, I was only half that monster.

Brad continued, "Now that we've heard the evidence, I want to hear your version of events because it's not as black and white as the prosecution suggests."

I swallowed again, preparing to be honest about my life for the first time. When Brad had walked me through how things were going to go and what he expected me to say, I'd been against it. Why did they need to know my past? What did my high-school years have to do with now? But he'd insisted and…I'd agreed.

Scanning the sea of angry, judging faces, I did my best to stay unaffected. To deliver what was needed and accept the consequences.

O.

I froze.

I did a double take.

Olin Moss sat in the middle of the audience.

My gaze snagged with hers.

I locked in place and was owned entirely by her.

Fuck, seeing her here.

What…what is she doing here?

She bit her lip, her eyes wide and worried. How long had she sat there, obscured by the crowd? Why had she come?

She shouldn't be here supporting me. I'd set her free, goddammit.

"Mr. Clark? Can you inform the court who Jeffrey Clark was and why you killed him?"

A murmur went around the silent jury, tearing my gaze from O's. I had so much to admit. Why had it been easier confessing to total strangers than it did to someone I loved?

My eyes sought hers again, and I found strength that I should've found years ago.

She was here.

She hadn't left me.

Fuck, I loved her.

Sitting taller, I balled my hands and prepared to answer.

To admit…everything.

"Jeffrey Clark was my father's brother. I'd never met him until a few years ago. He came looking for me when my father died."

"Your father who died of alcohol poisoning and raised you in a whore house?"

I didn't flinch. "Yes."

"And Jeffrey gained your trust?"

"Unfortunately."

"Why did he go out of his way to make you trust him if his sole intention was to kill women?"

"At the time, I thought it was because he was family. I didn't know he was a psychopath who killed my father's whores. I didn't know who he truly was and wanted to believe not all my family was bad."

"But what he told you turned out to be a lie, correct?"

"Not everything. He said he was a car painter and detailer—that was true. He said he shared my drive to create art—that was also true. But everything else was just a ploy to take my money—money I only started earning because of his tutoring and pushing me into a business idea that I would never have had on my own."

"And what business was that?"

I avoided looking at O, feeling suddenly seedy. "Painting mostly naked women for large advertising campaigns."

"Why didn't Jeffrey just do that himself?"

I shrugged. "Not sure. He had the talent to do it. He painted the fourth girl, after all."

An electrified murmur shot around the court. Brad held up his hand for quiet, continuing his line of questioning.

I added before he could speak, "When my business became successful, he wanted what I had. What he didn't realise was I would've shared it all with him. I was unbelievably grateful for his guidance. He didn't have to take it by force."

"How did Jeffrey Clark take it by force, even when you ran out of income?"

"He kidnapped my daughter and blackmailed me."

"Why didn't you go to the police?"

"Because I didn't want them to know Olive's origins."

"Why not?"

"Because I didn't want them tracking down her birth mother and forcing me to give up custody."

O flinched. But she never looked away. Never left me hanging or alone.

Brad consulted his notes for a second, asking, "The mother of your child is called Jane Tallup, correct?"

"Yes."

"And who is Jane Tallup to you?"

"Your honour, what is the point in dragging up the past?" The prosecution's lawyer interrupted. "This isn't relevant to the case."

"I beg to differ, your honour. It has everything to do with the case." Brad scowled.

The female judge peered at both lawyers then me before finally nodding, "Carry on, Mr. Clark."

I cleared my throat. "Jane Tallup was my teacher at high-school."

"And she's the mother of your daughter."

I nodded again, annoyed at his repetitive question but aware of why he did it. To add more power to the punch line.

The court moved restlessly, no doubt thinking I'd forced myself onto her.

That I was a rapist as well as a killer.

Brad paused, then said, "She raped you when you were a teenager, correct? She alienated you from your friends, forbid you contact with the girl you were in love with, and molested you."

I curled my hands. "I was a stupid kid who should've spoken out but didn't."

"That sounds like you're blaming yourself for what happened."

"I'm blaming myself for the consequences of not telling people when I had the chance."

"Hurry it along," the judge muttered. "Get to the point."

The jury shifted on their chairs, their attention fully on me. My eyes stayed on O's hazel ones, safe as long as I just focused on her. I wanted to do this. I needed to be honest. To finally purge the rot inside me, to eradicate the poison I'd carried alone for so long, but it didn't mean it was easy.

My life was full of regrets.

Today would not be one of them.

"So, not only were you raped in your youth, but your teacher—an adult in a position of power—stripped you of safety and dumped a baby on you...all because she didn't want it?"

I nodded but then shook my head, unable to let Olive be talked about as if she wasn't wanted. "Olive might not have been wanted by her mother, and I might have been a vulnerable son of a bitch, but the moment I held her, I knew I loved her. She was wanted by me with all my heart, I just didn't know it until I met her."

My lawyer strolled calmly around the courtroom, nodding as if what I said made perfect sense. "Once you met your daughter, you left your home and family behind."

"I did."

"Why?"

"Because I didn't want anything to jeopardise Olive's future. My father wasn't a good role model; my family environment was abusive and unstructured. The only good thing in my life was my girlfriend who I'd hurt when I'd tried to do the right thing by breaking up with her. I was prepared to walk away so Olive had things I never did. Safety and good food and a father who cared about her."

"Very noble," the prosecution lawyer muttered.

I glared at him. "I just did what any father would do."

"Not every father." Brad pinned me to the chair. "Tell the court what happened the night you confronted Jeffrey with Olin Moss as his next victim."

A rise of energy swept around the jury as I admitted, "He shot me in the back, leaving me for dead."

"So your uncle tries to kill you and your father regularly used you as a punching bag." Brad peered at the jury. "I'd say family hasn't been kind to you, yet you did everything humanly possible to protect and claim back your daughter."

"Of course. I would never stop fighting for her."

"Would you kill another to protect her?"

He'd warned me he'd start sweet and swiftly divert into dark. I'd been waiting for the hard questions but it still made my heart skip. "I think anyone would if it was justified."

"Did you kill those innocent girls?"

I sat taller, keeping my hands on my thighs. "No, I did not. My uncle, Jeffrey Clark, did."

"The same Jeffrey Clark you killed?"

I nodded. "I ended his life for killing those girls as well as hurting Olin Moss and kidnapping my daughter."

My eyes searched out O's. Her skin had turned white and lips bitten with nervousness.

"So you admit that you *are* a murderer."

"Of a man who'd murdered girls, blackmailed me, and threatened rape to the only woman I've ever loved, yes. I am. I killed him."

A buzz of energy came from the jury again.

Brad ignored them. "But you didn't kill the other girls?"

"No."

His eyes narrowed. "Then why was the same brand and batch number of your paint found on their skin?"

I braced myself. "Because I painted them."

The buzz of energy became a tidal wave of tension.

I stayed focused on my lawyer, trusting him to navigate through the next chaos.

"How is it that you painted them and didn't stop them from being killed? If you painted them for your uncle to murder, you knew what their fate was. That makes you an accessory. You had a moral and civil obligation to report the crime."

"I didn't know."

My lawyer scoffed before the jury could. Such a weak and useless answer. But it was the truth, regardless. "You didn't know? How did you not know? You painted them to match the undergrowth where they were killed."

"He did that."

"You're saying he staged each murder depending on how the girls were painted?"

"Yes."

"You do realise how this sounds? That you're asking the jury to believe in an unbelievable excuse that you didn't ...know?"

This was where he wanted me to play my trump card.

I'd rehearsed my paragraph. I had my truth. It wouldn't set me free, but it would grant some resemblance of peace.

Looking again at O, I said, "I've done many commissions over the past few years. Some are garish and bright, some are fantastical and mythical, others are natural and pure. Those are the jobs I love the most. The ones where I get to use nature as my palette. The designs where foliage and shadow, flora and fauna consume the model and make her a part of their world."

Some of the jurors rolled their eyes. Others stared at me with doubt. Only a few kept judgement from showing.

"The girls were painted because of me. I can show you the invoices and emails requesting that sort of camouflage. I can show you where the photo shoot was taken and even present a couple of magazines where the photos were used. What I can't show you is the location of where Jeffrey Clark put them because if you look very closely, they weren't designed to go with that body paint."

"So they were canvases you'd hired?"

"Yes." I nodded. "If you look at their bank accounts, you'll see payment for the time we spent together."

"How did your uncle grab them before they'd showered off their paint?"

I pinched the bridge of my nose, cursing once again for being an idiot. "The number of canvases who ask if they can keep the paint on to show loved ones before washing is extremely high. I always offer them a shower before they leave. Some take it, but most don't. I'm not responsible for them when they walk out the door."

"No, but you are responsible if they get killed."

I hung my head. "I'll always feel guilty for playing even a small part in their demise. I'm guilty for a great many things. But I didn't kill them. I didn't know they'd been targeted until it was too late. When the ransom demands came in, I always paid. I paid countless times and he held off killing—or at least, I hope he did. When the girls started showing up, I didn't know it was my paint they wore. After all, Jeffrey taught me. He was just as capable of the artwork as I was."

"But you had a suspicion?"

"By the second girl, yes…I worried."

"And why didn't you go to the police then? When you knew lives were being taken?"

"I honestly can't answer that." I sighed. "I was still afraid of Olive being taken away from me, but she'd already been taken so that wasn't such a big restriction. I guess, I knew I was in too deep. And if I was arrested, how could I keep working and paying him? How could I prevent him from killing Olive if I was in jail? She would die."

"So you kept paying him, hoping you could stop him yourself?"

"Yes. I paid until I was bankrupt. I sold my warehouse, my furniture, everything I could. On the nights when the demands came in, I'd trawl the streets until dawn, looking for him, searching for Olive, for a girl he might have taken. I walked up and down the length of England. I explored countless forests and estates. I kept trying, but I always failed."

"Is that why your footprints were found at the location of the fourth girl?"

"Yes. Jeffrey gave me her location. I hadn't painted anyone in camouflage that week and hoped…I hoped she'd still be alive to save." My head hung. "But he hadn't waited for nature to kill her. He'd done it himself somewhere else, then painted her to match the bluebells where he dumped her body."

"And you didn't report this?"

I winced, accepting how it sounded. "No."

More noise in the court. More hate.

Hearing it out loud was worse. Everything I'd done, I'd done for Olive. I'd sacrificed everything I could—my fortune, my freedom, my very fucking soul. But it wasn't up to me to play God and let those girls die.

I *had* killed them. I'd played executioner just by keeping silent. That was my true crime.

Staying silent when a teacher took advantage of me, staying silent when O came back into my life, staying silent when my daughter was taken.

Fuck.

Silence was my mistake.

For everything.

Brad paced for a moment, working up to his next question. "How many girls did you save by paying his ransoms?" He stopped and looked at me. "Do you know?"

I shook my head. "I can only go by what he told me. But he was a killer before he took Olive. I don't know how many lives he took while he had her."

"Just a guess is fine."

"Seven, eight? Enough to know at least my money saved a few girls, even if I couldn't save my daughter."

"And when you found him that night, when he went back on his word to trade the woman you loved for your daughter, you decided enough was enough?"

Temper curled through me. My mind shot back to the night in question. The guilt in my veins. The self-disgust in my heart. "Yes. It was pre-emptive."

"How so?"

"I bought succinylcholine, also known as sux, on the black market. It's a drug they use in anaesthesia."

"And you injected him?"

"Yes."

"But you almost died before you could."

"I did." I rubbed my side, poking at the soreness that still lingered. "I almost lost the two people I love most in the world with my idiotic behaviour. I thought I could fix what I'd caused. I tried to do the right thing."

"By killing someone."

"By killing a monster who'd already taken far too many lives."

Brad nodded and turned to face the jury. He spread his arms and delivered his closing statement. "Gilbert Clark is a boy from a bad neighbourhood, born to an abusive father, and someone who prefers to suffer in silence than ask for help. He's admitted to the crime he did. He's willing to pay for taking a life of a man who murdered an unknown number of innocents and kidnapped his daughter for over a year. A man who took every penny he had and left him homeless because he didn't want to involve the police in case his daughter was taken away for the second time by the courts. He's also a man who dedicated his time teaching art part-time at his daughter's school—even though his childhood was traumatised by a teacher who raped him. Living through these traumas has had profound psychological effects. He's now bankrupt after a year of failing to protect his daughter. Overall, Gilbert Clark is not a bad man. He's just one who fell into bad situations and didn't ask for help. Thank you."

Nodding at the judge, he added, "That's all, your honour." To me, he said, "You may leave the stand."

I stood, searched for O in the crowd one last time, then returned to my seat for sentencing.

Chapter Thirty

Olin

"ALL RISE FOR Honourable Judge Hoft."

I stood with the crowd, gritty-eyed and heart-racing, staring at Gil's back.

I hadn't slept at all last night.

I doubted he did either.

I worried that I hadn't been called to testify. If that was a good or a bad thing.

I worried about so many, many things.

After his time on the stand yesterday, the judge adjourned for the next day, giving the jury time to mull it over and for any other evidence to be presented when it wasn't so late in the day. I'd waited for the police to pop by again—prepared to battle on his behalf.

But no one knocked on my door, and I'd forced myself to stay away from Justin's, even though I basically had to chain myself to my apartment not to intrude on Gil and Olive's final night together. He hadn't expected the extra night. And I wouldn't get in the middle of an already excruciating goodbye with his daughter.

Instead, Justin had text me and filled me in. How Gil had told Olive the truth about what he faced today. About how jail worked and why he was going away. He said Olive had taken it okay but he feared how things would go when Gil didn't go home.

I'd tried to drown out my worry about Gil with concern about my own life. I hated my job. I despised my apartment. I was done living here alone and doing my best to settle for things I didn't want.

Gil was almost out of my reach.

Justin and Olive would become close.

I wasn't needed in their future anymore.

But that didn't stop me from returning to the crown court the next day. It didn't prevent me from sitting stiff with goosebumps as Gil and his lawyer returned in suits that didn't have a speck of paint on them.

He'd never looked so presentable or so tragic.

His hair was tamed off his face as he sat in front of the audience. His hands remained balled on the table even when his lawyer scooted closer to talk to him.

The aura of the court was hushed and waiting.

Judge Holt glanced over the jury as she settled on her podium. Smoothing her gown, she asked, "Is there any other evidence or closing statements from either party?"

Sweat rolled down my spine as both lawyers shook their heads.

She nodded and turned to the jury. "In that case, do you have a verdict?"

A slim woman with a blonde plait nodded. "We do, your honour."

"And?"

The woman opened an envelope.

Everyone held their breath.

I couldn't take my eyes off Gil as he stiffened and braced himself.

The woman locked eyes with him and read in crisp firm voice. "We find the defendant, Gilbert Clark, guilty for the murder of Jeffrey Clark."

The judge scribbled something down before looking up. "And the four painted girls?"

Tears prickled my eyes.

I wanted so much to hug Gil. To tell him I'd changed my mind. That I did have the strength to be his…if he still wanted me.

"Not guilty," the woman announced.

Gil's spine rolled. His hands dove into his hair, his elbows wedged on the table.

His lawyer patted his back with a rough slap.

The judge waited for the murmurs of the court to die down before rapping her gavel loudly. Her steely gaze caught Gil's. "Mr. Clark. After your testimony and the evidence presented yesterday,

I can say you are not a threat to society. You killed out of self-defense of those you loved, and, although your paint obscured the girls who were killed, you aren't directly responsible. However, you did take a life, and for that, you must pay. Taking the law into your own hands always comes with consequences. If you'd spoken up about what had happened, those four young women might still be alive today."

She shuffled a few pieces of paper. "The court demands you pay a fine to the families of the deceased of four hundred thousand pounds, one hundred thousand per family. You will not be charged with accessory before the act which carries up to fifteen years and instead will serve five years with one hundred hours of community service upon release."

Her gavel slammed down.

It was done.

My ears rang with the sentencing.

Five years?

Five years?

Such a long time, but really…incredibly short for murder.

He'd been lucky.

Life had finally been kind.

"Bailiff, please escort Mr. Clark to his new home. Thank you, jury, for your help in delivering justice today." The judge stood. "Court dismissed."

People sprang from their seats, journalists crammed to listen to what Gil's lawyer said to him, and I wriggled my way through the crowd to say goodbye.

All over again.

Gil seemed to sense my closeness, turning to catch me from the crowd before he was ushered out and into places I couldn't go.

I searched his eyes for panic or pain, but I only saw relief.

"You okay?" I asked softly, barely audible above the hum of other conversation.

He nodded. "I don't want to leave Olive. But I'm okay with serving what I owe."

"Five years is a long time."

"It is. But if it helps rid some of my guilt, then I'll do it without complaint." His eyes dropped to my lips. "My one huge regret in this is that I hurt you so much, O. There's no punishment that can take that guilt away."

My mouth went dry.

I ached with so many things.

Justin and Olive should be here.

They should be allowed to hug him, so he wasn't shuffled off without knowing he was loved.

Words crowded on my tongue.

Promises and commitments that I wanted so much to give to him.

But the bailiff pushed Gil forward, breaking our connection, ending the time we had.

"I'll come visit you." I walked with him on the opposite side of the rail, getting caught up in journalists and tape recorders shoved in Gil's direction.

He smiled softly. "I don't expect it." He held my eyes as the guard opened a side door and ushered him through. "Be happy, O. Find a new dream and forget me."

The door shut.

Gil was gone.

Chapter Thirty-One

Olin

MY APARTMENT WAS terrifyingly lonely.

After having Gil and Olive share it, after being painted and made love to, after all the sleepless nights thinking about him, the walls were ever more depressing. The sparse furnishing and lack of home—the aching loneliness…everything was a disease.

A disease I couldn't suffer anymore.

It hurt.

It stung.

I can't stay here.

All I could think about was Gil locked up for five years, his hardship of figuring out how to pay such a massive fine, and the knowledge that even when he was released, his punishment wasn't over.

I was being so selfish. So what if my flat made me claustrophobic with the need to run? Gil didn't have the luxury of his own place anymore and he *couldn't* run, no matter how much he wanted to.

God.

I hugged myself, unable to stop thinking about Gil in prison. Gil being shoved into inmate population. Gil dying inside a cell.

What about his art?

What about his need to create?

What about Olive?

I…I can't do this.

I needed to leave.

Immediately.

Grabbing my handbag, I swept out of my flat in the same cream blouse and black skirt I'd worn to court. Fighting tears, I summoned an Uber to take me to Justin's.

He answered the door before I could even knock, yanking me into his arms, his nose buried in my hair, his body tight and tall. "You holding up okay?"

I nodded, breathing him in, finding some resemblance of strength. "How's Olive?"

Pulling away, Justin closed the door and led me into his minimalist bachelor pad. The two-bedroom apartment had epic views over the Birmingham business district and the twinkling lights looked too merry for my liking.

Apart from the colouring pencils on his breakfast bar and a small purple hoodie thrown on his couch, it still looked like he lived alone.

Now, he lived with a little girl.

A little girl he was godfather to for a friend serving time for murder.

"She's about as expected." He cocked his head to the spare room which had become hers.

"Do you mind if I see her?"

"Not at all." He let his arm slip from around my shoulders. "She'd love that. She's learned to trust me but she still doesn't like living alone with me. She's going to take it hard. If I'm honest, I'm kind of terrified that I'm going to set her back. That I should find a good therapist so she has someone she can talk to when it all becomes too much."

I didn't really have an answer for that. "You're already doing a great job, Justin. You've got this."

"Not so sure about that." He squeezed the back of his neck. "Go on. Go see her."

Giving him a slight smile, I headed down the corridor and knocked on Olive's door. "Olive, it's me? Can I come in?"

Her tears were my answer.

I turned the handle and entered. Moving swiftly to her bed, I sat beside her as she cried with her face buried into a pillow. My hand rested between her tiny shoulder blades, rubbing soft circles. "It's okay. Everything is going to be okay."

She didn't look up, just cried harder. "*How?* Daddy's in prison. You're going away. And Justin works all the time, and I don't like the babysitter." Her cheeks glowed red as she looked up, anger and agony in her grey gaze. "I don't want this. I want to go home with Dad. I want him to come home with me. I miss him." Her tears became sobs as I pulled her into my arms. "I miss him *sooooo* much. How much longer do we have to live apart?"

I rocked her, kissing the top of her head. "Not long. Once this is over, you'll both be free to live the rest of your life together if you want."

Olive sniffed. "But five years is *forever.*"

It is.

It's so, so long.

"It will go by fast if you stay busy." I said that for her benefit but also reminded myself too. "You're going back to school. You'll make new friends and learn more skills. And when he's out, you can paint together all the time. A true family business."

"But it's so *long.*" Her shoulders drooped, more tears splashing. "I don't think I can do it."

"You can. You will." I kissed her head again. "It's a long time, but Justin is here. He'll take care of you and you can still see your dad. You can go visit him."

"Wait...I can?" Her eyes lit up instantly. "Can we go now?"

I didn't know what prison protocol was but I guessed they'd need him to settle into his new home before visitation. I stroked her glossy hair with a gentle smile. "I'll find out when you can."

"Can you come too?" She threw her arms around me, squeezing me tighter than I expected. *"Please?"*

Justin appeared in the door frame, his lips twisted into a half-smile, his body reclining against the wall.

I held his gaze as I squeezed Olive back. "Of course, I'll come for however long I'm in town."

My promise to leave tasted like ash in my mouth.

Could I leave?

Where would I go?

Why would I go when this poor little girl needed care?

She has Justin.

Gil set you free.

You have to leave.

If I stood any chance of finding who I truly was, I had to open my wings.

But...

What if I don't want to fly away? What if what I want is right here?

"I don't want you to go. All the people I love leave me." Olive pulled away, her face deadly serious and determined even as crystal tears rained. "Move in with us. Don't go away. Please, *please* don't go."

I froze.

Justin stiffened.

Olive arched her chin, defiant and ready to fight. "I like Justin. He's way nicer than Uncle Jeffrey, but...I don't want to be alone without my dad. I liked staying at your place. If you won't move in here, can I come live with you instead?"

Oh, no.

I tried to apologise silently to Justin over Olive's head. I didn't mean to destabilise her new home with him. I didn't want to ruin their fragile bond.

But Justin shrugged, saying quietly, "There's plenty of room if you want to join us, O."

My heart crashed blindly. "But I have an apartment."

"An apartment where your lease is almost up and you weren't going to renew it."

Damn for confiding in him.

"You know I'm planning on travelling."

"You need time to save and decide where to go. You could save more by moving in here."

"I wouldn't live here for free, Justin. I'd pay rent, same as any other place."

He nodded, appeasing me. "That's fine. But you have to admit, it makes logical sense."

I tried to think up another excuse why moving in with Gil's only friend and his lonely daughter was a bad idea. The truth was, it was a *terrible* idea because it kept me in Gil's stratosphere.

Justin seemed to sense my thoughts. "He let you go that night...didn't he?"

I jerked. "How do you know about that?"

"I didn't until now." He sighed. "When I saw him the next morning, he seemed different. Sad, definitely, but relieved too. Relieved that he'd set you free and wouldn't mess up your life any more than he already had."

"Isn't it up to me if I want him to mess it up or not?"

He chuckled. "I suppose." His eyes glowed with questions. "So...are you? Going to wait for him?" He looked at Olive. "Are you really thinking of putting your life on hold for five years?"

Olive watched us, cheeks glistening, chest heaving from her sobs. But she didn't interrupt, almost as if she knew this was one of the most important conversations of my life.

Justin was forcing me to answer a question I didn't know

how. Asking me if I would wait for the boy I'd been waiting for my entire existence.

Could I wait?

Should I?

Why would I when there was so much that'd gone wrong between us?

I wanted to move on.

I *needed* to move on.

I wouldn't survive five years pining after him.

And yet...

The thought of walking away, of finding him via a job advertisement, then just leaving?

God.

I knew what it was like to miss Gil.

I'd learned that lesson many, many times in the years we'd spent apart.

But that was yet another reason I *should* go.

Before it was too late.

Because missing him was too painful and living in limbo too great a toll.

I slouched, running my hand through Olive's hair. "I honestly don't know."

He gave me a half-smile. "You don't have to decide right now. That's the beauty of this situation. Gil isn't going anywhere."

I tried to laugh—to find humour in hardship. Instead, I cuddled Olive close and kissed her crown.

"So...?" Olive blinked. "Are you staying? You can move into my room with me. Can't she, Justin?" She looked at her godfather.

"She could." He nodded. "But she can also have my room, and I can take the couch."

I scowled. "I'm not kicking you out of your bedroom, Justin."

"Ah, so you are thinking about it?"

I shrugged again. "I don't know what to do anymore."

"But you haven't made any decisions on flying away yet."

"No...I've been looking at flights, but every time I go to book, something happens."

He chuckled quietly. "Could be a sign that you're meant to stay here."

"And here is just as complicated as there."

He sighed. "Isn't that the bitch."

I placed my hands over Olive's dainty ears. "Language, Mr. Miller."

Olive smiled through her sadness. "Dad swears far worse than that. I know all the swear words. Uncle Jeffrey said a lot of them too."

I tried to be stern. "Well, just because you know them doesn't mean you can use them."

"I know." She pouted, plucking at the comforter. "I miss Dad. Are you sure we can't go see him yet?"

"In a few days, pipsqueak," Justin said gently. "They'll need time to settle him into his new home."

"It's not a home. It's a jail." Her eyes flashed. "He should be here, with me."

"He should." Justin came in, squatting to his haunches by the bed and staring up at Olive. "But you know why he had to go away. We talked about it last night, remember? He stopped Uncle Jeffrey from doing bad things to other girls. He did the right thing by stopping him, but the rules of society means he has to pay for taking the law into his own hands."

"That's just stupid." Olive stuck out her bottom lip. "He should be given a gold sticker like they used to at school when you did good things."

I smiled, hugging her close. "How about we give him a gold sticker when we visit him."

"Can we?" She turned in my arms, her grey gaze so intelligent and fierce. "Can we go together all the time and let him know that we don't think he's bad."

My heart squeezed. "Of course."

Justin stood, looking down at both of us, his gaze pensive. "Stay at least tonight, O. You'd be doing me a huge favour." Lowering his voice, he added, "I'm not entirely sure I'm equipped to help if Olive has a panic attack tonight."

The thought of returning to an empty apartment and my chaotic thoughts was definitely not appealing. But staying would feel like a betrayal to Gil—agreeing to play families with Justin and Olive, all while he rotted in a cell.

Justin was my friend.

Platonic and sweet.

And I liked him.

But I didn't know if I could live with him.

"Is that a yes?" he asked gently.

I looked away, unable to keep his stare. "It's a maybe."

"No." Tears fell swift, Olive clung to me. Her chest rose and fell, faster and faster, her grief finding her all over again. "Don't go. *Please* don't go." Her arms were wiry and tight, locking around me.

And I did something stupid.

I let her keep me.

"Hey, don't cry." I wriggled a little in her embrace and brushed back her hair.

Her eyes met mine.

My heart pounded.

And I said, "I'll stay...for a little while."

Chapter Thirty-Two

Olin

"HELLO, GIL."

Gil stood beside the metal table in the visitation area, his love for me evident in his gaze.

My heart kicked, responded, replied.

It'd been eight days since I'd seen him.

Eight days since I'd listened to his sentencing.

Eight days since I'd come to the realisation that I was still stupidly in love with him and still stupidly unable to make a decision about my life.

I'd been a fool to think I could walk away.

I'd been an idiot to think I could stay.

Limbo was where I'd existed the past few years since my accident, and I couldn't seem to get free. Especially now that Gil had stolen the final pieces of my soul and became untouchable.

"O…hi." His voice licked around me with velveteen love. His affection no longer buried beneath ice. He seemed different. He was a ward of the crown, yet…he seemed freer than I'd ever seen. "It's so nice to see you."

The urge to hug him was agony.

But we'd been told hugging wasn't permitted. At least he'd been placed in a low security prison where face-to-face visitation was allowed and not maximum security where glass and phone was the only way to communicate.

That would've been an extra level of hell for Olive.

This was already unbearable.

I wanted to tell him what the last week had entailed.

How my lease ended in a month and I didn't know what I should do.

How Olive had begged me to sleep in her room at Justin's four out of the past eight nights, because she couldn't cope knowing he was gone.

How Justin had offered again for me to move in, and I didn't know what my answer should be.

My tongue tied.

Desperate to tell him everything. To ask him what he wanted. To hear him say he could never let me go, and that I should stay.

And wait.

But Olive barrelled past me, stealing Gil's attention.

"Olive Oyl." His entire body softened as he fell to one knee. His arms opened wide, looking like a proud father, starving man, and pained protector all at once.

"You can't hug—"

Too late.

Olive launched into his embrace, and Gil trapped her close. He buried his face against her sweet, strawberry smelling hair, and Olive clung to him like a baby spider monkey.

They didn't obey the rules as fresh tears rolled down Olive's cheek as she leaned back to kiss Gil's five o'clock shadow.

He kissed her back before pushing her painfully away and standing. A guard caught our gaze in warning, shaking his head at our affection.

Gil cleared his throat and pinned his attention back on Olive. "Wow, little spinach. You better stop growing because I swear you're already bigger than last week."

Olive smiled but didn't laugh. Her bubbliness had faded somewhat. But her joy at being with Gil was evident. "I'll stop growing. I promise I won't grow another inch until you're home."

"Nah, you can't do that. Ignore me. You have to grow into a gorgeous creature who will kill me on a daily basis with how awesome she is."

She blushed.

Now our reunion was over, the rest of the world came back into focus. Other families chatted with loved ones, the visiting room buzzing with relief and regret at seeing each other but still torn apart.

We stood in the corner; our own private oasis.

Olive's gaze skipped over other parents with their kids, grateful prisoners, stern guards, and doting wives and girlfriends.

The scene was sweet with so much affection but raw with so much loss.

I hoped she wouldn't have a nightmare tonight.

She'd suffered pretty bad since Gil had gone. She'd wake up screaming and only my touch could snap her out of it. If Justin tried to soothe her, he just made it worse.

On the nights that I hadn't stayed, he'd called in the early hours of the morning, begging me to talk to her. To help her know she was safe, that Jeffrey was dead, and Justin wasn't her uncle.

Child Protective Services had also called, checking in on Olive's living arrangements and providing the name of a therapist with skills in helping children overcome traumatic events. At least they were happy that Olive's best interests were upheld and allowed us to keep temporary custody.

We were all tired.

And confused on how best to make our new realities work.

Cupping Olive's cheek, Gil earned a scowl from a nearby guard. He reluctantly let her go and motioned to the metal chairs bolted to the floor. "Sit. Hang out with me."

Olive took one while Gil and I took the others.

Reaching across the table, Olive grabbed his hand and didn't let go. Even when another guard moved toward us and Gil dropped their grip beneath the table out of sight.

I waited to see if he'd be reprimanded, but the guard just narrowed his eyes and returned to his post, allowing a small kindness between father and daughter.

"Are you okay? No one is being mean?" Olive sniffed back tears.

Gil smiled and shook his head. "No, everyone has been very welcoming."

His eyes slid to mine, hiding the truth.

I doubted everyone had been welcoming. Shadows marked his jaw, and he'd sat stiffly—all signs I recognised of him being bruised from a fist.

I shivered, hating that he was locked in there and unable to escape brutality. Hating that I couldn't have a frank conversation with him because of innocent ears.

Was he truly okay? Was it true that men shed their human skins and became monsters in jail? That beatings and rapings were just a part of prison life, or was that merely conspiracies and gossip, designed to scare you into staying straight?

"Are you painting?" Olive asked, swiping her nose with the

back of her hand and blinking away more tears, as if she knew her grief was hard on her father.

"No. I don't have much inspiration. My muses are all back at home." His eyes flashed to mine again, holding my stare with a need so rich and deep, if it was a colour, it would've been a decadent red.

"Will you teach other prisoners how to paint?" Olive looked around at the bland beige walls. "Maybe you can graffiti in here like our rainforest wall. It's ugly."

Gil chuckled. "That would be an improvement to the place. I agree."

I leaned back, allowing the small family to have their conversations and privacy. I'd come as chaperone to Olive as Justin was working, and I'd been given the afternoon off. Shannon wasn't as friendly these days, and the mystery of me being used as a pawn in the painted murders had worn off. No one in the office liked me because I didn't make an effort to mingle.

I didn't go there to find company. I went there to earn money, and frankly, I didn't know how much longer I could stay.

It was yet another hurdle I had to jump.

Quit my job and have no income.

Give up my lease and have no home.

Walk away from everything and have no Gil or Olive.

I couldn't deny that watching Gil with his daughter made me more alive than I had been in days. I fell deeper into him, seeing such a tender side. My shattered trust stitched itself back together, witnessing a guy who wasn't the scared, icy boy anymore but a man who wore his mistakes with pride.

It punched me in the heart with hypocrisy.

I loved Gil.

I probably always would.

And now…when there were no more secrets keeping us apart, I was the one who hid the truth. Who didn't know if she was brave enough to admit that *this* was what she wanted.

Him.

Her.

A ready-made family who I'd fallen head over heels for.

Five years was an eternity.

But it was nothing in the term of a lifetime.

I sat stewing in my thoughts as Olive chattered and drank in her father. Gil smiled dotingly and gave her every scrap of attention.

Fifteen minutes later, a buzzer sounded, announcing the end of visitation.

Olive's eyes immediately filled with tears again. "No. I don't want to go. Dad, come home with us."

Gil cupped her cheek, sadness creating grooves in his forehead and deep brackets around his mouth. "I'd love nothing more than to go home with you, little spinach, but I can't. Not yet."

"Can I move in here with you then?" She stood and hugged him while he still sat in the chair. He squeezed her, even as a guard cleared his throat, encroaching with his rules. "This isn't a nice place for little Olive Oyls."

"Then where can we go to be together?"

Gil pushed her toward me, a plea in his gaze.

I stood, understanding what he needed. I opened my arms to catch her, to prevent her from clinging to Gil. It felt wrong to separate them. So, so cruel. "We just have to be patient, Olive. He'll—"

"No!"

I clutched her close, bending down to kiss her temple. "Remember what we talked about? How Dad will be home soon? And then you'll be together forever. This is the last time you guys have to be apart, okay? But you have to be strong."

Olive sniffed. "I don't want to be strong. I just want him to come home."

Gil swallowed back agony as another buzzer went. "I'll come home soon, Olive Oyl. I promise." Kissing her cheek, he looked at me with every weight of the world. "Thank you for coming, O. I'm sorry we didn't have a chance to talk."

He went to touch me.

A guard came toward him.

He sighed and followed the other prisoners through the door.

His gaze never left us until he was gone.

Chapter Thirty-Three

Gil

"JUSTIN...IT'S ME."

Justin swallowed a mouthful of food, surprise in his voice. "How are you calling me, Clark? It's in the middle of the day."

"Prison allows phone calls." I'd deliberately called during the week, and on his office line. This was a conversation just for us, and I couldn't afford to be weak and not do what I should've done a long time ago.

In reality, I'd already made this offer.

In a text while walking through a forest with an unconscious O in my arms.

"True, yeah. Cool. Hey, do you want me to get Olive? She's in the empty office next to me, drawing. She wasn't quite up for school today, but she's going tomorrow. She promised."

Fuck.

Poor thing.

So many things to adapt to and accept.

Me gone. Justin her guardian. Returning to school after so long away.

I worried that she'd be picked on and held back. That a teacher would touch her like one had touched me. Familiar rage and fear crested through me, and I couldn't swallow it back.

I just had to hope Justin was vigilant and wouldn't accept her silence for an answer if she started to shut down.

"Don't get her. This is just a quick call."

"Okay...what's up?" His voice turned serious. "Everything going okay in there? You safe?"

I nodded, even though he couldn't see me. "Yeah, it's fine."

"You don't sound fine."

"All good." I sidestepped the question. It wasn't that I didn't want to be honest, but he didn't need to know about the beatings I'd already taken or the threats. Other inmates didn't believe I wasn't involved with the girls' murders and dished out their own punishment.

I'd held my own.

I'd find my rank in the hierarchy.

Eventually.

"I didn't call to talk about me."

"Okay…what did you call to talk about?" His voice changed, turning wary.

As he should.

I couldn't seem to stop asking this guy for goddamn favours. "First, how *is* Olive? She all right?"

Justin cleared his throat. "As well as can be expected. She's still guarded around me at night, when it's just us. I don't push her, though. She's much better when O stays over."

My heart stopped beating. "She what?"

"Yeah, sorry, mate. I wanted to tell you but didn't know how. I wasn't coping the first few nights with Olive's nightmares. O seems to have a magic touch and agreed to help Olive adjust." He cleared his throat, pausing for a second. "Look, you should know that I asked O to move in with me." He rushed as if terrified that I'd throttle him through the phone line. "Her lease is almost up, she hates her job, and she's at a total crossroads on what to do with her life. While she figures out that shit, I invited her to stay with Olive and me. To help ease everyone into this new routine, you know?" He kept talking, not giving me a chance to interrupt. "You know O is thinking of travelling. At least this way she can save up some money before she goes. And…I can keep an eye on her for you. I know you'll worry about her, and if she does move in with me for a little while, you can relax knowing I have both of your girls safe."

He stopped.

The line crackled.

He asked cautiously, "Eh, Gil…you still there?"

I rubbed my face. "Yeah, I'm here."

"You…okay with what I just said."

"I'm okay as long as my daughter is happy. O doesn't belong to me anymore. She can stay wherever she wants."

"Okay…great."

I sighed heavily. I'd sounded like a bastard. I sounded as if I was jealous. Justin had just proven why this phone call was the best choice for all of us. He'd already taken the step toward the future I was willing to give up in gratitude for his help.

Squeezing the back of my neck, I asked softly, "Is there anything I can do?"

As if I could do anything trapped inside here, but I had to offer. Had to try.

Justin sighed. "Honestly, mate. Just get out early on good behaviour. Come back to your kid as fast as you can."

"I'll do my best, believe me." I was still shocked I'd only received five years. It felt like an eternity but also didn't feel long enough. I knew that was the guilt talking, but still…life had finally been kind to me and I didn't know how to accept it.

Looking at the dirty clock, fully aware that my phone privileges were running out, I said as firmly and as genuinely as I could, "Look, I'm glad you asked O to move in with you. You're a good bloke, Miller. And…your offer makes why I called easier." I laughed under my breath. "It's not fucking easy. It's the hardest thing I'll ever do, but…it seems fate is one step ahead of me."

"Oh?" He cleared his throat. "What are you trying to say?"

"I have another favour to ask." I groaned, leaning against the wall where the bank of telephones hung. "The last one I hope, but it's still another bloody favour."

Justin chuckled. "You don't need to feel so bad about asking, Clark. That's what friendship is."

I didn't want to argue again about friendship and how one-sided ours had always been. I didn't have the luxury of not asking, even though it would tear out my heart once and for all.

It wasn't really a favour.

It was an offer.

Fucking permission even though neither of them needed it.

It was just my way of coming to terms with everything.

Accepting my future.

"If O does travel, then I'm glad. I want her to be happy and won't stand in her way."

"And if she doesn't? If she stays in town?" Justin's suspicion bled through the phone line.

This was it.

No going back.

My knuckles tightened around the phone. "If she doesn't, if she moves in with you and finds happiness under your roof with you and my daughter…then…I give you my blessing to love her. Make her yours. Be together. Get married. Just…be happy."

Justin choked before coughing and blurting, "You're giving me *permission* to date Olin. To *marry* O?" His tone turned cool. "I don't need your permission, Clark."

My temper fired, but I kept it locked away. "I know. I just didn't want you to hold back if there came a moment where you two could be happy together."

"If O knew you'd said this to me, she'd be right pissed. You're acting as if she doesn't have a mind of her own."

"She does. Her heart is big and desperate to love, but she's also kind to a fault and far too generous to even consider being more than just friends with you out of fairness to me and our past."

"I think you should talk to O."

"I don't want to mess her up any more than I already have."

"Look, you're tired and missing home and thinking you'll never be happy again. I get it. Having your freedom taken away can't be easy, but, Gil, stay focused on the future. You will get out of there. You will have Olive back and raise her into a wonderful young woman. And who knows, maybe O will wait for you, and you'll all ride off into the sunset with your paintbrushes. Just focus on the possibility of—"

"Times up!" a guard shouted, waving his finger in the air and stabbing at the watch on his wrist.

"Shit, I've got to go." I turned my back on the guard, swallowing hard. "Just…just be open to the idea, Miller. If you still have feelings for her. If you want her, and she wants you. Don't worry about me. I just want her to have the best. And that isn't me. It never was. It's always been you. You guys are the same, Miller. Like should stick with like. Anyway, thanks for looking after my daughter. I promise one day, I'll find a way to pay you back."

I hung up before he could protest.

I walked back to my cell with images of O kissing Justin when he told her he still had feelings for her. Of her moving into Justin's bedroom and becoming a surrogate mother to my child.

They would move on.

They would live in domestic bliss.

I would remain here in limbo.

A prisoner with nothing and no one.

And I was okay with that.

I was *happy* with that if it meant the two girls I loved more than anything were protected and cared for by a man I trusted with my life.

Chapter Thirty-Four

Olin

GILBERT CLARK, the body painter from Birmingham responsible for killing the man who murdered at least four girls, with possibilities of countless more, has been incarcerated for the past six months.
Served five years for his role in the Painted Murders, the online community who demanded the death penalty and did their best to destroy his business has now faded into white noise on the web.
For such a prolific painter, Gilbert Clark refused to touch a paintbrush for five months where he's currently serving his sentence. However, just last week, three canvases have been placed up for auction by the prison itself, donated by Gilbert Clark who, according to our sources, has returned to painting and now teaches a class to fellow inmates.
This past year, the prison has been working on the education offered to its prisoners, along with rehabilitation programs. Painting has been proven to have a positive impact on both psychological issues and stress levels.
The canvases on sale depict scenes from inside the jail. One shows the cafeteria where the inmates eat, another the barbwire-enclosed field where exercise is encouraged, and the last of a cell itself—complete with sketches of Gilbert Clark's daughter, the woman he loves, and the friend who stuck by his side, blue-tacked to the cell walls.
If you wish to bid on one of these limited-edition canvases, please head to the prison website and click on the link provided.

I locked my phone as I entered Justin's building.

I'd finished work early and surfed the news on the bus.

I'd stumbled upon the article about Gil's return to painting.

My heart hurried in hope, grateful he'd finally embraced his gift again. I knew what it was like to live without such an outlet.

To no longer be able to dance. To no longer be allowed to paint.

Thank goodness he'd been permitted to indulge his gift inside, and how brilliant that the prison had accepted his donations to sell. Hopefully, they could put the profits toward providing better programs for the inmates.

For six months, I'd stayed in town.

For six months, I hadn't told Gil that I loved him.

For six long months, I still hadn't made up my mind.

Stay.

Go.

Commit.

Fly free.

Sighing, I unlocked the letterbox and pulled out new mail.

Two letters.

One addressed to me and one to Justin.

And one magazine from Kohls showing their new line.

Instantly, my breath caught as I traced the glossy magazine covered in cellophane.

Thanks to reading the news article about Gil, his presence already wrapped around me.

But now…I almost felt his touch.

Felt his brush upon my skin.

His paint upon my body.

Tearing open the magazine, I stared at myself.

At the green camouflage transforming me from human to department store logo. Along with the mannequins in the fellow letters, it punched the shopper with a unique offering. A symbolic advertisement that said if you bought things from them, you too could become anything you wanted.

I sighed, my heart hurting as I relived the changing room jealousy, the tension while painting, the awfulness of watching the police steal him away.

I should've known then that Gil's freedom was running out even though, at the time, it had been mine.

We'd both been victims of circumstances outside our control, and as I stood in Justin's apartment stairwell, clutching a magazine where my naked body was hidden beneath my lover's talent, I finally knew what I would do.

Finally knew the answer to the question I'd been too afraid to ask.

Where do I belong?

Easy.

With him.

With the man who'd terrified me, sacrificed me, almost died for me.

With the boy who'd claimed me, loved me, protected me.

With the body painter who saw past my colours and painted his own upon my heart.

NINETEEN MONTHS LATER

Chapter Thirty-Five

Gil

TIME HAD DIFFERENT speeds.

For the circumstances you couldn't accept, it went slow—tormenting and giving plenty of opportunity to either rebel against the current situation or finally accept the unacceptable.

For the events you *could* accept—the ones where joy was the main ingredient and life was good, time sped up, as if hurtling you toward the next catastrophe.

Prison had consisted of two versions of time.

The beginning was slow and miserable with no end in sight.

O kept chaperoning Olive for her weekly visits, and we stuck entirely to conversation about my daughter, her progress at school, and the life I was no longer a part of. The fifteen minutes always went far too fast, and the urge to grab O and demand she tell me what she wasn't saying built and built until I'd tremble in my cell at night, desperate to know.

At no point did she advise when she was leaving and to where. At no time did she put me out of misery and say she'd fallen in love with Justin.

And I was too gutless to ask.

The subject of her vanishing one day slowly buried beneath all the other topics we didn't discuss.

It fucking killed me to think that the past had repeated itself and Justin had claimed the love of my life, but if it meant she was happy, I would hide my pain forever.

All I could hope for was that every week, she'd turn up. And every week, she'd still be there.

As my friend.

As my family.

Their visits got me through the first few months of claustrophobia. The only bright speck in cell time, yard exercise, and prison monotony. I returned to sketching to keep boredom at bay, sending fortnightly letters to Olive, enclosed with drawings and renders of things created from memory, from my previous freedom.

Justin visited too.

His upbeat convo and antidotes of Olive helped keep me a little sane. He tactfully avoided the subject of O and their home life, and out of respect—to show him I meant what I'd said on the phone—I kept my questions silent.

By the time routine set in, and I accepted my new temporary home, minutes no longer made me suffer such long days. I agreed to lead a painting class for fellow inmates, using broken down easels and painted over canvases. The stock of paints ranged from dry oils to old acrylics, but I never complained.

They were colour.

They were small tubes of freedom into my craft.

I returned to painting normal canvases and not O's perfect skin.

I didn't care that some of the inmates would rather flick paint at fellow cellmates than follow my instruction. I didn't mind that the results of the class were worse than any kindergarten finger painting. It was nice to have a task and a relief to create.

It was also rewarding to conjure a scene that others might see outside of these walls and gave me purpose again when the warden said they'd hold an auction and use the proceeds to buy more supplies for my newly established painting school.

I painted a canvas for Olive, full of owls and ballerinas.

I painted a canvas for O, drawing her tattoo from memory.

Inmates took note of the skill it took to turn lines and shadow into recognisable things and my class attendance switched from taking the piss to dedicated.

I became a teacher.

I thought about Jane Tallup, our daughter, and O.

And through the medium that had always helped calm my thoughts, I somehow helped others too. Fellow prisoners relaxed around me. The stress in their eyes faded while focusing on pigment rather than regrets. I gained more freedom within the new world I inhabited, and I unofficially became someone they could talk to.

I didn't know how it happened, but the prisoners who took my painting classes seemed more centred and not nearly as violent.

The warden noticed.

He gave us more supplies.

Gave us more opportunities to use our passion for paint in other areas.

When a renovation budget was announced, we put up our hands to help refresh the jail. We painted it from top to bottom—grey walls and white windowsills.

Along with painting, I continued to volunteer for odd jobs and handyman tasks. The yards were redesigned. The gym equipment upgraded. The kitchen supplied with better facilities.

I had every intention of learning new skills, so when I was freed, I could be a reliable father to Olive. I had no idea if my Master of Trickery business would resurrect. I couldn't check my website or emails. I'd filed for bankruptcy and had nothing left apart from my wonderful daughter.

When I got out, I had no intention of being a failure to society. I planned on finding work straight away because I had no intention of making Olive feel anything but pride.

I wasn't a convict who had accepted his uselessness.

I was a man who'd paid the price of his mistakes and now was free to move on.

I was the person I always wanted to be.

*****

One day, eighteen months into my term, the warden called me into his office.

I'd had my monthly meeting with the in-house shrink, and my results were glowingly positive. The monthly conclusion was always the same: I wasn't likely to offend again.

My murderous tendencies were not a repeating occurrence.

I wasn't a danger to society.

The warden read my file with a frown etched deep into his forehead. He told me the prison was at full capacity, and he'd been instructed to select inmates he felt were rehabilitated enough to be released on good behaviour.

I would be monitored if released early. I would be expected to fulfil my community service.

But there was a chance…a small, small chance, I could go home.

I daren't let my hope explode.

I nodded calmly and agreed to yet more interviews and

assessments.

After a week of talking to people in suits, I was advised they'd be in touch.

I didn't tell O or Justin about the possibility of being released early. I didn't want to promise Olive something that I couldn't guarantee.

A month later, when I was called to see the warden, I refused to be hopeful. The chances of being told that serving nineteen months of a five-year sentence was enough to be freed were slim.

However, fate once again treated me kindly.

Within a week, I'd signed the paperwork, been advised of my parole officer and community service liaison, and given a date.

O and Olive were due to visit me three days after my freedom was reinstated.

I had the choice of telling them the good news.

I mulled over the options of sharing the celebration now— when I was penniless, unsure of my future, and homeless...or wait.

To keep one last secret so I could get back on my feet and prove to them that my past was behind me. I didn't know how O would take it. Would she be mad that I kept silent and didn't ask for help, or proud that I hadn't given up?

It was Olive who made the choice for me.

I called the night I was due to leave and asked how school was going. How things with Justin and O were. She'd said things were good, but she missed me and couldn't wait until we lived together again.

I'd promised it would happen sooner than we figured. The news of my parole itched to be said, but if I told her, I would break a promise because she couldn't live with me if I didn't have anywhere to keep her safe.

A halfway house for reformed felons was not ideal.

And so, I kept quiet.

One last time.

I told her I was coming down with something and to avoid me for a week because I didn't want her to get sick. I slept one last night in prison, traded my uniform for civilian clothes, and stepped from the gates far sooner than I'd hoped.

The guard signing me out asked if I had family to call or a pick-up arranged.

I just shook my head and strolled from the jail, destitute and in the same clothes I'd faced court in. I'd asked for too many favours of too many people. I would stand on my own feet from now on.

Otherwise, I really didn't deserve my daughter.

As I'd slinked back into society, I used the change in my pockets to rent a computer in a downtown Wi-Fi café and checked my business accounts.

My emails had dried up.

No commissions had waited nineteen months for a reply.

But at least my Facebook page was still up.

The visibility was obsolete and content buried with no traffic, but the photos and videos were still there. Emblems of my past. Reminders of a talent I once had.

Clicking on the last video I'd uploaded of me painting Olin in her flat that night, I tortured myself with our kiss.

I relived the connection we'd shared.

The goodbye I'd done my best to honour.

My finger hovered over the mouse.

I wanted to delete the video. To put aside those heart pangs for a girl who might be in love with my best friend by now.

But I left it.

I left it as yet another reminder not to ruin her happiness, and used the many videos and photos saved in my cloud to add new content. Previous commissions. Accolades from advertisement companies. Images of magazines and billboards and the many places where my creations had ended up.

I even uploaded a picture of Olive painting a kid from her school while dressed in her hockey uniform. The poor kid had ended up looking like some squashed marshmallow but both she and Olive had had a great time.

It showed in their smiles and splashed paint.

An image of powerful joy.

Once I'd scheduled and arranged a few posts that hopefully would get exposure, I updated my business description.

Experienced Body Painter willing to work for free.
Ex-convict, single-father, determined.
You supply the paint, canvas, and location.
I'll do the rest.

I was willing to start from the ground up again.

I'd brush the cobwebs off my fingers, raise my business from the ashes, and be worthy of all the wonderful people in my life.

And this time, there would be no one to blackmail or bleed me dry.

No uncle to steal my daughter.

No teacher to send me to jail for rape.

No secrets to make me lose my soul-mate.

People knew the truth.

It was time I accepted that I no longer had to look over my shoulder.

It was time to live.

* * * * *

That'd been four weeks ago.

I'd called Olive once a week—like I used to from jail—assuring her I was fine and not to come and see me. That I couldn't quite shake the flu and didn't want her to catch it. A few fake coughs and sneezes, and she agreed to be patient.

I hated lying.

I worried about keeping silent.

I was *desperate* to see her.

I barely slept with the need to ensure she was safe—to assure myself she was free and no longer prisoner like I had been.

But unlike the panic that'd filled me when searching for her, I could temper my desperation with the knowledge she was happy with Justin and O. She had everything she could ever want. She was loved and protected.

And if I stood any chance of providing for her half as well as Justin and O did…then I needed time to make myself a better man.

To ensure I could be the father she deserved.

And besides…I had a plan.

Four weeks had already given me enough time to paint and get the word out that I was back.

Thanks to the prison selling some of my work, my reputation had been patched up with the underdog tale of a guy incarcerated for putting a psychopath down.

People no longer hated me, and it wasn't the battle I'd feared to get noticed.

I did three free commissions.

One for a woman on her thirtieth birthday who wanted to wear her 'birthday suit' with paint embellishments.

Two for a small pet shop who helped rehome shelter animals and wanted two women painted as one stray looking for a home.

And three for an up-and-coming band with no cash who wanted their drummer to be covered in their logo for their banner and next week's show.

For each one, I uploaded the time-lapse video of creation, and each one got more and more traction online.

By the fourth one—a law firm who wanted a woman painted as a judge—I deleted the promise of free work and accepted my first paid gig in almost two years.

I slashed my usual rate for the right to share.

The second gig, I increased it.

And by the fifth, I was confident in my skills again.

Confident enough to charge higher prices, invest my new funds into fresh brushes, bottles, and sponges, and dared hope that I could step back into my role as Master of Trickery.

There'd been no hate directly into my inbox.

No beatings or awkward moments when I went to paint.

It was as if everyone had moved on. As if they no longer cared about something that happened so long ago, even if it was scandal and murder.

I didn't question the luck I had.

I scooped it up as fast as I could, focusing on my goal of a home for Olive and money to pay Justin for caring for my daughter.

I worked every hour I could.

Day and night.

I didn't rest, even when I had enough for a down payment on a rental only a block away from Justin's place. My parole officer helped vouch for me and acted as referee on my rental request. Luckily, the landlord took a chance and I signed the lease with a chest-full of relief.

The place came fully furnished, and the first night I slept there and not the halfway house provided for ex-prisoners, I knew I could do this.

I was done taking the scraps life threw at me.

I would make a success of myself and not feel guilty or undeserving.

There was also another reason for staying busy.

Each time my thoughts strayed to O, my heart would buck and writhe. I'd lost her. I'd let her go. And that was the biggest punishment of all.

Not jail time.

Not fighting from the ground up.

Just the knowledge that I'd grown the fuck up finally, I'd let down my guards, and it didn't matter.

Because the chance of a happily ever after was too late.

Chapter Thirty-Six

Gil

SCHOOL LET OUT in a gush of same-dressed students.

Nerves raced down my spine. Sweat broke out on my palms.

I waited until Olive spilled out with her satchel bashing against her side and her smile wide and confident.

She'd grown a lot in the past year.

She was no longer the tiny girl with hurricane love but a timid heart. She was closing in on ten years old and resembled the young woman she'd become.

Wiping sweaty palms on my jeans, I checked that my grey t-shirt was presentable and my new boots—that already held specks of paint—were tied, then crossed the road to surprise my daughter.

"Olive Oyl."

She slammed to a stop. Her bag swinging and mouth falling open. "Dad...*dad?*" Then she was running, bolting into my arms and leaping into me.

I swept her from the pavement and hugged her close. Her hair still smelled of strawberries. Her body still felt like her. She'd changed but was also so familiar.

"How? How are you here?" She squirmed in my embrace. "I thought you were sick! And...in jail."

I put her down, unable to stop grinning. "I wanted to surprise you."

"Did you break out?" Her voice lowered to a harsh whisper. "Are they gonna come arrest you for escaping?"

I laughed hard. "No. I didn't break out. I was released."

Her forehead furrowed. "But...it's not time yet. O and I have a calendar at home that shows when you'll be free, and it's not for ages."

I fought the urge to touch her ponytail. To cup her cheek. "I got lucky."

"So…you mean, you're out for real? Like forever?" Hope exploded in her pretty grey gaze.

I nodded.

She squealed and launched herself back into my arms.

Chuckling, I held her while she nuzzled into my neck, her legs kicking my knees in excitement. "This is *amazing!* This is so good. Yay!" Pulling away, seriousness bled through her joy. "So…are you moving in with Justin and O and me? We'll need to get a bigger place. There isn't another bedroom."

O had told me she'd moved in with Justin a while ago.

But I hadn't pried for more.

I battled the awful question. The question I couldn't run away from.

Were O and Justin sharing a bedroom?

Were they a true family, raising my daughter as their own?

I swallowed it back, shaking my head and that nasty thought away.

So what if they were?

I had to be happy for their happiness.

I would not ruin it just because I was out early and suddenly desperate to see if I could salvage the wreckage of O and I.

"I have my own place. Not far from Justin's."

She looked around, searching for the guards she'd grown used to tolerating whenever she came to visit me. "So…does that mean you don't want to live with us?" Her forehead wrinkled. "You don't want to live with me?"

I ducked to one knee, looking into her pretty eyes. "Of *course* I want to live with you. I was hoping…well, I hoped you'd come live with me in my new place. I got it for us." I brushed a lock of dark hair from her cheek, then captured her hand. "But I can see how that's rude of me to expect you to change your life so much. So…if you don't want to live with me, that's totally okay too."

My heart hurt.

I didn't like the stares of other parents or the high-pitched chatter of other kids.

I cursed myself for being so forward when I should've known Olive would grow attached to Justin and O. Why did I expect her to leap back into my arms when she had a great thing going with them?

She licked her lips. "It's not that. It's just…um…" She kicked a pebble with her patent black school shoe. "I just have to ask them if that's okay."

"Completely understand." I stood, glancing around at the mayhem of parents picking up children. I probably looked totally suspicious. Stepping back a little, I stared down a young woman who looked at me as if I was some paedophile.

Olive took my hand, tugging me gently. "I know. We can ask them right now!"

"Wait...what?" My eyes fell to hers, my body yanked into movement thanks to her tenacity.

Pulling me across the street, she grinned. "They're here. They pick me up."

"They do?"

"Yep." She skipped beside me. "Sometimes it's just O and sometimes Justin. But lately, they've both come to get me."

Lately.

I swallowed hard.

Was that a sign of true love finding separation excruciating?

She pointed up ahead. "That's O's car."

My legs suddenly turned into pillars of concrete. I stopped without thinking; fear a tangible thing in my blood.

O lounged against her car, waiting for my daughter. Her gorgeous face was framed by long dark blonde hair. Her smile was carefree and genuine.

And beside her was Justin.

My chest crumbled as he shoved her, mid-laugh, as if she'd ribbed him and he'd retaliated. Their body language was loose and happy, smiles full of affection.

I'd given Justin permission to chase her if she'd wanted to be chased.

I wouldn't stand in their way if they got married or wanted nothing to do with me now I was free, but I couldn't deny that my heart fell into a blender and sliced to pieces. A salsa of pain. A rain of ruin.

"Come on." Olive tugged my hand, yanking me toward the two people who meant so much to me in different ways. Doing my best to keep my face neutral and ordering my arms not to reach out and snatch O, I smiled the best I could as Justin's gaze met mine.

He froze.

O looked to where his eyes had locked.

She froze too.

For a second, guilt flashed over her face before a huge grin split her lips and she charged toward me. "Gil!"

I braced myself for her hug, unable to fight the urge to bury my face in the crook of her neck. She felt so warm and soft and right.

She felt like home.

Justin came over, pulling me into an embrace after O let me go. "Mate, how the hell are you here? Why didn't you tell us you were out?" He slapped me on the shoulder. "Did you just get released? We could've picked you up."

I hugged him back, gratefulness a warm Band-Aid over my bleeding heart. "Don't get mad but I got out a few weeks ago."

Olive's face scrunched up, dragging my eyes down to her level. "You didn't come see us straight away?"

Us.

Not me.

Us.

Like it or not, she'd made a family with O and Justin. Whatever our joint future held, I would share Olive with them. I wouldn't take her away. Not after nineteen months of them being together.

I kept my voice neutral of pain. "I wanted to have a home before I came to you, little spinach. I can still call you that, right?"

She frowned. "Yeah, but I don't know why you didn't come find us sooner. You wasted all that time when we could've been together."

"I didn't waste it. I used it to get my painting back on track and fix what I'd broken."

"Huh." She crossed her arms, still annoyed. "I still think you should've told us."

Her firecracker temper made me chuckle, but I swallowed it back, staying serious. "I agree. It was wrong. Can you forgive me?"

Her lips twitched. "I suppose so."

"Phew." My eyes trailed to O as understanding glowed on her face.

"You've been painting," she said softly. "I haven't been online lately…I should've checked your page."

"I wanted it to be a surprise."

"It is. A great surprise." She smiled. "So…you're working?"

I nodded. "A few commissions."

O's hazel eyes warmed with a thousand different things. "That's wonderful." She understood why I needed to repair myself on my own terms. She got why it was important that I came to them whole and not ask for more hand-outs.

"That's great, Clark." Justin patted me on the back. "Guess you'll be slammed with work again. No rest for the wicked."

"He's not wicked," Olive piped up. "He might've been sent to prison, but he isn't wicked." She stepped closer, and I wound my arm around her delicate shoulders.

"Thanks for having my back."

"Anytime." She winked, filling my chest with love.

O watched us, the same kindness and gentleness that'd always drawn me to her spilling from her soul. "Olive's missed you. We all have."

I couldn't look away from her. "I've missed you." Clearing my throat, I added, "All of you. I missed everyone."

O tucked flyaway hair behind her ear. "Do you...do you need somewhere to sleep? You're welcome to come home with us."

Two words that left literary power and became physical as knives.

Us and home.

So they were together, and they shared a home.

"Yeah, mate." Justin shoved his hands into his suit pockets. "You're welcome anytime. You know that. The couch is super comfy. I can vouch for it."

Justin only had a two-bedroom place.

Olive had one.

O most likely had the other.

And if Justin wasn't couch surfing anymore...that meant he and O shared a room.

And a bed.

Fuck.

I hadn't wanted to jump to conclusions, but it became impossible not to.

"That's very kind of you, guys, but..." I let Olive go, my feet backing up and putting distance between us. "I have my own place."

Stop being an ungrateful prick.

This was the price I'd been willing to pay.

So pay it.

"Besides, I've already been far too much of an imposition."

"You've never be an imposition, Gil." O's eyes burned. "You know that."

I didn't know what to say or how to deal with the wave of

emotion emitting from her. My skin prickled, my heart begged, life felt empty knowing I'd lost her.

But it *wasn't* empty.

It was full because I'd paid my sins, my conscience was clear, and for the first time, I had everything to look forward to.

Olive was safe.

I was free to protect her the way she deserved.

Free to spoil her, raise her, and love her until she became an adult in her own right.

That was what I focused on.

That was what I was grateful for.

I forced another grin. "I better let you guys go—"

"But you just got here." Olive pouted. "I want longer than the stupid fifteen minutes in prison."

"Yeah, Clark. You can't go yet." Justin smoothed his suit. "Tell you what, we need to celebrate! Let's go out. Have a drink. Catch up. All of us."

Olive bounced on the spot. "Yay! Let's go."

O sucked in a breath.

My every cell was attuned to her. She flinched as if going out to eat with me wasn't tolerable. "I don't know. You probably have a million and one things to do—"

"Nope. Done for the day," Justin interrupted. "Let's go to dinner."

"Dinner is hours away, silly." Olive wrinkled her nose. "I've only just finished school."

Justin held out his hand, letting Olive slap it as if he deserved being told off. "Okay, smartypants, call it a late lunch or pre-dinner. How about a lunner? Does that work? You know...like breakfast and lunch are combined to make brunch? Lunner."

He shrugged as O groaned, rolling her eyes. "What? It's a legitimate question."

"You're so weird." Olive giggled.

"Takes one to know one."

O laughed. "Both of you are weird."

"You're weirder," Justin shot back.

"I have to be to put up with you two." O's gaze sparkled with contentment.

The trio of togetherness while I watched in envy.

The ease between them.

The connection that'd grown while I'd been locked away.

I stood quietly, not sure how to untangle myself from this

family. Not sure how to claim back my daughter when she'd found something so special. And most of all, unsure how I could cope after losing both girls of my heart to a guy who deserved to be loved as much as he was.

Justin cleared his throat, noticing my stiffness. He tapped the top of the bronze sedan beside him. "Everyone pile in. Let's move this party to somewhere cooler than a pavement."

O inched toward me, hesitating before threading her arm through mine.

The second she touched me, my body reacted.

My heart pounded.

My blood gushed.

The chemistry and electricity that always punished us sprang into full force.

I shuddered. I couldn't breathe.

O murmured, "You'll come eat with us...won't you, Gil?"

There was that word again.

Once upon a time, I'd fought against such a promise. I'd told her there could never be an us because I was hiding so many goddamn things.

Now that word belonged to them, not me.

Shit.

Olive hugged me from the other side, putting me in the centre of an affection sandwich. I couldn't stand much more before I broke, so I untangled myself and said the simplest thing. The thing guaranteed to avoid an argument but also destined to destroy me. "Sure. Dinner would be nice."

And it would be.

Dinner out in the real world with my child and friends would be better than nice.

I just had to rein in my heart and force it to get the memo that O was off-limits.

"Great." O smiled.

My nervous system disagreed as O strolled to the car. Returned to Justin. Left me.

I drank in the way she moved. The dancer's grace that still ran in her blood. The kindness that was visible around her, a softness that made her ever more stunning.

I fell deeper into love with her when I should've been schooling myself into platonic boundaries.

Justin opened the door for Olive as she hopped in the back. O went to sit in the back with her but I leaped into action and ripped open the front door. "Please. I'll take the back."

"You sure?"

"Yeah. It'll be fun hanging with, what did Justin call her? The pipsqueak?"

Olive piped up from inside the car. "I'm not a pipsqueak anymore. I grew."

O chuckled and slipped into the car. "She has many nicknames these days. Pest being a favourite one."

"You're the pest." Olive stuck out her tongue. "The best pest."

O laughed again and I hid my gratefulness of their care and the agony of what I'd missed out on. Falling into the car, I forced a grin at my daughter. "I can see pest suiting you."

"You know nothing." She arched her chin, flicking her hair smugly.

I know some things, little spinach.

I know that I love you.

And O.

And you've both moved on.

And I know I'll do whatever it takes to not jeopardize the happiness you've found.

Justin turned the car on and switched into gear. "All in? Let's go."

Chapter Thirty-Seven

Olin

HOW COULD DOING something as mundane as going to a restaurant be equally strenuous and enjoyable?

I couldn't stop looking at Gil.

Couldn't stop pinching myself that he was out and free and back.

Nineteen months served.

An eternity for all of us.

Yet…it felt like yesterday that he'd painted me and we'd slept together and I'd vowed that I'd never turn my back on him.

Each time I'd visited him with Olive, I'd wanted to tell him that I would wait. That we weren't over. That I'd forgiven him and accepted that whatever madness we shared was worth fighting for.

That I finally knew I belonged to him, with him, and always had.

I wouldn't give that up.

For anything.

But each visit, I kept my secret.

Until one day, I no longer knew if he even wanted me in that way anymore. He'd given me no sign that he hungered for me. His smiles were warm but reserved. His animation and energy given to Olive while I was just his daughter's chaperone.

I appreciated why he'd pulled away.

In his mind, we'd said goodbye that night in my apartment.

And I'd moved in with Justin.

"What did they feed you in jail?" Olive asked, sucking on the paper straw in her raspberry coke.

Gil raked a hand through his hair, looking ruggedly

handsome. His messy dark locks were just as wild. His eyes just as piercing. He ought to have looked older thanks to almost two years in prison, yet whatever demons had hounded him had gone.

He no longer looked wary of the world or on guard to everyone around him.

He looked like the boy I'd fallen in love with.

"Bland, boring things mainly." He twisted in his chair, facing his adorable daughter. "They need a proper chef."

"I can cook okay." Olive stirred her straw. "O taught me how to bake banana muffins the other day."

"You did?" Gil's gaze caught mine.

My heart fluttered.

"I can't take the credit. The cookbook did all the work. We just followed the recipe."

"They were pretty tasty, though," Justin said, sipping an ice-cold pint. "Ten out of ten."

"Yeah, and you ate them all." Olive pretended to frown. "You didn't leave any for me."

"You're forgetting you ate three, you glutton. I only had two."

"Oh yeah? I think you should go back to school and learn how to count." Olive giggled.

"I'm an accountant, little pest. I know how to count. And you had three." Justin winked at Gil. "That's why she's grown so much. She's a piggy."

Gil laughed, sounding strained, almost as if he wished like hell he'd had the stupid volley match with Olive.

I worried we'd overstepped. Feared Gil would think we'd replaced him just because we bantered a lot.

In the months we'd all lived together, I'd come to love Olive to the point of disaster. If her father held my soul, she held my heart undoubtedly. I was unbelievably happy Gil was back, but if I was honest, I was also terrified.

Terrified of losing Olive.

Of losing the family Justin, she, and I had created.

I hadn't been lonely with them.

I hadn't been lost.

Gil would always be a missing piece of me but I'd found enough to be happy. That was another reason I hadn't needed to travel. I'd found contentment in the very same city where all my dreams had shattered.

"I'll bake you some, Dad." Olive touched Gil's forearm on

the table. "And you can have all of them. Justin gets none."

"Meanie." Justin wiped a fake tear from his cheek. "I get it. Now your dad's back, I'm forgotten." He laughed, but it held the same thread of fear I felt.

We both struggled.

Both ecstatic that Gil was home.

Both afraid that Gil was home.

Olive blew a kiss to Justin across the table. "I won't forget about you. Ever."

"Ah, shucks." Justin smiled, deeply genuine and relieved. "I'm going to hold you to that. I expect weekly hangouts. And daily updates."

"Wait…are-are you kicking me out?" Olive squeaked.

Justin glanced at me, panic in his eyes. "Of course not. I just figured with your dad back you'd want to—"

"Olive wanted to check with you guys first," Gil cut in. "I have my own place. I'm earning an income." He swallowed hard, taking a sip of his lemonade and avoiding my stare.

His abhorrence for alcohol hadn't changed in prison then. He still hated liquor. I doubted I'd ever catch him drunk again.

Gil rushed, "But I don't expect Olive to move out if you're not comfortable with that. If you guys are happy, then…I'm happy for her to keep living with you."

Everything in my chest ached.

He was once again willing to sacrifice the most important person in his world. He'd sacrificed me. He'd sacrificed Olive. He did it out of love, but I worried Olive might take it as if he didn't want her enough to fight for her.

Justin leaned forward, the green velvet bench seat we shared creaking under his weight. He looked seriously at Olive, asking her as an adult for her decision. "What do *you* want, Olive Oyl? You have three grown-ups wrapped around your little finger, so you get to choose."

She bit her lip, her gaze dancing from Gil to me to Justin and back again.

The ancient pub where we sat hugged us with smoke and stale beer. The low beams and dark walls cocooned us, making it seem like it was midnight and not late afternoon.

This was one of the few places still open and serving food at three-thirty in the afternoon. And in a way, it was fitting. A pub this old held so many secrets. Lives had changed, and friendships were tested, all hidden within its protection.

Just like now.

"Um…" Olive's eyes widened, feeling the pressure.

She loved Justin.

She loved me.

Those two facts I knew without a doubt.

But she would never love anyone as much as she loved her father, and that was exactly how it should be.

"It's okay, Olive. You don't need to rush. And you don't need to decide right away. Everything will work out, you'll see." I nodded in encouragement. "We're all family. Always will be."

Gil sucked in a breath.

Olive relaxed a little.

Justin picked up his beer and held it out for a toast. "To family."

Gil clinked his lemonade, Olive tapped her raspberry coke, and I raised my wine glass. "Family."

We all drank, sharing a tentative smile, all of us wondering what the future held.

Justin broke the tension by asking Gil, "So, you've been out for a few weeks, got your business back on track, and found a place. What else have you been up to?"

Gil slouched in his chair, comfortable with the easier topic. "I started my community service two weeks ago. I go every other day for a few hours."

"Oh yeah? What do they have you doing?"

"Last week, I helped out at a cattery. The week before that I helped move heavy furniture around a Salvation Army store. I think next week I'll be on food prep somewhere downtown at a shelter."

"Enjoying it?"

Gil nodded. "Actually, yeah. Seeing things I wouldn't necessarily see has been great for creative inspiration. It sucks to witness the hardships of others, but watching the other side of society has been beneficial. It's been almost healing to paint their sadness."

"I get that." Justin swigged back his beer. "Bet it's nice to be painting again. And not teaching untalented convicts."

He smiled. "It was actually kind of rewarding teaching. A lot of inmates found it calming. Teaching the class was probably a reason I was allowed out so early on good behaviour. Rehabilitation comes in many forms."

Gil's gaze caught mine, trapping me in the green icy depths

like only he could. "It didn't escape me that I actually started to enjoy it, after despising teachers all my life. Ironic that I found satisfaction in being the one thing I hated."

Hated one teacher in particular.

Jane Tallup who did her best to ruin him.

I'd stalked her online.

I'd found her still teaching English in Japan. A few months after Gil's imprisonment, I'd requested local authorities to file an arrest for her if she ever came back to England. To get justice for what she did to Gil.

Maybe one day I'd tell him, but not now.

Not when the past had been dealt with and the future beckoned bright.

God, I'd missed him.

I wanted to talk to him, but I didn't know what to say. How to say things. How he'd take them.

Almost as if he sensed my reluctance to share, Gil asked, "O...you still working at that place...Status?"

"Status Enterprises." I shook my head. "No. I quit not long after you were—"

"Incarcerated. I get it." His tone held no malice or meanness, but he couldn't hide the ache of loneliness. "Where do you work now then?"

I swallowed a mouthful of white wine. "Well, after giving up my lease and moving in with Justin and Olive...I still planned on travelling. I just couldn't stand going back to that office though. So...Justin had an opening for a personal assistant and...offered it to me."

Gil coughed. "You live and work together?"

Justin winced. "Yeah, O's become rather fundamental to our office. She basically runs my life and the other partner's."

"That's great." Gil looked as if he'd lost something all over again. "Sounds like a perfect fit."

I rubbed at the lacerating lightning inside my chest. I felt guilty all over again. Upset for upsetting Gil. Confused as to why he looked at me as if he wanted to stab himself through the heart.

He was the one who acted as if we were over.

He was the one who told Justin he could be with me—just like high-school.

Justin hadn't wanted to tell me what'd happened on the phone a fortnight or so into Gil's sentence. He'd come home steely-eyed and tense, hiding the truth until I kept bugging him for answers.

I'd been pissed off that Gil thought I would jump into Justin's bed the moment he was gone. Furious that he'd given his 'permission'.

What happened between Justin and I was our business and ours alone.

Silence became strained, growing tighter as a waitress came over with big bowls of fries, onion rings, and a basket of fish bites.

Olive stuck her hand into the onion rings straight away, oblivious to the stress between adults. "Yum."

This is stupid.

I wouldn't let tension ruin the celebration of having Gil back.

Reaching over the table, I placed my hand on Gil's, squeezing the heat and strength of him. "We missed you so much."

I.

I missed you.

He flinched but turned his hand up so we linked fingers. "I missed you guys too."

You.

I missed *you.*

Olive put her head on his shoulder. "But we never have to be apart again so that's the good thing."

Gil tugged his hand from mine.

I couldn't breathe through the pain still alive between us.

He grabbed a fry and grinned as wide as he could. "Exactly. We'll be together. Always."

Justin chewed a fish bite. "And that brings us back to living arrangements." He held up his hand when I went to remind him that we didn't need to rush, adding, "Decisions don't need to be made now. But…if Gil is okay with it. How about we head over to his place, check it out, and go from there." He smiled at Olive. "What do you say?"

Olive tapped her fingers against her mouth, thinking deeply. "Sure. That sounds good." She looked at Gil. "That okay, Dad? Can we go see your place?"

Gil nodded quickly. "Of course, that's okay. More than okay."

"Great." Justin wiped salt off his fingers. "It's a plan."

Gil went still, his gaze shifting from Justin to me, pinning us to the velvet bench. "Just so we're clear, I'm not going to demand or expect anything. Olive is yours as much as mine. I'm happy if you want to keep her, and I'll see her when you're free. Or vice versa."

The thought of not seeing Olive every day. Of not making pancakes with her or experimenting with other cooking with her. Of not watching her laugh and scream at the TV with Justin when he watched football. We didn't own Olive. We hadn't created her. But we had grown into something that meant a great deal to all of us.

"Of course." I nodded. "We're together now. That means all of us."

Us.

That pesky, damning word.

Gil's green stare shot right into my heart. "I love you." His cheeks pinked as he hugged his daughter and glanced at Justin. "All of you. We're family."

Those three little words wouldn't stop colliding in my chest.

I love you.

I

love

you.

I love you too.

Chapter Thirty-Eight

Olin

"WOW, THIS IS super cool." Olive drifted forward, inspecting Gil's new apartment.

Tiny in size but cosy.

Newer than my old apartment, the walls were a fresh white and the floors bamboo planks.

Gil's paints rested in a big box on the dining room table, reminding me that he still had a bunch of belongings in storage at Justin's.

The kitchen was modern with nice pendant lights, the bathroom with a shower over the bath, and two bedrooms: one with a queen bed, black sheets, and Gil's signature scent of citrus and paint, and a second with a king single, rainbow bedspread, and a huge stuffed owl waiting in a rattan chair by the wardrobe.

I moved toward the quaint lounge.

Olive would be very happy here. Happier than anywhere because she'd be with her father. Justin and I had been a temporary fix. We'd been there to nurse her nightmares and help her feel safe again, but there'd always been something missing, something we could never be.

"Did you want to stay the night here, Olive?" I asked softly. "We can go back to Justin's and pack a bag if you want?"

Olive paused, yet another huge decision for such a young girl to make. I hated putting her on the spot and I hated that all our lives would have to change from this point on, but I also refused to keep daughter and father away from each other.

"It's the weekend tomorrow." She frowned. "I have dance

practice."

Gil's head snapped up. "You dance?"

Olive nodded proudly. "O showed me a few moves when we stayed with her before you went to prison, remember? I was too busy with school to learn more, but last month she taught me a few new steps. But now I go to a fancy place because she said I have talent."

Gil looked at me, disbelief and awe in his gaze. "Are you dancing again?"

I blushed, hoping he didn't mind that I'd added an afterschool activity to Olive's life. I would continue paying for the lessons. Now I worked for Justin, I'd been able to squirrel money away. He overpaid me really but I was good at my job and worked hard.

We both did.

It was probably rare that we could live together, raise a child that wasn't ours, and work together without trying to kill each other.

Guilt squeezed me again, but I kept pushing it away. I had nothing to feel guilty about. Nothing.

"No but we had fun playing one night. She's a natural." I beamed, forgetting as I sometimes did, that Olive wasn't mine. That her skill at dancing didn't come from me but someone else. Maybe someone in Jane Tallup's family tree had been a dancer, lithe and limber like I used to be. "I was going to tell you…we wanted it to be a surprise next time we came to visit you." I smiled. "But you visited us instead."

Gil's gaze caught mine, holding for long enough to make my heart skip a beat. The green shone with gratefulness and pride.

He cleared his throat, saying, "She's always been quick to learn." Turning to grin at his daughter, he added, "You'll have to show me a few of your moves."

Olive's face lit up. "Why don't you come to my practice tomorrow? I'm still new there, but you can watch." Her eyes dipped with shyness. "Then maybe I could have a sleepover here…with you."

Gil's face turned serious and intense. "I'd love that. I've love that very much."

"Great." Olive spun in place, her arms flying out in a messy pirouette. "It's a date."

Gil looked at me again.

That hissing, licking need that always consumed me around

him raced down my spine.

It'd been almost two years since we'd talked in private.

Two years where his daughter hadn't been there—a sweet distraction from our honesty.

If Olive moved back in with Gil tomorrow, I'd lose my chance to be truthful.

To tell him exactly how I felt.

To tell him honestly what'd happened between Justin and me.

I owed him that.

I owed him transparency because he was home now, and we were family.

And family didn't keep secrets.

While Gil drifted off and made plans with Olive for tomorrow, I made plans to return tonight and fight for our future.

Chapter Thirty-Nine

Gil

I SAT AT the dining room table doing what I did best. Painting.

The sketch I'd done of a ballerina with musical notes dancing around her, signified both O and my daughter. Olive had been taking dancing lessons. What else had I missed while being in jail? *Everything.*

Dipping my brush into the water glass, I opted for a fuchsia watercolour, highlighting the ballerina's slippers.

I'd missed O and Justin getting close. I'd missed joking and arguing with Olive. I'd missed restaurants and moonlight strolls.

But at least the things I'd missed had given me redemption. They'd wiped my future clean, so I was at peace to enjoy those things. *Deserved* to enjoy those things.

Looking up, I studied Olive's bedroom. The apartment was small and both bedrooms entered straight onto the living area. The decoration I'd purchased and prepared, the hope I'd nursed, all sat hushed and waiting.

Tomorrow, I would get to see Olive dance. I'd no doubt suffer reliving a past where I'd watched another girl dance for me, and then I'd say goodbye to O and Justin and bring Olive home.

We'd start slow.

One night to see if she still loved me enough to live with me.

Another night if she wanted to stay.

Then possibly, *hopefully*, a whole week, where I'd be privileged enough to take her to school, cook her dinner, and help with her homework.

Swirling the brush in water again, I swiped the thin, soft

bristles in aquamarine to decorate the dancing notes and threads of music ribbon.

A knock resonated through my front door, wrenching my head up.

My eyes narrowed. Suspicion that'd saved me from a few beatings in prison made my instincts prickle. Who the hell would visit me at eleven in the evening?

The knock came again.

I stood and strode across the small lounge. With muscles tense for confrontation, I unlocked the door and ripped it wide.

O flinched, her hand flying to her chest. "God, you scared me."

I froze. "*I* scared *you*? You're the one on my stoop at almost midnight."

"Sorry, I—" She blushed; her tongue licked her bottom lip. "I admit it's a little late. I didn't wake you, did I?" Her skin glowed as if imagining me in bed made her hot.

Suspicion bled into lust in a single heartbeat.

She couldn't be here.

I didn't have the strength.

My hand curled around the door handle as I fought the urge to slam it in her face. Better that than snatching her wrist and jerking her into a kiss.

And not just any kiss but a full-blown nuclear meltdown of a kiss.

"You need to leave." I braced myself, inching the door to its closed position.

Her hazel gaze widened. Her mouth parted. "You're kicking me out without even inviting me in?"

The way she looked at me.

The way her entire body invited me to take.

I swallowed hard. "You can't come in, O. Not tonight."

Her face fell. "Why?" Her question was soft…almost a whisper, but it ricocheted through my blood.

I went to lie.

To tell her it didn't matter. That my reasons were my own.

But…I'd made a promise to stop staying silent.

Truth was the only way forward.

Every muscle locked in place as I muttered, "Because I'm recently released from prison. I haven't been with anyone in a very long time. The last person was you. And you've always been *my* person." I cleared my throat, my voice growing raspy and harsh.

"But you're not my person anymore. And I respect that, so I need you to respect my request for you to go."

Her arms wrapped around herself. "Wow, I wasn't expecting honesty."

"Yeah, well. That's what you'll get from now on." I raked a shaky hand through my hair. My self-restraint had frayed so much around the edges, and I was hanging on by a fucking thread. "Please, O. Go home. Go back to Justin."

O ducked her head, her eyes skating down my body with fire. "Not yet. I came to talk to you. It's important that we talk."

"Talking isn't going to be my strong suit tonight." I angled my hips away, doing my best to hide just how much my body *didn't* want to talk.

I was so hard, it hurt.

"I've been wanting to talk to you for almost two years, Gil. At least give me ten minutes." Her eyes met mine, emotion bleeding through her calmness. "If you don't like what I have to say, then I'll go. No questions asked. At least…at least I'll know I tried and can put it behind me."

Didn't she get it?

I let her into this flat and talking would swiftly end up beneath the clothes I'd rip from her body. I swallowed a groan as images of her naked and me inside her exploded in my mind.

Goddammit, I wanted her so fucking much.

"O, please don't ask me to let you in here." I dropped my head, glaring at her beneath my brow. "I don't have the best self-control, and I don't trust myself around you."

She stepped forward, placing her hand on the doorjamb. "Ten minutes, Gil." Her voice turned smoky and loose. "You won't do anything. I know you and your honour."

In a split second, my fist curled around her wrist, my arm yanked her inside, and the door slammed closed. My entire body burned as I pressed against her, wedging her against the wall.

She sucked in a heady breath, her eyes sparkling with need.

"I have no honour left. I have *nothing* left. And it's fucking liberating because I can start anew. I *have* started anew. Whatever I make is fresh and untainted by all the shit I did wrong." My hand cupped her cheek, holding her still. "And you were my biggest mistake, O. Just like it was your mistake to come here."

I already regretted my actions.

I already cursed what I couldn't stop.

But my lips ignored my loyalty to Justin and sought hers.

They crushed over her mouth. Her taste exploded onto my tongue. My knees wobbled. My breath stopped. And I shoved myself away from her as fast as I could.

"Shit." Pacing with my hands buried in my hair, I growled. "Please, go. I won't betray Justin. Not after everything he's done for me."

O stood plastered to the wall, her gorgeous eyes tracking me. "Gil, please...calm down."

"I won't fucking calm down. I can't be around you, O. You're not mine anymore. You're *his*."

"I'm not though." Her hands balled. "If you just listen to what I have to say, you'd—"

"Wha-what did you say?" My feet glued to the floor. My hands fell from my hair.

Her chin arched. "I'm not his."

"But...you live together."

"We do."

"You share a bedroom."

She smiled, laughing quietly. "No, we don't."

"What?"

"I share with Olive."

My heart hammered. "How...how is that possible?"

"We have two singles. We're roommates."

"Why would you bunk with a child?"

O sighed gently, infuriatingly patient. "Because that child had nightmares for months after you were locked up. She still has them occasionally. It made sense for me to be right there when she woke up screaming rather than have no one to soothe her."

"Fuck." I wrapped hands in my hair, overwhelmed all over again at the selflessness of this woman. "You truly are the kindest person I know."

"No...I'm not." Her face fell. "If I was kind, I would've told you this a long time ago. Instead of keeping a secret that's literally been chewing me alive."

I dropped my hands; a shiver ran down my spine. "What secret?" I shook my head, still unable to believe she wasn't with Justin after all the time they'd lived together, worked together, been together. "The secret that you're in love with Justin?"

She rolled her eyes. "No, dammit."

"Look, you don't have to lie to protect me. I'm happy for you. I'm glad you're both—"

She sighed dramatically. "Oh, my God, will you just listen?

And you're happy? Really, Gil? Honestly, how would you feel if I stood here and told you that yes, Justin and I *were* together. That yes, we sleep with each other every night. That yes, I'm madly in love with him and plan to marry him next week." She planted hands on her hips, her temper appearing. "Tell me, Gil. How does that make you feel?"

How did that make me feel?

Fuck.

I'd tell her.

She wanted to know so badly?

Fine.

Honesty was a disease because once you'd started, you couldn't fucking stop.

"I feel as if my heart has cracked into pieces and turned to dust. I feel guilty because I shouldn't want you and angry that I still do. I hate that I have my freedom and Olive is safe and I'm still not fucking satisfied. That I'll never be satisfied until I have you. Until we're together…just like we should've been since school. And I'm fucking furious that Justin gets to touch you, kiss you, love you when all along it should've been me."

"There." Her hands slipped from her hips. "Was that so hard?"

I groaned. "Don't ask me what's hard, O."

Her lips twitched with dark humour, her gaze trailing to my jeans.

My need was evident. Grotesquely eager after being caged for so long.

"It's a relief to finally hear you say it."

"Say what?"

"That you love me."

I stiffened. "I told you before. I told you so many—"

"You told me while tying me up to paint and sacrifice me. You told me when we were saying goodbye." O pushed off from the wall, coming toward me in the middle of the lounge. "You told me in texts and whispers, you told me…but you didn't make me believe you."

I trembled. "How was I supposed to do that? It was the honest to God truth. Still is."

"I believe you now."

"Why, what changed?"

"The fact that *you* believe that you love me. Your jealousy makes yourself believe."

Anger rippled through me. "You're saying I didn't love you even when I told you I did?"

"I don't think you trusted you had the *right* to love me. You wanted me, but you wouldn't have kept me if you thought I deserved better."

"Of course, I wouldn't. I was the puppet of a psychopath and then facing jail. Why would I trap you into a relationship with someone like me?"

"Because I love you, too. I never stopped."

The world screeched to a halt. Words stuck in the back of my throat. "You love me? Still?"

She smiled. "It seems it's a lifetime affliction."

"But...we agreed it was over. You didn't contradict me."

"I needed time. I needed to come to terms with the truth."

"What truth?"

"That I've always loved you, even when I shouldn't. That I always put you first, even when some might call that weak. That I believe we're meant to be together, no matter what nonsense life throws in our way." Her voice lowered, softened. "I've wanted to tell you for ages. Every time I came to visit you, I wanted to say I was waiting for you. Every time we said goodbye, I wanted to hug you and say it wasn't really goodbye. That you were it for me. For always."

My heart tripped and stumbled. "Then...why didn't you?"

I didn't dare believe her.

Couldn't figure out what this meant.

"Because Olive was there, and she took first priority. Our visits were for her. To assure her you were okay, even if you were trapped for a little while. I wouldn't take that away from her—"

She sighed, shaking her head slightly. "You know what? That's a lie too. I had plenty of opportunity to talk to you. I could've told you in a letter. I could've visited on my own. I could've just called you and told you that I was waiting, worried, and completely unable to get over you."

I swallowed, trembling. "You didn't tell me because you didn't want it to be real. You might've still been in love with me, but you didn't want to be."

She nodded, spearing a harpoon through my chest. "You're right," she said quietly. "And that's why I didn't tell you. That's the honest truth."

Truth had always been brutal, but now it cleaved me into pieces. "Look, O, if you came here to tell me you don't want to love me anymore, that's fine. I get it. But we can work out Olive's schedule without—"

"Stop." Placing her hand over my pounding, aching heart, she murmured, "Not telling you I was still in love with you was my one selfish choice. I wanted to feel no obligation or expectation by announcing that I would wait. I wanted to wait…for *me*, not you. I wanted the freedom to change my mind. I needed the space to choose you without feeling trapped." Her lips tipped into a shy smile. "You know…that's the first time I've been honest with myself too. I always made up excuses about why I hadn't told you. That I didn't know if you felt the same way anymore. That it wasn't the right time or place. That our complicated past meant our future could never work. But none of that matters because…it's always been you."

I shivered. "But…what about Justin?"

O spread her hands with a shrug. "What about him? I love Justin. He's one of the kindest, sweetest, most uncomplicated people I know. He's been so good to me, Olive, and you. Yes, I moved in with him because it made financial sense and because Olive was more comfortable having both of us there. But at no point has there ever been a romantic entanglement—even when we were kids. He always knew how I felt about you. He knew there was never anyone else for me."

A bright smile lit up her face. "You can ask him. He started dating a woman called Chloe a few months ago. She's super nice. Don't think it's going to last the distance, as she's a little too independent for a guy like Justin who just wants to dote, but it's nice to see him with someone."

She sighed again. "So…you see, I'm not with Justin. And you don't have to feel guilty for wanting me. You have me. You've *always* had me and—"

I didn't let her finish.

I grabbed her, wrapped her in my arms and kissed her.

Her spine melted.

Her body liquefied in my embrace. And her mouth opened, welcoming me to kiss her deeper, harder, forever.

Heads dancing. Tongues licking.

I couldn't get enough.

The chains around my heart broke away. Padlocks shattered. Ropes unbound. All the restrictions I'd placed on myself vanished the longer we kissed.

There was something special about this kiss.

Something new and honest and true.

This was real.

Real and promising eternity.

Her heart pounded against mine as I tripped backward, needing every part of her.

Immediately.

Now.

Unable to keep kissing her and navigating my new place, I scooped her into my arms, and stormed into my bedroom.

O shivered as I placed her onto the bed.

A bed.

We'd connected in so many erotic ways. With paint smearing us and cameras recording us, but we'd never done it somewhere that promised romance as well as sex. Somewhere that gave us the freedom to fall into each other, rather than drown out the love with the noise of why we couldn't.

Her hands landed on my chest, her fingernails scraping down my belly. Her touch ran over the scar from Jeffrey shooting me, and banished the last remaining bad memories. Maybe I'd get a tattoo like hers—colour and design that was already a part of me to cover up the ugly scars and mistakes of my past.

But then again, those mistakes had made me worthy.

Worthy of my soul-mate.

My mouth crushed hers again.

I kissed her.

And kissed her.

I kissed her with the softness I'd always wanted to treat her with. The respect, the worship, the undying affection where every touch bled with permanence.

I'd never experienced softness.

Never allowed myself to relax or trust enough to give myself entirely to another.

The sensation of falling into her and out of me, of creating something new together, wrapped around my heart and squeezed. It squeezed with joy and euphoria and a crushing amount of regret.

Regret at not experiencing this overwhelming closeness before.

Of not realising just how special our connection was when we were younger—before I almost ruined everything.

My pulse pounded as our kiss took on another dimension.

Of longing and longevity.

I would kiss this woman for the rest of my life and never get tired of her, never stop wanting her or being so fucking grateful that she waited.

That she had an endless well of forgiveness and strength to put up with all my mistakes.

She moaned as my fingers trailed to her belly, lifting her white t-shirt over her head and breaking our kiss. Hating the distance, I unzipped her jeans and shimmied them down her legs before kissing her again.

Our lips never stopped touching as I removed her bra, socks, and underwear.

Only once she was naked, did I stop.

I pulled away, looking down at her hair tousled on my bed, her perfect breasts rising and falling with erratic breath, and her lips red and swollen from mine.

She was the most perfect thing I'd ever seen.

And she belonged to me as surely as I belonged to her.

It wasn't a matter of possession.

It was a matter of undeniability.

Of two souls being one.

"My turn," she breathed. Arching up, she tugged my t-shirt over my head and unbuckled my belt.

I shuddered as her touch skimmed over my bare flesh.

I'd never get over how reactive I was to her. How much I craved her. How much I fucking loved her.

Her hands looked so delicate as she pushed aside my jeans, and I shifted to shove them down my legs. No boots, no socks, they slipped off the bed, leaving me in my boxer-briefs.

Her fingers wrapped around my erection, her skin hot even through the cotton.

"Wait." I clutched her wrist, my heart racing.

Her eyes flared. "Why?"

The urge to rock into her hand made me grit my teeth. I squeezed my eyes closed, doing my best to scrape together the last remnants of my self-control. "We do this, and there is no going back. Until death do us part, O."

Her hand fisted me, fierce and possessive. "No more secrets. No more sacrifices."

I bared my teeth. "No more being apart."

"I'm okay with that." Her grin was light-hearted even while everything about me was heavy. My blood was heavy. My desire heavy. My promise to always protect her heavy with utmost honesty.

I kissed her again, shuddering as she shoved down my boxer-briefs, and our skin connected bare to bare.

Heat. Softness. Overwhelming need.

Her hand found my cock again, this time without cotton separating us. She squeezed me, stroking up and down. My head tipped forward as I lay on top of her, trapping her arm between us, smothering her with my weight.

Our eyes locked. My heart overflowed. The past meant nothing because this was where I earned everything I ever wanted. Olive was safe. My soul was healed. And O still loved me.

Despite everything.

"I need you, Gil." She rubbed against me, her touch tightening in command.

My own hand slipped between her legs, finding her wet and wanting.

She cried out as I pierced two fingers inside her, claiming her, tormenting her.

I kissed her, harsh and dominating as her hips worked up and into my control. My own hips worked into her hand, both desperate to connect, impatient and hungry.

I wanted to take my time.

To touch every part of her, suck her nipples, grant her orgasm after orgasm, but…there was time for that. We had a lifetime to make up for the fast moments. We had forever to explore and experiment.

For now, this was a hello.

A long-awaited hi.

Withdrawing my fingers, I nudged away her hand and settled between her thighs.

She spread wider, her smile bright and blinding.

I couldn't help it.

I had to kiss her again.

Deeply, deliciously *kiss* her.

Her tongue danced with mine as my cock found her entrance. She gasped into my mouth as I slowly pushed inside.

I went slow, tantalisingly slow. This wasn't sex. This was so, so much more. This was us no longer fighting destiny.

We quaked as I finally slid the final inch and sheathed myself completely within her. Her body radiated heat and I struggled with the need to thrust. To push us both to the release just out of reach.

Instead, I paused.

I looked down at her, nestled beneath me, her lips still red, eyes liquid with love, and for the first time in my life...I trusted.

Truly, unquestionably *trusted*.

This woman was mine.

She always had been, always would be.

I would never doubt that again.

I pumped into her.

She moaned and dug her fingernails into my lower back, rocking with me.

My thrusts turned faster, deeper, plunging as far as I could.

And O demanded more.

We traded the slow rhythm for a primitive one. Chasing love and lust in its rawest form.

Our lips collided, quick and out of control.

Need galloped around my blood and an orgasm wrapped around the base of my spine.

O shuddered, her mouth parting as pleasure rippled through her. The bands of her release squeezed my cock. I grew harder, thrust faster.

"Fuck..." I groaned.

She cried out as I drove into her, burying my face into her neck and biting her as I lost control.

I came harder than I ever had before.

My stomach hollowed out. My muscles locked. I poured into her, giving her every part of me.

Over and over I came until I trembled and slowly returned from paradise to earth.

For the first time, I wondered about birth control. I'd slept with O without protection. We'd never discussed if she was on the pill. We should probably chat about our future dreams and goals regarding family, but for now, I was open to anything.

I didn't care if I spent the rest of my life loving O and Olive or if we'd add to our brood.

Either way, we were family.

Now and forever after.

＊ ＊ ＊ ＊ ＊

"Good morning." I smiled as O appeared from my bedroom.

Her answering smile was almost sheepish, her hair tangled and body loose. "Good morning."

"Coffee?" I poured a fresh cup for her.

"Please." Padding over to me in bare feet, I couldn't stop staring at her. Couldn't stop believing this was real. That I got this fucking lucky.

Passing her the mug, I couldn't stop myself from hugging her close and kissing her.

It was meant to be a short kiss.

It turned out to be a long, heated hello.

By the time I let her go, I was hard again and cursing the clock for not having enough time to get her back into bed.

Justin had text and congratulated me. He said he knew why O hadn't gone home last night and was glad I'd finally come to my senses. He also said to meet him and Olive at her dance practice downtown and not to be late.

My grin was stupidly big as O sipped the drink I'd made her and practically swooned. "How is it that life feels so much brighter? This coffee tastes better than any other coffee. The sun is prettier than any other sun. It's as if—"

"We've come alive again," I murmured.

"Yes, exactly." Her eyes snagged mine and once again my heart skipped a beat.

Without looking away, I pulled the small piece of paper from my pocket. "Here."

I hadn't planned on giving it to her so soon. But…this moment was perfect. This moment was just us, before we returned to reality.

"What is it?" Placing her coffee on the bench, she grinned.

"Read it."

Her eyes left mine, skimming the newly-penned job advertisement. If she accepted the job, there would be no terminations or quitting.

The position was for life.

Must be brave, stubborn, and impervious to the tempers of loved ones.
Hours are endless, pay is non-existence, quitting absolutely forbidden.
Able to function on no sleep, refrain from running when times get hard, and be more than just a living canvas but a lover…a mother.
Other attributes required: forgiving, opinionated, and not afraid to tell me when I'm wrong. Must also enjoy being touched and kissed at any time of my choosing.
Call or email 'YOUR HEART, HIS SOUL' if interested in applying.

Her head whipped up the moment she'd finished, her gaze searching mine. "What is this?"

I fought the weakness in my knees, going to her and cupping

her cheek. "It's exactly what it looks like."

I'd written it an hour ago as dawn arrived. I'd dared to dream I could have everything.

"What are you saying?"

"I'm saying that I want you in my life. My business is back in full work, and I only want to paint one canvas for the rest of my days. I want you there to scold me when I'm being an arse. I want you to continue loving Olive like you do. I want to share everything I have and am with you...forever."

"Gil, I—"

"You don't have to say yes...not straight away. I can wait."

"And if I say yes now?"

"Then it's binding. A contract for eternity."

She blushed. "Eternity is a long time."

"It's far too short." Gathering her in my arms, I kissed her gently. "I will never be as good as Justin. I accept that. I accept that I will never be as selfless as either of you and acknowledge that I will probably let you down at some point, but, O...I don't want any other canvas. I don't want any other mother for Olive. I want to share art with you. I want to paint and dance together. I want *you*."

She trembled under my touch. "I...I don't know what to say."

"Say you'll marry me."

Her lips parted. She gasped. "Are you serious?"

Instead of answering, I dropped to one knee. "Marry me, Olin Moss. It's always been you. It will always be you. I don't know how to survive without you."

O tugged at my hands, trying to bring me to my feet.

I fought her, waiting for a reply.

I would stay on my knee for weeks if that was what it took.

Slowly, a tear ran from the corner of her eyes. "Yes."

"Yes?"

She bit her lip, nodding. "Yes. Yes, I'll marry you."

And suddenly, I was that kid falling in love with a girl in a school corridor.

Possibilities were endless.

Love guaranteed.

She was my family.

Finally.

Epilogue

Gil

IT TOOK A year to pay off the fine and the donations to the victim's families.

I technically didn't have to pay. I'd filed for bankruptcy in prison and all debts against my name were null and void.

But...I wanted to.

I *needed* to.

I might not have killed those girls but my silence gave Jeffrey the freedom in which to take their lives.

I also paid Justin for his time and cost of looking after Olive in his home.

He tried to give it back.

Said it was insulting.

But I wrapped his hand around the thick envelope and begged him to take it.

Money was crass and not worth nearly what he'd done for me, but I needed to even the scorecard between us. Until he had a kid of his own that O and I could babysit, I didn't want anything outstanding between us.

I didn't want him to feel like I didn't appreciate what he'd done when he was as important to me as my daughter and wife-to-be.

It took another year to save enough for a new home for the three of us—four counting our regular guest, Justin.

Business was good.

Commissions were piling up.

O was my canvas every day.

She ran my page, liaised with companies, and ensured my

notoriety went global.

Without her, I would never have reached the levels I had. She ruled me and my creativity with her capable, wonderful kindness.

Working with her, living with her, I was aware I'd replaced Justin in both those roles. But at no point was there animosity between any of us. Justin hung out almost on a nightly basis—unless he had a date, and then he'd vanish for a week or so, figuring out if this new girl was worthy to join our extended family.

Once O and I had saved enough to buy a home, all of us went house hunting. We started in the city, looking for large warehouses like I had before. We investigated the suburbs next, traipsing through derelict homes and abandoned corner shops that could be renovated into the next location for our business.

In the end, we went into the country, door knocking on old farms with large barns, asking local villagers if they knew of estates coming up for sale.

And we found nothing suitable.

The hunt had been fun before it became frustrating.

I wanted a large studio with its own shower and lots of storage.

O wanted lots of sunshine and big windows.

Olive wanted a huge bedroom with a painting corner and chalkboard walls.

Justin wanted a guest suite with its own sitting room so he could come stay with us for days at a time and work away from the office.

Our hopes dwindled as we struggled to find anything remotely perfect.

Until...we finally found it.

A 1600s barn that had been converted into a four-bedroom, three bathroom home with modern editions of glass and steel. The ceilings soared above us with exposed centuries-old timber. Sun streamed in from big skylights and our wish list was complete with a private studio and guest suite dotted around the hobby farm.

Olive got a conservatory and O got her sunshine. Justin got his guest wing and I got a large studio for my business.

Life was good.

Better than good.

Life was perfect.

And I was so fucking grateful.

"Hey!" I chuckled as Olive dashed past me, stealing my

paintbrush.

"You're too slow." She waggled it, dropping ochre splashes on the polished concrete floor. I didn't care about the paint spots, this entire place would be covered when I started working. That was the beauty of paint. It belonged on the tools and walls as much as it did on the canvas.

I chased her, grabbing her around the middle and flipping her upside down. A couple of pennies fell out of her pockets along with a blue pencil and scrunched up piece of paper.

"Put me down!"

"Do you promise not to be annoying?"

"*You're* annoying." She giggled.

"You're the most annoying." I spun her the right way up and plonked her onto her feet. "The most annoying of annoying."

She stuck out her tongue, swiping the paintbrush over my cheek. "No. *You* are."

"Oh, now you're gonna get it." I launched at her, only to miss as she barrelled around O and tucked herself against the wall.

"Nu-huh. You will!" She laughed as I bear-hugged both of them, squishing O against me and Olive against the wall. "O will protect me!"

To be able to joke like this. To be stupid like this.

Fuck.

O rolled her eyes and laughed softly. "You two need to grow up."

"Tell him that." Olive stuck her tongue out again. "He's not painting. He's just standing there with a dopey look on his face."

O looked over her shoulder, kissing the tip of my nose. "I like that dopey look."

"And I like you," I murmured, placing my mouth over hers for a quick kiss.

I would never get used to that privilege, that sense of completeness. I was home. In every sense of the word. We'd found our dream house, but without O to share my heart and Olive to take care of, it would be meaningless and empty.

"Eww, you two are so gross." Olive wriggled out, returning to the huge mural we'd started this morning as a family.

Part graffiti, part geometric, part realism.

I'd taken inspiration from O's tattoo. The owl with its hidden animals beginning with O. This time, it was a design that incorporated all of us, and took up the entire two-story wall at the end of the studio, showcasing the art of paint and the master of shadow.

O had agreed to help paint the simple stuff—outlines and bold block colours—saying she didn't have enough talent to do more. Olive had exceeded all my hopes of her following in my footsteps, and her talent with a brush sometimes made me sit back in serious awe.

We returned to work, colours flowing harmoniously.

O glanced at the clock, her stomach rumbling. "In another thirty minutes, I'll put dinner on."

"Don't forget I have a dance lesson tonight," Olive said. "The teacher is coming here."

"And don't forget I asked for a lesson for me after." I chuckled. "Thought we could practice outside by the pond."

O spun to face me. "You asked for a dance lesson?"

"Yep."

"Why?"

Why? Because dancing had been torn from her life like Olive had been torn from mine. I'd been lucky enough to reclaim Olive, but O...she wasn't under false illusions that her body would always be a slightly bit broken.

I didn't want her to go through life without soul food.

So...I'd arranged ballroom dancing for us. Salsa and jive. I sucked and my coordination was laughable, but I would embarrass myself every night if O danced with me.

Because when she danced, the music whispered through her veins, and she glowed.

Glowed like the angel I always knew she was.

"I need the exercise."

She chuckled. "You work out every morning." She walked into my embrace, her lips seeking mine. Her eyes said she knew exactly my intentions. "You're so good to me, Gilbert Clark."

"I love you, Olin Moss."

She kissed me harder and I smiled around a secret.

I meant what I said about giving her what she needed, but I also had an ulterior motive for the dance lessons.

I was going to marry this woman.

Now my debts were settled and bank account flush, I was happy knowing I had enough to protect her for life. That I could afford to make her mine.

In two months' time, we would get hitched and our family would be official.

And after I made this wonderful woman mine, I would spin

her and dip her and waltz her into our future.
   Forever.

Epilogue Two

Olin

"QUIT MOVING." Gil's fingers latched on my hipbone, his voice strict and chilly like it did when his art stole his concentration.

"Quit tickling me then."

"Quit making me want to skip the wedding and go straight to the consummate part."

I swatted his ear, my gaze skimming over to Olive who stood in the bathroom fixing a final flower into her hair. I doubted she'd heard, but still. "Your daughter is right there."

"*Our* daughter." His eyes caught mine and my heart melted just like always. I would always be weak where he was concerned. Always have no future or home unless he was there.

I accepted that.

Embraced that.

I smiled as he dropped his attention and airbrushed crème and ivory over my skin. "I'm marrying both of you."

"And no divorce shall be given," he growled threateningly, but it ached with need.

I chuckled, loving all over again how carefree he was. How different he'd become now he actually communicated his hardships and shared his troubles. "You know you're not supposed to see the bride on her wedding day."

He bit his lip, angling the airgun to follow the shadows along my leg. "Not many husbands help dress the bride."

"You're not my husband."

His head tipped up, his eyes flashing. "Not yet. But in ten minutes, I will be."

I bent in half to kiss him, keeping my bouquet of white roses away from the perfection on my skin. All I wore was two pasties, a skin-coloured G-string, and his paint. I was about to walk down an aisle in front of my family, mostly naked, and I couldn't wait.

Couldn't wait to show them the talent of my husband-to-be.

After all, our relationship had started this way—our second chance. It was fitting that it would finish this way—marrying us for eternity.

"I love you, Gilbert Clark."

"And I love you, soon-to-be Mrs Olin Clark." He pressed a kiss right over my underwear before adding the finishing touches of my untraditional wedding gown. Only once my skin wore ice, alabaster, and snow did Gil put away his brushes, wipe his paint streaked hands on a rag, and slip into his tux jacket.

He frowned as his gaze slid over me, judging his creation, assessing if I was perfect.

"Oh, wow." Olive's mouth fell open as she came toward us. "That's...you look amazing, O." Her grey eyes, so intelligent and gentle sparked with love.

My own eyes prickled with overwhelming affection. She might not be mine by blood but she was my daughter through and through. "Thanks, lovely." Things grew hot and melty in my chest again. "I can't take credit. It's all this body painter's work."

"Helps that the canvas is beautiful to begin with," Gil muttered, adding a last-minute flourish.

More tears built.

Olive shook her finger at me. "Don't you start crying, O. You'll ruin Dad's art." She giggled. "And you know how much trouble you'll be in."

"He'd probably divorce me." I chuckled, sniffing back liquid that wasn't allowed to fall.

"He has to marry you first." Olive snickered.

"I married her the moment she made me pancakes when I was a teenager," Gil said. "She just didn't know it."

I wanted to laugh but kept my face composed so I didn't ruin the rhinestones Gil had embellished my eyebrows with.

Today was already perfect, and we'd only just dressed.

"So...are you done?" Olive asked her dad, moving forward to help close up the paint and box the bottles where they belonged. "Justin text me before. He said they're almost ready."

"Yeah, I'm done." Gil raked a hand through his hair, leaving behind a streak of white in his otherwise dark unruly mess. I didn't tell him. I liked the roguish imperfection.

"I'll go and see if he needs any help," Olive said, blowing me an air kiss. "Don't be too long! It's not raining but we don't want to push it."

Gil chuckled, his face soft and full of affection as Olive smoothed down her pretty grey bridesmaid dress and slipped from the guest apartment.

I had no doubt in five minutes, Olive would have everyone sat in the white wooden chairs, the music would be playing, and our small neighbourhood would be ready to witness our nuptials.

Together, we would walk through the studio to the manicured garden at the back. To the pond twinkling in the sunshine and over grass that looked like perfect green carpet. We would become betrothed beneath a small alter made from twisted old branches and flowers.

Justin would stand beside Gil as best man and Olive would stand beside me, and tonight, I hoped Justin might pop the question to his year-long girlfriend, Monique. A year wasn't a very long time, but when you met the right one, you only needed a day.

One day to understand that you could like others, love others, even marry others, but unless that person was approved by fate and your perfect other half, then it wasn't entirely your destiny.

Gil was my destiny.

Even though I'd tried to fight it.

Even though he'd tried to kill it and I'd walked away from it...the undeniability of us had won.

Gil moved toward me, keeping his hands to himself with a groan. "I'd give anything to smudge you. To grab and kiss you."

I blushed. "You can kiss me but you can't touch."

He groaned again. "I can't kiss you. I painted your lips too. If I do, they'll smear."

"Guess you're going to have to wait until the official kiss then."

"You're determined to kill me."

I smiled. "Determined to marry you." Spreading my arms, I added, "Thank you, Gil. For giving me such a wonderful gown."

Leaning in, he pressed his lips to my ear. "I'm far from done with you, O. I have another artwork in mind for the honeymoon."

I shivered in anticipation. Kissing his cheek, I pushed him away so I didn't leap into his arms. "Shoo. It's time for me to finish getting ready. You can't see this next part. It's a surprise."

Olive and I had put it together.

I wore Gil's paint, but I needed something that moved with me. Something that would dance around my legs and arms. Together, we'd sourced panels of sheer lace and organza, designing a dress that hung like a kimono, open down my chest and tied at the waist with a simple silver sash with the sides split, revealing my lace-painted legs and body paint.

The fabric would frame the masterpiece Gil had done.

He chuckled as Olive darted back into the room. "Everyone's ready. You guys coming?"

Gil brushed past her, giving her a quick kiss on her hair. "You're gorgeous, little spinach. A perfect wedding planner."

She blushed. "The wedding won't work if the bride and groom are late."

He laughed again. "Fine, I'm going." He looked back at me, drinking in his colours and creation but only seeing me beneath it. Loving me despite everything.

My heart swelled and spilled over.

An affliction of love that would happen every day for the rest of my life because I was so unbelievably lucky to marry my soulmate.

Gil winced as if he couldn't bear to say goodbye. "Guess I'll see you both soon."

"You will." I smiled softly.

"I'll be the guy waiting at the altar."

"I'll be the woman walking up the aisle."

"Don't make me wait too long." He drank me in one last time. Smiled at his daughter. And then, he left.

He left behind all the mess between us.

He walked into the future where all our dreams came true.

And I followed him.

THE END

UPCOMING RELEASE

GODDESS ISLES

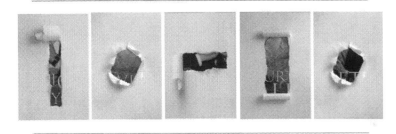

Dark Romance

Blurb

"There was a boy once. A boy who wasn't strong enough to save me when I was taken."

"There was a girl once. A girl called Tess Snow who sat with me in the dark waiting to be sold."

"There was an owner once. An owner who bought me, entrapped me, and made me his unwilling goddess."

Eleanor Grace is a naïve dreamer. Trusting and young, she believes her book-loving boyfriend can save her when her freedom is snatched and sold. Squirreled away to an island at midnight, delivered to a man even darkness won't touch, she's bound by a contract.

Four men.
Four fantasies.
Four pieces of her soul.

Sullivan Sinclair is the giver of fantasies. Any wish, any desire—he is the master at quenching even the filthiest appetites. His private paradise and perfectly trained goddesses are there for one purpose: to ensure every guest is extremely well satisfied.

He bought her.
He trapped her.
She belongs to him.

PLAYLIST

Imagine Dragons – Birds
Muse - Starlight
Keane – Somewhere Only We Know
Lady Gaga – Shallow
Rhianna – Stay
Bruno Mars – When I Was Your Man
Sam Smith – Too Good at Goodbyes
Gotye Ft Kimbra – Somebody I Used To Know
Hozier – Take Me To Church
Lady Antebellum – Need You Now

ACKNOWLEDGEMENTS

ANOTHER BOOK.

Another thank you.

It never gets easier.

To all my beta readers who helped perfect this conclusion—you guys truly are invaluable and I'm forever grateful.

To all my amazing readers who came with me into yet another genre and (hopefully) enjoyed Gil and Olin's story.

To the amazing bloggers who supported and shared, I couldn't do this without you!

To all those who left reviews and suggested the book to friends, you are incredibly amazing and deserve so many, many thank yous.

To those who found me by chance, read a book by an unknown, and stuck with me with my crazy tales, THANK YOU.

To the original street teams and book lovers, thank you.

I'm so grateful for all your support and kindness.

Words aren't enough.

But I'm always in your debt.

Pepper

xxx

OTHER WORK BY PEPPER WINTERS

Pepper Winters is a multiple New York Times, Wall Street Journal, and USA Today International Bestseller.

All Pepper's books are available in e-book, paperback, & audio (some titles still in progress).

UPCOMING DARK ROMANCE 2019
The Goddess Isles

COMING OF AGE ROMANCE
USA Today Bestselling New Adult Series 'The Ribbon Duet'
"Award winner for best tear jerker. An epic tale of love, loss, and life."
Start the Duet with
The Boy & His Ribbon

DARK ROMANCE
New York Times Bestseller 'Monsters in the Dark' Trilogy
"Voted Best Dark Romance, Best Dark Hero, #1 Erotic Romance"
Start the Trilogy **FREE** with
Tears of Tess (Monsters in the Dark #1)

Multiple New York Times Bestseller 'Indebted' Series
"Voted Vintagely Dark & Delicious. A true twist on Romeo & Juliet"
Start the Series **FREE** with
Debt Inheritance (Indebted #1)

GRAY ROMANCE
USA Today Bestseller 'Destroyed'
"Voted Best Tear-Jerker, #1 Romantic Suspense"

SURVIVAL CONTEMPORARY ROMANCE
USA Today Bestseller 'Unseen Messages'
"Voted Best Epic Survival Romance 2016, Castaway meets The Notebook"

MOTORCYCLE CLUB ROMANCE
Multiple USA Today Bestseller 'Pure Corruption' Duology
"Sinful & Suspenseful, an Amnesia Tale full of Alphas and Heart"
Start the Duology with:
Ruin & Rule (Pure Corruption #1)

SINFUL ROMANCE
Multiple USA Today Bestseller 'Dollar' Series
"Elder Prest will steal your heart. A captive love-story with salvation at its core."
Start this series for only **99c** with
Pennies (Dollar Series #1)

EROTIC ROMANCE
Brand New Release 'Truth & Lies' Duet
Start this duet with
Crown of Lies (Truth & Lies #1)

ROMANTIC COMEDY written as TESS HUNTER
#1 Romantic Comedy Bestseller 'Can't Touch' *"Voted Best Rom Com of 2016. Pets, love, and chemistry."*

UPCOMING RELEASES
For 2019/2020 titles please visit
www.pepperwinters.com

Made in the USA
Middletown, DE
12 November 2019